SUNY series in Latin American and Iberian Thought and Culture
Jorge J. E. Gracia and Rosemary Geisdorfer Feal, editors

Mothers, Lovers, and Others

The Short Stories of Julio Cortázar

∾

Cynthia Schmidt-Cruz

State University of New York Press

Published by
State University of New York Press, Albany

For information, address State University of New York Press,
90 State Street, Suite 700, Albany, NY 12207

Production by Judith Block
Marketing by Fran Keneston

Library of Congress Cataloging-in-Publication Data

Schmidt-Cruz, Cynthia.
  Mothers, lovers, and others : the short stories of Julio Cortázar / Cynthia Schmidt-Cruz.
    p. cm. — (SUNY series in Latin American and Iberian thought and culture)
  Includes bibliographical references and index.
  ISBN 0-7914-5955-1 (hc : alk. paper)
    1. Cortázar, Julio—Criticism and interpretation. 2. Women in literature. I. Title. II.
Series

  PQ7797.C7145Z7758 2003
  863'64—dc21   2003054615

10 9 8 7 6 5 4 3 2 1

To my father and in memory of my mother
To Jesús and Cristina

∾

The eternally youthful Cortázar, here fifty-four years old and in a characteristic ludic mode, poses with Magritte's apple. 1968 © Agencia EFE.

Contents

∾

Acknowledgments

Cortázar and his stories have intrigued me since I read my first Cortázar story as an undergraduate. Was it "Axolotl?" "La noche boca arriba?" "Carta a una señorita en París?" I don't remember. I met Cortázar only once, but I will never forget his huge, wide-set, penetrating eyes. I always thought I would see him again in person, but my next contact with him was when I visited his grave in Montparnasse Cemetery.

I have been reading, teaching, thinking about, and writing about Cortázar for many years. Once I became a mother, I began to pay more attention to his depiction of mother-child relationships, and I was fascinated by the complexity of this relationship as well as its profound impact on not only his representation of male-female relationships, but also on his personal construction of national identity and his denunciation of the "Dirty War" in Argentina. And thus, this study began. I have enjoyed every minute I have dedicated to Cortázar's stories, and sometimes I wonder if I will ever find another project that intrigues me as much as this one.

I have various individuals and institutions to acknowledge for their role in this book. Thanks to Peter Standish, Hortensia Morell, Carlos Alonso, Marie Murphy, Joan Brown, Alexander Selimov, Mary Donaldson-Evans, and Monika Shafi for reading portions of the manuscript in progress and providing me with valuable feedback. I am also appreciative of the insightful comments made by the anonymous readers, which helped me to improve the manuscript. Thanks to the staff at SUNY Press, in particular Michael Rinella and Judith Block, for their enthusiasm for my manuscript and their invaluable assistance and guidance through the editorial process. I am grateful to my colleagues in the Department of Foreign Languages and Literatures at the University of

Delaware for their support and friendship, especially Laura Salsini, Susan McKenna, and Annette Geisecke. I thank the University of Delaware for granting me a sabbatical leave, which gave me the precious commodity of time to make significant progress on the manuscript, and also for awarding me a General University Research Grant to carry out research at the Biblioteca Julio Cortázar in Madrid. And to the Fundación Juan March, I thank them for allowing me to research in the Biblioteca Julio Cortázar, where I had access to many hard-to-find articles and other publications about Cortázar's life and works.

My deepest gratitude goes to my wonderful husband, Jesús Cruz, for his great sense of humor, his constant encouragement and support, and his belief in my ability to write this book; and to my daughter Cristina for her love and understanding and for her interest and curiosity in most everything.

I thank the general editor of *Hispanic Review* for graciously allowing me to reprint in chapter 5 a revised version of the analysis of "Cambio de luces," which appeared in *Hispanic Review* volume 65, number 4, 1997. An earlier version of the analysis of "Deshoras" and "Historias que me cuento" in chapter 4 was originally published in *Latin American Literary Review,* volume 25, number 49, 1997, and is reprinted by permission of the publisher. I gratefully acknowledge permission from the Heirs of Julio Cortázar to reprint quotations from the following works of Julio Cortázar: *Bestiario* ©1951, *Final del juego* ©1956, *Las armas secretas* ©1959, *Todos los fuegos el fuego* ©1966, *Octaedro* ©1974, *Alguien que anda por ahí* ©1977, *Queremos tanto a Glenda* ©1980, *Deshoras* ©1982, and *Salvo el crepúsculo* ©1984; all ©Heirs of Julio Cortázar.

For use of the photo which appears on the cover, I gratefully acknowledge Sara Facio. She took this picture of Cortázar and his first wife, Aurora Bernárdez, in 1967 in their apartment on Place du Gènèral Beuret, Paris XV, where Bernárdez still lives today. Permission to reprint the frontispiece photo was obtained from Agencia EFE, Madrid, and the photo at the end of the book is courtesy of the Carmen Balcells Literary Agency, Barcelona.

Chronology of Cortázar's Stories

Abbreviations

  Cc 1: *Cuentos completos/*1
  Cc 2: *Cuentos completos/*2
  Oc 1: *Obra crítica/*1
  Oc 2: *Obra crítica/*2
  Oc 3: *Obra crítica/*3

Chapter 1

ℂ

Introduction: Cortázar's Female Space and the Configuration of Masculinity

Julio Cortázar is, by all accounts, a towering figure in twentieth-century Latin American letters. If we were asked to sum up, in a nutshell, the man and his work, we might focus on the enduring interest in his masterful and varied *oeuvre,* and the heated polemics sparked by his choice of residence and his stances pertaining to issues of politics and gender. Among the reasons for the continued fascination with Cortázar's writings are the multiple levels of interpretation they offer, combined with his startling honesty in depicting, albeit often in a veiled manner, his deep-seated obsessions. And the controversies whirling around him touched on some of the major social issues of the last half of the twentieth century: feminism, socialism, and the transition from modernism to postmodernism.

Feminists were furious when, in *Rayuela* (1963), he coined the term "*lector hembra*" to refer to the passive, uncritical reader. Cortázar's residence in France and his political views landed him in the vortex of virulent debates. Fellow Argentines and Latin Americans have attacked him for embodying Argentina's modernist fascination with Paris, and for presuming to write and speak about his country when he lived in France from 1951 until his death in 1984. The fact that he supported the Cuban, and later the Nicaraguan, Revolutions garnered him praise from some quarters, criticism from others. The most generous of his critics preferred to see his stance as well-intentioned naïveté, while the more severe said he was "using" the socialist cause for his own self-promotion. Then, during the Argentine military dictatorship, his statement about "genocidio cultural" in the country incensed many Argentine artists who were trying to continue producing from within the country.[1] And Cortázar, in his

1

interviews, letters, and speeches, was frequently responding, with utmost candor, to an attack provoked by something he had written or pronounced or done. Without a doubt, Cortázar's unrelenting drive to explore, attune, and articulate his position regarding major cultural polemics of his time bore fruit in his proliferous literary production.

The canonical image of Cortázar is currently undergoing a reexamination, initiated, in large part, by the important collection of essays entitled *Julio Cortázar: New Readings.*[2] Recently published correspondence offers fresh material for further reevaluations of Cortázar and his work.[3] A central aspect of Cortázar's work which, I believe, merits further examination is the portrayal of women. How can we understand Cortázar's female characters in the wake of the burgeoning importance of feminist and gender studies, and our increasing realization of the role played by gender in areas such as national identity and political discourse?

This book will examine the role of Cortázar's conception of the feminine, or female space, not only in the traumas that generate his psychological fantastic, but also in his political stances, specifically his construction of national identity and his denunciation of the "Dirty War" in Argentina. I have chosen the term *female space* to refer to the conceptualization of femininity in the title of this chapter and throughout the book in order to evoke the varied spatial meanings Cortázar's concept of the feminine encompasses, such as the maternal womb, the lover's body, the home and the homeland, the receptacle for "feminine" traits—qualities or psychic states that the male struggles to disown. But the attempt to contain this space proves to be a losing battle. The crisis in Western philosophy, explains Alice Jardine, involves a problematization and disruption of the boundaries and spaces given male and female connotations (71). An important source of Cortázar's creative energy, at least in his early stories, this book will argue, is his intuitive perception of this breakdown in boundaries and his defensive reaction to his troubling discovery.

The female space in Cortázar's *oeuvre* is first and foremost the mother, and then a series of substitutions for her. An examination of this space with female connotations leads us to concerns which are at the heart of Cortázar's universe: the fantastic, erotic desire, family, exile and expatriation, his *argentinidad*, human rights, and, ultimately, his constant search for meaning or fulfillment through the creative act.

Critics have analyzed the problematic love relationships in Cortázar's narrative, and more than one has pointed out the attenuation, in the latter part of his career, of the male chauvinism that colored Cortázar's depiction of female characters in early works.[4] However, with the exception of Ana Hernández del Castillo and René Prieto, few have recognized the overwhelming power of his maternal figures, or the web of female associations weaving through his concept of the "Other" and otherness. New critical approaches, specifically the intersection of feminist revisions of psychoanalytic thought with cultural studies, enable us to arrive at a new understanding of the pervasive role of the feminine in Cortázar's writings.

Psychoanalytic insights explain how the concept of the feminine, or female space, is shaped in large part by masculine projections and fantasies, pointing to the inextricable connection between the characterization of women and the construction of masculinity. The drive to sustain a rigid masculine identity, which depends on maintaining a difference or distance from the feminine, results in the attempt to situate femininity in a space outside the masculine self. Psychoanalytic theory related to gender construction enables us to view the internal tension characteristic of many of Cortázar's stories as a dramatization of the futile struggle to sustain a rigid boundary between traditional conceptions of masculinity and what is seen as the feared and desired "other" space, the feminine. Ultimately, Cortázar's intuition of his dependence on the female "other," which implies the fragmentation of self—or, from another perspective, the shifting ground on which a gendered identity is negotiated—espouses one of the fundamental tenets of postmodern thought.

Cultural studies explore the role of gender in structuring national identity and political ideology, explaining how erotic or sentimental investment in the state can generate "our passion for 'la patria' " (Sommer, *Foundational Fictions* 32) and how systems of gender identity become a metaphor for oppressor and oppressed. These studies inform my reading of how the political statements encoded in Cortázar's stories rely on gender polarity, casting the country he left behind as an abandoned woman, and using female bodies to evoke a beleaguered Argentina during the military dictatorship.

Cortázar's Psychological Obsessions: What's Mom Got to Do with It?

A basic structural paradigm of Cortázar's fiction that has been characterized and analyzed by many critics is the self/other dichotomy and the constant passage between these poles. Noé Jitrik's seminal work introduces the concept of *"zona sagrada,"* his term for Cortázar's idea of an inner irrationality.[5] "[L]as fuerzas invasoras están en nosotros mismos" (48), explains Jitrik, characterizing Cortázar's fantastic in opposition to Borges's, who places irrationality outside, in the world (49). These irrational forces, which emerge from "una interioridad profundamente resguardada, tal vez oprimida" (52) are opposed to "el mundo de los otros," who represent an oppressive, limited, and arbitrary order, the "anti zona sagrada" (56). The characters strive to hide or defend their zona sagrada from the rationality of others who would censor it. The zona sagrada and "el mundo de los otros" form the space within which the characters struggle; the fight is uneven and at times useless with dramatic consequences: usually either renunciation of the zona sagrada or suicide (54–55). Jitrik's study of this polarity in Cortázar's work focuses on the stories of *Bestiario* where integration with the persecutory others is impossible (55). At the same time, Jitrik maintains that the appearance of the zona sagrada persists throughout Cortázar's work, and that gradually "hay menos renuncia, hay menos negación de una perspectiva humana, es decir histórica, poco a poco Cortázar va encontrando que la 'zona sagrada' se da también y no simbólicamente, en todo lo humano" (61).[6] Jitrik never identifies, however, what is at the core of this zona sagrada.

The primordial role of the search for the "other" in Cortázar's ontology and aesthetics is elucidated by Sara Castro-Klarén.[7] In a statement evocative of Lacan, she explains how the self/other dialectic is the basis for the two main postulates in Cortázar's theory of literature:

> 1) Fundamentally, Cortázar posits a porous, non-substantial, open structure for the self, the world and knowledge. At the root of this vision of porousness is a feeling of incompleteness . . . which leads the poet to an awareness of existing alongside or parallel to something "other" (*lo otro*). 2) This in turn implies the eternal presence of the Other as the orientation of being. ("Ontological Fabulation" 141)

> For Cortázar, then, there is indeed anther world, but it is right here, imbedded in the present, in man's inability to coincide with himself. . . . As man fabulates the Other in his longing for it, he is actually fabulating his own being. ("Ontological Fabulation" 147)

The desire for the Other, then, according to Castro-Klarén, constitutes the essence of the self.

In another study analyzing Cortázar's psychological fantastic, Castro-Klarén points out the connection between transgression and the fantastic in several stories (*Escritura* 75). On the one hand are the defense mechanisms employed by Cortázar's characters—"estrategias de auto-decepción y negación de deseos transgresores" (*Escritura* 76)—and on the other are the prohibited desires that manage to break through "rajaduras de la conciencia que descuida su vigilancia" (*Escritura* 80). Thus the "rajaduras" or fissures become a type of conduit through which the repressed desires manifest themselves in the protagonist's quotidian reality. Castro-Klarén specifies the nature of the forbidden desires in several stories from *Bestiario*. For instance, in the story "Bestiario," she discovers that "[l]as caricias de Rema constituyen el deseo prohibido," and then elaborates: "en 'Bestiario' irrumpen dos deseos prohibidos— amar a Rema y matar al Nene" (*Escritura* 78). However, we still do not know the origin of these troubling desires, a discovery that would enable us to arrive at a master scheme to explain their pervasive and unsettling presence throughout Cortázar's work.

Doris Sommer's insightful article of 1986[8] traces the stages in Cortázar's quest for a utopia, focusing on how his experimentation with pronouns, those "slippery shifters," reflects the evolution of the relationship between self and other in his short fiction. Sommer sees a continuity of desire in Cortázar's stories within four distinct, if slightly untidy, periods that culminate in a Lacanian-type realization of endless desire, necessarily imperfect and frustrating, an impossible longing that makes us human. Sommer variously describes the harmony Cortázar was seeking as belonging to "the Imaginary realm, where the child perceives its mother as an extension of itself, so there is no contradiction between self-love and love for the other," and as "the paradise of being at one with the other" ("A Nowhere" 232). While these references seemingly allude to the maternal womb as the ultimate source and goal of Cortázar's desire, Sommer refrains from stating it explicitly, perhaps preferring to evade stasis, as did her slippery subject.

Finally, the work of René Prieto represents a breakthrough, as he pinpoints the source of Cortázar's obsessions in the birth trauma.[9] Prieto's grouping of symbols that haunted Cortázar—hands, breathing disorders, fear of darkness, claustrophobia, animals, bridges, and tunnels— and his detailed analysis of the stories "No se culpe a nadie," "Cuello de gatito negro," and "Noche boca arriba" detect the anxiety of separation from the maternal body in the coded language of Cortázar's phobias. Prieto concludes that the unconscious desire of Cortázar's characters "to return to the shuttered environment from which they have been so violently ousted" is the desire "from which all of Cortázar's fictional universe springs" ("Cortázar's Closet" 87). Thus, Prieto's insight exposes Cortázar's closeted secret—the essence of the zona sagrada, the origin of the forbidden desires, and the location of the sought-after utopia—as the conflicted longing for the maternal womb. Indeed, following through on the implications of Prieto's study, we can deduce that Cortázar's "Other" and "other space"—the zona sagrada which stands for his perception of inner irrationality—are primordially feminine, and the opposing term is the masculine self.[10]

With the help of recent psychoanalytic theory that explores how gender takes hold in the psyche, in particular the works of Stephen Frosh, Rosalind Minsky, and Jessica Benjamin, we can begin to uncover the broader and deeper implications of understanding the self/other dichotomy in Cortázar's work in terms of gender polarity. Cortázar's binary configuration corresponds to a basic mode of perceiving reality: the "traditional association of masculinity with rationality and femininity with irrationality" (Frosh 42). At times, the "category 'woman' becomes elided with the category of the 'Other,' " explains Frosh, and there is an implicit parallel between femininity and the unconscious (40, 42). "The designation of women as irrational, ultra-precarious and even mad," maintains Minsky, "is a necessary unconscious manoeuver to sustain the idea of men as rational and objective and conceal their envy and dependence on them" (209). Frosh further elaborates on this fundamental psychological structure and its implications for social organization, citing the claim that "since Kant and the Reformation, rationality has been the dominant western mode available for construing experience, and rationality and masculinity have been conflated so that each connotes the other" (90). Frosh explains that this contention has "implications for the marginalisation of femininity and the valorisation of a normative framework for action. It also relates to the way gender insinuates itself into the central polarities around which society is organised," he continues, "it is *reason* that is taken as marking out what is true and what is false, and reason is seen as something embedded in masculinity but not in femininity. Where reason breaks down, madness ensues; femininity and madness are consequently aligned" (90).

Cortázar's constant search for, and his apparent dependence on, this (irrational) female "other" can be seen as part of a generalized self-questioning of patriarchal discourse or the "master narrative." Jardine speaks of "crises in the narratives invented by men" (24), which she considers "the master narratives' own 'nonknowledge,' what has eluded them, what has engulfed them. This other-than-themselves," explains Jardine, "is almost always a 'space' of some kind (over which the narrative has lost control), and this space has been coded as *feminine*, as *woman*" (25). In this sense, we can consider Cortázar a "master writer" (a concept problematized in postmodern thought) who continually undermines his own mastery by demonstrating the instability of the (male) subject due to the surfacing of unconscious impulses. While binary logic pervades Cortázar's culturally transmitted knowledge of sexual identity, his unconscious—his dreams, which are transposed into stories—betray the deep fissures in this structure, ineluctably pointing to the untenability of sustaining a rigid "masculine" identity. The central role of the unconscious in gender identity means that it can potentially be subverted. And in the case of Cortázar, this instability translated into the generative mechanism for many compelling and unsettling tales.

Although I have spoken of a dichotomous structure in Cortázar's work (i.e., self/other, rationality/irrationality, masculinity/femininity), it is misleading to insist on the exclusivity of the two terms. The invasion of rational quotidian reality by the irrational is a Cortazarean constant. Cortázar explains how his idea of the fantastic depends on a momentary breakdown in binary reasoning, one that exposes a third term in the interstices: "The fantastic . . . presents itself in a way which we could call interstitial, slipping in between two moments or two acts in order to allow us to catch a glimpse, in the binary mechanism which is typical of human reason, of the latent possibility of a third frontier, of a third eye" ("The Present State of Fiction in Latin America" 30). In his critical writings and interviews, Cortázar reiterates his mistrust of a naive faith in reason, and emphasizes the importance of the irrational in his perception of reality and his creative work, frequently relating that some of his best stories were initially dreams (or nightmares).[11]

Cortázar's emphasis on the irrational, Sommer would remind us, pertains to what she categorizes as "his early or surrealist stage" ("A Nowhere" 238), consisting of the stories from *Bestiario* and *Final del juego*. His first stage, she points out, is characterized by "a surrealism that invited irrational desire to break through a brittle veneer of language" (231). In phase two, made up by the stories of *Todos los fuegos el fuego* and *Octaedro*, the gap between desire and its realization is mediated by the no-win game. "[T]he rules of the game are calculated to preclude the apparent goal of love," observes Sommer. "The only happiness found is an almost masochistic appreciation for the impossibility of love" (244).[12] By *Alguien que anda por ahí*, phase three in Sommer's categorization, the predictable games reach a dead end, and Cortázar experiments with the collective as a way to fuse with the other. In "Las caras de la medalla" this is accomplished through the collective persona—*nosotros*—and "Apocalipsis de Solentiname" envisions the collective through the continuity between art and politics (246–249). The last period, corresponding to *Queremos tanto a Glenda* and *Deshoras,* qualifies the hope of the previous phase by warning us of the violence inherent in fixing desire, while recognizing that striving after insatiable desire is what constitutes the human condition (232, 251).

Sommer's study has important implications for my reading of Cortázar's stories because it demonstrates that Cortázar's search for harmony or paradise was not static, but rather followed a specific evolutionary path. Her characterization of that trajectory shows how it developed from its most convoluted and defensive form to a more open and tolerant embrace of humanity. In the following sections of this introduction, I will use Sommer's categories of desire in Cortázar's fiction as a basis for examining the evolution of female space in his stories. At the same time, I will elaborate on and propose modifications in Sommer's grouping for the purpose of my study. In conjunction with this, I will explore how Cortázar's changing relationship to the feminine shapes his construction of masculinity.

It's Not Me, It's My Dream:
The Unconscious and the Unraveling of Sexual Identity

We can think of Cortázar's utopia, says Sommer, as "the very space in language that divides desire from realization and that provides the possibilities for happy slippage" ("A Nowhere" 232). I would like to consider that same space "that divides desire from realization" to be where Cortázar marks his distance from the feminine, and eventually begins to forge a tentative relationship with it, or in other words, as the space where he negotiates his gender identity.

That negotiation is fraught with tension generated by the confrontation between the traditional conception of gender categories as absolutes and the voice of his unconscious "truth," which works to deconstruct those categories. Cortázar grew up in a patriarchal society based on traditional gender categories, yet his exceptionally keen sensitivity to "otherness" and his unconscious voice fostered uncertainty and ambiguities. An acute tension is produced by the misfit between the socially transmitted belief in absolute gender categories—whereby masculinity is equated with reason and femininity with the unconscious—and his intuition of the irrational other within himself. The act of releasing this tension through his writings is an important source of Cortázar's creativity.

Indeed, due to Cortázar's extraordinarily penetrating intuition of gender instability, his work offers a uniquely rich source for a case study in the "crisis in the master narrative," or the precarious construction of masculine identity. Both Castro-Klarén and Prieto have noted Cortázar's singularity in regard to his obsessive concern with the (m)other:

> La postura central "del otro", de la otredad en los textos de Cortázar es algo que ha preocupado a la crítica de manera central, y esto tal vez se deba al hecho de que Cortázar maneje esta categoría con más lucidez, variedad e insistencia que ningún otro escritor moderno. (Castro-Klarén, *Escritura* 73)

> More than any other author, Cortázar spent his life reenacting in fiction the separation from the maternal body. (Prieto, "Cortázar's Closet" 86–87)

Whether we identify Cortázar's central concern as the presence of otherness or as the birth trauma, there can be no doubt that his singular— yet, at the same time, universal—psychological obsessions played a pivotal role in his literary production. His ability to transpose and articulate these into unforgettable, haunting masterpieces is crucial to his widespread acclaim.

Psychoanalysis, in the view of some theorists, "is a process that aims to enable the subject to be reconciled with otherness, to acknowledge the power of what lies outside" (Frosh 124). In this same manner, Cortázar's stories helped him cope with his obsessions. Indeed, he has often said that they functioned as therapy for him.[13] A comment Frosh makes in relation to Freud's analysis of his dreams could just as well apply to Cortázar's compulsion to write his stories: "By naming what is going on, we cease to be ravished by it" (125). Through his stories, Cortázar allows his unconscious to speak and in so doing frees himself from the grip of irrational fears. At the same time, he listens to it, and acknowledges its speech as something worthy of offering up to the world. Thus, by writing his unconscious, Cortázar harnesses it into social production, transforming his deep-seated fears and desires into literature.

Returning to the issue of the construction of masculinity, I will consider Cortázar's sensitivity to his unconscious impulses, which translate as a preoccupation with otherness or female space, as an intuitive recognition of the instability of gender identity. To better understand how the fundamental structure of masculinity depends on its representation of the feminine, and thus shed light on the processes underlying Cortázar's construction of self and other, I turn to Stephen Frosh and Jessica Benjamin. Since traditional "masculinity" focuses on dominance and independence, explains Frosh, men who strive to project this image turn away from emotion and intimacy, fearing this will make them vulnerable, dependent, and "womanly" (2–3). The struggle to differentiate oneself from the mother—of which one originally was part—is a central feature of masculine identity (88). On the one hand, the mother represents intimacy and dependence, which must be repudiated for the boy "to assert himself against her, against the feminine principle of oneness, against what has the opprobrium of 'regressive narcissism' " (112). Experiencing her power, the boy idealizes her and wishes for her, at the same time that he fears she will engulf him. This suggests that masculinity is essentially a negative identity, experienced as a flight from something, "rather than toward something with a clear and vibrant content of its own" (112). Frosh speaks to the precariousness of gender identity in general: "The ambiguities of sexual difference revolve around uncertainty over the content and fixedness of the categories 'masculine' and 'feminine,' " categories that "are always collapsing into one another" (65).

Femininity, Frosh observes, has "usually been defined as the negative of the masculine . . . constructed to offer a space which can be filled by projected male fantasies, becoming a receptacle for what is disowned and feared" (89). Seeking to overcome his anxieties, the man projects them onto the woman, who is then dominated and excluded (89). The reverse can also occur, with the woman becoming a space for idealization. In this scenario, sexual difference serves to maintain masculinity, because the woman is made into what the man needs her to be (89). "The powerful injunction against being the same as the woman," Frosh maintains, "produces a confusion in which all 'womanly' attributes are rendered problematic, made into something 'other' " (112).

Women are a spatial fantasy, Frosh explains, insofar as they are constructed as marginal to rationality, marking the boundary "between what can be controlled and what threatens to explode, engulf or subvert" (121). Female space, being on the outside, forms the boundary of containment around a safe terrain that holds unstable masculine identity in place and allows it to survive. The dangerous "feminine other" is excluded and repudiated from the safeguarded masculine self (122).

In her discussion of the Oedipus complex, Jessica Benjamin points to the repudiation of femininity as central to that process, and no less important than the renunciation of mother as love object:

> To be feminine like her would be a throwback to the preoedipal dyad, a dangerous regression. The whole experience of the mother-infant dyad is retrospectively identified with femininity, and vice versa. Having learned that he cannot have babies like mother, nor play her part, the boy can only return as an infant, with the dependency and vulnerability of an infant. Now her nurturance threatens to re-engulf him with its reminder of helplessness and dependency; it must be countered by his assertion of difference and superiority. To the extent that identification is blocked, the boy has no choice but to overcome his infancy by repudiation of dependency. This is why the oedipal ideal of individuality excludes all dependency from the definition of autonomy. (*Bonds* 162)

Once the boy looses inner continuity with women in the Oedipal experience, Benjamin explains, and encounters "instead the idealized, acutely desirable object outside, the image of woman as the dangerous, regressive siren is born. The counterpart of this image is the wholly idealized, masterful subject who can withstand or conquer her" (*Bonds* 164).

Maternal omnipotence—the fantasy that the mother is all-powerful and overwhelming—is also analyzed by Benjamin. While it is a psychic bedrock, common to both sexes, the male child's need to differentiate himself from, and then repudiate, the mother can intensify and prolong this fantasy (*Shadow* 81). In achieving masculinity, the boy cannot identify with the mother. The ensuing loss of and separation from the mother may stimulate "a more dangerous representation of the maternal sexual object as dreaded, engulfing, overwhelming, tantalizing" (*Shadow* 98). As the male becomes "the one" and the mother "the other," her subjectivity, her reality, is denied, and the void is filled with the fantasy of the powerful, controlling mother (*Shadow* 94).

Since femininity is a category full of masculine projections, a study of depictions of female characters can tell us as much about men as about woman, and "the activity of men in marking out, describing and exploring the feminine 'dark continent' can be understood as an attempt to deal with the anxiety produced by the unstable state of masculine identity" (Frosh 91). Thus, the psychoanalytic explanation of the process by which masculine insecurities construct a specific image of femininity enables us to understand, in Cortázar's work, the relationship between his negotiation of gender identity and female space. Or, to state it more precisely, we can view certain portrayals of female space in Cortázar's stories as a *consequence* of the effort to maintain a traditional masculine identity. For instance, certain traits possessed by the female characters are those that the male is struggling to disown. The more strongly and assertively the man attempts to dominate and control the woman, the more threatening he finds her, and the more fragile is his own sense of masculine identity. In contrast to this defensive stance, a man who is relatively at ease with the difference within himself will allow the woman to have her own voice instead of insisting on total control of her.

The Evolution of Female Space: A Cautious Rapprochement

The concepts outlined above provide necessary insight for analyzing how Cortázar stakes out his gender identity in relation to the feminine and how it evolves throughout Sommer's stages of desire, with which I concur, for the main part.[14] The body of this book follows a thematic organization according to specific male projections or preoccupations used to frame the feminine in Cortázar's stories, although there is a basic chronological development among the themes. The following pages discuss the earliest phase in order to help contextualize, within the trajectory of Cortázar's short stories, the depictions of female characters analyzed in chapters 3 through 7. This section presents an in-depth discussion of stage one because the remainder of the book concentrates on stories from subsequent phases. Additionally, phase one represents the starting point from which Cortázar's portrayal of female space will evolve, so a discussion of the earliest stage provides a base-line evaluation against which his progress toward a more balanced and less threatening view of sexual difference can be measured. In his early stories, the desire for the Other is ominous and threatening, so he strives to erect a hermetic boundary between himself and his terrible desire, attempting to barricade the masculine self from the feared feminine (m)other. Gradually he begins to reconcile himself to the feminine within, and cautiously lets down some of his defenses.

The stories of *Bestiario* represent the initial and most pathological expression of Cortázar's gender anxiety, when the desire for the mother is strongly censored, surfacing through phobic symptoms. The "brittle veneer of language" that articulates the conventions of "the correct bourgeois world" (Sommer, "A Nowhere" 231, 237) forms a barrier intended to protect the masculine ego from his incestuous desire. However, there are cracks in the shield. When the uncivilized passions burst forth from the safeguarded zona sagrada and meet the light of day, they wreak havoc and destruction.

Cortázar, in his description of the creative process of his irrational tales, stresses the threatening nature of these irrational impulses that must be exorcised through the writing of the story:

Un verso admirable de Pablo Neruda: *Mis criaturas nacen de un largo rechazo*, me parece la mejor definición de un proceso en el que escribir es de alguna manera exorcisar, rechazar criaturas invasoras proyectándolas a una condición que paradójicamente les da existencia universal a la vez que las sitúa en el otro extremo del puente, donde ya no está el narrador que ha soltado la burbuja de su pipa de yeso. Quizá sea exagerado afirmar que todo cuento breve plenamente logrado, y en especial los cuentos fantásticos, son productos neuróticos, pesadillas o alucinaciones neutralizadas mediante la objetivación y el traslado a un medio exterior al terreno neurótico; de todas maneras, en cualquier cuento breve memorable se percibe esa polarización, como si el autor hubiera querido desprenderse lo antes posible y de la manera más absoluta de su criatura, exorcisándola en la única forma en que le era dado hacerlo: escribiéndola. (*Último round* 66)

The terms Cortázar uses to describe his relationship with these "criaturas invasoras," such as "rechazar," "desprenderse de," and "[situarlas] en el otro extremo del puente," point to the fact that the impulses must be cast out of the self, disowned. We may consider what is being repressed and disowned to be the desire for the utopia of oneness with the mother, a desire that threatens his masculine identity.

So strongly censored is the forbidden desire in *Bestiario* that there is only one longed-for maternal figure in the entire collection: Rema in "Bestiario." Instead, the dangerous impulses surface in the twisted form of phobic symptoms. The formation of phobic symptoms is a process characteristic of anxiety hysteria whereby the anxiety is liberated by displacing it onto a specific external object (Laplanche and Pontalis

37–38). The beasts depicted in the stories—miniature rabbits, a tiger, candied cockroaches—are the external objects onto which the anxiety is bound. At the same time, the animals embody the repudiated sexuality, which is relegated to the category of the bestial, producing fascination and fear (Frosh 104). Consider, for example, the translator who vomits tiny rabbits in "Carta a una señorita en París." In his working hours, the translator pursues the "masculine" activity of knowing and ordering, while the pesky rabbits convey the supposedly "feminine" activities of embodiment and disruption.[15] The translator is initially fascinated with his creatures, and struggles to conceal them from Sara the maid who represents the bourgeois conventions. Finally, however, they escalate out of control. Realizing he can no longer maintain a façade of "normalcy," the translator commits suicide. The story dramatizes the repudiation of the feminine within; it is a compulsive reenactment of the birth trauma that finally overwhelms him. The following statement, which Frosh uses to summarize the sexual ambivalence betrayed by Freud in *The Interpretation of Dreams,* could just as well apply to the protagonist of "Carta a una señorita en París": "right at the heart of this text . . . is an uncertainty over gender: a masculinity that plays with, represses and expresses, its own fragmentation and ambivalent feminine identifications . . . [raising] continually the question of the sexual identity of dreamer and interpreter" (43). Thus, the phobic symptoms in Cortázar's early stories can be considered a manifestation of the author's hysteria over the fear of being feminized by his desire for the womb (or to *be* the womb), a desire that interferes with the necessity to differentiate himself from the mother.

The hysterical women frequently found in Cortázar's early stories embody the irrationality and neuroses that the male characters are struggling to disown. It is as if the author were trying to cast off this unwanted part of self onto his female characters, but it invariably returns to haunt him. The story which immediately comes to mind in this regard is "Las Ménades" (*Final del juego*)—a vivid depiction of the protagonist's persistent attempts to disassociate himself from the hysterical feminine other. The frenzied women become a receptacle for the "feminine" hysteria that is disowned by the detached and haughty narrator who takes great pains to establish his noninvolvement in the women's hysterical admiration of the orchestra conductor. At the end of the story, however, he admits to his gnawing guilt about his supercilious indifference, calling his behavior "el escándalo final y absoluto de aquella noche" (*Cc* 1, 326). Is he referring to the fact that his horrified fascination with the hysteria paralyses him into inaction when the maestro is devoured? Is he implying that his role as passive spectator turns him into an accomplice of the irrational frenzy? Whatever the reason for his guilt, he finally owns up to the fact that he is somehow implicated in the hysteria, it somehow impinges on him.[16] Another story from *Final del juego*, "La puerta condenada," hauntingly portrays the narrator's ultimate identification with the female hysteria that he initially disowns. At first the traveling businessman is certain that the phantom cries of a child that keep him awake at night in his hotel room come from a hysterical woman on the other side of the wall. But after callously driving the woman away by mocking the sounds, he continues to hear the whimpers. Thus, a psychological fantastic interpretation leads us to the conclusion that the infant's cries emanate from within him. These stories illustrate how Cortázar's male protagonists try to turn women into a receptacle for their disowned hysteria; anxiety is produced when the man realizes it cannot be contained in the other, but spills over to implicate him. Man tries to distance himself from the hysteric other, but discovers it within himself.

Feminist readings of Freud's case study of Dora provide an instructive model for understanding the encounter between the patriarchal male and feminine hysteria. The studies collected in the anthology *In Dora's Case: Freud-Hysteria-Feminism*[17] analyze how Freud invented psychoanalysis on the basis of his clinical experience with hysterical patients, most of them women. In the introduction to this collection, Claire Kahane observes that Freud read "hysterical discourse by experiencing its source within himself" (22). In other words, the gaze he turned on these hysterics was productive precisely because it revealed what was 'reading' within himself (Frosh paraphrasing Felman 23). In reference to the Dora case, Toril Moi explains "psychoanalysis is born in the encounter between the hysterical woman and the positivist man of science. . . . Freud more or less unwittingly opens the way for a new understanding of human knowledge. . . . Freud's . . . act of listening represents an effort to *include* the irrational discourse of femininity in the realm of science" (Moi 196–197).[18] Following this reasoning, we could say that Cortázar's stories are born of the encounter between the hysterical discourse of his unconscious and the rational and ordering activity of the lettered man who is horrified by what he has dreamt, and wants to exorcise it through his writing. In this process he universalizes and raises to the level of social production the hysterical discourse.

Finally, to summarize the gender anxiety in stage one of Sommer's scheme, the stories of *Bestiario* and *Final del juego* speak of a fragile and defensive gender identity, with the protagonists battling vainly to maintain a border between their precarious ego and the feminine.

By the second phase, the maternal figure is no longer under interdiction, and two of Cortázar's most powerful mothers appear in "Cartas de mamá" (*Armas secretas*) and "La salud de los enfermos" (*Todos los fuegos el fuego*). Variations of the mother-son dynamics reappear throughout the remainder of Cortázar's literary production, as he apparently continues to work through those issues via his writing. During stage two, lovers begin to appear, and the protagonists relate to them with the same ambivalence as directed toward the mother. Since sexual love is a reenactment of the earliest love relation with the mother, the protagonists fear their desire, associating it with dependence and loss of mastery. When faced with demands for intimacy and mutually dependent relationships, they react with incapacity and terror.[19] Sommer has explained that in Cortázar's second phase the no-win games serve to keep the would-be romantic partners at a safe distance, "Manuscrito hallado en un bolsillo" (*Octaedro*) being a prime example of this phenomenon. The erotic and dangerous game serves as a buffer zone where "play" with the feminine as erotic partner is allowed, but intimacy is kept at bay by designing the rules of the game so as to preclude the possibility of winning.[20]

The two final phases of Sommer's categorization can be collapsed into one for my purposes. Here the feminine is experienced as less threatening; Cortázar is able to lower his defenses and negotiate an easier relationship with it, in some instances even coming to respect and admire the difference, and accept the feminine within himself. Female characters are less controlled, and women sometimes subvert the power play of a domineering male, for instance in "Cambio de luces" (*Alguien que anda por ahí*) and "Diario para un cuento" (*Deshoras*). The "deliberate embrace of others" (Sommer, "A Nowhere" 250) becomes a way to arrest the narcissistic mother fixation. Sometimes this is achieved through a political cause, such as in "Apocalipsis de Solentiname" and "Recortes de prensa," and sometimes through an unyielding desire for a totalizing romantic love, accompanied by a Lacanian acknowledgment of the unattainability of that desire, for instance in "Orientación de los gatos" (*Deshoras*) (Sommer, "A Nowhere" 251). At the same time, progress toward an easy relationship with the other, female, space is uneven, with setbacks along the way. It seems that total renunciation of a lingering patriarchal mind-set was impossible for Cortázar; indeed, with his characteristic candor, he did at times manifest an awareness of his own limitations in this regard. Thus, to characterize Cortázar's overall evolution, his stories initially reveal a sense of horror and denial in face of the incestuous desire, accompanied by the ill-fated struggle to establish differentiation, and eventually arrive at a tentative coming-to-terms with the feminine, resulting in a critique of dead-ended categories and exploration of new possibilities.

In this way, Cortázar negotiates his gender identity through a constantly changing dance with the feminine, a continual play of difference, at first an obsessive distancing and then a cautious approach. On this shifting ground he constructs his precarious masculine self. Many of Cortázar's stories can be read as the unraveling of gender identification. The instability of the male subject results from its total and overwhelming dependence on the Other. "Masculine" identity, as such, is untenable because it is impossible to sustain rigid boundaries between traditional masculine and feminine essential qualities or functions. In this sense, Cortázar's (post)modernity consists in the decentering and problematizing of male experience—the deconstruction of traditional patriarchal masculine identity.

A biographical anecdote reveals that Cortázar's critique and deconstruction of machismo was not entirely unconscious on his part. Cristina Peri Rossi reports Cortázar's expression of regret and rectification for having implied that women are passive readers: "—Me equivoqué . . . Pertenezco a una generación muy machista y cuando dije eso, respondía a un código cultural reaccionario y atrasado . . . .Pero sabés bien que me he corregido y soy un hombre nuevo, es decir, medio mujer" (70–71). Thus with two words—"medio mujer"—Cortázar lets down his defenses and blows open the boundary between "masculine" and "feminine."

This brief overview of the evolution of female space in Cortázar's short stories provides context for the analysis of selected stories in the chapters that follow. As mentioned above, the chapters are organized thematically, but with consideration given to the evolution of female space in Cortázar's work. Each chapter draws on different theoretical readings to inform its approach.

Before launching into the analysis of female characters, chapter 2, "The Personal and Cultural Context" offers a glimpse of Cortázar's relationships with women and the feminine in his personal life, and also examines cultural values attached to motherhood in order to understand Cortázar's portrayal of mothers within a larger cultural context.

Chapter 3, "The Omnipotent Mother," inspired by Benjamin's study of maternal omnipotence, focuses on the dominant mother figures in "Cartas de mamá" and "La salud de los enfermos." Using Benjamin's feminist insights to elucidate the dynamics between the mother and her children enables us to get beyond the "Terrible Mother" archetype that pervades existing studies of Cortázar's mothers. In conjunction with this, attention will be given to how the stories dramatize the idealized and oppressive status of motherhood in Western and Argentine culture.

Chapter 4, "Mothers and Lovers," deals with complementary phenomena that are pervasive in Cortázar's *oeuvre:* the conflicted desire for/ dread of the mother, which is then projected onto potential lovers, thwarting the ability to sustain a complementary love relationship. The depiction of unresolved Oedipal desire in "Deshoras" and "Historias que me cuento" is analyzed in depth, taking its cue from Madelon Sprengnether's analysis of the pre-Oedipal mother in Freud's writings. Next, we will examine four stories that depict the ambivalent relationship between the boy and his mother, or a maternal figure. Last, this chapter turns to the frustrated love relationships in Cortázar's stories, understanding them as a consequence of the maternal obsession. Since numerous critics have analyzed these romantic relationships, this section features a general presentation and discussion of the variations of the love theme, with a concise analysis of selected stories.

As mentioned above, in the latter part of his career Cortázar becomes less controlling with female characters, allowing himself to be surprised by them (Sommer, "A Nowhere" 236). Chapter 5, "Defiant Women, or Coming to Terms with Difference" focuses on Luciana in "Cambio de luces," one of Cortázar's first female characters who resists the male protagonist's attempt to control her. Using Shoshana Felman's feminist strategies of reading, which show us how to reclaim female desire in a male-centered text, we discover how this seemingly retiring and submissive woman ends up undermining her lover Tito's bid to remake her according to his desire. Preceding the analysis of "Cambio de luces" is a brief discussion of other stories in which we can perceive Cortázar's new attitude toward his female characters.

The last two chapters shift to Cortázar's concerns with national identity and politics, focusing on the centrality of female space in his conception of these. Chapter 6, "*Eurídice, Argentina:* Women and the

Guilty Expatriate," deals with the crucial role played by Cortázar's female characters in his quest to reconcile his divided allegiance to Argentina and France. Based on the stories "El otro cielo," "Cartas de mamá," "Recortes de prensa," and "Diario para un cuento," this chapter analyzes how female space functions as the site where Cortázar problematizes his feelings of guilt and loss in regard to his expatriation. Carlos Alonso's *The Burden of Modernity* helps to understand and contextualize Cortázar's ambivalent relationship to his homeland, while *Foundational Fictions* by Doris Sommer provides a conceptual framework for the allegorical reading in which national destiny is married to personal passion. Also important for my understanding of the image of the feminine in masculinist ideologies of nation are the studies of Mary Louise Pratt and Francine Masiello.[21]

"Women and the 'Dirty War,' " the final chapter, explores the role of gender in Cortázar's narratives, which denounce the military dictatorship in Argentina, studying how he uses systems of gender identity as metaphors for the oppressor and the oppressed. My understanding of how the ideology of the regime depended on alternatively demonizing and idealizing the feminine is indebted to Diana Taylor's *Disappearing Acts*. I have also found useful Francine Masiello's article "Cuerpo/presencia: mujer y estado social en la narrativa argentina durante el proceso militar," which explains the role of women in literary production during the years of the dictatorship. The first part of the chapter focuses on how the female body represents the beleaguered Argentina in Cortázar's stories "Pesadillas" and "Graffiti," while the second part analyses how Cortázar depicts politicized mothers who opposed the regime in "Recortes de prensa" and the essay "Nuevo elogio de la locura." In these last two pieces, I will focus on the portrayal and meaning of "maternal madness." In "Recortes" the narrator Noemí's identification with victimized mothers has a nefarious outcome, as it results in her participation in another atrocity. However, Cortázar's identification with the *supposed* madness of the *Locas de la Plaza de Mayo* in "Nuevo elogio" has the opposite meaning—it represents a profoundly positive and life-affirming value. In this nonfictional piece, female space becomes the "me-too" instead of the "not-me." I will consider the essay "Nuevo elogio" as the culmination of Cortázar's evolution in regard to the feminine because, through the human rights agenda, Cortázar embraces and celebrates the power of the maternal bond. Instead of envisioning maternal space as a place to project his fears and fantasies, it becomes a force for truth and justice.

Chapter 2

ॐ

The Personal and Cultural Context

En caso necesario, trátelo amablemente de machista, y poco a poco dejará
de serlo.

—Dunlop and Cortázar, *Los autonautas de la cosmopista*

Cortázar and Women, Cortázar on Women, Cortázar's Women

A look at Cortázar's life provides insight into the probable genesis (or
trigger) of his obsessions—the absence of his father and the close but
conflicted relationship with his mother. Accounts of his three most important romantic relationships along with his statements about women
provide a fuller picture of his experiences and detail the evolution of his
attitude toward femininity over the course of his life. Thanks to the fact
that Cortázar was an amazingly prolific letter writer—hundreds of his
letters were published in a three-volume set in 2000—and that he gave
many interviews, three of them book-length, we have access to his own
words on a wide variety of issues. Statements made by his sister and his
friends, along with several recently published biographies,[1] provide additional information about his life and opinions.

Cortázar's father abandoned the family when Julio and his sister,
Ofelia, were young, and various sources describe the emotional bond
between Cortázar and his mother. Perhaps the most vivid statement
comes from his sister: "Ofelia asegura que Julio y su madre eran 'carne
y uña' " (Castelo and Guerriero 2). His mother was only twenty when he
was born, and their relationship continued to be intense until his death
(she outlived him). She gave him his first books, and he shared with her
an interest in reading and telling stories (Goloboff 12–13). Ofelia reports that he wrote his mother regularly—"Cada quince días, llegaba
una carta para mamá, en toda la vida que ha estado lejos"—and goes on
to explain that in her old age, his mother, concerned about who might
get hold of his letters, had them burned: "¿en manos de quién, esto que

21

es todo cariño, que es todo intimidad, entre un hijo y una madre, en manos de quién iba a parar? Ella prefirió que todo eso se quemara" (Goloboff 16).

But, as a matter of fact, not all of the letters to his mother were burned—eleven letters written between 1980 and 1983 are included in the published collection. However, few of these appear in their entirety— practically all have ellipses indicating omitted material. Most of the portions that have been published describe what Cortázar is doing—his work, his travels. Among the parts made public, the most personal passage appears in the letter of 1981 in which he assures his mother that he has no objection to her having the letters burned:

> hablando de cartas . . . si Ángel las convierte en humo, como decís, tanto vos como yo nos vamos a quedar tranquilos. Lo que teníamos que decirnos en nuestras cartas a lo largo de tantos años, fue dicho, y los dos recibimos nuestros mensajes que eran solamente para nosotros. ¿Qué razón hay para dejarle a otros esas cosas que fueron nuestro diálogo de madre a hijo y de hijo a madre? Creo que tu punto de vista no tiene por qué dolernos ni a vos ni a mí; lo que tenemos que decirnos lo seguiremos diciendo en nuestras cartas, y nadie tiene que meter la nariz en ellas. De modo, mamita, que si seguís pensando que es mejor quemar esos papeles, no dudes ni un minuto, porque yo te acompaño en eso como en cualquier cosa. (*Cartas* 1718)

Cortázar's response implies that the letters that were to go up in smoke contained highly private discussions between mother and son. The author revealed some of his most intimate secrets through his interviews and writings, but the bulk of Cortázar's lifelong correspondence with his mother is forever lost to peering eyes.

Declarations made by Cortázar in various interviews confirm the close relationship with his mother, along with his respect for her. To Omar Prego he explains the importance of his mother in his early formation and throughout his career, concluding "mi madre fue una gran iniciadora en mi camino de lector primero y de escritor después" (42). He expresses admiration for her struggle to give her two children a good upbringing after her husband left, and appreciation that she understood his extraordinarily precocious and voracious addiction to reading. For instance, when a doctor recommended that he be forbidden to read for a period of time, he says his mother, being "sensible e inteligente," did not enforce the prohibition (Soler Serrrano 70). Other references to his mother are enigmatic, leaving much to the imagination. For instance, in speaking of his childhood, he admitted to Bruno Berg "había cosas que me dolían. Hubiera querido tener un contacto más de adulto con mi madre" (128). The most telling allusion comes in his interview with Julio Huasi, when he says coyly, "Y de la adolescencia, no vamos a hablar, que lo hagan la Srta. Cora o la mamá de Roberto, si mis lectores se acuerdan de ellas" (62). Yes, we do recall those stories. "La señorita Cora" is about Pablo, a fifteen-year-old boy who is hospitalized for an appendectomy. In his hospital bed, he is smitten by Cora, the pretty young nurse who tantalizes and teases him as she gives him medical attention. "La mamá de Roberto" refers to the story "Ud. se tendió a tu lado." Roberto appears to experience a strong sexual attraction to his mother, who is struggling herself with conflicted feelings about keeping him close to her, as opposed to giving him independence to pursue a relationship with a girl his age. What could la Srta. Cora or Roberto's mother tell us about Cortázar's adolescence, other than the tale of a young boy who is confused and tormented by his strong attraction to a young maternal figure?[2]

René Prieto, in his analysis of the domineering mother figures in Cortázar's stories speculates: "It is likely (whether consciously or not is immaterial) that Cortázar blamed his own mother for a traumatic separation that seems not to have been resolved for many years" (*Body of Writing* 54). This may be true, but in my opinion, there is stronger evidence suggesting that Cortázar felt *too* close to his mother, and struggled for many years to establish his emotional independence from her. And these difficulties in separation could have resulted in a type of defensive retaliation, embodied in the manipulative "Terrible Mother" figures that populate his stories.

Cortázar does confess to an incest complex—not with his mother, but with his sister, Ofelia, who was fourteen months his junior. He discusses it in his revealing interview with Evelyn Picón Garfield, saying that initially he was shocked when a reader of *Bestiario* told him he had a problem with incest. He then discovered that it was true: "Yo empecé a pensar y a descubrir que efectivamente a través de mis sueños yo tengo un problema incestuoso con una hermana mía . . . yo me he despertado muchas veces impresionado porque me he acostado con mi hermana en el sueño" (43). It is important to note, as pointed out by Prieto, that due to the strong self-censorship at work in regard to incestuous feelings for the mother, the son may displace these feelings to a sister (*Body of Writing* 67).

A possible explanation for his obsession with *"otredad"* or femininity is that he was raised among women. Cortázar was six years old when his father abandoned the family, and from then on he was brought up in a household consisting of his mother, his maternal grandmother, a female cousin of his mother, and his sister (Goloboff 15). When Picón Garfield asks him what it was like to "crecer entre mujeres" (100), his response is intriguing for its unintentional revelations:

> Como es lógico, como todo chico que se cría entre mujeres, cuando entré en la adolescencia tuve que quitarme algunas costumbres femeninas, que se van pegando, ciertas maneras de hablar, ciertos gustos. Pero eso en un chico de tendencias normales, que no está destinado a ser un homosexual o un invertido o la peor forma de homosexualidad, el hombre que quiere ser una mujer, eso, claro, un chico se lo quita muy fácilmente en el colegio secundario. Porque son sus compañeros que con maldad o sin maldad se lo hacen notar inmediatamente, o le imitan cuando dice alguna frase con una cierta inflexión que puede sonar un poco amanerada o femenina, se la repiten tomándole el pelo, y el chico reacciona naturalmente y no lo vuelve a hacer. De manera que eso no, realmente no fue un problema para mí. En poco tiempo entré en un mundo perfectamente coherente sin esa clase de problema. De modo que la influencia femenina no creo, en fin, que haya una presencia demasiado marcada. (100)

In a single statement Cortázar assures us *no less than six times* that he got rid of feminine traits—and quite easily and naturally at that. His insistence reveals a need to assert his masculine gender identity, which meant establishing the division between himself, as a "normal" male, and the feminine, and then strongly repudiating the feminine as the "not-me" (or at least the "no-longer me"). His statement points to his acute—and even painful since he implies the other boys teased him— awareness of the boundaries between the masculine and feminine, and his vital need to shore up his masculinity by eliminating any mannerisms that could identify him with femininity.

Although Cortázar hardly ever spoke about his father, it is likely that his absence played an important part in Cortázar's seemingly obsessive need to distance himself from (and even denigrate) the mother and femininity in general. Psychoanalyst Jessica Benjamin's explanation can shed some light on Cortázar's circumstances:

> The "father hunger" shown by sons of absent fathers is primarily a reaction to lack of homoerotic love. In heterosexual men it becomes an im-

pediment to loving women, not simply because there is no "role model" but because the erotic energy is tied to the frustrated wish for recognition from the father. . . . Frequently, the thwarting of paternal identificatory love pushes the boy to deny his identificatory love of the mother on whom he depends too exclusively, spurring an exaggerated repudiation of femininity. (*Like Subjects* 67–68)

Thus, based on Benjamin's observation, the absence of a father figure could have been a decisive factor in the problematic nature of Cortázar's love relations in his fiction, his portrayals of "terrible mothers," and his repudiation of femininity.

In Cortázar's rambling reply to Picón Garfield, cited above, he also implies that he does not harbor homosexual tendencies. Much like the feminine, homosexuality is depicted as the repudiated "not-me," and his references to it in his fiction and in his statements are ambiguous. For instance, in "Las babas del diablo," the homosexual man who is trying to procure a young boy is depicted as grotesque and sinister. In the same interview, while admitting that "Las babas" does present "un aspecto negativo de la homosexualidad . . . una tentativa de corrupción, de envilecimiento de un menor" (122), Cortázar insists it would be the same problem if the man were trying to procure a young girl. From a political standpoint, Cortázar expresses an illuminated view in regard to homosexuality, stating his complaint with socialism's backward stance: "El socialismo en general sigue considerando la homosexualidad como una enfermedad, como una tara, concepto que el psicoanálisis, la medicina y la psicología profunda han destruido hace muchísimo tiempo" (Picón Garfield 121). A statement made in the last year of his life represents an unqualified condemnation of *machista* homophobia: "el tema de la homosexualidad . . . ahora es también objeto de una discusión fraternal pero muy viva con los nicargüenses cada vez que voy para allá. Yo creo que esa actitud machista de rechazo, despectiva y humillante hacia la homosexualidad, no es en absoluto una actitud revolucionaria" (Prego 195).[3]

As an adult, Cortázar had important romantic relationships with three women. While he was still living in Buenos Aires, however, he was sure he would remain a bachelor: "De 1946 a 1951, vida porteña, solitaria e independiente; convencido de ser un solterón irreductible" (*Cartas* 1154).[4] But in 1953, at the age of thirty-nine, he married Aurora Bernárdez, an Argentine woman four years his junior, whom he met before his departure for Europe, and who later joined him in France. In a letter to a friend, Cortázar describes their happiness together: "Lo pasamos muy bien, aunque Aurora tiene conmigo el trabajo que te puedes imaginar: cocinar, lavarme, arreglar la cama, etc. Pero estamos juntos, y en realidad nos divertimos mucho" (*Cartas* 272). Goloboff tells us they had "fuertes afinidades, sobre todo intelectuales" (97); Herráez calls Bernárdez his "alma gemela" and mentions "[l]a connivencia casi mágica entre ambos" (98). In many letters, Cortázar alludes to their sharing of literary conversations and opinions. He obviously had a great deal of respect for her literary instincts, as exemplified in the following passage in a letter to his editor, Francisco Porrúa: "el libro [*Rayuela*] sólo tiene un lector: Aurora. Por consejo suyo, traduje al español largos pasajes que en un principio había decidido dejar en inglés y en francés" (*Cartas* 483).

Mario Vargas Llosa, who considered Cortázar and Bernárdez soulmates, has a vivid recollection of the last time he saw them together in 1967: "nunca dejó de maravillarme el espectáculo que significaba ver y oír conversar a Aurora y Julio, en tándem. Todos los demás parecíamos sobrar. . . . La perfecta complicidad, la secreta inteligencia que parecía unirlos era algo que yo admiraba y envidiaba en la pareja" (13). " 'La pareja perfecta existe,' " Vargas Llosa recalls telling his wife Patricia, " 'Aurora y Julio han sabido realizar ese milagro: un matrimonio feliz'. Pocos días después recibí carta de Julio anunciándome su separación," continues Vargas Llosa. "Creo que nunca me he sentido tan despistado" (22).

In his letters of 1968, we read how Cortázar explains their separation to several friends. To Julio Silva he writes: "Quiero terminar esta carta con algo de tono muy personal y muy penoso. . . . Una crisis lenta pero inevitable, un largo proceso de cuatro años, nos ha puesto frente a una situación que, como gente inteligente y que se quiere y se estima, tratamos de resolver de la manera menos penosa posible" (*Cartas* 1256– 1257). To Vargas Llosa he admits: "Estoy bastante destruido por dentro" (*Cartas* 1277). Goloboff provides two reasons for the end of their relationship: Aurora did not share Julio's newly militant political convictions, and the romantic attraction (probably on both sides) had ceased some time ago (170). Peri Rossi, who had hoped for a reconciliation between Julio and Aurora, witnessed Cortázar's sadness: "Cortázar arrastraba cierta tristeza, una nostalgia por ese matrimonio deshecho que posiblemente sólo le podía confesar a una mujer" (55). Peri Rossi says that Bernárdez asked for a divorce because of his involvement with Ugné Karvelis. In spite of their painful separation, they maintained their friendship and mutual affection and respect (Herráez 202). In December 1982, a year after the death of his second wife, Cortázar gave Bernárdez rights to his literary production. She cared for him in his final days, and was at his bedside when he died. Bernárdez has prepared posthumous editions of many of his early unpublished works, as well as the three-volume collection of his letters.

At the time his marriage to Aurora Bernárdez was coming apart, Cortázar met Ugné Karvelis, a Lithuanian woman who was a literary agent for the Gallimard publishing house, working in the area of Latin America. They had met briefly in France, at the publishing house, and their relationship blossomed when they coincided in Cuba in 1967 (Goloboff 170–171). Once he separated from Aurora, Cortázar and Karvelis lived together, but never married. Karvelis was a loyal supporter of the Cuban Revolution, and it is said that she was influential in Cortázar's deep commitment to both the Cuban and Nicaraguan Revolutions. Additionally, her friends say she was instrumental in the international diffusion of Cortázar's work. Herráez, however, disputes those who believe that Karvelis played a decisive role in Cortázar's politicization and growing literary fame (209).

The relationship between Cortázar and Karvelis was stormy, and explanations given for their eventual breakup include her abuse of alcohol and her competitive spirit that could not tolerate being reduced to the companion of an increasingly famous man. Peri Rossi relates various incidents illustrating Karvelis's intense and hostile jealously that poisoned their relationship (56–58). In several letters to friends, Cortázar expresses his desire to maintain a friendship with her, but says it is impossible due to "una agresión demasiado agotadora" (*Cartas* 1637)[5] and "sus reacciones y sus manera de ser" (*Cartas* 1729).[6] His strongest statement about Ugné appears in a letter to Picón Garfield: "me temo que no habrá posibilidad de la menor relación amistosa: hasta ahora por lo menos tengo que defenderme de una agresividad permanente y vengativa que a veces se vuelve insoportable" (*Cartas a una pelirroja* 68). The definitive end to their relationship came in 1978, several months after Cortázar met the "love of his life," Carol Dunlop (Goloboff 170–173).

Cortázar and Dunlop met in Canada when he was on a lecture circuit. Born in the United States in 1946, she was thirty-two years younger than Julio (Ugné was 22 years younger). Dunlop went to live in Canada as a result of her opposition to U.S. involvement in the Vietnam War. Residing in Quebec, she adopted French as her written language;

like Cortázar she was a writer of fiction (Goloboff 249–250). The attraction was immediate. "[L]a vio como una predestinada aparición," reports Goloboff (250), and they had an intimate and harmonious relationship until her premature death. Peri Rossi remarks the tenderness between them and the sense of harmony they transmitted, and another friend describes Cortázar as radiant when he was with Carol, characterizing her as humble yet self-possessed.[7] Still another testimonial of their happiness together comes from Carlos Fuentes: "Nunca vi a Cortázar más contento que la útima vez que lo vi, en enero de 1982, casado con Carol Dunlop . . . la alegría de Carol y Julio era la del perfecto encuentro de dos imaginaciones amorosas" (1). Dunlop shared Cortázar's love for Nicaragua and its people, and his enthusiasm for the Nicaraguan Revolution. Their last sojourn together in Nicaragua was cut short when Carol's deteriorating health forced then to return to Paris, and she died in early November of 1982 (Goloboff 275–276). Cortázar was devastated by her death. Also in poor health, he declined rapidly after loosing Carol, and died on February 12, 1984.[8] Cortázar and Dunlop are buried together in Montparnasse Cemetery in Paris.

A tribute to their love is *Los autonautas de la cosmopista*, the chronicle of their unconventional car trip from Paris to Marseilles, in which they took thirty-two days to complete the 800-kilometer (480-mile) drive. The rules of their odyssey dictated that they stop in every other rest station, spend the night in the second, and never leave the highway. Cortázar completed and published the book relating their adventure of mutual discovery after her death. On the last page, he calls their voyage: "ese avance en la felicidad y en el amor del que salimos tan colmados que nada, después, incluso viajes admirables y horas de perfecta armonía, pudo superar ese mes fuera del tiempo, ese mes interior donde supimos por primera y última vez lo que era la felicidad absoluta" (305–306). Tomás Borge, the commander of the Nicaraguan Revolution, who came to be a close friend of the couple, perceives a connection between Cortázar's love for Dunlop and his devotion to others: "Fue capaz de amar de un modo tan integral a su compañera, lo que a su vez refleja la capacidad de entrega que posee Cortázar para con las otras personas" (cited by Goloboff 278). Thus, perhaps the fact that Cortázar achieved such an intimate and fulfilling relationship in the final years of his life, along with his enduring friendship with Bernárdez, can be considered a reflection, in his personal life, of his warm and expansive nature, of his ultimate embrace of humanity.[9]

In his professional life, the change in Cortázar's attitude toward women is evidenced in his creation, and later retraction, of the derogatory term *lector hembra*. He coined the concept in *Rayuela* (1963) to connote a passive, uncritical reader, a gaffe that he never seemed to be able to live down. His repeated apologies provide concrete evidence of his evolution from a cavalier machismo to a more enlightened attitude, although he does reveal—in isolated statements and stories—persisting ambivalence. One of the first of many sincere recantations came in the 1973 interview with Picón Garfield:

> [P]ido perdón a las mujeres del mundo por haber utilizado una expresión tan machista y tan de subdesarrollo latinoamericano, y eso deberías ponerlo con todas las letras de la entrevista. Lo hice con toda ingenuidad y no tengo ninguna disculpa, pero cuando empecé a escuchar las opiniones de mis amigas lectoras que me insultaban cordialmente, me di cuenta de que había hecho una tontería. (117)

Peri Rossi also comments on his regret for that statement: "Se había arrepentido mucho de esa declaración.—Me equivoqué, Cristina—me dijo" (70).

Notwithstanding this apparently heartfelt regret, his backhanded apology in a 1981 interview with Julio Huasi represents another of those memorable moments when Cortázar unwittingly reveals much more than he intended:

> Según algunas de ellas [críticas escritas o dichas por mujeres] yo he escrito siempre como un tremendo machista, mis personajes femeninos tienden a la inconsistencia, a la pasividad y a la tontería en diversos grados. Nunca me perdonaron aquello de "lector-hembra" con que *Rayuela* se caracterizaba al que se somete a la hipnosis de lo que lee en vez de mantener una distancia crítica y una complicidad vigilante. De nada me ha valido excusarme en muchas ocasiones por esa expresión, desde luego desafortunada, porque las chicas vuelven a la carga cada vez que pueden. Lo malo es que han llegado a acomplejarme. . . . [A]dmito que, al igual que casi todos los escritores latinoamericanos, soy un macho peludo garrote en mano y ramo de flores. (61)

What calls our attention is how he exposes the ambivalence of his attitude toward women, in particular with his complaint: "De nada me ha valido excusarme en muchas ocasiones . . . porque *las chicas* vuelven a la carga cada vez que pueden" (emphasis added). Can we accept that he really has attained a progressive view of women when he apparently does not realize that he is patronizing female critics by calling them *girls*? He depicts them as irrational, hysterical women who won't listen to reason—no matter how many times he apologizes, "the girls" come back with the accusation. What is more, their hysteria has infected him: "Lo malo es que han llegado a acomplejarme." With his characteristic candor and self-mocking humor, he describes himself as an old-fashioned Latin American "macho peludo garrote en mano y ramo de flores." Here, he seems to be joking about his identification with the traditional *machista* image, a stereotype he also links to his peers— other Latin American writers. His tongue-in-cheek characterization of his masculinity—"garrote en mano y ramo de flores"—speaks of the age-old dual denigration and idealization of women: a staff to represent authority and possibly violence, and flowers to woo her.

Cortázar continues his confessional response to Huasi with references to the shortcomings in his view of femininity and the crossover between the women in his life and his literary creations:

> Sin duda, fui y soy torpe en mi visión de lo femenino; sin duda, su lectura por una mujer puede mostrar flaquezas y falencias en esa visión que no por apasionada alcanza a ser lúcida. No sé, ellas están ahí, vienen desde el fondo de mi tiempo, más vivas y queridas que muchas de carne y hueso. Si algo discrimina en mí, no es mi yo consciente; si algo las ofende o las menoscaba, en todo caso no puede ser mi amor y mi ternura. Y todo esto que digo de mis personajes mujeres vale igualmente para lo personal, puesto que es una sola y misma cosa. (61)

With disarming candor, Cortázar admits to clumsiness in his vision of femininity. His profession to have the same "amor y tenura" for both his female characters and real women in his life, since, as he puts it "they are one and the same thing," points to the inextricable connection between his life and his literature. According to Cortázar, then, his portrayal of women in literature closely reflects his own attitude toward women in his life. As several critics have pointed out, at times Cortázar's fiction appears to be a thinly veiled autobiography.

Perhaps Cortázar felt at ease to speak his mind in the interview with Huasi because he was talking with his good friend. In any event, at the time of another interview, conducted by Radio France and one of his last, he articulates a detailed and unequivocal apology for the *machista* attitude in *Rayuela*:[10]

A propósito de esa demoninación de "lector hembra," me acuerdo que hace casi cuatro años, en Venezuela, en una reunión en la universidad, me excusé públicamente frente a las oyentes de haber utilizado esa expresión en *Rayuela*, que me había valido muchas y muy justificadas críticas. Yo creo que *Rayuela* es un libro machista, es decir, dentro de la ignorancia, dentro de la inocencia general en que ese libro fue escrito; es decir: inocencia en materia de historia, ignorancia del contexto histórico de mi época, *prescindencia* de la historia y también *prescindencia* o ignorancia de algunos de nuestros principales defectos latinoamericanos, entre los cuales el machismo es uno de los más graves. . . . El sentido crítico de esto me ha venido después; si lo hubiera tenido en ese momento, jamás hubiera utilizado la expresión "lector hembra" para designar un lector pasivo, y además fui muy duramente castigado por eso. Es el momento de hacer la verdadera autocrítica, porque cuando empecé a recibir una correspondencia muy nutrida con respecto a *Rayuela* descubrí que una gran mayoría de lectores eran mujeres, y eran mujeres que habían leído *Rayuela* con un gran sentido crítico, atacándola o apoyándola o aprobándola pero de ninguna manera en una actitud pasiva, con una actitud de "lector hembra"; es decir, que eran lectoras pero no tenían nada de hembras en el sentido peyorativo que el macho tradicional le da a la palabra hembra. (Blázquez and Chao 1, 4)

Significantly, in this statement, he situates his machismo in a historical, cultural, and political context, and also acknowledges that he has learned of his error from experience with his female readers. Thus, he seems to have reversed his attitude from both a theoretical and an experiential standpoint. In this statement he also alludes to the fact that his consciousness-raising in regard to feminist issues occurred as part of his general political conversion or awakening that came with his "discovery" of the Cuban Revolution in 1963, and his participation in the student protests of Paris in 1968.

Cortázar's life span and experiences encompassed extremes in regard to cultural attitudes toward women, from the deeply ingrained and unquestioned machismo that characterized Argentine society during the 1920s, 1930s, and 1940s, to the heady period of the French feminist movement centered in Paris during the late 1960s and early 1970s. His recantation of earlier *machista* attitudes demonstrates the sensitivity he acquired in regard to feminist issues. At the same time, we could consider his statements in the 1981 Huasi interview as a moment when he lets down his guard, revealing a lingering attitude of condescension toward women. Although Cortázar's struggle to deal with feelings of ambivalence toward women may have continued throughout his life, his fulfilling, if tragically short, union with Carol Dunlop seems to speak of his ultimate achievement of a sense of peace and harmony in a love relationship.

Values Associated with Motherhood

Resonating in the work of Cortázar are images of motherhood that reflect an intricate weave of values originating in Western culture in general, in Hispanic culture, and in Argentine culture. Since many of these concepts will be discussed further in subsequent chapters where they are relevant to my analysis of specific female characters, here I will provide an overview of cultural attitudes and behaviors that underlie Cortázar's depictions of mothers.

In the previous chapter I explored psychoanalytic thought that offers insight into male identification with the mother. Here we will consider feminist studies of motherhood as an institution. These studies address how the image of motherhood, as well as the mother's self-image, is constructed as a result of values and unconscious associations attributed to it in Occidental culture. Adrienne Rich's classic and groundbreaking work, *Of Woman Born,* identifies motherhood as an as idealized and oppressive institution constructed for male need and desire. Selflessness is a basic requisite for mothering because mothers are obliged to subordinate their personal objectives and put the needs of others first, devoting themselves to the well-being of other family members, loving and giving unconditionally (Polatnick 35). Several authors have pointed to the lack of maternal subjectivity; as Luce Irigaray puts it: "So what is a mother? Someone who makes the stereotypical gestures she is told to make, who has no personal language, who has no identity. Mothers and the women within them have been trapped in the role of she who satisfies need but has no access to desire" (50–51).

In a similar vein, Sara Ruddick asserts that maternal thought has emerged out of maternal practices that basically consist of satisfying the child's demands for preservation, growth, and acceptability ("Maternal Thinking" 215). According to Ruddick, mothering continuously calls for a radical kind of self-denial, which is particularly tempting in societies where mothers are rewarded for their failure in self-preservation ("Maternal Thinking" 238). Ruddick also discusses the issue of mothers' power, asserting that "the 'vast apparatus of hatred' attributes to mothers and their work amazing power," and mothers do, in fact, have immense power over their children's emotional needs. However, this power lies, in part, in the eye of the beholder. A mother sees herself as relatively powerless: on the one hand, she is subject to the workings of nature—death and illness of the child frustrate her efforts; on the other hand, if she is expected to serve the needs of the father and society in general, she is impotent in a social sense. From this perspective, Ruddick points out, the powerlessness of mother is notorious (*Toward a Politics* 34–35).

While self-denial and repression characterize maternal practices in general, the tradition of *marianismo* and strong patriarchal values serve to accentuate this pattern of behavior in the Hispanic world. *Marianismo*, which compliments machismo, is named after the Virgin Mary, who is considered the model of sacrifice and devotion to family and children. It teaches women they must sacrifice everything for their family, particularly the male members. They are solely responsible for bringing up the children and attending to the household, and must stoically put up with husbands who stray or fail to support the family. Evelyn Stevens defines *marianismo* as "the cult of feminine spiritual superiority, which teaches that women are semi-divine, morally superior to and spiritually stronger than men" (91). On the one hand, *marianismo* creates a pattern of repressive social expectations that a traditional woman may use as a standard for her own behavior. On the other hand, it elicits a sense of respect and even reverence for the figure of the morally superior yet submissive and self-abnegating mother.

Finally, several cultural critics have noted the exacerbated maternal sentiment particular to Argentina. Argentine writer Horacio Vázquez-Rial observes that the highly maternalistic strain in Argentine culture may be due to "la profunda marca de las dos culturas más maternofílicas, o edípicas, del mundo: la italiana y la judía" (39). And it is possible to identify other factors that have intensified the sense of maternal duty as well as the emotional charge attached to the concept of motherhood in Cortázar's homeland: a mothering campaign connected to European immigration, popular sentiment as expressed through tango lyrics, and the phenomenon of the Madres de la Plaza de Mayo.

The impact of southern European immigration in the creation and development of a governmentally sponsored campaign to foster good mothering is explained by Donna Guy. Between 1880 and 1914, Buenos Aires experienced a huge influx of poor Europeans from Catholic countries where a high rate of infant mortality was accepted and an extensive system of church orphanages encouraged high rates of child abandonment (Guy 156, 169). To counter these values and behaviors, government entities, principally the Buenos Aires municipal government, "devised mothering campaigns that ultimately became incorporated into national policies" (Guy 156). Secular and medical authorities, as well as upper-class women, constructed and disseminated new images of appropriate mothering through classes for women, legislation, and campaigns sponsored by private and governmental agencies. The ideal mother, according to the new socially and politically constructed image, zealously tended to her children's health as well as to their emotional nurturing, providing tenderness and caring, and even placing "devotion to children above devotion to spouse" (Guy 157). The mother was urged to fulfill her responsibility to provide proper love and care in order to play her part in the creation of a vibrant democracy. "By the 1930s," concludes Guy, "the bodily and symbolic nature of mothering had been challenged, reshaped, and redefined. Mothers were important not only for their wombs and breasts but also for their knowledge, emotional commitment, and awareness of patriotic duty" (Guy 170). Guy's research illustrates that specific concepts of what constitutes a good mother are not inherent to mankind, but rather a social and political construct.

Popular culture also plays an important role in capturing, disseminating, and immortalizing the mother's role, as seen in the example of the quintessentially Argentine musical expression, the tango. Eduardo Archetti has analyzed how masculinity is constructed in tango lyrics through the juxtaposition between romantic love and a mother's love. In this discursive context, the images of the ungrateful son and the treacherous *milonguita* (a young woman from the lower-middle classes who goes to the Buenos Aires cabarets seeking excitement and pleasure) are contrasted to the idealized mother. "Maternal love is exalted and closely associated with ideas of purity, suffering, sincerity, generosity, and fidelity. A mother's love is the only permanent feeling . . . For a loving mother there is no place for calculation, second thoughts, or hidden intentions. The idealized mother is the source of boundless love and absolute self-sacrifice" (Archetti 203). Romantic love, in contrast, may be a malevolent deceit. Since the mother cannot be chosen, she represents an absolute contrast to the stream of fickle or unfaithful girlfriends: "The mother is depicted as a model of fidelity and continuity" (Archetti 203–204). Thus, the tango's poetics serve as a means to model, and perhaps perpetuate, gender identities in the public sphere (Archetti 205). The lyrics of tangos such as "Madre," "Madre hay una sola," and "La casita de mis viejos" portray a maudlin relationship between a long-suffering mother and a repentant son who, after abandoning his mother for worldly vices and temptations, finally realizes that Mother is the sole source of unconditional love and forgiveness.

The values associated with motherhood found a unique manifestation in the Madres de la Plaza de Mayo, a women's protest movement which sprang up to protest the "disappearances" of the Argentine "Dirty War" (1976–1983). The Madres, composed mainly of mothers of young people who had been kidnapped, and frequently tortured and killed, by the military dictatorship, organized a courageous and visible resistance movement to the brutal regime that "succeeded in seriously damaging the junta's legitimacy and credibility" (Taylor 189).

They marched silently around a central plaza in Buenos Aires, transforming their private and personal grief into a public and political statement (Navarro 251). It is important to note that they purposely chose to demonstrate *as* mothers, thus exploiting and manipulating stereotypical images of motherhood that had previously controlled them (Taylor 195). Modeling themselves on the stoic and suffering Virgin Mary, they tapped into the cult of *marianismo*. The respect for and almost mystical veneration of the mother in Hispanic society afforded them some degree of (but not complete) protection from retribution by the military. Claiming that they were acting out their responsibility as mothers to take care of their children, they were carrying out the "good mother" role they had been taught by the dominant classes; or, in other words, their actions were "a coherent expression of their socialization" (Navarro 255).

The mothers' protest created a problem for the junta because, as staunch defenders of the mystic of maternity and patriarchal society, they could not openly condemn the women for fulfilling their family duty (Rossi 147). Feminist critics argue that, from the standpoint of positive roles for women, the Madres movement was unfortunate in that it served to reinforce a highly traditional, limited, and repressive definition of womanhood.[11] At the same time, it must be kept in mind that the Madres' campaign was highly effective in calling attention to the atrocities of the military regime.

The following chapter focuses on Cortázar's most powerful fictional mothers—of "Cartas de mamá" and "La salud de los enfermos," who coincidentally are wresting with the tragic loss of a young adult son. While these mothers predate the Madres de la Plaza de Mayo, we could say, in a Borgesian sense, that the Madres create and give meaning to their literary predecessors. Cortázar's later writings, specifically "Recortes de prensa" and "Nuevo elogio de la locura," immortalize his solidarity with this brave group of women who defied military authorities to demand justice for their missing children.

—

Chapter 3

❧

The Omnipotent Mother

[A]mong the few roles open to Argentine women, the suffering mother is
the most popular and certainly the most socially rewarding.
—Taylor, *Disappearing Acts*

The impact of fantasized maternal power on grown children is dramatically portrayed in "La salud de los enfermos" and "Cartas de mamá."
While maternal figures appear frequently in Cortázar's work, the strong-
minded and manipulative mothers in these two stories represent
Cortázar's most penetrating and memorable depictions of motherhood.
The first story recounts the meticulous care given to a fussy and demanding bed-ridden matriarch; the second focuses on the feelings of
dread elicited by the letters an Argentine mother sends to her son in
distant Paris. In both stories, the mothers exercise a powerful control
over the emotions of their adult children.

René Prieto's study explains how Cortázar's personal experience
was transformed into fiction in his stories (*Body of Writing* 18). What
Cortázar's fiction is continually expressing, Prieto demonstrates via his
analysis of various stories, is the primal longing for the maternal body
and anxiety of separation from it. Against this background explanation,
Prieto discusses the portrayal of numerous maternal figures in Cortázar's
work, stressing their perverse and cruel nature. Their depiction as domineering, calculating, hard-hearted, and revengeful, says Prieto, communicates Cortázar's feelings of anger and resentment toward mothers (*Body
of Writing* 50–55). Ana Hernández del Castillo's earlier study of Cortázar's
female characters also focuses on the "Terrible Mother" figure.

This chapter approaches the mothers in "La salud" and "Cartas"
from another perspective: it attempts to resurrect the mother's subjectivity by examining the maternal subtext of desire and despair.[1] Instead
of adopting exclusively the child's view, I will explore social and psychological dynamics that shape both the child's and the mother's thinking.

37

Reading Cortázar's stories in light of research into the mother-child relationship enables us to understand how the negative representation of the mother comes about when the child converts her into his fantasy object. Feminist critiques of the institution of motherhood, presented in chapter 2, explain how social norms that glorify the role of the self-sacrificing mother cause her to play into and perpetuate the maternal "ideal." And psychoanalytic studies that unpack the values and obsessions projected onto the maternal role allow us to detect and examine the fantasies attached to motherhood that drive Cortázar's tales.

Coppélia Kahn, in her discussion of how an understanding of the phenomenon of mothering can lead to the reinterpretation of both psychoanalytic and literary texts, concludes with the following directive:

> For [Freud], the [unplumbable] "navel" of psychic development is identification with the mother. It is "unknown" to him not because it is unknowable but because he is a man, because manhood as patriarchal culture creates it depends on denying, in myriad ways, the powerful ambivalence that the mother inspires. Part of our task as feminist critics, I suggest, is to excavate that gray, shadowy region of identification, particularly male identification with the mother, and trace its influence on perceptions and depictions of women in patriarchal texts. (88)

In this chapter, I would like respond to that challenge, and delve into that "shadowy region" of identification with the mother through the analysis of two of the most powerful mothers Cortázar has created.

"La salud de los enfermos" and "Cartas de mamá" dramatize the consequences for mothers as well as children when the fantasy of maternal omnipotence persists into adult life. The concept of maternal omnipotence, developed by Jessica Benjamin as part of her intersubjective theory, explains how this fantasy of the all-powerful mother originates and is perpetuated.[2] According to Benjamin, the unconscious image of Mother as omnipotent—either all-powerful and overwhelming or engulfingly weak—is a psychic bedrock. Benjamin explains that the child does not see the mother as a separate subject in her own right, but as his or her needed object and fantasy. Benjamin's studies not only provide a more fully elaborated understanding of why the child experiences the mother as terrible and dreaded, as is the case in "Cartas de mamá," but also accounts for the behavior of the mother in "La salud de los enfermos," who participates in—or at least fails to dissipate—this fantasy. Her research on maternal omnipotence helps us see beyond the "Terrible

Mother" archetype that obliterates the mother's subjectivity, and understand the psychic processes that drive the behavior of the children and the mother.

Both stories deal with a family tragedy in which the mother is made to embody the emotions that the children refuse to confront. In "La salud de los enfermos" the grown children ostensibly attempt to protect their ailing mother by keeping her ignorant of the fact that Alejandro, her youngest son, has died. Clues in the text alert us to the fact that the mother eventually figures out the truth but keeps the heart-rending discovery to herself, thus enabling the children to maintain an illusion of a live Alejandro in her eyes. Her children's scheme actually has to do with their attempt to spare themselves the sense of narcissistic loss they would suffer if they shared the reality of his death with mamá. In "Cartas de mamá," Luis steals away his brother Nico's girlfriend, and Nico succumbs to tuberculosis shortly after their wedding. Feeling responsible for his brother's death, Luis takes his bride, Laura, from Buenos Aires to Paris to try to escape his sense of guilt and start a new life. However, this proves to be impossible because every letter from mamá reactivates his guilty conscience. In this situation, Luis projects his deep-seated but unacknowledged desire to be punished for his actions onto his mother whom he makes into his accuser and punisher.

Such a powerful hold have Cortázar's mothers over their adult children in each story that, on the occasion of their brother's death, the surviving children anticipate their mother's wishes and make them their own, thus internalizing and attempting to manage what they construe to be the mother's desire. The deaths of Alejandro and Nico, each in their own way, trigger a power struggle of sorts between the mother and children in which the relationship of domination is based on controlling that death (Bronfen and Goodwin 17). Instead of acknowledging the mother's need to grieve her son's death on her own terms, the children can only envision her as an extension of their own need, and their manner of interpreting her desire turns out to be a reflection of their own desire. In both cases, as is characteristic of all relations of domination, the mother's subjectivity is denied when she is converted into an object to fulfill her children's psychological needs, but at the same time, she wields tremendous power in determining their actions and the course of their lives.

At first glance, it seems curious that both of Cortázar's stories that portray the mother's power are set in motion by the death of her beloved son. But if we consider the power inherent to the representation of death, the relationship between those deaths and maternal omnipotence becomes clear. "Representations of death," Bronfen and Goodwin explain, "necessarily engage questions about power: its locus, its authenticity, its sources, and how it is passed on" (4–5). Death is an independent power in itself, "but other forms of power rely on death to disclose and enforce themselves," and "[t]he dead body presents above all a site where a multitude of fantasies, often complex and contradictory, converge" (Bronfen and Goodwin 5, 17). Cortázar's stories explore the relationship between family members by presenting the family in this extreme situation, and their ways of dealing with the deaths serve to expose and highlight the fantasy of maternal omnipotence. In both stories, maternal power utilizes the son's death to manifest and impose itself.

Initially, the mother in these stories is seen as powerless because she could do nothing to prevent that tragic death. The death of a child represents a radical failure of motherhood's most basic aim: the preservation of the life of one's child. As if to intensify the tragedy, in both stories the necessary work of mourning with its attendant gradual healing process is suppressed and replaced with a dysfunctional response: the refusal to mourn that death as a family. The failure to share the mourning process represents a lack of recognition of the other's subjectivity, and therefore omnipotence at its strongest. Benjamin explains that the solution to the omnipotence dilemma can be found in the intersubjective space of mutual recognition and understanding (*Like Subjects* 92). In Cortázar's scenarios, that space is absent. The upshot of the family's refusal to share the recognition of Alejandro's and Nico's deaths is that the mother ultimately becomes the sole controller of how the young man's untimely death is represented. Due to the denial of the mother's subjectivity and the resulting fantasy of maternal omnipotence, the children unwittingly relinquish that claim to her. As principal mourner, she accrues and despotically wields supreme power over the survivors by controlling the representation of that death—or, to be more precise, the refusal to represent it. Thus, Cortázar's twice-told tale of the death of the son is ultimately about maternal power because the mother legislates his death, utilizing it to manipulate her family.

Another explanation of why death becomes the domain of the mother has to do with the gendering of death. Bronfen and Goodwin discuss this phenomenon:

Death, as the limit of cultural representation, has been associated with that other enigma, the multiply coded feminine body. As the mother, "woman" is the original prenatal dwelling place; and as Mother Earth, she is the anticipated final resting place. Freud has made this much clear: femininity and death are Western culture's two major tropes for the enigma. At the same time, our culture posits death and the feminine as radically other to the norm, the living or surviving masculine subject; they represent the disruption and difference that ground a narcissistic sense of self and stability in a cultural system. But the system must also eliminate them or posit them as limit in order to survive. (13–14)

So the stories express the writer's desire to explore and control, via the written word, the complementary and intertwining enigmas of death and the feminine.

These considerations provide a springboard for tapping into the maternal subtext by reading between the lines, mamá's gestures, her silences. In both cases, the mother's grief is not openly expressed, but rather buried and transformed into a muffled and coded response. The latent drama of the mother's despair and desire must be sought in the gaps—the maternal subtext—and in order to begin to "decode" this subtext, it is necessary to explore the ambivalent and changing power relationships that sustain the fantasy of maternal omnipotence in Cortázar's stories.

"La salud de los enfermos": Caring Exquisitely for Mamá

What can be said about a mother who reduces the grown-up members of her family to lying in order to preserve her own health and the stability of her personal world? Isn't hers the ultimate perversion: to turn her children into slaves while, bedridden and overindulged, she rules over the entire household? (*Body of Writing* 50)

Prieto thus describes the manipulative mother in "La salud de los enfermos" from her children's perspective. But every story has more than one side to it, and, as Benjamin points out, domination is two-way— those who exercise it, and those who submit to it (*Bonds* 5). So let us give mamá and motherhood a fair and equal hearing.

In "La salud" the relationship between this Argentine mother and her family illustrates the traditional concepts associated with motherhood. As an institution at once idealized and oppressive, it corresponds to mamá's paradoxical powerful/powerless status. The family members lovingly refer to their house as "casa de mamá" (*Cc* 1, 526), underlining mamá's intimate connection with the home and the fact that the household revolves around her. But mamá has paid a steep price for this veneration. Mothering and domesticity seem to be her only concerns, and having sacrificed herself to her home and family, she appears to have no life outside the family home. In this sense, mamá's status as a bedridden invalid is an appropriate metaphor for her state of social subjugation.

This close-knit family—mamá; her four children, Pepa, Rosa, Carlos, and Alejandro; and Aunt Clelia and Uncle Roque (presumably mamá's sister and brother)—live together in a large house in Buenos Aires. When Alejandro, mamá's youngest son, dies in an automobile accident, and Aunt Clelia falls ill and eventually dies, the other family members, convinced that the shock of the tragedies would be detrimental to mamá's already-failing health, hasten to conceal the facts. According to Dorothy Dinnerstein, since the mother is able to bestow happiness, the child undertakes to do what will pleasure her, takes the initiative, anticipating her wishes, making them its own. In this way, Dinnerstein tells us, the child changes submission into mastery, is ruled at its own behest by a powerful and loved creature whose power and love it thereby incorporates within itself (165). Dinnerstein's observations offer us insight into the family members' behavior in "La salud." The children seem to be incorporating and turning back mamá's power and love when they anticipate her desire that Alejandro and Clelia be alive, act on it, and make it a "reality."

Initially, the family accrues power over mamá by containing death and replacing it with life. Although we may accuse mamá of being manipulative, actually it is the family members who are constantly scheming to fool mamá. In order to let no trace of Alejandro's death penetrate mamá's room, the family censors all material that could leak the tragic news, and in order to convince mamá that Alejandro is alive in Brazil, they supply proof of his residence there and invent plausible arguments that indefinitely postpone his return to Buenos Aires. They construct an elaborate discourse to stand in for the departed Alejandro, beginning by telling mamá that the young engineer has been hired by a Brazilian firm to install a cement factory. The family's complex scheme involves multiple aspects: the temporary suppression of radio news, the censoring and rewriting of newspapers, the creation of spurious conversations, the falsification of gestures and facial expressions, and finally, the central component, the concoction of a make-believe correspondence between Alejandro and mamá. In their mission, the family takes advantage of mamá's confinement to her bedroom, and mamá is stripped of all physical recourses for discovering the truth.

The family taps into mamá's value system to rationalize their actions as well as to create a discourse that will be acceptable and convincing to her. Since health matters are an obsession in this household and the doctor is a respected authority figure, the family uses their perception of mamá's frailty to justify concealing the bad news from her, and attempts to shift the blame for their deception to the doctor:

La pobre está tan delicada, no se puede ni pensar en . . . (*Cc* 1, 529)

a mamá no se le podían dar noticias inquietantes con su presión y su azúcar, de sobra sabían todos que el doctor Bonifaz había sido el primero en comprender y aprobar que le ocultaran a mamá lo de Alejandro. (*Cc* 1, 524)[3]

To convince mamá to accept what they promise will be a temporary separation from her youngest son, they appeal to her sense of maternal pride in her children's professional successes, celebrating Alejandro's new position as "una gran oportunidad para un ingeniero joven" (*Cc* 1, 528). In order to justify why Alejandro had to travel immediately to Brazil without taking leave of his mother, they play off the industrialists as the bad guys who possess antimaternal values: "Mamá tenía que comprender que eran nuevos tiempos, que los industriales no entendían de sentimientos, pero Alejandro ya encontraría la manera de tomarse una semana de vacaciones a mitad de año y bajar a Buenos Aires" (*Cc* 1, 525). So by taking advantage of mamá's paralysis and concocting ruses that engage her value system, the family is able to fool mamá, at least temporarily.

But mamá has her own power sources, which can be read in the maternal subtext. Compensating, in part, for her immobile state, is her acute and uncanny capacity of perception, described as a nearly magical, telepathic type of power: "el oído tan afinado de mamá y su inquietante capacidad para adivinar dónde estaba cada uno" (*Cc* 1, 524). The day of Alejandro's funeral, although the family takes great care in mamá's presence not to leak hints that anything unusual is going on, she is described as being "dolorida y difícil" (*Cc* 1, 525).

Tuning into the maternal subtext, we discover that mamá seems to figure out the truth when the family gives her the first piece of bad news regarding Alejandro. This occurs when mamá's repeated insistence that

Alejandro come to Buenos Aires for a visit has them at wit's end, and they decide to tell her that he cannot travel due to a fractured ankle. With this news, mamá takes ill. Why would hearing of Alejandro's minor mishap make her ill unless this is when she put together the pieces of the puzzle and realized that she would never see her son again? Two days later she recovers sufficiently to ask Pepa to write Alejandro, but now her attitude has changed. Apathy and disinterest replace her initial intense participation in the correspondence with Alejandro.

The maternal subtext—her silent despair—can be read in the gestures and silences that veil her true feelings. In her first stage of inner mourning, she closes her eyes as if to prevent the family from reading her grieving soul through her eyes:

> Cuando Pepa . . . vino como siempre con el bloc y la lapicera, *mamá cerró los ojos* y negó con la cabeza. —Escribile vos, nomás. Decile que se cuide. (*Cc* 1, 529, emphasis added)

> Seguía *con los ojos cerrados* y no los abrió hasta la hora de la tisana; parecía . . . estar pensando en otras cosas. (*Cc* 1, 530, emphasis added)

Next, she looks away, perhaps to avoid the glance of mutual recognition, of shared grief: "Carlos, que leía la carta en voz alta, tuvo la impresión de que mamá no lo escuchaba como otras veces. De cuando en cuando *miraba el reloj*, lo que en ella era signo de impaciencia" (*Cc* 1, 530, emphasis added). When Uncle Roque talks of Alejandro's success, mamá only replies "—Ah, sí—. . . *mirando el cielo raso*—. Decile a Pepa que le escriba, ella ya sabe" (*Cc* 1, 531, emphasis added).

Then, she responds with indifference, declining to comment, failing to care about anything associated with Alejandro: "[C]ada tres semanas recibía sin comentarios las noticias de Alejandro; le decía a Pepa que contestara y hablaba de otra cosa, siempre inteligente y atenta y alejada" (*Cc* 1, 531). When Uncle Roque makes up a story about diplomatic tension between Argentina and Brazil in order to create another excuse for the postponement of Alejandro's trip, mamá does not mind if he makes mistakes in his reading (inventing) of the newspaper articles, nor does she seem to worry about the obstacles this could create for Alejandro's journey to Buenos Aires. Finally, mamá even plays along with the game by providing the appropriate responses. When Aunt Clelia takes ill, she tells them to write Alejandro about it, but adds without missing a beat: "Ya vas a ver que tampoco podrá venir él" (*Cc* 1, 534). In a supreme gesture of radical self-denial, mamá never seeks to overtly confirm her suspicions or share her grief with anyone. She has sacrificed herself to her family for so long that it seems natural to her to allow them believe that they have succeeded in their merciful deceit.

Nonetheless, mamá's subjectivity, her true feelings, come out in a visit with María Laura, Alejandro's fiancée:

> La primera en hablar fue María Laura, esa misma tarde. Se lo dijo a Rosa en la sala, antes de irse, y Rosa se quedó mirándola como si no pudiera creer lo que había oído.
> —Por favor—dijo Rosa—. ¿Cómo podés imaginarte una cosa así?
> —No me lo imagino, es la verdad —dijo María Laura—. Y yo no vuelvo más, Rosa, pídanme lo que quieran, pero yo no vuelvo a entrar en esa pieza. (*Cc* 1, 530)

The dead son's girlfriend, the would-be daughter-in-law and rightful heir to her son's love, has a special link with mamá, and the two undoubtedly have experienced a rare moment of mutual recognition in which they communicated their shared grief through the gaze.

Although the family members know that María Laura may well be right, they choose to dismiss her observation as a fantasy: "En el fondo a nadie le pareció demasiado absurda la fantasía de María Laura" (*Cc* 1, 530). In order to evade acknowledging what they know to be the truth, they submit to the authority of the unwritten household rules: "Pero Clelia resumió el sentimiento de todos cuando dijo que en una casa como la de ellos un deber era un deber" (*Cc* 1, 530). The duty to which Clelia refers seems to translate as: protect and venerate mamá at any expense.

The family eventually realizes that mamá has figured out the truth, so why do they persist in playing the game of deceit once it has become meaningless? The answer is that mamá is their scapegoat. The family members project onto mamá the weakness they refuse to acknowledge in themselves. All loss is experienced as narcissistic trauma, and narcissistic identification with a suffering person can be unbearable (Cassem 9, 12). By keeping this figment of Alejandro alive in the farce they continue to perform for mamá, a part of them does not have to accept the truth of Alejandro's death, and what is even more significant, they spare themselves the heartbreakingly painful experience of witnessing mamá's inconsolable grief brought about by the loss of the son she holds so dear.

And what about mamá? Why does she submit to this farce, this domination on the part of her family long after she has discovered the truth? What gives her the strength to bury her grief deep inside and not share it with anyone? The key to mamá's mystery is in her last words: "—Qué buenos fueron todos conmigo—dijo mamá con tenura—. Todo ese trabajo que se tomaron para que no sufriera. . . . Tanto cuidarme . . . Ahora podrán descansar . . . Ya no les daremos más trabajo" (*Cc* 1, 535). Mamá's final utterances reveal that she *wanted* her family to look after her in this way, and that she understands their protection from the tragic truth as an expression of their loving care. Her way of reciprocating or returning their love is to allow them to maintain the illusion of omnipotence. As Benjamin tells us, the mother who clings to the fantasy that she can provide a perfect world for the child, allows the child to feel that he or she has succeeded in controlling mommy (*Like Subjects* 89). By playing along with their farce and keeping her grief to herself, she spares her family from having to come to terms with a profound sense of narcissistic loss. In other words, *mamá fears destroying her children by finding her desire.* She is the perfect mother of fantasy, always ready to sacrifice herself for her children. This traditional Argentine mother has not only fallen into the trap of radical self-denial, but thrives on it, burying her desire when she lets her children believe they control her. She relishes being the center of attention, and sees it as proof of their love, even if it means denying her own subjectivity. To recall Benjamin's observation, domination is two-way—those who exercise it, and those who submit to it. Domination is anchored in the hearts of the dominated, and mamá docilely submits to her children's domination because she understands it as an extension of the bonds of love (*Bonds* 5).

In "La salud," the lack of a shared reality—in this case, the mutual recognition of mourning—feeds the fantasy of maternal omnipotence, and in "casa de mamá," each party feels compelled to maintain this fantasy. In a healthy relationship, according to Benjamin, the mother has to relinquish the fantasy that she can provide a perfect world for the child and injure the child's sense of complete control over her, and the child must accept mother's being disappointing (*Like Subjects* 110). Mourning means accepting imperfection, and the labor of mourning requires the solidarity of the other (*Like Subjects* 113). The defensive fantasy of omnipotence blocks an intersubjective relationship and cannot tolerate imperfection; consequently the family cannot share the reality of

Alejandro's death. Thus, the children annul mamá's tragic reality and replace it with the fantasy of a perfect life in which everything is lightness, laughter, and gaiety. Family members are not sick or sad, and beloved sons do not die in car crashes; to the contrary, they are successful and conquer the world. And conversely, mamá thinks she has to provide them with a perfect world, which, in this case, means allowing them to fabricate a perfect world for her. Thus, instead of attributing mamá's behavior to sheer perversity, we can understand the complicity of both the children and mamá, as well as the weighty values attached to motherhood, in this pitiful farce.

"Cartas de mamá": Fantasies of Persecution

If "La salud" presents maternal power as benevolent insofar as it is well-intentioned (i.e., mamá does what she thinks she must to preserve her children), "Cartas de mamá," in contrast, depicts the mother's power as malevolent and destructive. In this story mamá becomes a hapless victim of the unequal power struggle between her two sons. Mamá is delighted to be introduced to Laura as the girlfriend of her son Nico, and she seems to bond with Laura immediately: "le había caído como una hija" (Cc 1, 187). When Nico takes ill on the eve of a local dance, she approves that his brother Luis accompany Laura to the dance. But Laura quickly abandons the sickly and timid Nico—"el hijo de mamá" (Cc 1, 184)—for his more aggressive and self-confident brother, and the two marry in a hasty civil ceremony. Nico's defeat culminates in his "melancólico refugio en una muerte de tísico" (Cc 1, 184), and after the "turbio intercambio de reproches, del llanto y los gritos de mamá" (Cc 1, 184), Luis decides that the couple will leave Buenos Aires for Paris. Luis later recalls his callous behavior toward mamá: "Todo había sido brutal en esos días: su casamiento, la partida sin remilgos ni consideraciones para con mamá (Cc 1, 182)." Thus, mamá has been triply victimized: first by having to witness the betrayal of Nico, her mama's boy, by his brother, next by the loss of Nico to death, and thirdly by Luis's abrupt abandonment of her. In a letter to Luis, Uncle Emilio stresses mamá's solitude: "Se notaba que estaba muy sola en la casa de Flores, lo cual era lógico puesto que ninguna madre que ha vivido toda la vida con sus dos hijos puede sentirse a gusto en una enorme casa llena de recuerdos" (Cc 1, 189). As in "La salud," this traditional Argentine mother is closely identified with her sons and the family home; an empty home means a diminished life.

The maternal subtext in "Cartas" is more deeply buried than that of "La salud," in part because the story is narrated from Luis's perspective, and once he goes to Paris, the reader can only access mamá through her letters. But more important, Luis's fantasy all but subsumes her subjectivity. However, there are some indications of the emotions of the real person behind Luis's fantasy. Luis recounts that when Nico dies, her reaction is of wailing and recrimination—thus at first she openly mourns her son, and blames Luis for his death. Next, we learn of her consuming dread of being abandoned. Recalling mamá's expression in the final days before his departure, in retrospect Luis becomes aware of her overwhelming and terrifying sensation of powerlessness:

> Cada vez recordaba con más claridad la cara de mamá en las últimas semanas de Buenos Aires, después del entierro de Nico. Lo que él había entendido como dolor se le mostraba ahora como otra cosa, algo en donde había una rencorosa desconfianza, una expresión de animal que siente que van a abandonarlo en un terreno baldío lejos de la casa, para deshacerse de él. Ahora empezaba a ver de veras la cara de mamá. (*Cc* 1, 190)

And, in fact, mamá's deepest fears are realized when her surviving son and new daughter-in-law leave Buenos Aires for Paris. As noted above, Uncle Emilio comments on how very lonely she appears to be. Luis mentions that she is alone with Nico's clothes still hanging in the closet, a pitiful allusion to her solitude in face of this agonizing loss.

Surprisingly then—but to Luis's relief—after her initial surge of emotion, mamá appears to quickly come to terms with Nico's death, showing no further outward signs of grief:

> Mamá había parecido comprender, ya no lloraba a Nico y andaba como antes por la casa, con la fría y resuelta recuperación de los viejos frente a la muerte. (*Cc* 1, 182)

> Lo mejor de mamá era que nunca se había abandonado a la tristeza que debía causarle la ausencia de su hijo y de su nuera, ni siquiera al dolor— tan a gritos, tan a lágrimas al principio—por la muerte de Nico. Nunca, en los dos años que llevaba ya en París, mamá había mencionado a Nico en sus cartas. (*Cc* 1, 181)

The reader can surmise that mamá keeps her pain within, refusing to mourn openly; conceivably the bitterness she harbors toward Luis causes her to wall up her emotions. Since mourning is a healing process, the family's failure to engage in it means that Nico's death remains an open wound. The feelings of guilt and aggression among the family members are not worked out via the creation of an intersubjective space which could contain these strong emotions.

Mamá's newsy letters show that she immerses herself in everyday life, perhaps as a way to try to deny or evade her sorrow and anger. But denial results in a morass of unattached guilt, anger, and despair (Cassem 9). Pathological forms of mourning are those in which the subject holds him- or herself responsible for the death that has occurred, denies it, or believes to be influenced or possessed by the dead person (Laplanche and Pontalis 486). In the case of Luis and mamá, the two pathologies feed into each other: guilt and its punishment. And the lack of shared feelings gives rise to Luis's fantasy of persecution.

Luis's tragic flaw seems to be his inability to acknowledge his feeling of guilt; he refers to it only under the sign of negation: "las [cartas] de mamá le traían un tácito perdón (pero nada había que perdonarlo)" (Cc 1, 182). This passage reveals his highly ambivalent feelings and also implies that he makes his mother into his judge and jury. As a result, Luis's guilt is projected onto his mother and all his anxiety is seen as a product of external attack rather than his own subjective state. In other words, his paranoia is a consequence of the fact that he cannot contain or admit to the notion "I feel guilty," and instead tells himself "mother is persecuting me." The profound suggestive power he attributes to mamá is dramatically portrayed through the devastating effect her bland letters have on Luis:

> Cada carta de mamá . . . cambiaba de golpe la vida de Luis, lo devolvía al pasado como un duro rebote de pelota. . . . las cartas de mamá eran siempre una alteración del tiempo, un pequeño escándalo inofensivo dentro del orden de cosas. . . . Cada nueva carta insinuaba . . . que su libertad duramente conquistada . . . cesaba de justificarse, perdía pie, se borraba . . . No quedaba más que una parva libertad condicional . . . Y desazón, y una necesidad de contestar en seguida, como quien vuelve a cerrar una puerta. (Cc 1, 179)

Although Luis has struggled to re-create his life in another continent and free himself from guilt, this piece of paper, an extension of mamá, makes all his accomplishments crumble. He feels compelled to answer each letter immediately, as if this were the only way he could escape from the spell it casts over him. Mamá has become an omnipotent fantasy mother for Luis because his acute but unadmitted feelings of guilt make him so vulnerable to her domination. A masochistic craving to be punished for his misdeeds turns mamá into his accuser and punisher.

This process by which the mother becomes an object of dread, especially for males, is elucidated by Benjamin. In the introductory chapter, we saw how Cortázar's portrayal of the feminine, or female space, can be perceived as a result of the desire to "shore up" the masculine self, casting off feminine identifications. Benjamin explains how this polarized constellation of heterosexual identity, which demands confinement to circumscribed gender categories, feeds the omnipotence fantasy and causes it to be more intense and prolonged for boys than for girls (*Shadow* 104–105). The male child's need to disidentify with feminine attributes involves the repudiation of the mother and the denigration of the mother-baby dyad. Since the boy cannot identify with the mother, he experiences a frightening sense of separation and loss that "stimulates a more dangerous representation of the maternal sexual object as dreaded, engulfing, overwhelming, tantalizing" (*Shadow* 98). The problem, Benjamin explains, is not that man dreads woman, if he recognizes that he dreads her. The trouble is when he thinks she really is like his fantasy. This symbolic equation—she is malignant, a beast, a witch, and so on—signifies a collapse of reality and fantasy (*Like Subjects* 86). In this situation, Benjamin tells us,

> All that is bad and dreaded is projected onto the other, and all the anxiety is seen as the product of external attack rather than one's own subjective state. The problem, then, is not simply that male children disindentify with and then repudiate the mother. It is also that this repudiation involves the psyche in those projective processes—"she is . . ."—that intensify the fear of the other's omnipotence as well as the need to retaliate by asserting one's own omnipotence. (*Like Subjects* 86)

Thus, Luis's refusal to admit mamá's grief or the guilt he feels toward her creates a barrier between the subjectivity of mother and son, and the resulting substitution of the real mother with a vengeful monster.

Mamá's ultimate weapon is that she wields the power of Nico's death. And Nico, the mama's boy who was powerless in life, becomes powerful in death. Mamá terrorizes the couple by daring to name the dead man, and the act of naming Nico is so potent precisely because Luis and Laura have silenced all reference to him in their two years in Paris: "la repentina mención de su nombre era casi un escándalo" (*Cc* 1, 181). What truly confounds Luis and Laura is that mamá refers to Nico in her letters as if he were alive. As in "La salud," by virtue of her close bond with this cherished son, mamá seems to possess special power to breathe life into the "undead." First, she mentions that Nico inquired about them, next, that he is planning to go to Europe, and finally, her letter announces the date, time, and train number of his arrival.

Although he is loath to admit it, Luis has been cruel and unfeeling in his treatment of both Nico and mamá. When mamá retaliates by naming Nico, Luis falls victim to the pattern of behavior described above by Benjamin: he does not experience her as outside of himself—she *is* his fantasy of the dreaded, avenging mother. Within Luis's paranoiac state, Laura becomes the accomplice of mamá: "Cómplices como nunca, mamá le estaba hablando a Laura de Nico . . . le estaba anunciando que Nico iba a venir a Europa . . . [a] una casa donde se fingía exquisitamente haberlo olvidado" (*Cc* 1, 186). Similar to María Laura in "La salud" (curiously, both daughters-in-law have the same name), Luis's wife has a special relationship with mamá, and he imagines that mamá's power has extended to Laura, her agent, who conspires with her to wreak their just revenge. The unspoken guilt felt by both Luis and Laura is poisoning their relationship, and instead of recognizing his role in the failure of their marriage, Luis projects the blame onto mamá.

Luis and Laura attempt to dismiss mamá's mention of Nico as a sign of mental illness or senility, repeatedly referring to it as such, as if to convince themselves: "un anuncio de senilidad" (*Cc* 1, 181), "la insania . . . se [estaba] poniendo chocha" (*Cc* 1, 185), "el delirio de mamá" (*Cc* 1, 186), "se ha vuelto loca" (*Cc* 1, 189). Thus, in the power struggle with mamá, they attempt to discredit her through the attribution of mental illness, tapping into a long-standing social practice used to control unruly women.[4] Nevertheless, on the day of Nico's announced arrival, both Luis and Laura go separately to the train station and see an Argentine who bears a resemblance to Nico. That evening at home, neither comments on the event, but as Luis begins his letter to mamá, he looks up and sees Laura looking at Nico.

The story's tension and the surprise ending hinge on the ambivalence surrounding mamá's mental state and Nico's actual corporeal presence in Luis and Laura's apartment. Luis's second thoughts in regard to how to deal with mamá—"Matilde comprendería la urgencia . . . de proteger a mamá. Pero, ¿realmente . . . había que proteger a mamá, precisamente a mamá?" (*Cc* 1, 190)—seem to indicate that he suspects she is not really deranged and helpless. Luis finally seems to deny that mamá is mad—"¿Para qué fingir . . . que mamá estaba loca?"(*Cc* 1, 191). What does he mean by this? Does he think that mamá's mention of Nico is actually a calculated, even malevolent, gesture to disturb him and Laura, or is he starting to believe that the "undead" Nico is actually coming to Europe?

And how can we understand Nico's apparition in Paris? While we could dismiss Nico's supposed passage to Europe as a product of mamá's imagination or invention, what about the mention that Luis and Laura see Nico in their apartment? Have they gone mad as well? Has their guilt driven them to madness, believing Nico's ghost has returned to demand its revenge and claim its rightful place between them? Or is Nico's appearance a supernatural event? Precisely in the ambiguity and the reader's hesitation lies the fantastic, which Cortázar so aptly employs to dramatize psychological states.

And what is the outcome of the power struggle between Luis and his mother? After going to the train station and seeing the Argentine who resembles Nico, Luis determines to write to mamá without mentioning what he calls "the ridiculous episode." As the story draws to a close, we see him laboring to begin a letter to mamá "como debía," first writing "querida mamá," then throwing the paper away and writing simply "mamá," just at the moment Nico seems to appear in the apartment. Luis's difficulty in writing the letter shows that this time, he is not going to be able to exorcise mamá's hold over him by answering her letter. The apartment feels suffocating to him, a psychic projection of his oppressive guilt. Finally, Luis remains trapped in the spell of the omnipotent fantasy mother and his treachery has been corresponded—his attempt to start a new life in Paris has been thwarted, just as he shattered the lives of Nico and mamá.

But how can we judge mamá, this enigmatic woman who never reveals her innermost thoughts, unlike the mother in "La salud" whose final words explain the reason for her actions? The central question concerning mamá seems to be this: Is she really demented or does she feign dementia in order to get even with Luis?

On the one hand, it is entirely possible that mama *is* deranged and writes that Nico is coming to Paris because she has lost touch with reality. But if this is the case, Nico should not be showing up in Luis and Laura's apartment. In other words, if Luis believes mamá is crazy, *he* should not see Nico in his apartment, because *this is his mother's delusion*, not his. So, from this perspective, the more feasible explanation is that mamá is merely feigning insanity or senility to get her revenge. After all, Luis's rhetorical question—"¿Para qué fingir que mamá estaba loca?"—seems to be implying just that. But we still don't have an explanation for why Luis sees Nico.

On the other hand, Luis's insinuation that mamá is being perverse and deliberate in her mention of the dead brother could be a product of his persecutory fantasy. That is, perhaps mamá *is* confused, but in Luis's paranoid state, he reads her confusion as calculated revenge. And even though Luis may believe, or at least strongly suspect, that mamá is actually sane and concocting a bizarre type of retribution, such is her power over him—intensified by her control of Nico's death—that the mere suggestion of a visitation by Nico produces in Luis a paranoid hallucination, a delusional return of the repressed. This hallucination could be considered a regressive wish fulfillment, corresponding to Luis's masochistic desire to be punished for his cruel treatment of Nico and mamá.

At the story's conclusion, the omnipotence fantasy is so strong that there is never a point where the real person manifests herself, and the persecutory fantasy mother totally subsumes the real person. The reader is drawn into the fantasy, having neither an external or objective perspective whereby to judge mamá, nor an outside witness as to whether or not Nico was present in the apartment. (It is true that Laura also sees Nico. But Laura—at once co-conspirator with mamá as well as a guilty party—can hardly be considered an objective witness.) The most feasible solution, then, is to consider the "undead" Nico as the delusion of *both* mamá and Luis: mamá's desire for revenge and Luis's masochistic desire for punishment. Both desires feed off and complement each other in the omnipotence fantasy.

Thus, the ultimate message we can glean from the attempt to recover the maternal subtext seems to be that the only way mamá could manifest her desire for revenge was under the guise of insanity, or alienation from herself. On a symbolic or metalevel, this corresponds to how society would categorize her actions—only a crazy mother would engage in the premeditated destruction of her son, sane mothers do all they can to save their children, sacrificing their desire to the well-being of the child.

Finally, then, we could say that the mother in "Cartas" does escape, in a convoluted sort of way, from the trap of radical self-denial, but it is only through madness, be it feigned or real. Compared to the mother in "La salud," we see a stark contrast with this woman who stays lucid to the end while willingly submitting to self-denial for the sake of her children. These two unforgettable characters and their juxtaposition convey an eloquent and alarming message regarding the concept of motherhood in Argentine society, as it is depicted in Cortázar's stories. When the regressive fantasy of maternal omnipotence persists into adult life, the mother who practices self-denial to save her children is lucid, while the mother who finds her desire, but in so doing destroys her child, is insane. And the tragic shortcoming that fuels the omnipotent mother fantasy in both cases is the inability to cope with strong, conflictive emotions, or share the tragic dimension of life.

In conclusion, the discourse on motherhood has been hampered by our failure to understand and contend with a myriad of unconscious associations to the mother and maternal practice in general (Bassin 14). Feminist and psychoanalytic theory help us uncover infantile and regressive systems, and look at texts in new and challenging ways. Using feminist thought regarding motherhood and domination to inform our reading of Cortázar's stories, we see how they dramatize the oppressive status of motherhood, and how the powerful bonds between mother and son are inextricably tied up to despair and desire for all those caught in their tangled threads. The following chapter analyzes another manifestation of the obsession with the maternal figure—the Oedipal desire.

Chapter 4

ℂ

Mothers and Lovers

murmur · n *1* a subdued continuous sound, as made by waves, a brook, etc. *2* a softly spoken or nearly inarticulate utterance. *3 Med.* a recurring sound heard in the auscultation of the heart and usu. indicating abnormality. *4* a subdued expression of discontent.

—*Oxford English Reference Dictionary*

In Louis Malle's 1971 film, *Murmur of the Heart* (*Le Souffle au Cœur*), the adolescent protagonist makes love to his beautiful young mother. After their unplanned moment of passion, the mother tells him: "I don't want you to be unhappy or ashamed or even sorry. We'll remember it as a beautiful moment . . . one that will never be repeated." "What will happen now?" asks the boy. "Nothing," his wise and gentle mother reassures him. "We will never talk about it. It will be our secret. I'll remember it without remorse, tenderly. Promise me you'll do the same." In this bold remake of the Oedipal scene, Malle portrays the ultimate taboo and the ultimate fantasy: union with the yearned-for mother without guilt or punishment. Although Cortázar's protagonists may eternally long for this very moment, it is a desire that will only be fulfilled through their active fantasy lives—dreams and daydreams, sometimes committed to paper, sometimes just imagined—and never without sanctions.

One of the reasons why Cortázar's stories hold such a strong grip over many readers is undoubtedly because they often portray seemingly unnatural or "perverse" instinctual urges that threaten to unravel the very fabric of our civilized society, but that are ultimately kept in check by their status as literary fantasies. Many of Cortázar's stories unfold through a dynamic tension between the characters' routine quotidian lives and an underlying world of intense and frustrated desires. The characters view this submerged realm with a mixture of fear and longing. On the one hand, they may feel compelled to explore, understand, and even participate in it; on the other hand, there is sense of horror when it erupts into "este lado," the mundane, bourgeois routine, which

55

is governed by reason and logic and cannot tolerate the disruptive nature of intense passions. As explained in chapter 1, Prieto's study reveals that this disturbing latent content, the "wellspring from which [Cortázar's] stories flow" (*Body of Writing* 18), is indeed the forbidden longing to return to the womb. His incisive analysis makes apparent the pervasive, albeit camouflaged, presence of this guilty yearning in Cortázar's writing.

The previous chapter, "The Omnipotent Mother," probed the causes, consequences, and implications of the mother's psychological power over her children in two of Cortázar's stories; this chapter focuses on stories that are driven by the libidinal desire to possess the maternal body. Subsequently, we will consider how this obsession plays out in stories that portray the mother-adolescent relationship as well as how it carries over to love relations with "other" women.

A Freudian Fallacy

The Freudian theory of human civilization rests on the incest taboo, or successful resolution of the Oedipus complex, the function of which is to deny the child his (or her) primordial love object—the mother. Thus Freud maintains that civilization itself depends on the male subject's detachment from and transcendence of the mother. Yet, as Madelon Sprengnether argues in her work *The Spectral Mother: Freud, Feminism and Psychoanalysis*, Freud was never able to integrate the pre-Oedipal mother, meaning the figure of the mother in the earliest phase of the child's development, with the Oedipal construct (2, 181). "If anything," she maintains, "the dyadic mother-child relationship threatens to subvert the triangular Oedipal structure. The concepts of repetition compulsion and the death instinct appear to give lie to the progressive model of development based on the paternal threat of castration and the male child's renunciation of desire for his mother" (182). Sprengnether argues that in *Beyond the Pleasure Principle* and *Inhibitions, Symptoms and Anxiety*, which focus on questions of origins (infant separation from the mother) and conclusions (death), Freud undermines his own progressive model of human civilization, and, at the same time, of Oedipal masculinity, by exposing the undertow of regressive urges focused on the desire to return to the maternal body (140).

Emblematic of this contradictory stance is Freud's characterization in *Beyond the Pleasure Principle* of a game invented by his one-and-a-half-year-old grandson. The child tied a wooden reel to a piece of string and draped it over the side of his bed. He would repeat *Fort!* (go away) at its disappearance and greeted its reappearance with a joyful *Da!* (there) (Freud 8–11). Sprengnether points out that while Freud initially presents the game as the efforts of a small child to gain mastery over the condition of separation from his mother, the game enacts not only the child's desire for control over her departure, but also his wish for her return (128–131). "The fort/da game, based on a little boy's memorialization of his loss of his mother," she explains, "institutionalizes both the act of renunciation and the impulse toward regression that inheres in it" (135). Throughout his work, Sprengnether maintains, Freud is never able to come to terms with this seductive pre-Oedipal mother because she is too threatening to his theory of patriarchal authority.

Cortázar's stories confirm this powerful undertow of the urge to recuperate the lost paradise of oneness with the mother. My reading of "Historias que me cuento" and "Deshoras" focuses on how the narrator's desire to recover the lost object of infantile bliss is played out through his fantasies.[1] The fact that in these stories the narrators' desire is deflected from the actual mother onto a mother figure or surrogate mother reflects the power of the taboo while at the same time attesting to the strength of the attachment to the maternal object.[2] Through their fantasies, the narrators attempt to transcend their mundane existence as they articulate their longing for an unattainable reunion with the beloved source of goodness and nurture. The narrators' fantasy has the power of evoking the absent mother and bringing her temporarily under their control, much as the child's game described by Freud. Both pursuits strive to master the separation anxiety at the same time that they memorialize the loss of the mother.[3]

"*Historias que me cuento*": *The* *Walter* *Mitty* *Complex*

In "Historias que me cuento," the façade of a man's fantasy life of heroic adventures and manly conquests is rent asunder to expose the radical instability of his masculine identity. The narrator is a self-described "Walter Mitty porteño" who indulges in a rich fantasy life.[4] The few details he offers about his waking life characterize it as solitary and unfulfilling. He often sleeps alone when his partner, Niágara, works the night shift at the hospital, and the bed suddenly seems enormous and cold. The nights she does spend with him, she comes home from work so tired that she immediately falls into a deep sleep, so he feels alone even when she is in bed with him. Thus, it seems that her job caring for others at the hospital leaves her with little energy to nurture her needy husband. Perhaps feeling inferior to his hardworking wife, the narrator remarks that his daily activities are not very memorable, and that he considers himself incompetent in his job. He makes only one reference to his name: Marcelo Macías.

Marcelo's nighttime fantasies seem to be a type of antidote to his lackluster existence—they are characterized by "un intenso dramatismo muy trabajado" (*Cc* 2, 401), and he is almost always in the central role. Unlike the narrator of "Deshoras" who will spin out his fantasy on paper, writing down his stories seems inconceivable to Marcelo. "Un hombre tiene que tener sus lujos secretos," he declares, and he connects the prohibition of writing his stories to "nociones de transgresión o de castigo" (*Cc* 2, 401). Thus the fantasies take on an aura of forbidden pleasure that must be kept hidden from those who would judge and censor their content.

One of his favorite fantasies is that he is a trucker: "Ser camionero siempre me ha parecido un trabajo envidiable porque lo imagino como una de las más simples formas de la libertad, ir de un lado a otro en un camión que a la vez es una casa con su colchón" (*Cc* 2, 402). The description of the truck's hollow but cushioned interior that permits the narrator to move about within its protective cocoon lends the vehicle a uterine quality. In these trucker fantasies, Marcelo often picks up and makes love to women who ask for rides. They are always unknown women whom he has seen in a movie or a picture, and the only physical description that he offers categorizes them as exotic and "other": the redhead, the mulatta, the little Indian girl, the gypsy, the Japanese girl, the Norwegian tourist. The fact that they represent a different nationality, ethnicity, or color may reassure the narrator that they have no place in his quotidian life and helps to maintain the separation of the two realms, preventing his illicit dream life from encroaching on his respectable, if mediocre, waking existence.

The narrator relates in detail a fantasy in which he, as Oscar the truck driver, picks up Dilia who is hitchhiking by the side of the road in a deserted mountainous area. Dilia and her husband Alfonso are friends of Marcelo and Niágara, so it is shocking that someone from his own world has appeared in his fantasy, and he puzzles over the question many times: "Ver a Dilia fue entonces más que una sorpresa, casi un escándalo porque Dilia no tenía nada que hacer en esa ruta. . . . Dilia y Alfonso son amigos que Niágara y yo vemos de tiempo en tiempo . . .

seguirlos de lejos en su vida de matrimonio con un bebé y bastante plata. Qué demonios tenía que hacer Dilia allí" (*Cc* 2, 403). In his description of the fantasy, he stresses the difficulty of the route and Dilia's helplessness: "vi la frágil silueta de Dilia al pie de las rocas violentamente arrancadas de la nada por el haz de los faros, las paredes violáceas que volvían aún más pequeña y abandonada la imagen de Dilia" (*Cc* 2, 402–403). The evocation of a minute, fragile Dilia against the purplish walls of the rock face repeats the womb imagery. Unlike the other fantasized women who are often cold or timid, Dilia is a willing and even seductive sexual partner, and the sensuous story of their fortuitous encounter lasts all night.

Some time later, Marcelo and Niágara are invited for dinner at the home of Dilia and Alfonso, and, to his astonishment, the narrator learns that his fantasy had paralleled an episode that actually occurred. Dilia had traveled to another town to accompany her ailing mother who died a few days later. Upon Dilia's return, her car broke down in the mountains, she was alone and terrified at night, and a trucker finally came by and picked her up. Alfonso remarks "—Se ha quedado traumatizada. . . . Ya me lo contaste, querida, cada vez conozco más detalles de ese rescate, de tu San Jorge de overol salvándote del malvado dragón de la noche" (*Cc* 2, 407). To which Dilia replies "—No es fácil olvidarlo . . . es algo que vuelve y vuelve, no sé por qué" (*Cc* 2, 407). Dilia says she does not know why she cannot forget this episode, but the narrator realizes that "en el otro lado" Marcelo the daydreamer materialized as Oscar the trucker to rescue Dilia, and they shared a night of tender love.

In the nocturnal rescue episode, Dilia is helpless and in need of comfort and protection. The mother of an infant who has recently lost her own mother, Dilia feels overwhelmed by her doubly new status of orphan and mother. She must become a source of sustenance and strength to her helpless infant precisely at the moment when she herself feels most vulnerable, no longer having her own mother to turn to for guidance and support. The fragility of her mental state intensifies the trauma of being stranded in the wilderness: "la noche vacía y una interminable espera al borde de la ruta en la que cada pájaro nocturno era una amenaza, retorno inevitable de tanto fantasma de infancia" (*Cc* 2, 406–407). So traumatic is this situation that she experiences a type of infantile regression and relives childhood terrors, the most vivid of which for many children is the death of the mother. Dilia's condition of dependency creates the opportunity for Marcelo, in his "incarnation" as Oscar the teamster, to demonstrate his valor by rescuing her. Dilia's eagerness to sleep with the truck driver can be seen as her expression of gratitude and reward for the brave deed as well as an urge to seek comfort in his arms. The interior of the truck's cab, described as "la cabina tibia" (*Cc* 2, 407) when the shaken but grateful Dilia enters, continues to evoke a womb that nurtures and protects both the exhausted driver and the fragile woman. In this way, the union of the two suggests the desire for comfort in the mother-child dyad.

The rescue fantasy, according to Otto Rank, which usually involves the son liberating the mother from the father's violence, is highly significant in human sexual life and is a product of the individual's longing for his mother's love and his wish for the absence of the disturbing competitor (65, 100, 137–138). Significantly, when Alfonso snidely refers to the trucker as "tu san Jorge de overal," he betrays a note of jealousy and resentment at the same time that he unwittingly elevates the event to mythic proportions. The legendary Saint George, patron of warriors and travelers, is famed for having slain a ferocious dragon, which was terrorizing a city, and rescuing the king's daughter who was to be sacrificed to the dragon. In later versions of the legend, Saint George is transformed into a knight of chivalry who marries the princess (Holweck 423, Coulson 196–197). Thus, in the incident, its retelling, and its psychic and mythic dimensions, there is a slippage of identity at the points of the triangle occupied by Dilia, the daydreamer/trucker, and Alfonso. The truck driver is at once rescuer, seducer, son, and lover. Dilia mutates from motherless child to seductress, unfaithful wife, and mother; while Alfonso degenerates from jealous husband and symbol of the law who denies son access to the mother, to night terror/dragon. Once the dragon (or night terror/husband/father) is eliminated, the lovers (or mother and son) can realize their longed-for but adulterous (or incestuous) union, and the triangle collapses to a dyad. The shifting of identity that characterizes the wilderness rescue scene foreshadows the final scene of the story that occurs at the dinner party.

After Dilia and Alfonso have recounted their version of Dilia's nocturnal adventure, to his amazement and also to his horror, the narrator begins to desire Dilia "de este lado." The baby cries, Dilia runs upstairs to get him, and takes him into the bathroom for changing. Marcelo follows her, taking advantage of this opportunity to have some privacy with her. "Y era como si de algún modo ella supiera cuando le dije Dilia, yo conozco esa segunda parte" (*Cc* 2, 407) he says, meaning there is a mutual recognition of what she has not told Alfonso—that she slept with the trucker who rescued her. Now, Marcelo's desire for Dilia intensifies, and he focuses on her breasts as if he had a right to them: "Sentí mis ojos como dedos . . . buscando los senos. . . . El deseo era un salto agazapado, un absoluto derecho a acercerme a buscarle los senos bajo la blusa y envolverla en el primer abrazo" (Cc 2, 408). Here, the narrator's sudden urge to lunge at Dilia's breasts equates him to her suckling baby. But Dilia is changing the baby's diaper. Marcelo gets a whiff of "el olor de un bebé que se ha hecho pis y caca" (Cc 2, 408) and hears Dilia calming the baby to stop him from crying. In the story's surprising final image, the baby has replaced the narrator as the object of Dilia's attention:

[V]i sus manos que buscaban el algodón y lo metían entre las piernas levantadas del bebé, vi sus manos limpiando al bebé *en vez de venir a mí* como habían venido en la oscuridad de ese camión que tantas veces me ha servido en las historias que me cuento. (Cc 2, 408, emphasis added)

This scene is startling because Marcelo realizes that the baby, not Dilia's husband, is his rival. But in another sense it is even more unsettling: the image of Dilia's hands cleaning the baby's genitals instead of touching the narrator as they did in "el otro lado" superimpose the baby in what was once the narrator's place. The tables have turned: the fearless truck driver/rescuer has vanished, now Dilia is in control, and an infantilized vision of himself as a helpless baby flashes before Marcelo's eyes. This mental image undoubtedly constitutes for him a shocking realization about the meaning of his desire for Dilia and the truth behind his daydreams. Does he desire Dilia because she is the mother of an infant son? Was his desire for Dilia actually a desire to return to a state of oneness with the mother? In his fantasies he may be a virile male rescuing damsels in distress, but "en este lado" he sees himself in the passive role of an infant whose condition of radical dependency requires that his mother calm his wailing and clean his excrement. This is so startling and threatening to the narrator that he immediately invokes his "camión" and his "historias" in an attempt to recast his desire for the pre-Oedipal mother into his trusty masculine narrative of conquest and performance, thus regaining a sense of mastery and protecting his ego from the condition of helplessness.

The last words of the story, "en las historias que me cuento" (Cc 2, 408), echo the opening line: "Me cuento historias cuando duermo solo"

(*Cc* 2, 401). In this circular construction, life appears to be going back-ward. The narrator remains trapped in his daydreams because if he lets go of his fantasies of manly feats, he fears reengulfment by the maternal womb. The narrator's desire for Dilia has led him to a strange but famil-iar place—the site of the uncanny—the mother's body. Mother, the child's point of origin, is also its goal and destiny, but will only be realized in death, thus, the mother is a focus of dread as well as longing (Sprengnether 231).[5]

The narrator's daydreams of conquering the outer world collapse to expose the desire to retreat, and the urge to tell these stories turns out to be an attempt to defend himself from the strong regressive drive to return to the pre-Oedipal mother.[6] Thus the Walter Mitty fantasies may provide an illusion of self-sufficiency and mastery, but in so doing, they encode the trauma of infantile helplessness they seek to control. Finally, the Walter Mitty syndrome speaks of the precariousness of a carefully constructed masculine identity that threatens to unravel when confronted by the sen-sation of helplessness brought on by the lure of the pre-Oedipal mother.

"*Deshoras*": *Desperately Seeking Sara*

The desire to reunite with a cherished mother figure from the past motivates a man's evocation of his childhood in "Deshoras." The child-hood events are framed by the present time of the adult as he puts his memories down in writing and reflects on his purpose for transcribing these recollections. When the time frame switches from the present of the adult to the evocation of past events, the narrative person changes from first to third, and the narrator refers to himself as "Aníbal."[7] Al-though the narrator begins by denying any ulterior intent behind his memoir: "Ya no tenía ninguna razón especial para acordarme de todo eso" (*Cc* 2, 470), he soon admits that it is the image of Sara, his playmate Doro's older sister, that draws him to the task. Because Doro's mother was an invalid, Sara was obligated to take care of Doro, to become "una joven madre de su hermano" (*Cc* 2, 471). The narrator describes the games Aníbal played with Doro, and vividly recalls his obsessive but unrequited love for Sara. As the story continues, he recounts his family's move to Buenos Aires that occurred shortly before Sara's marriage, two events that marked his separation from her. Many years later, as an adult, Aníbal sees Sara on the street. The two have a drink, recall old times, and end up in a bedroom where they consume their mutual passion. At this moment, the story returns to the scene of writing, and we realize that the encounter with Sara did not really occur, but was fantasized by the narrator through his writing.

As the narrator's tale transports him to his world of memories, he establishes Sara as his surrogate mother by stressing the bond between himself and Doro, thus depicting the playmates as doubles: "Tan inseparables habíamos sido . . . [que] [v]erlo [a Doro] era verme simultáneamente como Aníbal con Doro, y no hubiera podido recordar nada de Doro si al mismo tiempo no hubiera sentido que Aníbal estaba también ahí en ese momento" (Cc 2, 470). However, a major and painful difference between the boys, as far as Aníbal is concerned, is his access to Sara's attentions and affection. Aníbal learns that Sara takes care of Doro as a devoted mother would, caressing and bathing him, curing him when he is sick. Aníbal feels excluded from the bubble of nurture between Sara and Doro, which he seems to idealize as a lost paradise (Benjamin, Bonds 163). When Aníbal returns to play at Doro's house after an extended absence due to a bout of bronchitis, Sara expresses concern for Aníbal's health and gives him special attention. This incident sets up his nighttime fantasies in which Sara comes into his bedroom to care for him. In one version of the fantasy, Sara tends to a cut on his leg:

A la hora en que cerrando los ojos imaginaba a Sara entrando de noche en su cuarto, acercándose a su cama, era como un deseo de que ella le preguntara cómo estaba, le pusiera la mano en la frente y después bajara las sábanas para verle la lastimadura en la pantorrilla, le cambiara la venda tratándolo de tonto por haberse cortado con un vidrio. La sentía levantándole el camisón y mirándolo desnudo, tocándole el vientre para ver si estaba inflamado, tapándolo de nuevo para que se durmiera. (Cc 2, 473)

In this fantasy, Aníbal's reception of Sara's attention is predicated on illness, a state of vulnerability and dependency. In his description of Sara's ministrations, the distinction between care of his injury and seduction becomes blurred—his imagined need for medical attention veils his desire to be seduced by Sara. As the passive recipient of Sara's care and gentle reproach, Aníbal is feminized and infantilized. Sara, as his fantasized mother/nurse, becomes a powerful figure—she possesses the power to comfort, the power to shame, the power to seduce. In this way, questions concerning seduction—perhaps too dangerous and disturb-ing to be accrued to his real mother—can be projected onto the figure of Sara as substitute maternal object.[8] This ambiguous relationship be-tween the boy and nurse figure appears in several Cortázar stories, most notably, "La señorita Cora," to be discussed in the next section of this chapter.

It is Sara herself who enforces the incest taboo, putting an end to Aníbal's fantasies of her. One day, while playing in their secret place on the banks of a gorge hidden by thick overgrowth, Aníbal looses his foot-ing, grabs onto Doro, and the two boys fall into the murky water. They splash around, terrified, until they manage to pull themselves out, filthy and covered with mud "[que] olía a podrido, a rata muerta" (*Cc* 2, 474). The incident, immediately following a description of the intensity of Aníbal's secret love for Sara, evokes a symbolic descent into the depths of guilty, forbidden passion. The muddy boys try to sneak back into Doro's yard unnoticed, but Sara sees them and orders them to bathe—a purification ritual, of sorts. In the shower, the boys forget their fear and begin to cavort in the water and suds until they realize that Sara has entered and is watching them. Aníbal is deeply humiliated because she has seen him naked, and subsequently can no longer evoke her in his nocturnal fantasies. Implicit in Aníbal's feeling of humiliation is the fact that Sara has the right to walk in and look at him because he still has the penis of a child. Her gaze forces him to acknowledge that she has beheld his bodily immaturity, and consequently, he cannot be her lover because his penis is too small. This enactment of the castration complex functions at two levels. On one level, Aníbal experiences the anxiety men feel in sexual intercourse associated with the fear of insufficiency and inability to satisfy woman's desire (Frosh 100). At another level, in the absence of a father figure, Sara performs the normative and prohibitive function of the castration complex—namely, the denial of the child's access to the mother as a sexual object—which is traditionally carried out by the paternal au-thority (Laplanche and Pontalis 56–59).[9] Sara acted decisively to curtail the incipient erotic attraction between them, thus fostering Aníbal's mas-culine identity and separation from her. Perceiving that she had become a dangerous siren for the young boy, Sara generously played the liberating role normally attributed to the father, giving Aníbal his independence, and protecting him from his own desire (Benjamin, *Bonds* 151). Aníbal is thus forced to confront the fact that a union between them is impossible, and must orient his desires toward other women.

With Sara's courtship and marriage, a paternal figure of sorts appears on the scene to further reinforce Aníbal's separation from her, although Aníbal is at no loss for motives to denigrate his rival: "lo vio [al novio] de azul y gordo, con lentes, bajándose del auto con un paquetito de masas y un ramo de azucenas" (Cc 2, 475). By describing Sara's beau as grotesque and eager to please, Aníbal discredits his authority as well as his worthiness to possess Sara. Aníbal's attitude reveals the typical hostility toward the rival father figure. Notwithstanding Aníbal's evaluation of the suitor, the marriage takes place, and Doro's words help Aníbal visualize its consummation: "no necesitaba cerrar los ojos para ver contra el fondo del follaje el cuerpo de Sara que nunca había imaginado como un cuerpo, ver la noche de bodas . . . desde la voz de Doro" (Cc 2, 476). Aníbal's curiosity regarding the wedding night is aroused by his fantasies of Sara and desire for her. Imagining the "parental" coitus, or primal scene, gives rises to sexual excitation as well as castration anxiety (Laplanche and Pontalis 335). With the realization that Sara belongs to her husband, Aníbal must give up hope of possessing her and come to terms with the limits of his relationship with her. By accepting that Sara and her new husband have gone off together without him, now Aníbal is free to go off without Sara.[10]

Aníbal moves to Buenos Aires, loses touch with Doro and Sara, and has his sexual initiation with other women, but Sara remains in his thoughts:

> Un día . . . la vio nítidamente [a Sara] al salir de un sueño y le dolió con un dolor amargo y quemante, al fin y al cabo no había estado tan enamorado de ella, total antes era un chico y Sara nunca le había prestado atención como ahora Felisa o la rubia de la farmacia, nunca había ido a un baile con él como su prima Beba o Felisa . . . nunca lo había dejado acariciarle el pelo como María. (Cc 2, 477)

Aníbal's repudiation of Sara—"al fin y al cabo no había estado tan enamorado de ella"—demonstrates his continued vulnerability to her power over him. In his ongoing struggle to let go of this threat to his autonomy and establish new bonds, he needs to deny his love for her. Instead of clinging to the image of lost perfection, he denigrates and spites her, assuming the attitude: "Mother doesn't need me, so I don't need her" (Benjamin, Bonds 175). As the years pass, Aníbal takes on adult responsibilities and settles down to a routine existence: "Aníbal aceptaba sin aceptar, algo que debía ser la vida aceptaba por él, un diploma, una hepatitis grave, un viaje al Brasil, un proyecto importante en un estudio con dos o tres socios" (*Cc* 2, 477). In other words, he seems to lead a normal life, and has achieved a modicum of success.

One day he suddenly spots Sara walking down the sidewalk and hurries to meet her. They have a drink in a café and talk about their lives. Aníbal finally asks her the questions that is burning on his lips: "¿Y tu marido?," to which Sara's reply is laconic: "Bebe" (*Cc* 2, 478). With this one word, by indicating that all there is to say about him is that he drinks excessively, Sara eliminates her husband both as a deserving partner for her and a worthy figure of authority as far as Aníbal is concerned. His rival cast aside, the field opens for Aníbal. He confesses to Sara that he loved her and fantasized about her as his "mamá joven" (*Cc* 2, 478), and tells her how mortified he felt when she saw him naked in the shower. Sara reveals that she did it on purpose, implying that she, too, was attracted to him, but felt she had to cure him of his sexual fantasies of her. She ends her confession saying, "Y ahora sí otro whiskey, ahora que los dos somos grandes" (*Cc* 2, 479). Her admission that she repressed her reciprocated love for Aníbal in the past because of their age difference, and her allusion to their mutual maturity in the present, following the disavowal of her husband's authority, signals the final lifting of the prohibition. The sexual union soon occurs:

> la casi inmediata, furiosa convulsión de los cuerpos en un interminable encuentro, en las pausas rotas y rehechas y violadas y cada vez menos creíbles, en cada nueva implosión que los segaba y los sumía y los quemaba hasta el sopor. (*Cc* 2, 479)

The consummation of the erotic union with the maternal object, the return to the lost paradise of infancy, is thus described by the narrator as an overwhelming sensation of bliss.

Once the written words arrive at their desired outcome, the narrator lays down his pen, and the scene shifts abruptly to his present reality. He admits that, up to a point, the words had represented "una memoria fiel" (*Cc* 2, 480), but that when they spoke of the reunion with Sara, "mentían . . . nada era cierto" (*Cc* 2, 480). The narrator fabricated this encounter in an attempt to satisfy his deepest longing.

But the fantasy cannot continue because it is not compatible with the predictable, routine life he leads: "pero cómo seguir ya, cómo empezar desde esa noche una vida con Sara cuando ahí al lado se oía la voz de Felisa que entraba con los chicos y venía a decirme que la cena estaba pronta . . . y los chicos querían ver al pato Donald en la televisión de las diez y veinte" (*Cc* 2, 480). The voice of Felisa, presumably his wife, and the mention of his children return him to quotidian reality where he is the husband of a woman other than his mother—in other words, a union sanctioned by society—and the father of her children. Just as Sara enforced the prohibition when he was a child, now it is the role that he has taken on as paternal authority—his own internalized sense of guilt or responsibility—which intervenes, rescuing him from the siren call of the engulfing maternal womb and bringing him back to civilized society. Yet his written words remain to memorialize his longing for the unattainable reunion.

"While civilization still rests on the incest taboo, it is a precarious construct, subject to the undertow of regressive urges focused on the desire to repair the first rupture from the mother's body" (Sprengnether 140).[11] Masculinity has no secure basis of its own because it is premised on "separation from that which the infant knows—the mother and all her feminine power . . . [masculinity is] always in danger of collapsing under the force of the fantasised plenitude of femininity" (Frosh 109). The message of Cortázar's stories corroborates these observations, as his narrators bear witness to the seductive and threatening nature of the pre-Oedipal mother. Through their depiction of the persistence of the primal urge to regress to a state of oneness with the maternal body, the stories point to the instability of masculine identity. In "Deshoras," the fact that this regressive drive is contained and controlled through the fantasy is a way of acknowledging its impossibility and allowing for a "safe return" to "civilized," quotidian reality. However, in the unsettling conclusion of "Historias que me cuento," the image of the virile male is virtually effaced by the siren call of the pre-Oedipal mother. Lurking as they do beneath the façade of self-mastery, the incestuous desires of the Cortazarean protagonists expose the power of the maternal bond as well as the primal fantasies that structure the imaginary life of the adult.

Prieto maintains that "Cortázar's scenarios evolve toward a resolution of primal anxiety" (*Body of Writing* 48). He bases this assessment on a comparative analysis of the Oedipal scene in "Bestiario" (*Bestiario* 1951) and "Los venenos" (*Final del juego* 1956). In "Bestiario," Prieto points out, the child Isabel brings about the demise of her rival, El Nene, and thus ends up in exclusive possession of the maternal body (her aunt

Rema). "Los venenos," in contrast, explains Prieto, portrays an integration of castration: after the protagonist discovers that the pretty neighbor girl he adores, Lila, prefers his cousin, he floods the ant tunnels (which emblematize the maternal body) with poison and destroys his prized possession—a little tree he planted in Lila's yard. While "Bestiario" depicts an unsustainable fantasy, in "Los venenos" the hero acknowledges he cannot have the maternal body and accepts castration, thus signaling Cortázar's "conspicuous psychological evolution" (*Body of Writing* 48). Prieto concludes his exposé of the presence of the primal anxiety in Cortázar's stories by determining that the author's obsession with incest ended with "Deshoras" (*Body of Writing* 73). He bases this judgment on the fact that Aníbal (as Cortázar's proxy) fulfilled his desire for the maternal body and punishment was not meted out; with this dramatized fulfillment, Cortázar put the notion of incest to rest (*Body of Writing* 71).

This logic seems foolproof, but if "Los venenos" represents "conspicuous psychological evolution" on Cortázar's part, how can we account for the fact that "Historias que me cuento"—part of a collection published some twenty years after "Los venenos"—depicts a highly regressive Oedipal scenario resulting in anxiety and escape into a defensive fantasy world when the narrator discovers the true nature of his desire for Dilia? On the one hand, the recurrence of the fear-inspiring regressive urge seems to indicate the enduring nature of this obsession and the uneven progress toward freedom from it. Or perhaps we can consider the story's final twist—when Marcelo sees himself in the baby's place—to be the flash of a jarring awakening that paved the way for the narrator's mature acceptance of the impossibility of Aníbal's desire in "Deshoras." Aníbal does resolve his primal anxiety—he momentarily possesses the maternal body through his penned fantasy, but once he gets her, he knows he can't keep her, and gives her up. Thus, Cortázar ultimately depicts his protagonist's judicious and sober-minded coming-to-terms with what could never be.

Mother's Darling

Cortázar's stories dealing with adolescents and boys present a striking and poignant portrait of the male protagonists' situation of dependency in relation to maternal power. A mixture of love and hate characterizes the intense and ambivalent relationship with the mother. The portrayal of the mother as a seductive, aggressive woman who arouses desire situates the boy in a passive position. He simultaneously revels in and suffers from being the focus of the mother's attention, receiving her ministrations with both pain and pleasure. Cortázar's favored nurse-invalid scenario to depict the boy's relationship with his mother or maternal surrogate is a fantasy that implies the surrender of an aggressive male role. The indeterminacy of the distinction between medical attention and seduction is also central to this relationship. The debilitated, needy condition of the patient coupled with the nurse's capacity to soothe, heal, and arouse imbue her with power and harken back to the infant's initial state of helplessness and dependency.

"La señorita Cora" is the story that immediately comes to mind as Cortázar's most memorable version of the nurse-patient script. Fifteen-year-old Pablo is in the hospital for what should be a routine appendectomy. His bossy, overprotective mother is irked by the young pretty nurse, Cora, whom she finds impertinent and whom she sees as a rival for her son's care and attention. A complication arises during the operation, Pablo's condition gradually deteriorates, and the story concludes with his death. A central preoccupation of the story is the relationship between Pablo and the two women. As dual and opposed female caregivers, they represent the splitting of the maternal figure into two women: the (excessively) nurturing real mother, who is seen in nonsexual terms, and Nurse Cora, the tantalizing medical professional, who is seen in sexual terms.

Both women humiliate the boy, although in different ways. The mother embarrasses him with her solicitous and overly protective manner. She infantilizes him, seeming to be unwilling to accept the fact that he is growing up and becoming self-sufficient. The story opens with her thoughts indicating her reluctance to relinquish the idea of Pablo as her mama's boy: "tiene apenas quince años y nadie se los daría, siempre pegado a mí aunque ahora con los pantalones largos quiere disimular y hacerse el hombre grande" (*Cc* 1, 548). With Cortázar's ingenious use of shifting points of view in the story, we have access to the boy's reaction to his mother: "mamá cree que soy un chico y me hace hacer cada papelón" (*Cc* 1, 548). When the mother imposes her doting attitude toward the boy on Nurse Cora, implicating her competency—"Le agradeceré que lo atienda bien, es un niño que ha estado siempre muy rodeado por su familia"—the boy is furious with his mother: "me hubiera querido morir de rabia" (*Cc* 1, 551).

But the humiliation Cora causes Pablo is much more intense and excruciating: she performs hygienic and medical procedures on his body that he finds acutely embarrassing because she is so young and attractive. The invasive procedures violate his intimacy and strip him of his adolescent male dignity. When Cora takes his temperature with a rectal thermometer, Pablo turns bright red. This is only the beginning of a series of torments Cora forces Pablo to undergo. The next incident involves the removal of hair in his groin area in preparation for the appendectomy. We are given a detailed description of the scene from Cora's perspective:

> "A ver, bajate el pantalón del piyama", le dije sin mirarlo en la cara. "¿El pantalón?", preguntó con una voz que se le quebró en un gallo. "Si, claro, el pantalón", repetí, y empezó a soltar el cordón y a desabotonarse con unos dedos que no le obedecían. Le tuve que bajar yo misma el pantalón hasta la mitad de los muslos, y era como me lo había imaginado. "Ya sos un chico crecidito", le dije, preparando la brocha y el jabón aunque la verdad es que poco tenía para afeitar. "¿Cómo te llaman en tu casa?", le pregunté mientras lo enjabonaba . . . tanta era la vergüenza . . . me pareció que se iba a poner a llorar mientras yo le afeitaba los pocos pelitos que andaban por ahí . . . casi me daba pena verlo tan avergonzado . . . (*Cc* 1, 551)

Here, Cora takes the active role, beginning with her order that Pablo undress, thus injuring his sense of manliness. As her patient, Pablo has no other alternative but to passively bear it while she lowers his pajama pants to expose his attributes. She even takes the liberty to comment on his development, all the while fully aware of how embarrassing this is to him. Having his pubic hair lathered and shaved off by the pretty young nurse, who manipulates the blade so close to his penis, is both titillating and threatening of castration.

Pablo may have thought things could not get any worse, but they do when Cora appears with a hose to give him an enema:

> Cuando vio lo que traía se puso tan colorado que me volvió a dar lástima y un poco de risa, era demasiado idiota, realmente. "A ver, m'hijito, bájese el pantalón y dése vuelta para el otro lado", y el pobre a punto de patalear como haría con la mamá cuando tenía cinco años . . . pero el pobre no podía hacer nada de eso ahora, solamente se había quedado mirando el irrigador . . . yo colgaba el irrigador en la cabecera, tuve que bajarle las

frazadas y ordenarle que levantara un poco el trasero para correrle mejor el pantalón y deslizarle una toalla. "A ver, subí un poco las piernas, así está bien, echate más de boca, te digo que te eches más de boca, así". Tan callado . . . por una parte me hacía gracia estarle viendo el culito a mi joven admirador, pero de nuevo me daba un poco de lástima por él, era realmente como si lo estuviera castigando . . . (*Cc* 1, 553-554)

No details are spared in the disquieting description of how Cora experiences a mixture of amusement and pity as she commands Pablo to assume a prostrate position, and then carefully poses him so she can insert the irrigation hose into his anus. The woman whom he is enamored of has taken him from behind against his will—an act evoking forcible sodomy. The scene is typical of a male masochistic fantasy, with the subject in a feminine position (Laplanche and Pontalis 245). Cora's assault on Pablo's manliness continues with more rectal thermometer incidents, injections in Pablo's thigh, and finally, after the operation, Cora makes him urinate while lying on his back.

Cora realized that Pablo was smitten by her, and she says several times that she finds it amusing to perform these acts on her young admirer. The brisk efficiency with which she carries out the humiliating medical procedures is indicative of her desire to put him in his place, punishing him both for his mother's petulance and his own precocious sexual awareness. And despite the mortification Cora has caused him, Pablo finds it difficult to stay angry with her because he is so attracted to her; he fixates on her youth and beauty, her sexy voice, her shining hair and fresh smell:

[T]iene una voz muy grave para una chica tan joven y linda, una voz como de cantante de boleros, algo que acaricia aunque esté enojada. (*Cc* 1, 553)

Tiene un pelo precioso, le brilla cuando mueve la cabeza. Y es tan joven, pensar que hoy la confundí con mamá, es increíble. . . . Me gustaría decirle que es tan linda, que no tengo nada contra ella, al contrario que me gusta que sea ella la que me cuida de noche. (*Cc* 1, 556)

Siempre parece que se acaba de bañar y cambiar, está tan fresca y huele a talco perfumado, a lavanda. (*Cc* 1, 559)

Pablo's mixed emotions toward Cora are vividly portrayed as she completes the task of shaving his private parts. He is seething with humiliation and anger, but then opens his eyes to see her hair nearly touching his face and smells its fragrance: "hubiera querido morirme, o agarrarla por la garganta y ahogarla, y cuando abrí los ojos le vi el pelo castaño casi pegado a mi cara porque se había agachado para sacarme un resto de jabon, y olía a champú de almendra" (*Cc* 1, 552). Clearly, Cora is torturing and seducing the impressionable young boy at the same time.

In his revealing interview with Picón Garfield, Cortázar tells her (twice) how much he suffered while writing "La señorita Cora" because *he was Pablo* (77–78). Our examination of this story makes it evident why Cortázar suffered—the author must have writhed as he penned in prurient detail Pablo's abuse at Cora's hands. The humiliation is overdetermined, as Cora repeatedly violates and penetrates Pablo's pubescent body with the protocol procedures. In the same interview, Cortázar describes the genesis of the story. When he was twelve years old and precociously sexually aware, his mother sent him to be seen by a young woman dentist who humiliated him by treating him like a child and using the familiar form of address with him.[12] He says he was infatuated with her and fascinated by the fact that she subjected him to physical violence, pulling his teeth and causing him pain. "Es decir, allí se mezclaban sexualidad, masoquismo, y el aparente sadismo de ella" (79), Cortázar explains. All these never-forgotten emotions are reenacted and relived in the interaction between Pablo and Cora.

The flip side of masochism—sadism—is rehearsed in Pablo's imagination after the tormenting enema incident: "nadie puede imaginar lo que lloré mientras la maldecía y la insultaba y le clavaba un cuchillo en el pecho cinco, diez, veinte veces, maldiciéndola cada vez y gozando de lo que sufría y de cómo me suplicaba que la perdonase por lo que me había hecho" (*Cc* 1, 554). Harming Cora by plunging the knife into her chest is an aggressive phallic act, a fantasized restoration of his sense of virility, of which he has been divested (Harvey 102).

Perceptive beyond his years, Pablo realizes that it is because of the nurse-patient relationship that Cora has the power and authority to humiliate him. He surprises her with the observation: "Si yo estuviera sano a lo mejor me trataría de otra manera" (*Cc* 1, 553). And he repeats: " 'Usted es mala conmigo, Cora.' . . . 'Usted no sería así conmigo si me hubiera conocido en otra parte' " (*Cc* 1, 560). His comments imply that he envisions their meeting in a neutral situation in which they would be on equal grounds, and he could behave like a man. But what seems to make Pablo the most resentful of all is his discovery that Cora is romantically involved with Marcial, his anesthesiologist. He witnesses them kissing in his room when they think he is unconscious. This is a type of primal scene, and Pablo experiences the hostility children feel toward both parents when they see or imagine the parents having sexual relations (Prieto, *Body of Writing* 60).

Having depicted the mortification that Pablo suffers at Cora's hands, Cortázar must have taken delight in the crushing revenge he wreaks on the sadistic young seductress. First of all, although Pablo does not know it, Cora is clearly attracted to him. She makes several observations to herself about how good-looking he is, for example: "Es bonito su nene, señora, con esas mejillas que se le arrebolan apenas me ve entrar" (*Cc* 1, 551) and "hasta me molestaba que fuera tan bonito y tan bien hecho para sus años" (*Cc* 1, 552). Then, after Pablo's second operation, when his condition is grave, Cora demonstrates her preference for Pablo over Marcial: "hubiera querido que Marcial se fuera y me dejara sola con él" (*Cc* 1, 562). Marcial, as the father figure, is supposed to break up the dyad, according to the sanctioned outcome of the Oedipal drama. However, Cora definitively rejects "the father" for the child, declaring she wants to stay with Pablo "esta noche y todas las noches" (*Cc* 1, 563). Having beat out the father figure, the boy is in sole possession of "the mother," who begs his forgiveness, imploring him that he call her just Cora without the "señorita." But now that Pablo has Cora precisely where he wants her, he rejects her pleas and spurns her, asking for his mother: "Me gustaría que viniera mamá" (*Cc* 1, 563). In his moment of death, he requests the enveloping, nurturing mother, and casts off the dangerous, taunting siren. He finally realizes his ultimate desire and deals Cora the culminating blow by dying as she caresses him. Cortázar fulfilled Pablo's wish and killed him off to punish Cora (Prieto, *Body of Writing* 62). And perhaps through his elaboration of this fantasized wish fulfillment the author got even with that tormenting dentist.

"Ud. se tendió a tu lado" paints a much less sinister, if equally ambivalent, portrait of the boy's relationship with his mother. As in "La señorita Cora," Cortázar employs an innovative narrative structure—the third-person narrator alternatively addresses "Ud.," presumably the mother, and "vos," her son.[13] Fifteen-year-old Roberto and his mother, Denise, are vacationing at a beach resort. As is typical of Cortázar's stories, there is no father figure for Roberto, so Denise takes it upon herself to talk to her son about sex. Since Roberto has been spending time with young Lilian, Denise asks him if he'd thought about birth control. It turns out that, yes, it did occur to him, but he is too embarrassed to go into the pharmacy and buy condoms. His mother offers to buy them for him, makes the trip to the pharmacy, and that night imagines the details of the scene as Roberto looses his virginity. However, the next morning he confesses to his mom that Lilian was afraid to go through with it.

The relationship between the boy and mother is ambivalent: at times he seems to need her motherly affection and nurturance as when he was a child; at other times he wants to behave as a grown-up with her. The fluctuation in how he addresses her—alternatively "mamá" and "Denise"—is emblematic of his adolescent vacillation between childhood and adulthood. Denise, by helping Roberto with his sexual initiation, is promoting his independence from her. She appears to be eager for him to get involved with Lilian: she changes the topic of conversation to the girlfriend, and brings up the delicate issues he is reluctant or embarrassed to talk about.

But why is Denise so anxious to push her boy out of the nest? Does she fear that they may be excessively close? Does she think that Roberto's sexual involvement with a girl his age will be the solution, will set the limit between the attractive, youthful mother and her rapidly developing, yet clingingly affectionate son? The story's opening line—"¿Cuándo lo había visto desnudo por última vez?"(*Cc* 2, 140)—sets the tone, reflecting Denise's awareness of (or shall we call it "obsession with") her son's sexuality. A leitmotiv of the story, thoughts related to her son's sexuality are never far from her mind.

Roberto is equally close to his mother—he even seems to prefer her company to that of his new girlfriend. The scene when Lilian makes her debut defines the dimensions of their triangular relationship. While Roberto and Denise are playing together in the water, Lilian appears in the distance: "en la playa empequeñecida la silueta repentina de Lilian era una pulguita roja un poco perdida" (*Cc* 2,141). Her image has been shrunken down to the size of her importance relative to the tight bond between mother and son. Additionally, she seems a bit lost—her role in the drama will be uncertain.

When Denise realizes that Roberto does not have the nerve to go into the pharmacy and buy condoms, and that she must do it for him, she recalls how she intervened in a similarly embarrassing incident in which Roberto needed her help. One day, when he was seven, he came home from school complaining of an itch in his private parts, fearful that he had caught mange while horse riding. She inspected the area between his legs and found insect bites. She calmed him down, reassuring him that it was nothing, and gave him relief with rubbing alcohol and ointment. This incident represents, for Roberto's nostalgic mother, a lost age of innocence when he could confide in her and she could attend to his intimate medical problem. But now it occurs to her that this lost time has been recuperated, as the resemblance between the two incidents lends them a sense of continuity: each moment is marked by the boy's embarrassment and his anxious, yet humiliated, expectation that his mother will intervene and take care of everything for him.

Both the attention to the suspicious itch and the purchase of condoms re-create the nurse-patient relationship in which the mother is in a position of power relative to her passive, needy son. Her care-giving tasks are infused with erotic implications: she is curing, holding, enveloping his penis, participating in his sexual initiation. Roberto's submissive position in relation to his queenly mother is memorably etched in an image of the two in the water: "de nuevo te acercaste sin mirarla, nadando como un perrito alrededor de su cuerpo flotando boca arriba" (*Cc* 2, 143).

Once Denise has purchased the condoms for Roberto, she behaves coldly toward him. When Roberto finds the package from the pharmacy on his bed, he is ready to thank her in his childish, effusive manner, but she establishes a new distance between them: "Escotada, muy joven en su traje blanco, te recibió mirándote desde el espejo, desde algo lejano y diferente" (*Cc* 2, 145). Denise appears virginal and seductive, but she is not to be for Roberto—he must go off with another woman of the horde.

Reading alone in her bed that night, Denise imagines Roberto making love to Lilian. At once a virtual voyeur and vicarious participant, she wishes she could intervene to help her son carry it off: "el súcubo hubiera querido intervenir sin molestarlos, simplemente ayudar a que no hicieran la bobada, una vez más la vieja costumbre, conocer tan bien tu cuerpo boca abajo que buscaba acceso entre quejas y besos, volver a mirarte de cerca los muslos y la espalda" (*Cc* 2, 146).

The morning after, Roberto is affectionate and solicitous toward his mother on the beach, showering her with attention: "Vos . . . te levantaste de un salto y envolviste a Denise en la toalla, le hiciste un lugar del buen lado del viento" (*Cc* 2, 146). But Denise continues to enforce the new distance between them—she realizes that their cuddly relationship must evolve and that she is the one who must establish the limit. Perhaps that time is right now; perhaps this will be the last time she caresses his back. But soon we realize the reason for Roberto's cloying behavior: he makes his humiliating confession that the act with Lilian was not consummated. Suddenly Denise envisions things sliding backward:

> Todavía era posible que uno de estos días la puerta del baño no estuviera cerrada con llave y que usted entrara y te sorprendiera desnudo enjabonado y de golpe confuso. O, al revés, que vos te quedaras mirándola desde la puerta cuando usted saliera de la ducha . . . ¿Cuál era el límite, cuál era realmente el límite? (*Cc* 2, 147)

So maybe there is no limit—the abyss beckons. Would they/could they repeat the tender/scandalous scene from *Murmur of the Heart*? But at this very moment in steps little Lilian and sits down between them, rescuing them, perhaps, from the unspeakable act. The danger seems to have been averted, at least for the time being. For a moment the mother and boy appeared to be powerless to set the necessary limit: an outside force was needed to break up the dyad. The sense of urgency for Roberto to establish a relationship with an "appropriate" woman in "Ud. se tendió a tu lado" speaks to the difficulty of separating from the mother. As mentioned in chapter 2, Cortázar deferred to his fictional mother figures to describe his own adolescence: "de mi adolescencia no vamos a hablar, que lo hagan la señorita Cora o la madre de Roberto, si mis lectores se acuerdan de ellas" (Huasi 62). Apparently the ambivalent relationship, the dangerous maternal attraction, was a vividly experienced sensation for the author.

The Oedipal scene is also central to Cortázar's masterpiece, "Las babas del diablo." While this story presents an ingenious expression of Cortázar's concept of how a short story works, here we will focus on its kernel plot.[14] Michel, an amateur photographer roving about Paris, spots a couple that look like they could be mother and son, but at the same time, he knows they are not. The photographer sizes up the scene and imagines that the woman is a prostitute attempting to seduce the nervous young boy. When he takes a picture of the pair, the woman angrily confronts him, and the boy flees. A man who appeared to be reading a newspaper in a nearby car gets out, infuriated with Michel for what has happened, and approaches them. At this moment Michel realizes that the woman was procuring the unsuspecting boy for the man, and is glad that he disturbed the scene with the act of taking the photo, thus giving the boy a chance to run off.

Once Michel develops the photo of the woman and boy, he likes it so much that he makes an enlargement of it and puts it on his wall. Suddenly, the people in the photograph come to life. The boy escapes again, the man enters the scene, and Michel is now in the place that was once the boy's. The man comes into the foreground of the photo, approaching with raised and outstretched hands until his body occupies the entire picture. Michel closes his eyes, covers his face, and begins to cry "como un idiota" (Cc I 224). What is Michel's destiny? Is he killed by the man? Did he survive to tell the story? Or did both happen? The story leaves the issue of Michel's fate ambiguous. "Las babas" depicts still another permutation—surely the most sinister—of the Oedipal dynamics: the mother's seduction of the son and the father's angry revenge. The promise of sweet sex with the mother flips over to reveal the hell of violent penetration by the father. "Las babas" encloses a fantasized enactment of the latent sexual violence implicit in family ties.

The fourth story of this group, "En nombre de Boby," may shed some light on the origins of the conflicted mother-son relationship frequently at the heart of Cortázar's stories. This story reaches farther back to a more remote childhood event, opening with Boby's eighth birthday celebration. The domestic situation in this story resembles Cortázar's experience as a child brought up by unmarried aunts (Standish, "Adolescence" 646). Another autobiographical detail is the reference to the divorce of the child's mother. (As noted previously, Cortázar's father abandoned the family when he was six.) The aunt, who is the story's narrator, mentions the parental breakup to explain the reason for her sister's hypersensitivity, and thus the need to keep Boby quiet:

> [B]ien que me acuerdo de cuando Boby era chiquito y mi hermana estaba todavía bajo el golpe del divorcio y esas cosas, lo que le costaba aguantar cuando Boby lloraba o hacía alguna travesura y yo tenía que llevármelo al patio y esperar que todo se calmara, para eso estamos las tías. (Cc 2, 151)

This passage capsulizes Boby's pathetic situation: any type of disruptive behavior on his part must be immediately reined in due to his mother's physical and emotional fragility. He is constantly reminded to suppress, for his mother's sake, the release of emotions and high-spirited playfulness, normal and necessary components of a child's emotional development.

The aunt and the mother seem to be excessively worried and anxious about everything associated with Boby—also an echo of the author's childhood: biographer Herráez reports tht Cortázar had "una infancia llena de cautelas y precauciones" (29). Boby's mother fears, for no reason since he is an exemplary student, that Boby might come home with bad grades and they will have to cancel his birthday party. Then, when he receives a soccer ball as a birthday present, the women worry that with his enthusiasm he may break the flowerpots on the patio.

As mentioned above, when Boby was small his mother was so traumatized by her divorce that she could not tolerate the slightest acting-up on his part, and the aunt had to remove him from her presence and calm him down. Later his mother was bedridden with pleurisy and even after she was cured, she was still suffering from lingering effects. During all this time, the aunt zealously protects her sister by enforcing on Boby the idea that he must be especially good. But since he is such a good boy anyway, he does not give his aunt any problems. He always complies with her wishes, and does not even ask to play the piano, something he loves dearly.

In fact, submissiveness appears to be Boby's most salient character trait. The aunt makes repeated mention of Boby's model behavior; for example, he compliments his mother on the lovely birthday cake, "como el niño bien educado que es" (*Cc* 2, 148), and serves it first to the ladies, repeating the expression of appreciation to his mother: "primero las damas ... Boby le dijo de nuevo a mi hermana que la torta estaba muy rica" (*Cc* 2, 148). Boby is always good to his mother: "A mi hermana no pedía nada, era muy atento con ella" (*Cc* 2, 152), and to his aunt: "nadie le ganaba en servicial conmigo" (*Cc* 2, 153). With sixteen references to Boby's good behavior in the story—"Boby era *tan* obediente y *tan* bueno" (*Cc* 2, 153, emphasis added)—this trait is overdetermined.[15]

But something is amiss with the good boy. One morning he asks his mother "por qué ... ella era tan mala con él" (*Cc* 2, 150). His mother and aunt are shocked by this accusation because, according to the aunt, his mother "es una santa, eso dicen todos" (*Cc* 2, 149). But once they realize that the alleged abuse occurs in his nightmares, they dismiss Boby's concerns, telling him he should not worry about what happens in his dreams. When he continues to be tormented by nightmares, they attempt to identify possible physical causes—perhaps he has pinworms or appendicitis, or maybe it is because he eats too much bread at night.

Not only are the women's reactions totally ineffectual in dealing with the boy's psychological disturbance, but also the aunt exacerbates it by making him feel guilty about his mother's involvement in the nightmares. The aunt admonishes him:

> me apuré a explicarle . . . [que] tenía que darse cuenta de que nadie lo quería tanto como su mamá . . . y Boby escuchaba muy serio, secándose una lágrima y dijo que claro, que él sabía, se bajó de la silla para ir a besar a mi hermana. . . . era una lástima que Boby las tuviera [las pesadillas] justamente con mi hermana que tantos sacrificios había hecho por él, se lo dije y se lo repetí y él claro, estaba de acuerdo, claro que sí. (Cc 2, 150)

What is worse, the aunt asks him not to bother his mother again by talking about his anxiety because she is still weak from her bout with pleurisy. Of course Boby agrees to everything his aunt says because he is such a reasonable and obedient little boy. The aunt, by repeatedly reminding him of how much his mother loves him and has sacrificed for him, makes him believe that there is no justification for him to have these bad dreams involving his mother. His traumatic fears are therefore not legitimized; he is expected to repress them or get over them by himself. Thus, the psychological control of the little boy is intense and insidious: first the women use his mother's fragility as a justification for the repression of his boyish energy and potential rambunctious behavior, then they make him feel *guilty* when his nightmares reveal the traumatic toll their constraining, heavy-handed upbringing has taken on his psyche. And worst of all, as far as Boby's mental health is concerned, because he is naturally duteous and submissive, he never rebels, but rather yields docilely to their damaging psychological coercion.

The nightmares intensify, and the aunt reports several fits of hysterical wailing by the boy, when she and his mother are at a loss to console him. Finally, Boby describes a fragment of the dream's imagery to his aunt: "habló de unos trapos negros, de que no podía soltar las manos ni los pies" (Cc 2, 150). As he recounts this sinister oneiric scene, the aunt witnesses his genuine fear and how very troubling the dream experience is to the boy, finally aware he has a serious problem.

One day the aunt notices Boby's skittishness when she is handling the long kitchen knife, and realizes that she has identified a clue to her nephew's puzzling behavior. The source of the boy's anxiety becomes clearer to her when she observes the uneasy way he looks first at the knife and then at his mother. The aunt recounts how she finally cures Boby of his nightmares by forcing him to confront his dread of the long knife. When she is working in the garden, she asks Boby to bring her the long knife, which she has intentionally left in plain sight. Dutiful little Boby comes running, but with a smaller knife, to which she reprimands him "Éste no sirve" (*Cc* 2, 154). With this, he collapses sobbing in her embrace, and she believes he has experienced his last of the recurring nightmares.

How can we understand Boby's problem? The convergence of Boby's dream of forcible restraint and immobility, and his phobic fear of the long knife points to castration anxiety. Boby's continual self-abnegation and uncomplaining acquiescence to the women's demands place him in a passive, feminine position. He feels as if he is being dispossessed of his masculinity, as if the women's constant and insidious repression of his impulses has infected him with their femininity. At the same time, he may also be experiencing a type of sympathetic identification with his mother's traumatic abandonment by his father. After all, he was abandoned along with his mother and thus denied his father's love. And since he was a small child when his father walked out on the family, he had no recourse to prevent it from happening, thus he was another passive victim, just like his mother.

To compound matters, the mother and aunt may unconsciously associate the boy with his treacherous father who has caused so much suffering, and project on Boby their hostility toward the father—all things considered, he *is* the man's son, and of the same gender. The women may unknowingly be taking out their anger toward that man, or perhaps toward men in general, through Boby, repressing certain behaviors on his part that they associate with masculinity. According to psychoanalytic thought, the threat of castration emanates from the active hostility women feel toward men (Sprengnether 85). And Boby, as a highly suggestible child, may unconsciously internalize his own identification with the wrongdoing father, and consequently accept, or even seek, punishment by assuming the position of victim. Thus, at one level the hypersensitive son incorporates and accepts the women's emasculation of him, but at another level, the nightmares reveal that he is deeply troubled by it.

And, finally, what connection could there be between Boby's domestic trauma and Pablo's supplication at the hands of Nurse Cora? We can perceive a continuity in the pattern of the boy's sense of victimization. Fifteen-year-old Pablo's accusation of Cora, " 'Usted es mala conmigo, Cora' " (*Cc* 1, 560), echo eight-year-old Boby's protest to his mother: "por qué . . . ella era tan mala con él" (*Cc* 2, 150). In *Beyond the Pleasure Principle*, Freud theorizes that the compulsion to repeat traumatic events or painful emotions is greater than the avoidance of unpleasure. The subject deliberately places him- or herself in a distressing situation, acting out an earlier traumatic experience that may have been repressed or not fully understood. Thus, "La señorita Cora" may represent an acting out of the earlier trauma, dramatized in "En nombre de Boby," which was revived by the author's moments of agony in the dentist's chair. The act of writing the stories has a restorative effect—they function as a working-off mechanism to dissolve the tension by changing the conditions. After all, doesn't the storyteller possess absolute control over his characters' fate?

Love Affairs: Frustration, Betrayal, Violence

What bearing does the unresolved Oedipal desire have on the depiction of love relationships in Cortázar's stories? The highly problematic nature of romantic relationships in his work has been remarked by numerous critics. An aura of violence and foreboding pervades his early stories, as sex is associated with taboo and death. Betrayal is a leitmotiv—practically every collection of short stories contains at least one narrative centered on treachery in a love affair. Later stories depict relationships tinged with sadness and doom; marriage becomes a tedious routine void of spontaneity and passion. While the protagonists' dread of women is eventually attenuated, love relationships are still unsustainable—there continues to exist the fear of commitment, the presence of betrayal, or stagnation in an unfulfilling routine. Thus, although Cortázar's male characters constantly desire and actively seek out romantic relationships with women, these relationships are rarely positive or fulfilling, invariably resulting in separation, frustration or ennui, or worse, violence and death.

It hardly requires a giant leap of imagination to conclude that the desired women, as substitutes for the forbidden maternal figure, embody the male subject's fantasies directed at her. This can explain the male characters' tendency to idealize women, as well as their highly ambivalent attitude toward their female counterparts, simultaneously desiring and dreading them. While union with the mother or mother substitute remains their deepest longing, they fear her power to castrate, overwhelm, or reengulf them, at the same time that they fear punishment for their guilty desire. The reactions of mastery, control, and distance of Cortázar's male characters toward women are a type of defense mechanism against the experience of helplessness in face of their overpowering desire for the mother.

Many of Cortázar's early works depict a dangerous, threatening woman, his archetypical "novia-araña." The image of the fatal spider woman is vividly evoked in his poem "Las tejedoras":

> Las conozco, las horribles, las tejedoras envueltas en pelusas,
> ....
> en cada patio con tinajas crece su veneno y su paciencia
> ....
> Teje, mujer verde, mujer húmeda, teje, teje,
> amontona materias putrescibles sobre tu falda de donde brotaron tus hijos
> ....
> en los fríos lechos matrimoniales tejen de espaldas al ronquido.
> ....
> y nuestra voz es el ovillo para tu tejido, araña amor . . .
> ....
> la muerte es un tejido sin color y nos lo estás tejiendo.
> (*Salvo el crepúsculo* 66–67)

These monstrous, revolting knitters are mothers, girlfriends, and wives concocting their poisons and knitting the death of their victims.

The "mujer terrible" is put in action to work her evil in "Circe," the tale of lovely Delia Mañara whose first two suitors met untimely deaths.[16] Her third fiancé, Mario, lives to expose her villainy when he breaks open a chocolate bonbon she has confected for him and discovers inside minced cockroach parts. "Circe" relies on woman-as-insect imagery to convey Delia's malevolent repugnance, which she craftily disguises beneath her delicate ways. Her last name, Mañara, evokes "araña." "Delia había jugado con arañas cuando chiquita" Mario learns, "las mariposas venían a su pelo" (*Cc* 1, 145). The third-person narrator uses chromatic imagery to isolate a moment when Delia's true hideous nature is exposed. Delia is playing the piano in the shadows, and when someone turns on the light, "a Mario le pareció un instante que su gesto ante la luz tenía algo de la fuga enceguecida del ciempiés, una loca carrera por las paredes" (Cc 1, 149). These same fingers, which dance and tremble over the piano keys, capture and crush the cockroaches bathed in liquor that lurk within Delia's exquisite and laboriously crafted chocolate candies. The multiple vibrating, undulating, scurrying legs of the predatory centipede, to which Mario compares Delia in the above quotation, convey the sensation of her repulsive feminine excess that machinates to entrap, engulf, and put to death its victims.

In his study of Shakespeare's *The Winter's Tale*, Murray Schwartz elaborates on the meaning of spider symbolism: "Psychoanalysis has shown that the spider, like the serpent, is an over-determined symbol. On one level, it represents the sexually threatening mother, contact with whom signifies incest. On a deeper level, it signifies the horror of maternal engulfment, frequently confused with the child's own oral-aggressive impulses" (270). Thus, the spiders and centipede superimposed on the diabolic fiancée in "Circe" betray her identification with the engulfing mother.

Spider imagery is also a leitmotiv of "Manuscrito hallado en un bolsillo." In this story the narrator plays a mating game in the Parisian subway. If his reflection in the glass crosses with that of the young woman seated across from him, the game is initiated. He can follow her as long as she takes the route he has predetermined; if she goes down another tunnel, he must give her up. Each time that his hope and excitement is aroused, he feels in his stomach "el pozo donde la esperanza se enredaba con el temor en un calambre de arañas de muerte" (Cc 2, 66). Since the spiders spur him on to play game after game in search of a woman, they represent the conjunction of longing and dread. The imagery used to describe the subway tunnels likens the dark corridors to a repulsive womb. Referring to the reflections in the glass, the narrator explains that "la oscuridad del túnel pone su azogue atenuado, su felpa morada y moviente" (Cc 2, 66); recalling the forking underground tunnel where he lost a game he says "Montparnasse-Bienvenue . . . abre su hidra maloliente a las máximas posibilidades de fracaso" (Cc 2, 67). Playing the game means flirting with engulfment in the viscous, vibrating, foul-smelling womb. It is no wonder then, that "the rules of the game are calculated to avert romance rather than engender it" (Sommer, "Playing" 57). Since he longs for, but at the same time fears the woman, the game functions as a safety buffer, separating him from his dangerous desire.

When the protagonist makes up his mind to transgress the rules of the game and approach a woman who entered the wrong tunnel, the end result is catastrophic for the narrator. "Manuscrito" establishes the paradigm of the game of love that Cortázar's protagonists play in different variations, always to be lost. Other stories in which Cortázar's characters play and loose the game of love are "Todos los fuegos el fuego," "Cuello de gatito negro," and "Vientos alisios."

Cortázar's first "decepción amorosa," he reveals to Picón Garfield, came when he was ten years old, and the classmate he secretly adored proved to be a cruel tattletale. He made the mistake of writing the little girl's name in ink on the school bench, and she immediately turned him in to the teacher who shamed him publicly, giving him a lecture, and making him rub out the writing in front of the class. Meanwhile, the stool pigeon sat "con un aire justiciero digno y satisfecho." The young Cortázar felt a deep sense of betrayal: "No podía imaginar que me iba a traicionar de esa forma, con tanta maldad, con tanta frialdad" (Picón Garfield 104). While he recalls this incident in order to explain the genesis of "Los venenos," the betrayal scenario is portrayed over and over again in his stories.

But another, even more intensely felt childhood breach of faith surely had a greater role in the generation of Cortázar's stream of treacherous or fickle female characters; he confesses to an interviewer that the incident in question "[f]ue un gran traumatismo" (Soler Serrano 71). Some poems the young Julio wrote ended up in the hands of an uncle who told his mother they could not possibly have been written by a child, and must have been copied from an anthology. At bedtime his mother came to ask him if the poems were really his. "Me acuerdo siempre de lo que aquello fue para mí: un dolor de niño, un dolor infinito, profundo y terrible," Cortázar recalls. "El hecho de que mi madre pudiera dudar de mí fue desgarrador, algo como la revelación de la muerte, esos primeros golpes que te marcan para siempre" (Soler Serrano 71). These childhood incidents, which might have been shrugged off by another type of child, left deep scars in the psyche of the hypersensitive young Cortázar. His perception of his mother's disloyalty is undoubtedly the most powerful source of the betrayal paradigm, which is compulsively repeated throughout his writings.

"Los venenos," mentioned earlier in this chapter, relates a young boy's loss of innocence when he discovers that Lila, the neighbor girl he likes, has been two-timing him. The narrator's cousin, Hugo, comes to spend time with the family, and the children play together in the yard. Hugo is something of a lady-killer. All the girls in the neighborhood are crazy about him, including, to her brother's disgust, the narrator's sister. After Hugo leaves, the narrator discovers that Lila has accepted from Hugo his prized peacock feather. Since the narrator has just given Lila his beautiful jasmine plant, "lo mejor que yo tenía" (*Cc* 1, 306), he realizes that Lila and Hugo have made a fool of him. The triangular structure is a reenactment of the Oedipal scene, Prieto points out, an evocation of the boy rivaling his father for the mother.[17] Other stories in which the omnipresent betrayal motif appears include "Continuidad de los parques," "La señorita Cora," "Instrucciones para John Howell," "Todos los fuegos el fuego," "Liliana llorando," "Los pasos en las huellas," "Cambio de luces," "Tango de vuelta," and "Clone." While in some stories the characters struggle to come to terms with their sorry lot, as is the case in "Los venenos," "Liliana llorando," and "Cambio de luces"; in others, for instance "Todos los fuegos el fuego," "Tango de vuelta," and "Clone," the price of treachery is death.

Sexuality and eroticism in Cortázar's fictions is laced with violence. A pointed assessment and explanation of this aspect of Cortázar's work comes from Antonio Planells:

> Los personajes de Cortázar son incapaces de amar; solamente conocen el deseo y la posesión. Buscan desesperadamente la reafirmación de su ego; barrera infranqueable que impide la intercomunicación amorosa, la fusión de un ser en otro, la unión perfecta. La mera idea de un amor que exija el ego a cambio, espanta a los personajes cortazarianos y los lleva al desequilibrio, al caos.
>
> Observamos que en los cuentos de Cortázar el acto sexual representa la última puerta por abrir, la tentativa final, la posibilidad de escape. Pero luego de consumado dicho acto, sobreviene el fracaso, la vuelta al principio inhibidor, la destrucción total, el suicidio. ("Represión sexual" 233)

Sexual desire void of love in Cortázar's fiction, Planells's statement implies, cannot produce the desired human connection. Fleeting physical union with the other only makes patent, paradoxically, the impossibility of a utopian perfect and eternal union, because once the act is consummated and the lovers disengage, they become more painfully aware of their irreconcilable separateness. This realization may be one of the causes of the desperation and violence so often acted out by Cortázar's lovers. A constant in Cortázar's fiction, violence in the form of homicide or suicide is linked to sexual relationships in the following stories: "Continuidad de los parques," "El río," "El ídolo de las Cícladas," "Las babas del diablo," "Las armas secretas," "Todos los fuegos el fuego," "Verano," "Lugar llamado Kindberg," "Cuello de gatito negro," "Vientos alisios," "Recortes de prensa," "Tango de vuelta," "Clone," and "Anillo de Moebius."

Sometimes violence is retribution for treachery, other times it is intrinsic to the sexual act—the husband or lover contains the rapist/assassin. Perhaps the most haunting stories in this regard are "El río" and "Las armas secretas" for the seamless and subtle manner in which the lover is transformed into rapist and murderer. In "El río," a micromasterpiece, the narrator belittles his wife's insistence that she is going to drown herself in the River Seine. His reaction to her suicide threats and angry desperation is marked by insensitivity: "hace tanto que apenas te escucho cuando dices cosas así . . . Me das risa, pobre . . . uno se pregunta si realmente crees en tus amenazas, tus chantajes repugnantes, tus inagotables escenas patéticas" (*Cc* 1, 297). Despite his exasperation, the narrator desires to make love to her. She refuses and resists him, but he overcomes her: "Tengo que dominarte lentamente" (*Cc* 1, 298). In the final scene we discover he is making love to her water-soaked and lifeless body, which has just been pulled from the river.

"Las armas secretas," a much longer story with a complex plot, centers on the relationship of Michèle and Pierre, French youths who are dating. Michèle professes to love Pierre, but each time that they are about to consummate their relationship, she rejects him. At the same time, Pierre struggles to understand his flashbacks, strange recollections, and a sense of déjà vu—repeated mental images that seem to belong to someone else. Putting the clues together, the reader comes to the realization that Pierre is gradually being possessed by the spirit of a German soldier who raped Michèle seven years earlier, and was executed by her friends. In the body of Pierre, the German soldier returns to avenge his death by harming Michèle.[18] The double in this story—the timid would-be lover with vague memories of a shadowy "other scene"—is an eerie evocation of Freud's topographical notion of the unconscious, often conceptualized as a palimpsest, a manuscript on which the original writing has been effaced to make room for another writing. The rapist and assassin who lurk within the mild-mannered boyfriend are akin to the repressed contents of the unconscious: the other writing that has been rubbed out, but not forgotten.

John Turner's edifying study of these two stories focuses on the reactions of the male reader to violence done to women. Reminding us of Cortázar's declaration "me vi obligado a escribir un cuento para evitar algo mucho peor" (*Último round I*, 69), Turner understands the stories as an exorcism of the compulsion to violence as well as a critique of male domination of women. The moral core of "El río," Turner explains, condemns "man's cruelly inhuman domination of the woman." The "text subverts the cultural stereotype it deals with, not only by depicting it with such frightening lucidity but by forcing us to re-enact it and feel its inherent contradictions" (47). In his analysis of "Las armas secretas," Turner identifies the clue to Pierre's emotional problems as unresolved Oedipal attitudes toward the mother, focusing on the moment in which Pierre imagines Michèle arranging his room as a mother would do: "la madre asoma en todos sus dientes" (*Cc* 1, 267). Later in the story, Pierre compares Michèle to Delilah because she threatens to cut off a lock of his hair that hangs over his forehead, thus evoking Michèle as a castrating woman. Michèle, as a mother figure, threatens Pierre's "insecure manhood and becomes the object of his fear/aggression" (Turner 56). Turner explains that the male reader identifies with the protagonist, and the reader's unconscious view of male sexuality is shaken up as he shares the character's shock when he realizes that he is making love to his wife's corpse, turning into his girlfriend's rapist (54).

"Anillo de Moebius," another particularly disturbing story, portrays the rape of Janet, an English schoolteacher who is cycling through the French countryside, by Robert, a French farmhand and social misfit. Janet dies of suffocation while Robert is violating her, and after his trial and conviction, he hangs himself in his jail cell. In her afterlife, Janet awakens to her sensuality and desires Robert, metamorphosing from one form to another as she seeks a state in which she can achieve harmony and union with Robert's spirit. Not surprisingly, the critical assessment of this story has been divided, pointing to its polemic nature. Peter Standish finds it disturbing because it implies that the girl enjoys being raped (*Understanding Cortázar* 47), and Estela Cedola sees it "casi como una apología de la violación" (125). Willy Muñoz views the story from a different perspective, considering it Cortázar's restitution to women for his earlier sexist attitudes. Janet is possibly the only female pursuer in Cortázar's literature, Muñoz argues, and through her Cortázar recognizes the woman's sexual desire and right to erotic pleasure (107). Muñoz concludes that at the end of the story "Janet es ahora parte activa en la formación de su propio destino: su deseo se convierte en acción, pero su propósito no es sólo liberarse de las lacras culturales que la han alienado del varón, sino también liberar al hombre de su machismo" (114). Sommer, while admitting that the construction of Janet's responses to rape is dubious if offensive, singles out "Anillo" as a representation of the striving toward utopian harmony due to its imagery of the Moebius strip that "breaks the earlier image of dichotomy between self and other" ("A Nowhere" 256). "Instead of single-voicedness," Sommer explains, "Cortázar tunes into lovers who can't meet each other, but still want to" ("A Nowhere" 256).[19]

The mixed critical reaction reflects the seemingly irreconcilable dimensions of the story: it poetically depicts a woman aspiring to experience sensual pleasure, but this quest is set in motion by her rape and asphyxiation at the hands of the man she comes to desire. Cortázar's remarks regarding "Anillo de Moebius" in a letter to Jaime Alazraki seem to indicate another instance of his lingering insensitivity toward women: "Me divertí con tu referencia a la crítica feminista posible sobre la violación, porque ya mi traductora francesa me saltó encima con todas las uñas. Siempre me parecerá una lástima que violar y ser violado no coincidan en el plano del placer; pero si fuera así, claro, no habría violación, y es mejor dejar la cosa sin más comentarios" (*Cartas*, 1732).

Frustrated and doomed love affairs, another face to Cortázar's fictional relationships, could be considered a trademark of his stories. In Cedola's words, "los encuentros contienen el germen de su destrucción, son desde el comienzo desencuentros" (123). In many of his narratives, these affairs are characterized by their transitory nature. For instance in "La autopista del sur," the love relationship that blossoms between two car owners during a fantastically long traffic jam, dissolves once the cars start moving again, and in "Cuello de gatito negro" as well as "Lugar llamado Kindberg" the one-night stand has tragic consequences. But *Octaedro* and *Alguien que anda por ahí* portray tender and seasoned relationships that also end in failure. "Las caras de la medalla" depicts a man and woman who attempt to enter into a romantic relationship, but due to different tastes and different lifestyles, are not able to coincide, like the two sides of a coin. Sommer observes that in "Las caras de la medalla" Cortázar makes clear his obsessive need to lose the game of love, and as in "Manuscrito hallado en un bolsillo," plays on the impossibility of human contact. The narrator blames his own cowardice for this thwarted romance, which brings remorse to both partners ("Playing" 60).

Both "Verano" and "Vientos alisios" feature a married couple whose long-standing relationship has grown tedious and predictable because it is based on practiced routine rather than spontaneity and passion, adventure and surprise. In "Verano," Mariano and Zulma agree to take care of a neighbor's young daughter in their house overnight. As she sleeps, the couple hears strange noises and sees a white horse that crashes against their door and window as if it wanted to get in. Mariano tries to calm the hysterical Zulma and gently leads her to bed, where she turns her back to him, "como tantas otras noches del verano" (*Cc* 2, 79). After Mariano drops off to sleep, Zulma suddenly sits up in bed, terrified again, insisting that the little girl is in their home precisely to let the horse in. Mariano replies that he does not care whether or not the horse comes in, and makes love to Zulma against her will. "No quiero, no quiero, no quiero nunca más," protests Zulma, "no quiero, pero ya demasiado tarde, su fuerza y orgullo cediendo a ese peso arrasador que la devolvía al pasado imposible" (*Cc* 2, 80). Planells analyzes the symbolism in this story, explaining that the little girl and the horse are outer manifestations connected to inner experiences: sexual repression, frustrated maternity. The girl represents Zulma's desire to be a mother, the inside of the house is Zulma's sex, the horse is the sexual act and the penis. "El caballo (pene) quiere penetrar la casa (vagina) y eso aviva el terror a la violación que yace en la subconsciencia de Zulma" ("Represión sexual" 236). In the González Bermejo interview Cortázar admits to autobiographical elements in the story: "Es el producto de un mal momento de mi vida, y ese caballo que pugna por entrar a la casa condensa mis propios fantasmas . . . ese caballo blanco es un poco la encarnación del sentimiento de culpa de los dos personajes que están llegando al final de una relación personal" (González Bermejo 138–139). Undoubtedly, Cortázar is referring to his separation from his first wife, Aurora Bernárdez.

"Vientos alisios" is another, and this time, fatal, version of the desperation resulting from that breakup. Facing yet another boring vacation, Mauricio and Vera, who have lived together for twenty years, decide that this trip will be different—they will each go separately to the same resort in Mombassa. This will be their way to "jugar el juego, hacer el

balance, decidir" (*Cc* 2, 127). At the resort, each becomes involved in an
exhilarating affair with a new partner: Mauricio with Anna, a languid,
sensual Scandinavian; and Vera with Sandro, a passionate Italian. The
game's success is fatal. Mauricio and Vera return home together, each
pretending to be their partner's holiday lover. Together they take an
overdose of pills, and in a final embrace, wait for death to come. Their
discovery of renewed vitality and passion via the game, the new partners, made them realize that they can neither revive the lost passion in
their relationship, nor can they continue to live without it. Death is their
only solution. In Sommer's view, Cortázar hints that their frustration is
a lack of children, because Vera is a pediatrician but not a mother ("Playing" 58). Perhaps this can partially account for, in both stories, the characters' sense of leading an empty, futile existence. Or more likely, it is
one element within two complex human realities.

Cortázar's final love story is "Orientación de los gatos," a tribute to
Carol Dunlop, his second wife. The narrator knows that Alana, his wife,
looks at him with absolute candor and openness, yet he senses that she
possesses other dimensions he does not know.[20] He admits that Alana
and their cat Osiris have their own special relationship, one that he cannot enter. He says he can tolerate his lack of understanding Osiris, but
his love for Alana cannot accept that distance from his wife—he desires
to know her totally. In order to capture every nuance of her being, he
secretly watches her expression in moments of self-revelation, when she
is listening to music or looking at paintings. As part of his "project-
Alana," the narrator takes her to a gallery to spy on her reaction to the
paintings, apprehending other Alanas with each picture she views. He
anticipates leaving with a perfect and infinite love for his wife. But the
final picture, of a cat identical to Osiris looking out a window at something beyond the painting, retains Alana's rapt attention. When Alana
finally returns her gaze to her husband, he realizes she has remained in
the painting, and he can no longer see himself in/through her eyes. He
realizes he cannot appropriate her gaze because he cannot see what she
sees, he cannot see through her eyes, in other words, he cannot posses
her completely. There can be no utopia, the story seems to be saying, but
that does not stop the narrator from trying, from striving toward it
(Sommer, "A Nowhere" 259).

Desire is endless, what is important is the search. "Orientación de
los gatos," a story which we could consider the culmination of Cortázar's
frustrated search for a perfect union, expresses the narrator's admission

of the impossibility of totally possessing the desired woman, and a recognition of his struggle to come to terms with her irreconcilable difference. And this is precisely the topic that we shall continue exploring in the next chapter.

Chapter 5

ॐ

Defiant Women, or Coming to Terms with Difference

Tanto Ludmilla como Francine le dicen más de cuatro verdades a Andrés,
y creo que eso habría que tenerlo en cuenta antes de lapidarme del todo.
—Cortázar, *Cartas*

My female characters *do* tell off the male protagonist, Cortázar points out (in the epigraph above) to Laure Bataillon, his French translator who apparently disapproved of the depiction of women in his novel *Libro de Manuel* (1973). Jokingly pretending that he thinks Bataillon is about to stone him, in his self-defense he argues that he is not totally blind to issues women have with men. To state his case, he provides her with a brief history of his awakening to his own *machista* biases, admitting to his continued objectification of women, despite his desire to be more open-minded:

> Te diré que comprendo cada vez más tu punto de vista, pues no eres la única en protestar por el machismo latinoamericano que como ves se infiltra incluso en quienes quisieran ir más allá y tener una visión más amplia y justa del dominio erótico. La cosa empezó hace tres años, cuando diversas lectoras o amigas me reprocharon aquello del "lector-hembra" de *Rayuela*. Hice "amande honorable", incluso en un reportaje por escrito, pero ahora al releer el *Libro de Manuel* compruebo una vez más que el erotismo está visto de manera prácticamente exclusiva desde el punto de vista masculino, y que las mujeres, a pesar de mi amor y mi respeto, están siempre un poco "reificadas" o cosificadas, como quieras llamarle. (Cortázar, *Cartas* 1531)

As we have seen in the previous chapter, the love relationships depicted by Cortázar are invariably highly conflictive. And Bataillon, in her presumed complaint, was in good company—it is well known that

93

Cortázar took (and continues to take) a lot of heat for the way he represented women in his fiction. *Rayuela* has been declared profoundly dated due to its egregiously aggressive machismo,[1] and many critics have sought to define the various treatments of female characters in his stories and novels, with descriptions ranging from "woman as intermediary or helper" and "woman as idealized goddess" to "woman as object of man's fear and aggression" and "woman as perverse beast." Female subjectivity is suppressed, critics point out, and the woman plays a role defined by a chauvinistic and patriarchal system.[2] Within these diverse portrayals and critiques, the common denominator is the objectification of women within a male-centered perspective.

And yet, in some of Cortázar's later stories we can perceive a subtle change. Doris Sommer has noted that "Cortázar moves beyond a cavalier sexism . . . Instead of considering women to be predictable, Cortázar increasingly allowed himself to be surprised by them and to narrate through their personae" ("A Nowhere" 236). As explained in chapters 1 and 2, there exists an evolution in Cortázar's attitude toward women, which can be evidenced in both his public statements and his fiction. Cortázar's narrators eventually let down some of their defenses and become less controlling toward women, showing more tolerance of difference and a willingness to try to reconcile themselves to it. But, as Cortázar himself acknowledged, a perspective free of sexism did not come easily to him, and his machismo sometimes carried the day in spite of his best intentions.

Numerous stories in Cortázar's last three collections—*Alguien que anda por ahí* (1977), *Queremos tanto a Glenda* (1980), and *Deshoras* (1982)—reveal his greater openness or sensitivity toward women, often expressed via a critique of *machista* attitudes. A brief overview of the stories in question demonstrates the contours of this evolution in his thinking.

"Las caras de la medalla" would have been one more typically Cortazarean drama of a frustrated romance if it were not for the author's experimental use of pronouns, employing the *nosotros* form to convey a spiritual connection, as well as a type of parity, between the would-be lovers. Sommer views the story as representative of what she calls Cortázar's "utopian experiment" because, by means of the first-person plural, the man and woman "are identified as equal partners in a new category" ("A Nowhere" 248). Sommer also considers "Anillo de Moebius," discussed in the previous chapter, to be an example of Cortázar's new "utopian grammar" because the image of the Moebius strip breaks down the barrier between self and other ("A Nowhere" 254–255). And, at least in the view of one critic, it represents Cortázar's restitution to women for his earlier sexism because it presents a female pursuer who takes an active part in her destiny and search for erotic pleasure.[3] Notwithstanding these assessments, in my opinion, "Anillo de Moebius" remains a dubious story in regard to whether it reflects an enlightened attitude toward women due to its depiction of a violated woman who eventually comes to desire her rapist.

"La barca o Nueva visita a Venecia," Cortázar explains in his preface to the story, was first written in 1954 and entitled simply "La barca." Not entirely satisfied with the original version, he never published it. Twenty-two years later he took it out of the drawer, and instead of rewriting the story to correct its flaws, he decided to resurrect Dora, a secondary character in the early version, to rectify the narrator's skewed perspective that gave the text a ring of falseness. In the new version Dora interrupts the narration, taking the (supposedly) omniscient narrator to task for his ignorance or hypocrisy regarding what transpired between three tourists in Italy—Valentina, Adriano, and Dora herself. Dora's interpolations insinuate that unacknowledged sexism led the narrator to focus on Valentina's affair with Adriano, downplaying Dora's presence and ignoring or pretending not to be aware of the importance of the lesbian attraction between the two women. "Diario para un cuento," to be analyzed in depth in chapter 7, is similar to "La barca o Nueva visita a Venecia" in that it also uses a female character to expose the narrator's shortcomings. In "Diario," the narrator invokes Anabel, an Argentine prostitute, to indict himself for his cowardly and hypocritical treatment of her and of the urban proletariat in general. "Recortes de prensa," which will be studied in chapters 6 and 7, has an urgent, agonic tone, featuring women who struggle against grave cases of social injustice: a mother who dared to confront the reign of terror unleashed by the Argentine military regime, and two women who take deadly revenge on a sadistic wife abuser.

Finally, "Orientación de los gatos" and "Queremos tanto a Glenda," along with "Cambio de luces," reveal the dangers inherent in the attempt to achieve total control over a beloved woman. "Orientación de los gatos" (also discussed in the previous chapter) is at once a tender love story and a critique of a male project of mastery over a woman.[4] When the narrator, who wishes to possess his wife Alana in her totality by knowing her completely, takes her to an art gallery to "read" her reaction to each painting, his project backfires on him. The last picture portrays a cat staring out the window, and by means of her spiritual communion with the cat, she perceives the "invisible vision" that it is seeing. Alana has stepped into another dimension, eluding her husband's possessive curiosity, and due to the powerful sympathies of her nature, she—instead of her husband—becomes the one in possession of new knowledge (Lohafer 229). Not only is the narrator left in the dark, but he is "zeroed out" by his own desire because when Alana looks back at him, she sees what is invisible from his perspective (Lohafer 218). "Orientación de los gatos" is a "postmodern parable," "a brilliant, almost mathematical deconstruction of rational, goal-oriented action, of male hubris, of the 'I' itself," as Cortázar admits to "male inadequacy before female mystery" (Lohafer 230, 233).

"Queremos tanto a Glenda" can be read as a warning against the idealization and objectification of women. A group of fans of the actress Glenda Garson love her so much that they realize they cannot tolerate the imperfections they perceive in her films. They pool their resources to edit the portions of her movies that they consider aesthetically flawed, and then secretly replace all existing copies of the films with their perfected versions. Thanks to their meticulous labor, each movie becomes "exactamente idéntico al deseo" (*Cc* 2, 334). When the Glenda fan(atic)s view the splendid corrected version of one of her movies, they are ecstatic: "supimos que la perfección podía ser de este mundo y que ahora era de Glenda para siempre, de Glenda para nosotros para siempre" (*Cc* 2, 335). Just when they have completed the project, to their delight, Glenda announces her retirement from the cinema. Now their grandiose project of editing Glenda and making her equal to their ideal of her takes on biblical dimensions in their minds: "Vivimos la felicidad del séptimo día, del descanso después de la creación" (*Cc* 2, 336). The image of Glenda so carefully wrought by these demigods will be perfect throughout eternity. But alas, a year later Glenda, showing she is only human, reverses her decision, announcing she will return to the screen. The fans are horrified that their perfect work will be ruined and sadly recognize that there is only one thing to do: they must eliminate Glenda. "Queríamos tanto a Glenda que le ofreceríamos una última perfección inviolable," explains the narrator (*Cc* 2, 337). This story is a parable of the danger of fixing an ideal, of searching for utopia in a woman, and trying to shape her to fit that static concept of perfection. Human reality is messy and imperfect, and loved ones can never live up to a predetermined ideal, the story seems to be telling us, but the only alternative is death.

To recapitulate the scope of the new attitude toward women revealed in stories from the latter part of Cortázar's career, some enclose a search for a new type of harmony between men and women; in others, his female characters confront and unseat chauvinistic and domineering males; and, similarly, other stories critique male hubris. Within Cortázar's stories that articulate his quest to come to terms with sexual difference, an especially rich and nuanced story in this regard and the focus of the rest of this chapter is "Cambio de luces." Using feminist reading techniques to reclaim the voice of Luciana, the female protagonist, we discover her ultimately successful resistance to a male protagonist who attempts to control and repress her.

"Cambio de luces": What Does Luciana Want?

In her insightful work, *What Does a Woman Want? Reading and Sexual Difference,* Shoshana Felman illustrates how the careful reader can reclaim the female voice in texts with a male-centered perspective. To this end, she proposes a reopening and radical displacement of the now-notorious Freudian query "What does a woman want?" This question posits femininity as the problem that perpetually baffles men; it is a dark and unknowable continent. Felman theorizes that great texts "are self-transgressive, with respect to the conscious ideologies that inform them" (6), and her readings of three male texts show how they "enact female resistance, even as they struggle with it and attempt to overcome and erase it" (4). Felman's readings "seek to trace within each text . . . its own specific literary, inadvertent *textual transgressions of its male assumptions and prescriptions.* Although this literary excess, this self-transgression of the text," continues Felman, "might be at first invisible, inaudible, because it exceeds both the control and the deliberate intention of the writer's consciousness, I am suggesting that it can be amplified, made patent, by the desire— and by the rhetorical interposition—of a woman reader" (6). Jardine, in a similar vein, calls for a rethinking of the master narrative in an effort to identify a space of some kind over which the narrator has lost control, a space that can be coded as feminine. She posits a problematization of the representation of women in contemporary thought and texts written by men (25).

"Cambio de luces" presents an intriguing example of a self-transgressive text. By reclaiming the suppressed female voice, we can see how the female character foils patriarchal norms, despite the controlling male narrator. I will make use, in particular, of some of the feminist strategies of reading that Felman practices in her work. Felman bases her discussion of sexual difference on Luce Irigaray's critique of the status of womanhood in Western culture. According to Irigaray, in the polarity of masculine/feminine functions in Western thought, the male term is privileged: "Theoretically subordinated to the concept of masculinity, the woman is viewed by the man as *his* opposite, that is to say as *his* other, the negative of the positive, and not, in her own right, different, other, otherness itself" (Felman 23). Within this perspective, woman is excluded from the production of speech, and identity is conceived as male sameness. This conception of identity represents a theoretical blindness to woman's actual difference, and it is this blindness, this failure to take into account women's otherness, her subjectivity, her desire that ends up subverting the male-centered narrator in the texts under study.

Felman's rereading of Balzac's "Adieu" provides a model for my approach to Cortázar's "Cambio de luces." In both stories the male protagonists, Philippe and Tito, respectively, cannot conceive of female identity outside of the masculine measure of identity and value: "men are identified with the prerogatives of discourse and of reason" whereas women are reduced to "an *object* that can be known and possessed" (Felman 32–33). Philippe's mistress, Stéphanie, has gone mad; she cannot speak except to say "adieu," and she cannot recognize Philippe. In former times, Philippe perceived Stéphanie as " 'the queen of the Parisian ballrooms' " (34). Felman points out that queen here implies a king—Philippe—and Stéphanie represented "above all, '*the glory of her lover.*' 'Woman,' in other words, is the exact metaphorical measure of the narcissism of man" (34). Philippe hatches and executes an elaborate scheme to cure Stéphanie, but at the moment she regains her sanity and recognizes Philippe, she dies. Felman's analysis shows how "the text subverts and dislocates the logic of representation that it has dramatized through Philippe's endeavor and his failure" (38). In "Cambio de luces," Tito's plan to mold his lover, Luciana, to fit his ideal image boomerangs when she leaves him for *her* ideal man. Thus, in both stories the male protagonists attempt to build monuments to themselves by putting a woman in a place that will glorify them, and these projects come to naught when the women ultimately refuse to play the roles assigned to them. The men fail because they operate from a phallo-logocentric position of reason and power that ignores the women's desire. My analysis of "Cambio de luces" will attempt to expose the fallacious reasoning on the part of Tito coupled with Luciana's subtle resistance that lead to the downfall of the male project of mastery.

Felman's perception of the self-transgressive nature of Balzac's text in regard to male assumptions is relevant to the Cortázar story, and this approach can shed new light on our understanding of the psychic structures underpinning Cortázar's work. Despite certain differences, both Balzac's and Cortázar's texts speak to the male encounter with femininity even as they enact female resistance to the male narrator. By following Felman's inspiration to encroach on the female desire in Cortázar's text and expose the consequences of the narrator's blindness to female subjectivity, we can decenter the male frame of reference in the text and take a fresh look at the depiction of gender roles in this story.

Like so many of Cortázar's fictions, "Cambio de luces" is the tale of a failed relationship. Tito is an actor for the *radioteatro* of Buenos Aires who always plays the part of the villain. One day he receives a letter from Luciana, a woman listener who professes to admire him despite the nefarious characters he portrays. When Tito writes back to thank her for the kind words, she responds with an invitation to arrange a meeting. Both Tito and Luciana had preconceived notions as to what the other would look like, and neither conforms to the expectations. Nevertheless, they get along well, and soon Luciana moves in with Tito. Tito previously had a four-year relationship with another woman but this had come to an end, and he was living alone. Gradually Tito instigates changes in Luciana's appearance and surroundings in an attempt to make her more closely approximate his ideal. When he thinks he has achieved perfection in his re-creation of Luciana and truly loves her, he spots her coming out of a hotel in the embrace of another man, strangely, a man who corresponds to Luciana's ideal image of Tito.

"Cambio de luces" is a story about identity and desire, and a woman's role within patriarchal society. Who is the desiring subject, who is the object of desire, and are these roles interchangeable? What will a woman do to please a man? To what extent will she sacrifice her identity to make him desire her? Why will a man delude himself about the character of the woman he professes to love? How can he be so blind to her real needs? And can he ever be certain about his own needs and identity? In "Cambio de luces," the male narrator never bothers to ask himself "What does Luciana want?," thus my rereading of the story will resurrect that question, and others that spin off it. For instance, why did Tito fail to recognize or acknowledge that Luciana could have needs and desires of her own? How did Luciana go about trying to get what she wanted? The attentive reader can discover in Luciana what the narrator failed to see due to his blind spots.

Highly stylized social settings—nineteenth-century Parisian ballrooms and radio soap operas—define the concept of ideal masculinity and femininity for Philippe and Tito, respectively.[5] These artificial worlds of posture and pretense revolve around the pairing of heterosexual couples with rigidly defined codes of appearance and behavior for both male and female. Those who subscribe to these codes achieve their sense of self-worth according to how closely they fit the image defined by these sociosexual stereotypes, and the male role accrues its value in relation to its complementary female role. After all, how can there be a leading man in a love story without a leading lady, or a king of the ball without his queen? Thus, Philippe and Tito value Stéphanie and Luciana not for themselves, but rather for how well they can play a feminine role that glorifies their male companion. The men seek in their beloved a reflection of their own self, and she becomes "an object whose role is to ensure, by an interplay of reflections, his own self-sufficiency as a 'subject,' to serve as a mediator in his own specular relationship with himself" (Felman 36).

This soap opera "culture" plays a central role in "Cambio de luces." Tito's romanticized but illusory version of himself is inspired, in a confused sort of way, by the *radiodrama,* and their plots, all monotonously alike with their predictable ending—"el inevitable triunfo del amor y la justicia según Lemos" (*Cc* 2, 124)—prefigure the outcome of the Tito-Luciana love story. These stories of romance and intrigue become a text-within-the-text, a repeated configuration in Cortázar's stories. Tito seems to be particularly vulnerable to the appeal of this artificial melodramatic world because he is dissatisfied with his own life. He uses his artistic expression as a way of coping with the tedium and void he experiences in his daily life in Buenos Aires, spending his afternoons practicing and polishing his sinister roles in the radio dramas. His professed purpose is to "vengarme de esos papeles ingratos . . . haciéndolos míos" (*Cc* 2, 120). Thus, his approach is one of transformation and appropriation; his revenge on the unflattering roles will be, paradoxically, to *be-*

come the villain. Indeed, this willful confusion between his own identity and his theatrical roles has become a cornerstone of Tito's life.

However, Tito's narcissism and desire for adulation is poorly served by his "papeles más bien secundarios y en general antipáticos" (*Cc* 2, 119), and he secretly covets Jorge Fuentes's crush of female fans. The day he receives Luciana's letter—the only letter in three years—he compares this meager missive to the hero's legion of admirers: "nuestro galán Jorge Fuentes . . . recibía dos canastas de cartas de amor y un corderito blanco mandado por una estanciera romántica" (*Cc* 2, 119). Tito unwittingly reveals his excessive pride when he describes his first meeting with Luciana: "era lógico que se hablara sobre todo de mí porque yo era el conocido . . . por eso sin parecer vanidoso la dejé que me recordara en tantas novelas radiales" (*Cc* 2, 122). His disavowal "sin parecer vanidoso" serves to call attention to what it represses—his vanity, which fuels a desperate desire for an adoring fan who will confirm his fame and talent. By allowing Luciana to focus on his artistic representations instead of his off-stage self, Tito promotes a type of "misidentification" on which he will ground their relationship.

Not surprisingly, Tito projects the fictional world of the love stories onto his relationship with Luciana, casting himself as the leading man and Luciana as his leading lady. He says that his meeting with Luciana would have given Lemos, the author of the dramas, an idea for another plot, but in Lemos's story, the boy would discover that Luciana was identical to his imagination of her. The fact that Luciana is different from his image of her proves, according to Tito, that these theories only work in Radio Belgrano—the world of artifice. At one point he refers to an actress as "la alternera muchacha que lentamente yo envolvería en mi consabida telaraña de maldades" (*Cc* 2, 121). This, of course, is what he will attempt to do with Luciana—he will try to wrap her in his web, subordinating her to serve his aggrandized vision of self. For Tito, Luciana is an object that can be mastered and possessed. When he projects his final move in his plan to conquer Luciana: "volverla definitivamente mía por una aceptación total de mi lenta telaraña enamorada" (*Cc* 2, 125), he repeats the spider web image he had used to describe the radio character's manipulations, again fusing his real life identity with his theatrical roles, but changing the web of evil into a web of love. This replacement is another indication that he is trying to switch codes and take on the appearance of the *galán*. However, no matter how he qualifies it, a spider web is still something woven for the purpose of trapping and retaining a hapless victim in its tangled threads in order to feed on it, and it aptly describes his urge to nourish his ego with Luciana's admiration for his talent.[6]

In any event, his amorous project is ultimately doomed to failure because Tito has internalized the role of villain, and is destined to repeat it despite himself. In the love triangles that invariably structure Lemos's plots, the *galán* always gets the girl, and Tito forgot he must play the villain, who never gets the girl and is foiled at the end. Thus, justice according to Lemos *does* eventually prevail, and, contrary to Tito's previous observation, his life *does* imitate his art because he willingly projects his fictional roles onto his behavior with Luciana. He tried to exploit the artistic experience as a way of overcoming his limitations, but that depended on him playing the leading man, not the villain—a stretch that, in the end, he could not execute. Finally, the artistic role does not constitute self-transcendence as he imagined, but rather fatalistic self-entrapment.[7] Tito's precarious construct of self depended on two layers of self-deceit: first, he attempted to live vicariously through the melodramatic roles, and second, finding insufficient food for his needy ego in his typecasted "bad guy" roles, he jealously tried to usurp the role of *galán*. And of course, since a *galán* is defined by his ability to woo a beautiful and adoring damsel who will unproblematically reflect back his noble and virile image of self, Tito tries to cast Luciana in that role.

Tito falls for the Pygmalion lure: the dream of a perfect woman as a man's work of art, a monument to his narcissism. From the moment she walks into the tearoom, Luciana's appearance and personality are a problem for Tito. Her hair and eyes are too dark, she is too tall, and she is spirited and lively, not sad and pensive as Tito imagines his perfect romantic heroine. However, since she is his one and only fan, he sets about remaking her. A mirror image of "Queremos tanto a Glenda," in which the actress's admirers edit her films according to their ideal, here it is the actor who will impose his image of perfection on his fan.

What leads Tito to believe he can transform this woman according to his desire? First of all, he revels in the control he exerts over his dramatic roles—he masters, perfects, and appropriates them. Perhaps this sensation of control over the characters he brings to life in the *radioteatro* convinces him that he can also sculpt Luciana according to his will. Second, he considers the prose of Luciana's letters to be "sencilla y tímida," and thinks she must be the same way. From simple and timid, Tito can readily extrapolate "malleable," and thus deludes himself into thinking that she will docilely submit to his makeover of her. Finally, when Luciana tells him about her past, which includes a boyfriend who left her for a job in Chicago and a failed marriage, Tito hears it "como si ella no hubiera hablado verdaderamente de sí misma ahora que parecía empezar a vivir por cuenta de otro presente, de mi cuerpo contra el suyo, los platitos de leche a la gata, el cine a cada rato, el amor" (*Cc* 2, 123). Here, Tito reveals that he sees Luciana as the object of his desire, existing only for him and his world. He chooses not to conceive of her as a person with a past, something that would force him to admit that at one time she had desires independent of his existence and control.

Tito's feminine ideal is like still another text-within-the-text, the script he will use as he resculpts Luciana. As soon as he reads Luciana's first letter, he constructs a mental image of her: "Esa mujer que imaginaba más bien chiquita y triste y de pelo castaño con ojos claros" (*Cc* 2, 120). In his imagination, Luciana's pensive spirit is echoed in the atmosphere of her home, characterized by penumbra and melancholy: "cada vez que pensaba en Luciana la veía en el mismo lugar . . . una galería cerrada con claraboyas de vidrios de colores y mamparas que dejaban pasar la luz agrisándola, Luciana sentada en un sillón . . . el pelo castaño como envuelto por una luz de vieja fotografía, ese aire ceniciento y a la vez nítido de la galería cerrada . . . en una casa . . . donde habitaba la melancolía" (*Cc* 2, 121–122).

Tito gradually goes about the transformation of Luciana. First he asks her to lighten her hair, and then he ties it back, assuring her it looks better that way. To complete his ideal image, he changes the environment around Luciana, buying her a wicker chair and writing table, and moving the lamp away from her so that only the dim, shadowy light of the afternoon is cast on her. Once the setting is perfect, Tito brings home a recording of one of his soap operas, and seats Luciana in the shadows to be his ideal audience. He has effected a "cambio de luz," a "cambio de Luciana." He rejects the extremes—bright light and black hair—for moderate midtones: dim, grayish light and chestnut hair. Akin to the "altanera muchacha" that the radio villain would wrap in his evil spider web, the initial Luciana is too spirited for Tito—her smiling eyes should have been sad, her free-flowing black hair should have been controlled and light brown, she should have drunk tea instead of whiskey. Tito is afraid of this vitality because it threatens his ability to control her; he prefers to repeat what he knows—art and imitation, midtones and melancholy—instead of daring to experience Luciana's liveliness and spontaneity. The chromatic symbolism evoked in the story's title speaks of Tito's attempt to dim Luciana's brilliance. Luminous Luciana shone too brightly to reflect back Tito's specular image. He needed to tone down the light to be able to see his shadowy self-image in the penumbra.

Observing Luciana's reaction while she listens to the soap opera seems to bring back a moment of lost perfection for Tito: "Me hacía bien mirar a Luciana atenta al drama, alzando a veces la cabeza cuando reconocía mi voz y sonriéndome . . . me sentía bien, reencontraba por un momento algo que me había estado faltando" (*Cc* 2, 124). In contrast to the loving husband of "Orientación de los gatos" who spies on his wife as she listens to music and looks at paintings in order to get to know her better, Tito's objective is not to learn more about Luciana, but rather to bask in the glow of his own reflection in her admiring eyes.

Finally, he believes he has achieved perfection in his transformation of Luciana: "la besé largamente y le dije que nunca la había querido tanto como en ese momento, tal como la estaba viendo, como hubiera querido verla siempre" (*Cc* 2, 125). However, Luciana's response to Tito's outpouring of affection and enthusiasm for her made-over self is silence: "Ella no dijo nada . . . estuvo quieta, como ausente ¿Por qué esperar otra cosa de Luciana . . . ? Ella era como los sobres lila, como las simples, casi tímidas frases de sus cartas" (*Cc* 2, 125). Tito rationalizes Luciana's lack of an appropriate response because otherwise, if he were to recognize that the changes he has made in her do not suit her, do not represent her authentic self, he would have to ask himself what she really wants, admitting she is a creature of desire who may want *something other* than the image and life he wants to mold for her. Since the hushed, distant woman fits into his ideal, he chooses to interpret this modification in her behavior as an extension of the traits he found in her letters.

Tito's project pitted art against life. To the vital woman with a will of her own, he preferred a lifeless artifact modeled on a stereotypical image of ideal femininity, something he could control that would not threaten him with desires and meaning of her own.[8] He misread Luciana's letters, her words, and her silences because within his narcissistic, male-centered perspective in which he constructs himself as the origin of Luciana's meaning and identity he cannot see her for who she is. He is interested in her only insofar as she compliments and confirms his own (mistaken) identity.

In order to recover or reconstruct Luciana's voice in a text that is narrated by a controlling male, we must look beyond Tito's misreading of her, which constitutes a type of smoke screen only partially covering over Luciana's desire. Using Felman's words, we must "encroach . . . on the female resistance in the text," (4) scrutinizing the passages where Luciana's voice or Luciana's consciousness filters through the narrative voice: the text of Luciana's letters; her discourse that is reported by the narrator; and her actions, looks, gestures, and silences.

In reality, Luciana's letters are not at all simple and timid as the narrator chooses to characterize them. Her first letter constitutes a strong appeal to Tito's masculine ego. She professes to know that he is not like the evil characters he portrays, and flatters his talent, saying she understands and admires him: "me hago la ilusión de ser la sola que sabe la verdad: usted sufre cuando interpreta esos papeles, usted pone su talento pero yo siento que no está ahí de veras . . . me gustaría ser la única que sabe pasar al otro lado de sus papeles y de su voz, que está segura de conocerlo de veras y de admirarlo más que a los que tienen los papeles fáciles" (*Cc* 2, 119–120). Unlike Stéphanie in Balzac's "Adieu" who, "by virtue of her madness, resists her 'woman's duty' . . . refusing . . . to reflect back simply and unproblematically man's value" (Felman 4), Luciana plays to the hilt the role of adoring female in order to win Tito over. Ironically, the trait that enables her to admire Tito—her belief in her intuition—will eventually lead her to see through his villainous manipulations.

Luciana's second letter includes an invitation to meet in a tea room, something she realizes is unfeminine behavior: "no me corresponde tomar la iniciativa pero también sé . . . que alguien como Ud. está por encima de muchas cosas" (*Cc* 2, 122). Luciana acknowledges that she is violating the accepted norm, but expresses her conviction that Tito is above such social conventions, thus implying he possesses a type of moral superiority. In this way, Luciana astutely and subtly recasts her aggressive behavior as a virtue in Tito.

Tito describes their first meeting in the following manner: "No se disculpó por la invitación, y yo que a veces sobreactúo . . . me sentí muy natural. . . . De veras lo pasamos muy bien y fue como si nos hubieran presentado por casualidad y sin sobreentendidos, . . . era lógico que se hablara sobre todo de mí porque yo era el conocido . . . por eso sin parecer vanidoso la dejé que me recordara en tantas novelas radiales" (*Cc* 2, 122). Tuning in to the woman's role, once again we can see Luciana's feminine strength and skills at work. Tito's remark that she did not excuse herself for taking the initiative shows she is poised and self-confident, not self-deprecating as it seems he expected her to be. Luciana's conversational skills are witnessed in her success at putting at ease a man who is normally unnatural in social situations, and she continues to stroke his ego by talking about him and his roles. Although Tito tells us several times that he is not vain, his positive reaction to her flattery speaks louder than his words. His narcissism proves to be a weakness that Luciana initially uses to her advantage to win him over, but which ultimately impedes his ability to know Luciana and understand her needs.

Luciana's observation regarding her expectations of Tito surprises him: "casi al final me dijo que me había imaginado más alto, con pelo crespo y ojos grises; lo del pelo crespo me sobresaltó" (*Cc* 2, 123). While he felt it was natural for him to create a mental imagine of her, Tito is taken aback when Luciana assumes the role of desiring subject with Tito as the fantasized object.

Luciana's overall reaction to the changes Tito instigates in her appearance is one of *apparent* acquiescence and passivity. When he first asks her to lighten her hair, she laughs and says "si querés me compro una peluca . . . y de paso a vos te quedaría tan bien una con el pelo crespo, ya que estamos" (*Cc* 2, 123). Thus, her first idea is to turn the tables by recalling her ideal image of him, and in so doing, casting herself as a speaking and desiring subject. But when Tito repeats the request, ignoring her crack about the wigs, she realizes that this is important for Tito, and that she cannot expect reciprocity on his part, so she cedes on this minor point—her hair color—for a greater strategic compensation—keeping Tito happy with the relationship. When Tito assures her that she looks better with her hair tied back, "[e]lla se miró en el espejo y no dijo nada, aunque sentí que no estaba de acuerdo y que tenía razón, no era mujer para recogerse el pelo, imposible negar que le quedaba mejor cuando lo llevaba suelto antes de aclarárselo" (*Cc* 2, 124). Here Tito offers a candid interpretation of Luciana's silence as the disapproval of a woman who knows herself and how she looks best, thus providing an allusion to her self-confidence as well as to her silent resistance.

The afternoon that Tito has Luciana listen to a recording of a radio episode, first moving the lamp away from the sofa so that she is seated in the shadows, she knows that something is unnatural about his manipulation of her environment: "por qué cambiás de lugar esa lámpara, dijo Luciana, queda bien ahí" (*Cc* 2, 124). But instead of belaboring the point, she protests that he treats her too well: "Me mimás demasiado, dijo Luciana, todo para mí y vos ahí en un rincón sin siquiera sentarte" (*Cc* 2, 124). Luciana's remarks when Tito presents her with the wicker chair and writing table also reveal her recognition that something is awry. Nevertheless, she immediately compensates for her initial objection by expressing her willingness to comply and praising Tito's choice: "No tiene nada que ver con este ambiente, había dicho Luciana entre divertida y perpleja, pero si a vos te gustan a mí también, es un lindo juego y tan cómodo" (*Cc* 2, 125). Thus, although Luciana may be beginning to perceive Tito's self-serving intentions, instead of confronting him she continues to go along with his whims and to flatter him. Finally, Luciana's speech evaporates into silence, and her last action speaks louder than words possibly could: as we know, Tito spots her coming out of a hotel in the loving embrace of a tall, curly haired man.

Paradoxically, Luciana meticulously carried out her "womanly duty"—affirming her male companion's value—as a way of keeping him under her control. Luciana's *seeming* docility was actually a careful strategy on her part to keep Tito happy, even while she was inwardly resisting. Her outward compliance gave Tito the illusion that he was in control of her, but in reality, it was *Luciana* who controlled the relationship from the very beginning—she chose Tito after listening to his voice on the radio and fantasizing about him for three years, she wrote him carefully crafted letters to pique his interest in her, and she took the initiative to invite him out on their first date. In order to lure him, she reflected back to Tito a trumped up and highly flattering image of himself, something his vanity found irresistible. She made him think he desired her when what he really desired was the narcissistic mirror she provided for him, and then took the initiative to replace him when she found this relationship unsatisfying. Not at all a shrinking violet as Tito made her out to be, *Luciana is a woman who knows how to get what she wants.*

Luciana and Tito communicate through their mutual dissatisfaction—both are lonely, living derivative existences, and both envision a perfect companion who they think will provide fulfillment and transform their lives. In order to fancy himself as a soap opera *galán*, Tito seeks a woman who will resemble his fictional heroine and adore him unconditionally. He could only conceive of Luciana as the object of his desire and mirror of his soul, thus suppressing her voice and her subjectivity. But Luciana turns out to have desires of her own. She subverts and castrates the narrator when she deceives him with another man, turning Tito into not only an object, but also a rejected object. The final scene is a manifestation of the uncanny when Tito realizes that his rival is actually his double—or Luciana's fantasized version of him.[9] Luciana's insistence on her fantasy, her right to being a desiring subject, finally prevailed.

While the character of Tito, the narrator, plays out male blindness, the role of Luciana, the resisting female, ironizes Tito's narcissistic ignorance to her needs. In the final twist of "Cambio de luces," we see another familiar Cortazarean technique, what I like to call "the Cortazarean boomerang": the character who is punished for his or her inauthentic behavior. And curiously, this story is about a seemingly submissive and fawning woman who ends up undermining chauvinistic male behavior. Thus, Cortázar's story transgresses its assumptions of male prepotency as it exposes its lack of control over the feminine consciousness, which finally dethrones the male narrator. Tito's fate is destitution from his mastery, from his desired role of *galán*, and reinstatement as the villain in the invariable love triangles that structure the soap opera plots. But are these textual transgressions entirely inadvertent? Or are they a manifestation of Cortázar's self-irony? Is this the winking eye of a man who knew himself to be an incurable male chauvinist, but at the same time, was compelled to call into question his own assumptions and certainties, realizing that ultimately, he could not get away with suppressing female subjectivity forever? At this juncture, we recall Sommer's words: "Instead of considering women to be predictable, Cortázar allowed himself to be surprised by them and to narrate through their personae" ("A Nowhere" 236). And in Luciana, he met a version of Lucifer, the angel of light who rebelled against God. Lucid, luminous Luciana, whose silence marked her inner rebellion, had desires of her own which ultimately refused to be subordinated to the male desire.

Felman's feminist strategies of reading, which show us how to reclaim the female desire in a male-centered text, inspire our reading of sexual difference in "Cambio de luces," and thus provide a new interpretation of both the male and female roles, as well as Cortázar's attitude toward women. Once we find a way to break away from the controlling male's hold on the text and explore the female consciousness in "Cambio de luces," we uncover hidden meaning: a strong-willed woman who eludes male domination and a man who is foiled by his ignorance to her desire. This perceptive portrayal of a woman who subverts patriarchal behavioral norms is a subtle example of Cortázar's realignment of his *machista* attitudes. In the last two chapters, our study of Cortázar's female characters shifts focus from family and love relations to their role in his formulation of Argentine national identity and politics.

Chapter 6

ꝏ

"Eurídice, Argentina":
Women and the Guilty Expatriate

> It may be that men always feel as if they have "lost something" whenever
> they speak of woman or women.
>
> —Jardine, *Gynesis*

Legendary is Cortázar's attempt to come to terms with his divided allegiance to Argentina and France through his writing and his use of women as bridges or mediums in that quest. One of his poems from *Salvo el crepúsculo* draws from classical tradition to offer a striking image of how woman and nation are linked in his poetic vision:

> *Me fui, como quien se desangra.*
> Así termina Don Segundo Sombra, así termina la
> cólera para dejarme, sucio y lavado a la vez,
> frente a otros cielos. Desde luego, como Orfeo,
> tantas veces habría de mirar hacia atrás y pagar
> el precio. Lo sigo pagando hoy; sigo y seguiré
> mirándote, Eurídice, Argentina. (345)

The last two words of the poem, "Eurídice, Argentina," in which Cortázar evokes his abandoned homeland as Orpheus' lost beloved, dramatically synthesize his concept of Argentina as sacrificial woman and also reveal the inextricable bond between his politics, poetics, and passions.

This chapter focuses on Cortázar's use of female space in his stories as the site where he problematizes his feelings of guilt and loss vis-à-vis his decision to reside in France. While certain female figures elicit an irreparable sense of guilt, at the same time they are a type of anchor or repository of national identity or connectedness, serving to safeguard the expatriate protagonist's Argentineness, and thus his authority to his claim to be an Argentine writer.

Cortázar's identity crisis can be understood in terms of Carlos Alonso's explanation of the ambivalent relationship of Spanish American writers to the discourse of modernity. Alonso studies the "strategies used by Spanish American writers and intellectuals to take their distance from otherwise explicit adoption of and commitment to the discourses of modernity" (*The Burden of Modernity* v). "It is an axiomatic belief of social and cultural criticism in Spanish America," writes Alonso, "that the economic and intellectual elites of Spanish America mortgaged the future of the continent in their relentless pursuit of the modern at the expense of the real needs of the region or of their individual countries" (172). Alonso qualifies this belief by demonstrating that Spanish American cultural discourse was not "unreflectively beholden" to metropolitan values (171), but rather "[t]he commitment to modernity created a crisis of authority for the Spanish American writer that was addressed through the disavowel of modernity at another level of his text" (173).

Cortázar's voluntary expatriation to France in 1951 made him into, for many, a quintessential example of the legendary Argentine infatuation with Paris as the supreme metropolitan model. His constant and often vehement self-defense in face of accusations of francophilia from his fellow Argentines showed he was by no means insensitive to the reasoning on which the attacks were based. Cortázar's guilt for apparently having turned his back to Argentina and its problems found expression in his search to formulate an interstitial identity. While he never attempted to deny his enthrallment with France, at the same time, he made a point of asserting his continued allegiance and commitment to Argentine reality.

This conflict between foreign influences and the perceived native values—or in other words, the radical division created by identification with the modern and the resistance to it—is considered by Nicolas Shumway to be the principal "guiding fiction" of Argentine nationhood in the nineteenth century (xi). The enlightened minority, possessing an unabashed elitism, explains Shumway, lived facing Europe. They were suspicious of the lower classes, and associated the pampas with barbarism (42). Cortázar's depiction of his own identity crisis engages the dichotomous concepts that form the basic paradigm of the guiding fiction of Argentine identity. The terms of this divisive rhetoric are variously defined as civilization versus barbarism, elite culture versus popular culture, Buenos Aires versus the interior, Paris versus Buenos Aires, center versus periphery. Another polarity put into play by Cortázar is bohemian intellectualism versus bourgeois materialism. Alonso's study shows us that the Spanish American intellectuals' engagement with the discourse of modernity—embodied by the first term of each polarity—was by no means unquestioned. Rather, there was a complex negotiation between the metropolitan model and local or regional values, as the movement toward modernity was followed by a recoil from it.

I would argue that Cortázar represents a special case in regard to the relationship between Spanish American intellectuals and the discourse of modernity as explained by Alonso. Cortázar's residence in France did create, at a certain level, a crisis in authority for him, and there can be no doubt that it occasioned intense feelings of guilt. However, after his "political conversion," he vigorously refuted his critics who excoriated him for living distant from his homeland and its struggles. Cortázar insisted that his move to Paris enabled him to obtain a more informed and equanimous perspective on Latin America, resulting in his reencounter with Latin American and Argentine reality. His first detailed defense came in his well-known 1967 letter to Roberto Fernández Retamar, in which he points out the paradoxical benefit of his residence in Paris:

> Si tuviera que enumerar las causas por las que me alegro de haber salido de mi país . . . creo que la principal sería el haber seguido desde Europa, con una visión des-nacionalizada, la revolución cubana. . . . ¿No te parece en verdad paradójico que un argentino casi enteramente volcado hacia Europa en su juventud, al punto de quemar las naves y venirse a Francia, sin una idea precisa de su destino, haya descubierto aquí, después de una década, su verdadera condición de latinoamericano? (*Oc* 3, 34–35)[1]

In this letter, he justifies his modernist pursuit as the engine of his midlife political engagement with Latin America. This response to his critics is reiterated in the 1978 González Bermejo interview with his oft-quoted statement: "París fue un poco mi camino de Damasco, la gran sacudida existencial" (12). Thus, Cortázar insisted that his expatriation to France ultimately served to help him recover his Latin American identity. In this way, he countered the axiomatic belief that the pursuit of the modern is carried out at the expense of the needs of the region. To the contrary, thanks to his modernist fascination with Paris he achieved a profound commitment to his vision of the needs of Latin America.[2]

Notwithstanding Cortázar's repeated defense of his residence in Paris because it made possible his political conversion, he continued to experience a sense of loss and ambivalence vis-à-vis Argentina. Regardless of his insistence: "El hecho de que yo haya venido a Europa . . . no me quitó nada de latinoamericanidad, ni de argentinidad" (González Bermejo 14), it seems that the need to reconcile his distance from Argentina persisted throughout his career. And this ongoing process of reconciliation takes us back to the role of female space in the articulation of his *argentinidad*. Although his uneasy conscience may have abated, we can identify female characters that continue to represent his feelings of guilt toward the homeland he has sacrificed. At the same time, there is an important evolution in the female space, which serves to offset his European affinity. At first these Argentine woman characters, mamá in particular, represent values of the Argentine petit bourgeois that were in conflict with the *europeizantes*, in other words, the women embody values that Cortázar found objectionable. But after his "discovery" of Argentine and Latin American reality, these female characters represent universal values that he embraces.

This chapter considers how Cortázar's evolving (but invariably guilty) relationship with his homeland is conveyed through a dynamic sequence of female characters. In the stories analyzed here, the protagonists' absence from Argentina is depicted as the betrayal of an Argentine woman. The connection between women and Argentine nationhood in Cortázar's work reflects a psychic structure that makes territory (and nature) female, and employs female icons as national symbols.[3] It is not uncommon for gender to play a role in cultural imaginings, as illustrated by Francine Masiello's study of how the positioning of men against women in literature serves as an allegory of larger historical events (*Between Civilization* 2). Masiello hypothesizes that "when the state finds itself in transition . . . we find an alteration in the representation of gender" (*Between Civilization* 8). An analogous process of alteration or development can be found within the trajectory of Cortázar's work: his formulation of the "native" or Argentine space, which countered his European attachment, evolved along with changes in global geopolitics and his own political consciousness.

Returning to Cortázar's poetic evocation of Orpheus and Eurydice, an examination of the myth and its interpretation points to the generative and productive dimensions of Cortázar's anguished relationship to his homeland. The tale conjures up a constellation of images, which set the tone for Cortázar's overall conception of the role of the feminine in his national and personal identity. To briefly sketch the myth, we recall that Orpheus was a bard possessing magical powers and prophetic vision.[4] When his bride, Eurydice, died from the sting of a venomous serpent, Orpheus enthralled the gods to petition Eurydice's return and descended into Hades to retrieve her. The only condition for her return was that he refrain from looking at his beloved until they reached the upper world. However, unable to resist the temptation to view her face, he turned back toward Eurydice, and consequently lost her a second time. He returned to the upper world alone and disconsolate, and wandered about, singing songs to his lost beloved. Finally, the jealous Maenads tore Orpheus apart, but his severed head continued to sing as it floated down the river.[5]

Some of the main themes of the Orphic myth are regeneration, memory, and renewal. According to the romantic poets, Orpheus renews himself through the descent into hell and separation from Eurydice; after losing his beloved, he resolves to conceive all future activity in her image. Orpheus' resurrection costs him Eurydice, but he transmutes her into song (Strauss 243, 75–76). Although Eurydice cannot accompany him, she gives meaning and direction to his terrestrial life, the production of poetry being dependent on the fertile longing for the absent beloved (Hasty 46).

Thus, by likening himself to Orpheus who constantly looks back toward his lost "Eurídice, Argentina," Cortázar sets up Argentina as the sacrificial woman whose loss has regenerated him and enabled him to regain his poetic voice. He says he keeps looking back, which implies he is continually suffering both the anguish of having lost Argentina and the guilt for having betrayed her, feelings that he transmutes into his writing. "Eurídice, Argentina" provides him with an identity and sense of direction, but the price is a constant feeling of guilt.

Through the appositive that fuses Argentina with Orpheus' beloved bride, Cortázar manifests his "passionate patriotism," casting his patriotic desire as erotic desire (and vice versa), binding his sexual identity to his national identity.[6] This beloved, feminized embodiment of Argentina serves as a type of counterbalance to the undeniable allure of *"la belle France."* Eurydice/Argentina is the partner on whom his identity depends—as a writer and as an (expatriate) Argentine. The abandoned nation and the abandoned woman are coterminous and inextricable, the symbolic woman-nation embodying the knot of guilt and identity.

Following the same process, in the stories under question Argentina as sacrificial woman is transposed into female characters. As mentioned above, the image of these women is dynamic, reflecting Cortázar's personal evolution. From 1951, when he left Buenos Aires definitively for Paris, until his death in 1984, the manner in which Cortázar experienced and articulated his displacement from his homeland went through a series of transformations as his political commitment intensified. Additionally, during Argentina's military dictatorship (1976–1983), Cortázar no longer considered himself an expatriate, but rather a political exile. While his belief in socialism and his involvement in the defense of human rights probably served to attenuate his feelings of estrangement, it seems that he was never completely free of the gnawing guilt feelings.

To recapitulate, the changes in how Cortázar conceived his relationship with Argentina can be traced through the succession of female characters that symbolize his distant homeland, as the women embody distinctive values Cortázar associates with Argentina. The texts under consideration portray three distinct stages in the depiction of his conflicted national identity. In the first phase, which is represented in the stories "El otro cielo" and "Cartas de mamá," it is a family matter—his distaste for the bourgeois values of his social class and his guilty departure from Argentina are conceived as intimate betrayals of the mother. "Recortes de prensa" marks the second stage in this process. Written during the military rule in Argentina, Cortázar's anguish and guilt are of a political nature, directed at his inability to help victims of the repressive right-wing regime. In "Diario para un cuento," the narrator, now an old man, reflects on his behavior during his last months in Buenos Aires, expressing regret for his insensitivity toward Anabel, a woman from the popular classes. The narrator struggles with the realization that he is not able to manipulate Anabel according to his writerly desires; rather she throws a mirror up to him, forcing him to come to terms with his past actions, specifically, those motivated by his own petit bourgeois elitism.[7]

The Family Allegory

"El otro cielo": Dispassionate Patriotism

"El otro cielo" and "Cartas de mamá" each cast the protagonist's disaffection with Argentina as a family allegory. The young man's preference for Paris over Buenos Aires is depicted as a betrayal of his mother and fiancée in "El otro cielo" and of the extended family in "Cartas de mamá," but always with mamá as the central figure onto which the restless son's guilt is projected. The stories can be considered a complementary pair in that together they dramatize the no-win situation of the two alternative destinies for the disaffected Argentine: he can either conform to a tedious, lackluster existence in Buenos Aires to please his mother, as does the narrator of "El otro cielo," or else, like Luis in "Cartas de mamá," make the break to go to Paris and suffer intense feelings of guilt and self-recrimination for having abandoned his mother(land).

The protagonist of "El otro cielo," a young man, time-travels between two worlds: Buenos Aires of the 1940s and Paris around 1870. His life in Buenos Aires is pervaded by his resistance to the demand for respectability elicited by his middle-class life, which centers on his mother, fiancée, and his position at the stock market. This rebellious streak has him wandering through the red light district of Buenos Aires, from which he is magically transported to the bohemian life of Paris during the Second Empire. There he delights in the company of a young prostitute named Josiane and the intense Parisian underworld she inhabits.

The representation of national identity in "El otro cielo" has been discussed by several critics. Dieter Reichardt points out that the story summarizes the existential ambivalence of the *"allá"* and *"acá"* of *Rayuela*. Josiane, as the mythical *"querida francesa"* represents the allure and attraction of Paris while the narrator's emotionally sterile relationship with Irma, his Argentine *"novia-araña,"* can be read as the author's indifference to, or discomfort with, Argentine reality during the period corresponding to the rise of Peronism (Reichardt 205–208). Richard Young notes that the juxtaposition of the two incompatible realities communicates the feelings of anguish and guilt experienced by the narrator due to his conflictive existence ("El contexto americano" 8).[8] In sum, the contrasted categories of women—the mother-fiancée couple in Buenos Aires versus the Parisian mistress—are used to embody the protagonist's opposing national allegiances.

The conceptual framework developed by Doris Sommer in *Foundational Fictions* enables us to further elaborate this allegorical reading. The "foundational fictions," or national romances of Latin America, explains Sommer, have in common their coupling of national projects with heterosexual love and marriages in which national destiny is married to personal passion (2, 27). In these romances, national constituencies to be reconciled or amalgamated are cast as lovers destined to desire each other; thus, this productive sexuality provides a figure for nonviolent consolidation (6, 24). Sommer observes that the Boom writers repudiated "the erotic rhetoric that organizes patriotic novels," and she reads their resistance to these national romances as "a symptom of unresolved dependence" (2–3). Following the tracks of Sommer's argument, we can detect in "El otro cielo" Cortázar's repudiation of "erotic patriotism" in the protagonist's lack of desire for his intended bride. The double life led by the story's narrator is his reaction against the bourgeois national romance championed by his mother and fiancée. The narrator struggles against his mother's design of domestic romance, but ultimately capitulates to it. This story can be read as Cortázar's self-ironization of his ultimately futile resistance to the values of the bourgeois classes who enriched themselves with Argentina's industrial expansion during the second half of the 1940s. The private passion of the time-traveling protagonist, represented by his fascination with bohemian Paris, was counterproductive to the industrialist mentality that sought to benefit from wartime prosperity. The protagonist's eventual surrender to his mother's desires can be read as Cortázar's testimony to his vulnerability to maternal and societal pressures to conform.[9]

Historical references in the story—the final events of World War II and another military dictatorship in Argentina[10]—situate the narrator's Argentine existence in the mid-1940s. By the end of the story, economic volatility caused by the bombing of Hiroshima requires his presence at the stock exchange, thwarting his yearning to pursue bohemian pleasures in Paris. Mamá and Irma embody the bourgeois values that the narrator finds so distasteful. Both are depicted as genteel society women: "Para ella [Irma], como para mi madre, no hay mejor actividad social que el sofá de la sala donde ocurre eso que llaman la conversación, el café y el anisado" (*Cc* 1, 591). Irma possesses the lofty qualities of a noblewoman: the narrator describes her as "la más buena y generosa de las mujeres" (*Cc* 1, 591), and is certain that she would be scandalized if she knew of his fondness for frequenting the red light district. The narrator drops details that clue us into the fact that both he and Irma come from affluent backgrounds: he mentions that his late father's friends are helping him solidify his career as a stockbroker, and that Irma's parents own a summer home on an island of the Paraná River. Quite possibly, Irma's landed family is "old money" while the protagonist's family represents the *nouveau riche* who made their money during the industrialization of the 1940s. Since the narrator professes to feel no passion for Irma, his engagement to her may be a strategic maneuver on his mother's part to improve the family's social status and solidify their financial situation. Their marriage of convenience will ensure consolidation and continuity of the bourgeois sector through their children who will be, in the words of the narrator, "los tan anhelados nietos de mi madre" (*Cc* 1, 591). In this tale of dispassionate patriotism, the tedium the narrator voices in regard to the values of his mother and Irma can be read as a critique of the social structure that will prosper due to the strategic union of the two families.

The narrator acts out his resistance to the bourgeois materialism of his mother and fiancée by immersing himself in the culture of bohemian Paris on the eve of the Franco-Prussian Wars. The narrator finds his paradise as a *flâneur* in the red-light district of Paris, a space in sharp contrast to the domain occupied by mamá and Irma. The two women are seen in terms of their domesticity—their kingdom is the home, the private sphere. Their goal is to keep a tight rein on the protagonist, at the same time that he struggles to assert his independence. In addition to her respectable family background, Irma is valued by mamá for her reproductive potential. Immediately after mentioning his mother's longing for grandchildren, the protagonist allows: "Supongo que por cosas así acabé conociendo a Josiane" (*Cc* 1, 591–592). In this way, he opposes his mother's domestic romance based on the ideal of "productive sexuality at home" (Sommer, *Foundational Fictions* 6) with a nonproductive liaison with a prostitute. Josiane's status as a representative of the world of vice and sin makes her an ideal counterpart to Irma's and his mother's respectable bourgeois existence. The lure of illicit erotic experience presents a welcome opportunity to violate the social norms his mother holds dear. The narrator's escape to a literary Paris shaped by the poetry and the figures of Lautréamont and Baudelaire[11] reiterates Argentine francophilia. His modernist and writerly fascination with Paris provides a seductive alternative to the stifling domesticity and bourgeois materialism he detests about 1940s Buenos Aires.[12]

If we base our interpretation exclusively on the confronted female characters, the story's message is fairly straightforward: the narrator's desire to escape the demands of mamá and Irma represents his critique of bourgeois Argentine values, while his libidinal desire for Josiane and her world is an allegory of the passion and freedom that bohemian Parisian culture represents for him. However, a close reading of the male "triple" in Paris reveals a sinister twist. While Josiane is the figure that draws him to this world and he does not fail to appreciate the pleasure and gaiety he derives from their superficial relationship, it is through her that he finds out about Laurent and the *sudamericano*. His connection to these two men is clearly more significant, albeit steeped in enigma. Emir Rodríguez Monegal convincingly explains how *el sudamericano* and Laurent function as doubles for each other. Both figures refer to Lautréamont, the pseudonym for the Uruguayan Isadore Ducasse who lived in Paris, and thus a type of parallel for Cortázar, explains Rodríguez Monegal.[13] Rodríguez Monegal does not, however, discuss the narrator's identification with *el sudamericano* and Laurent, nor does he develop in depth the implications of Cortázar's identification with these characters.[14]

Several passages in the story allude to the time-traveler's link to these characters. For instance, the connection first appears when he tells us that Josiane initially thought he might be Laurent the strangler: "cómo nos reíamos esa noche a la sola idea de que yo pudiera ser Laurent" (*Cc* 1, 592). Thus, the first identification between the two men is presented under the sign of negation. The story's conclusion reinforces the triple identity when, in reference to the death of the *sudamericano*, the narrator says it seemed "como si él hubiera matado a Laurent y a mí con su propia muerte" (*Cc* 1, 606). Thus the three men vanish from the Parisian underworld at about the same time.

The story is divided into two parts; the first emphasizes the exhilarating times in Paris, while in the second section the narrator's Parisian existence gradually unravels. In the first part, the narrator is tempted to approach the *sudamericano* and talk to him in Spanish or ask him about his origin, but decides against it, reflecting on the "la fría cólera con que yo habría recibido una interpelación de ese género" (*Cc* 1, 596). Does the narrator's imagined visceral response to such an inquiry mean that he fancies himself passing for French, ignoring his roots, or that he is attempting to deny that, as a displaced Latin American, he is a marginal person in Paris? Or could this be a pretext to disguise another, unadmitted reason for his reluctance to approach the solitary figure? In any event, the first half of the story ends with the narrator's expression of regret for not having spoken to the *sudamericano:*

> ahora no soy más que uno de los muchos que se preguntan por qué en algún momento no hicieron lo que habían pensado hacer... [N]o me acuerdo bien de lo que sentía al renunciar a mi impulso, pero era algo como una veda, el sentimiento de que si la trasgredía iba a entrar en un territorio inseguro. Y sin embargo creo que hice mal, que estuve al borde de un acto que hubiera podido salvarme. Salvarme de qué me pregunto. Pero precisamente de esto: salvarme de que hoy no pueda hacer otra cosa que preguntármelo, y que no hay otra respuesta que el humo del tabaco

y esa vaga esperanza inútil que me sigue por las calles como un perro
sarnoso. (*Cc* 1, 597–598)

In this mysterious passage he implies that a contact with his fellow
sudamericano could have saved him from something he finds impossible to define. Could this have been a reconciliation with his other, true,
self—his "South-Americanness"—in Paris? Possibly he thinks that if he
had come to terms with this part of himself instead of trying to deny or
repress it, he could have salvaged his life in Paris. But instead he maintained a strict schism between the two realms, and this repressed identity returned to exclude him from his Parisian paradise.

But let us delve deeper into the question of why he could not
bring himself to approach the *sudamericano*. Perhaps it is because this
identification would link him to Laurent the assassin—a horrifying
identification that must be repressed. Since the strong denial attached to
his connection to the serial murderer of prostitutes makes it impossible
for the narrator to recognize Laurent as a double, their coupling is
mediated by *el sudamericano*. If Laurent, as well as *el sudamericano*, is a
double for the Argentine time-traveler, can we consider Laurent's killing
of prostitutes to be a projection of a homicidal impulse on the narrator's
part? If so, how can we account for this misogynist fantasy?

A study of serial murderers reports that in cases of sexually motivated compulsive murder of women there was found to be unhealthy
emotional involvement with the mother. This resulted in a displacement
of affect from the mother to other women, culminating in a displaced
matricide (Giannangelo 28). Does the Argentine narrator of "El otro cielo"
have "issues" with his mother? One of the topics of conversation with
Josiane is "mis problemas de hombre soltero" (*Cc* 1, 592). Clearly "el hijo
que vive todavía en casa de su madre" (*Cc* 1, 592), as he refers to himself,
resents the emotional control his mother has over him, a control that
impinges on his sexuality. "Mi madre sabe siempre si he dormido en casa"
(*Cc* 1, 592), he complains, alluding to the watchful eye his mother keeps
on his pursuit of a sex life. When he does stay out all night, his mother
reacts as if it were a personal offense to her: "durante uno o dos días me
mira entre ofendida y temerosa" (*Cc* 1, 592). But what does she fear? That
he was "betraying her" with another woman? He believes that she has no
right to continue controlling his actions—"me fastidia la persistencia de
un derecho materno que ya nada justifica" (*Cc* 1, 592)—but nevertheless
gives in to her affectations of injury, appeasing her with gifts each time.
His proximity to his controlling mother feminizes and castrates him.

The prostitute embodies the promise and fantasy of unbridled sexuality at the same time that she represents a fantasmatic threat to male mastery. We recall that one of the prostitutes refused service to the *sudamericano* due to a perversion related to erotic voyeurism he asked her to perform, a perversion that the narrator says was not such a big deal after all. Could this allude to a sexual dysfunction that the narrator projects onto the *sudamericano*? To further complicate, or perhaps explain, his troubled sexuality, his mother's silent disapproval makes the narrator feel guilty about carousing with prostitutes. But the prostitute is not seen exclusively *in opposition to* the mother, because, as a type of devouring woman, she represents a degenerated version of his mother. Thus, the prostitute must be punished for making him be unfaithful to his mother and she must be feared because, as a version of the mother, she threatens engulfment. Therefore, within this twisted reasoning, the slain prostitutes are doubly deserving of their grisly fate. They have to pay for arousing his sexuality and for making him disappoint and betray his mother. In this way, his yearning for self-punishment is converted into a homicidal fantasy.

If this reading seems to imply that Cortázar himself possessed these violent fantasies, it is true that he never shirked from owning up to this aspect of his representation of sexuality. Turning once again to his revealing interview with Picón Garfield, we read Cortázar's response to her query regarding sadistic eroticism in his work:

> Yo creo que si he insistido en diversos pasajes de diversas obras sobre esta modalidad erótica . . . es porque sin duda forma parte de mi propio ciclo personal . . . . Evidentemente [mi erotismo personal] contiene elementos de agresión que por lo menos en el plano literario se cumplen de una manera muy explícita y muy franca. Me parecería hipócrita disimularlos en la literatura si responden a pulsiones profundas de mi propia persona. (102)

Finally, what does the murder of prostitutes have to do with national identity? The narrator sees himself as a misfit in both societies— his rejection of the values of his Argentine bourgeois class makes him feel marginalized in his homeland, while the side of him aligned with Mr. Hyde ultimately drives him out of bohemian Paris. Immersing himself in French "civilization" could not provide the narrator's sought-after antidote to Argentine "barbarism" because he carried a type of barbarity within himself. If he had approached *el sudamericano*, and, through him, owned up to his repressed link to Laurent, or his criminal instincts, perhaps he could have addressed and resolved these destructive fantasies. But he does not confront this pair of doubles, which represent two aspects of his conflicted self—*el sudamericano*, his repudiated regional identity, and Laurent, his troubled sexuality. Mamá, of course, is at the heart of both problems. Instead, he denies these thorny issues and retreats to what seems to be the lesser of evils: satisfying his mother by marrying Irma and settling down to a lackluster existence in Buenos Aires as a bourgeois husband. The dead French prostitutes are his scapegoats; their death has atoned for the guilt he feels for nearly spoiling his mother's Argentine domestic romance.

But now let us push ugly Mr. Hyde back down into the deep recesses of the psyche, his natural habitat, and refocus on the good Dr. Jekyll who became a celebrated writer.[15] Similar to many of Cortázar's works, the autobiographical projection of "El otro cielo" is obvious: as noted above, the protagonist's submission to his mother's plan can be seen as Cortázar's statement regarding the coercion to conform. Cortázar is criticizing the cultural values prevalent in his social class, ironizing his sensitivity to family pressures, and imagining what his destiny might have been if he had succumbed to those pressures. Omar Prego asked him if he ever wondered what would have happened to him if he had stayed in Buenos Aires, to which he replied:

> [M]uchas veces, después de ocho o diez años de estar viviendo en Europa he tratado de imaginar un doble mío en Buenos Aires y me he preguntado: ¿Qué hubiera hecho yo en estos diez años que he pasado en París si me hubiera quedado allá? Y tengo que decir que siempre sacaba una sensación, un sentimiento negativo. La impresión de que si yo me hubiera quedado allá, en esa época, en ese momento, me hubiera anquilosado, me hubiera enfermado, hubiera aceptado los parámetros de la época en Argentina. (125–126)

The contrite narrator at the conclusion of "El otro cielo" is a version of that "doble mío en Buenos Aires," obediently listening to his pregnant wife as he sips maté on the patio among the plants, not too different from these vegetative forms of life.

In *Salvo el crepúsculo* Cortázar's contempt for Argentine infatuation with bourgeois materialism around midcentury is palpable when he speaks of his relatives who bought an electric refrigerator and to celebrate it, "*hicieron una fiesta* a la que tuve que ir" (343, emphasis in original). Directly following this remark is his bitingly satiric poem about the new refrigerator entitled "Entronización": "Aquí está, ya la trajeron, contempladla: oh nieve/ azucarada, oh tabernáculo!" (344). Cortázar tells us that he left Argentina soon after the party for the new refrigerator.

"Cartas de mamá": Mamá in the Empty House

A symbolic rendering of Cortázar's own path is presented in "Cartas de mamá," which dramatizes the other side of the coin by depicting the guilty son who abandons Argentina for Paris. In this story, expatriation from one's homeland is portrayed allegorically as betrayal of the brother and abandonment of the mother. The inclusion of disapproving aunts, uncles, and friends brings in the notion of the larger community that the expatriate is leaving behind. Since Luis's projection of his feelings of guilt onto mamá is discussed in chapter 3, "The Omnipotent Mother," here we will focus on mamá and the family home as symbols for Argentina.

On one level, this is the story of a family broken apart by a love triangle. Luis stole his sickly brother Nico's girlfriend, Laura, and during Luis and Laura's honeymoon, Nico surrendered to tuberculosis. Shortly afterward, Luis and his bride embarked for France. The repeated mention of mamá being left alone in the enormous family house triggers the allegorical reading. For instance, when Luis receives a letter, it brings to mind elements of his daily life in Buenos Aires centered on *"el caserón de Flores, mamá"* (*Cc* 1, 179). He recalls his resolution to leave in the following terms: "se había jurado escapar de la Argentina, del *caserón de Flores, de mamá* y los perros y su hermano (que ya estaba enfermo) . . . *Mamá se quedaba sola en el caserón*, con los perros y los frascos de remedios" (*Cc* 1, 182). Luis has guilty memories of this departure, when he left behind, *"la casa ahí con toda la infancia"* (*Cc* 1, 182). Concerned about mamá's mental state when she writes that Nico (who is dead) is coming to Europe, Luis asks Uncle Emilio to check on her. The uncle admonishes Luis in his reply: "Se notaba que [mamá] *estaba muy sola en la casa de Flores*, lo cual era lógico puesto que ninguna madre que ha vivido toda la vida con sus dos hijos puede sentirse a gusto en *una enorme casa llena de recuerdos*" (*Cc* 1, 189). (Emphasis added in all of the above quotations.)

The obsessive mention of the house, nearly always in the same breath as mamá, begs an allegorical reading of the connection between the house and the protagonist's affective ties to his mother and Argentina. Ana Hernández del Castillo analyses the identification of the house with the mother in the stories of *Bestiario*, explaining how these stories are connected to the incest theme. While in "Carta a una señorita en París" the protagonist is expelled from the house, Hernández del Castillo points out, in "Cefalea" he is engulfed by it, and "Casa tomada" represents the theme of escape from the confinement of a house that "freezes" the siblings in a prolonged childhood (53, 50). A trait Hernández del Castillo notes regarding the house in "Casa tomada" also characterizes Luis's Argentine home in "Cartas de mamá": the house as container of the past and childhood memories. These qualities of the house in "Casa tomada" are illustrated in the story's opening line: "Nos gustaba la casa porque aparte de espaciosa y antigua . . . guardaba los recuerdos de nuestros bisabuelos, el abuelo paterno, nuestros padres y toda la infancia" (*Cc* 1, 107).

The house in "Cartas de mamá," in addition to evoking the protagonist's childhood, can be considered to be a representation of the Argentine national space. The term *caserón* creates a spatial metaphor for Argentina, the augmentative suffix "-ón" alluding to its expansive territory. The mother, through her identification with the spacious, empty house, is linked to the vast, unpopulated land of the Argentine nation, which is a source of barbarism according to Sarmiento and his contemporaries. In this way, mamá is tied to the autochthonous values that oppose the *europeizantes*. Mamá's presence there is Luis's anchor to his homeland. Mamá is the sacrificial woman incarnating the country he has left behind in his attempt to start a new life, and each letter reactivates the guilt he has worked so hard to escape. His connection to mamá, through the letters, is permeated by his intense and relentless sensation of culpability. At the same time, her letters represent his anchor to a realm marked by stability and permanence: "le recordaba la economía familiar, la permanencia de un orden" (*Cc* 1, 183).

Luis mentions that the stamps on mamá's letters bear the likenesses of Argentine national heroes José de San Martín, a patriot general during the wars of independence, and Rivadavia, an influential political leader who was briefly president of the United Provinces (of which Buenos Aires was part) from 1826–1827. Both men ended their lives defeated and exiled in Europe, a parallel of sorts to Luis's fate. Luis remarks that they are also names of streets, thus they convey simultaneously quotidian Buenos Aires and the historical tradition of exile in Europe of those Argentines whose national projects ultimately met failure in their homeland.

Returning to Luis's view of life in Buenos Aires, its principal component is boring domesticity, as seen in the letters from mamá and his recollections. Mamá's entire existence revolves around the house and domestic matters, and she fills the letters with dull news of her daily routine: her conversations with the cousins, the payment of her pension, the dogs who might have caught mange and the remedies she's been advised to try. Buenos Aires is certainly a homey place for Luis—"donde vivía la familia, donde los amigos de cuando en cuando adornaban una postal con frases cariñosas" (*Cc* 1, 180)—but his references to it are invariably derisive. He belittles the corny sonnets of Buenos Aires matrons: "el rotograbado de *La Nación* con los sonetos de tantas señoras entusiastas" (*Cc* 1, 180), and characterizes the city itself as outdated and faded: "un mundo caduco en la lejana orilla del río" (*Cc* 1, 180). He says that when Nico and Laura were dating, they probably went to all the movie theaters on "toda la rambla *estúpida* de la calle Lavalle" (*Cc* 1, 183, emphasis added). As a consequence of his guilt, he needs to disparage the world he left behind. According to Luis, Buenos Aires is embued with the provincial mediocrity he traded in for a new life in the metropolis.

But what about his life in Paris? Does it continue to provide the same allure of bohemian lifestyle and erotic adventure that the narrator of "El otro cielo" briefly enjoyed there? Certainly it does not. Once Cortázar's protagonist makes a definitive break and goes to make his life in Paris, it is no longer seen as an exciting escape and alternative lifestyle. It consists of a daily routine that is tolerable, even pleasant, but never exhilarating or joyous. There is no Frenchwoman analogous to Josiane who represents erotic pleasure and escape. To the contrary, he has brought with him all the burdensome baggage of his *porteño* existence: the Argentine wife who was first Nico's girl; the unrelenting memory of Nico, made even keener by Laura's refusal to mention him; and, of course, the weekly arrival of letters from mamá. He gains no emotional support from his wife Laura, sensing in her a colluder with mamá—both women continue to silently blame him for Nico's death, thus stoking the fires of his guilt.

Laura's presence in Paris spoils his new life, preventing him from establishing a fresh start. As mamá's accomplice, she is an accuser who constantly reminds him of the order he wanted to escape: "a la vez odiaba ese orden y lo odiaba por Laura, porque Laura estaba en París, pero cada carta de mamá la definía como ajena, como cómplice de ese orden que él había repudiado" (*Cc* 1, 183). Just like mamá and Irma in "El otro cielo," the Argentine mother-wife couple is his ball and chain that block his bid for freedom. He cannot fully enjoy the metropolitan amenities Paris has to offer due to his unshakable guilt and remorse.

Thus, in "Cartas," unlike "El otro cielo," Paris is not epitomized by a sensual woman. Once he possesses it, it seems to have lost its allure. It was a temptress when it was beyond his reach, but now that he has installed himself there, it is cold and gray and his overwhelming sensation is that of guilt toward Argentina. The contradiction involved in the solution envisioned by Luis (and Cortázar)—and the reason for its failure—is remarked by Santiago Colás. In his discussion of Horacio's unsuccessful strategy in *Rayuela*, Colás points out that Cortázar appears stuck in the mode of the colonial intellectual who "seeking refuge from an alienated colonial existence—in which meaning or referent is always elsewhere; namely, at the metropolis—goes to the metropolis, literally and figuratively" (41). The inevitable inferiority complex of the colonialized Argentine traveler to Europe is revealed in Luis's description of two Argentines he spots in the train station: "dos de los hombres que pasaban cerca debían ser argentinos por el corte de pelo, los sacos, el aire de suficiencia disimulando el azoramiento de entrar en París" (*Cc* 1, 191). Like these intimidated tourists, Luis cannot escape the paltry provincialism of Buenos Aires—it is an inextricable part of him through his binding family ties, characterized by the incurable mediocrity he senses in mamá, Laura, and Nico.

To summarize this phase of Cortázar's identity crisis, in both stories national identity is, above all, about family connections. Mamá safeguards the protagonists' Argentineness and represents the culture of domesticity and bourgeois values. Cortázar's stories convey an intimate expression. They serve to work out the reasons why he left Argentina, and the intense guilt occasioned by his expatriation. At their literal level, the stories speak of abandonment of family—as Cortázar undoubtedly experienced most intensely his decision to leave his homeland—but allow the double reading of abandonment of nation. The woman-nation connection fuels the allegorical reading—the female space embodying the Buenos Aires provincialism rejected by the narrator also contains the deep-seated guilt. Mamá is a version of the betrayed Eurydice safeguarding Cortázar's Argentineness and the focus of his creative writing.

The corrosive sense of guilt felt by the protagonists of both stories for having disappointed their mothers undoubtedly reveals how Cortázar himself struggled with his feelings. In *Salvo el crepúsculo* he addresses this issue in his own lyric voice. Immediately after speaking of his departure, he voices his profound sense of pain for not being able to fulfill his mother's dreams for him:

> Desembarqué en un Buenos Aires del que volvería a salir dos años después, incapaz de soportar desengaños consecutivos que iban desde los sentimientos hasta un estilo de vida que las calles del nuevo Buenos Aires peronista me negaban. ¿Pero para qué hablar de eso en poemas que demasiado lo contenían sin decirlo? La ironía, una ternura amarga, tantas imágenes de escape eran como un testamento argentino de alguien que no se sentía ni se sentiría jamás tránsfuga pero sí dueño de vender hasta el último libro y el último disco para alejarse sin rencor, educadamente, despedido en el puerto por familia y amigos que jamás habían leído ni leerían ese testamento.

La madre

> Delante de ti me veo en el espejo que no acepta cambios . . . Lo que veo es eso que tú ves que soy, el pedazo desprendido de tu sueño, la esperanza boca abajo y cubierta de vómitos. . . . Eres una columna de ceniza (yo te quemé). . . . [N]o puedo ser . . . el hijo verdadero y a medida de la madre, el buen pingüino rosa yendo y viniendo y tan valiente hasta el final, la forma que me diste en tu deseo: honrado, cariñoso, jubilable, diplomado. (329–330)

The poem's forceful images—the son who describes himself as his mother's hope lying face-down covered in vomit and the mother as a column of ash burned by him—convey the depth of remorse felt by the lyric speaker for not having lived up to his mother's expectations.

"Recortes de prensa": Rage and Impotence during the Proceso

At the same time that Cortázar's move to Paris seems to have produced a profound sense of guilt for having abandoned personal, family commitments in Argentina, it shook him from his detached stance in regard to politics. His involvement in public activities and pronouncements on political issues would continue until his death.[16] His first trip to Cuba, in 1963, turned him into a fervent supporter of the Cuban Revolution and of socialism as the future for Latin America. José Shafer expresses in the following manner the role of the Cuban Revolution in Cortázar's life: "Es cierto, Cortázar se fue a París. Oliviera [the protagonist of *Rayuela*] se fue a París, pero el pajarito argentino siguió torturándolo sin tregua. . . . [D]e no mediar la Revolución Cubana, [Cortázar] habría terminado como Oliviera. . . . [L]a Revolución . . . le permitió salvarse" (48–49). The reference is to the end of *Rayuela* when Oliviera is on the brink of jumping out of the second story window of a mental institution. Thus, Shafer implies that Cortázar's obsession with his conflicted allegiance and his guilty conscience for having left Argentina might have pushed him to the brink of suicide or madness if his commitment to Cuba and the socialist cause had not given new meaning and direction to this life.

Indeed, now he had an unequivocal response to his detractors who accused him of francophilia. Begging to differ with those who would argue that his modernist fascination with France distanced him from the needs of his country and region,[17] Cortázar credits his "European perspective" for winning him over to the socialist cause and the Cuban Revolution. As noted earlier in this chapter, he insisted that, paradoxically, in Europe he discovered his condition of Latin American.

But with Cortázar's new adhesion to political causes, the burden of guilt for the expatriate merely seems to have shifted from its fixation with family to political and cultural matters. As mentioned above, during the 1976–1983 Argentine military dictatorship, Cortázar no longer considered himself a voluntary expatriate, but a political exile. Daniel Mazzone believes that Cortázar's need to insist he was a political exile— something, which Mazzone points out, irked those who left in less ideal conditions than Cortázar—indicates the guilt he felt for abandoning the fight in Argentina. This guilt, in turn, according to Mazzone, reflects the sincerity of his political commitment:

> Parecería que en ese día de 1951 en que Cortázar decidió cortar amarras se anudan claves cuyo rastro puede seguirse en su obra y en sus dichos. . . . Parecería que para quien como él, modificó el rumbo ideológico, irse de América Latina representó mucho más que un traslado físico o cultural. Su culpa es la de quien abandona la trinchera que no debió ser abandonada. No dejó de sentirse un desertor, lo que a su vez indica cuán hondamente creyó en su papel como escritor más allá de su oficio. (14)

Cortázar's uneasy conscience for "abandoning the trenches," as Mazzone puts it, or being distant from the struggle finds its most penetrating expression in "Recortes de prensa." In this story two Argentines exiled in Paris, Noemí—a well-known writer and the story's narrator— and an unnamed sculptor, focus their guilt on a mother of victims of the

"Dirty War." Their horror in face of the extreme cruelty of the Argentine military regime, and their inability to help the mother in her plight to seek justice result in intense feelings of futility and rage. Since the issue of the politicization of motherhood in this story will be addressed in chapter 7, here I will discuss the Argentine mother as the abandoned Eurydice who generates guilt at the same time that she safeguards the identity of the Argentines in Paris.

In "Recortes," the sculptor and Noemí voice sentiments that they share as exiled Argentines during the dictatorship. The sculptor has asked Noemí, a type of female alter ego for Cortázar, if she will write a text to accompany the brochure for his exhibition. The story opens as Noemí arrives at the sculptor's apartment to view these figures, which represent forms of violence. "Algo sabíamos de eso," she remarks in reference to the theme of violence, "una vez más dos argentinos dejando subir la marea de los recuerdos, la cotidiana acumulación del espanto a través de cables, cartas, repentinos silencios" (*Cc* 2, 360). When she comments to the sculptor that if she writes the text it will not be too facile or obvious, the sculptor replies: "Yo sé que no es fácil, llevamos tanta sangre en los recuerdos que a veces uno se siente culpable de ponerles límites, de manearlos para que no nos inunden del todo" (*Cc* 2, 361). Here the exiled Argentines experience their common identity through their horror at what is happening back home—the extreme cruelty with which the military are repressing supposed subversives. The sculptor articulates their impossible situation: if they let the anger take over, it overwhelms them; but if they try to control it, they feel guilty. With his observation, the sculptor unwittingly foreshadows Noemí's fate: she will allow these images of torture to overwhelm her, and act under their influence. Noemí's reference to the "cables, cartas, repentinos silencios" expresses what it is like to experience the horror unfolding in their homeland from a distance: the dull panic of not knowing what has happened to friends, while fearing the worst.

"Cables" and "cartas" are forms of bridges between France and Argentina, between the exiles and their friends, family, and other fellow Argentines back home. The crucial bridge in this story is, of course, the press clipping which Noemí has recently received in the mail and takes out to share with the sculptor. It recounts the heart-wrenching story of Laura Bonaparte Bruschtein who has lost her husband and a daughter to the torturers, and whose second daughter and son-in-law are missing. "[M]e sentiré mejor si también vos lo leés" (*Cc* 2, 361), says Noemí, thus seeking a minimal consolation in the feeling of solidarity that comes from sharing her horror and grief with a fellow Argentine. The reading of the clipping creates one of Cortázar's famous interstitial moments:

> ese agujero en que estábamos como metidos los dos, esa duración que abarcaba una pieza de París y un barrio miserable de Buenos Aires, que abolía los calendarios y nos dejaba cara a cara frente a eso, frente a lo que solamente podíamos llamar eso, todas las calificaciones gastadas, todos los gestos del horror cansados y sucios. (*Cc* 2, 362)

Interstitiality, the feeling of living between two worlds, is another function of being distant from one's homeland. This time, that space is the no-man's land of the unspeakable horror they know all too well.

The details of the torture are horrific, and the mother, Laura Bonaparte Bruschtein, has been repeatedly victimized. With the reading of her petition, the exiles' feelings of rage, impotence, and guilt crystallize around her. Female space, once again, becomes the locus of the guilty identity. Although several murdered or kidnapped men are mentioned in the declaration, the assassinated daughter and her justice-seeking mother become the iconic victims.

The sculptor and Noemí deal differently with their outrage. The sculptor expresses his profound sense of frustration, futility, and guilt for being thousands of kilometers away and occupying himself with the details of his upcoming exhibit. They can do *something* from their place of exile: "vamos a congresos y mesas redondas para protestar" (*Cc* 2, 362–363), but this activity seems futile in the face of reports like that of Mrs. Bruschtein. Noemí, in a show of pragmatism, advises the sculptor not to get involved in self-recrimination: "—Bah, querido . . . No empieces a autotorturarte, ya basta con la verdadera, creo" (*Cc* 2, 363). However, she is the one who will act out her rage, perhaps as a consequence of her initial attempt to repress or deny its intensity. After she leaves the sculptor's apartment, she stumbles on a scene of domestic abuse—a man torturing a bound woman by burning her body with a cigarette. In a daze, she knocks the man unconscious with a stool, frees the woman, and the two women torture the man. The reader does not learn of the fate of the man until Noemí receives, several days later, a second press clipping reporting that the man was sadistically murdered. Clearly, Noemí vented her pent-up wrath when she came across the torture scene in France, and her own capacity for violence shocked her.

Noemí's Argentine identity was experienced through her seething fury accompanied by a sensation of impotence. When she came across the torture scene in France, she found a way of reversing that feeling of helplessness through direct participation. Since she could not rescue Laura Bruschtein Bonaparte's family or kill the henchmen who tortured them, she rescued a substitute victim and killed a substitute victimizer. Her out-of-control rage demonstrated to her the violence of which all human beings are capable.

The space of the victimized woman is where the (guilty) identity is focused and then acted out. Why did Cortázar use a female alter ego to narrate the story and release his pent-up rage? Perhaps it is because the torture scenes in both Argentina and France correspond to traditional gender roles in a situation of physical abuse: woman as victim and man as victimizer. Cortázar's female avenger could identify more readily with the victim, and also alter the gender-based cycle of abuse.

How does Laura Bruschtein Bonaparte, the sacrificial Eurydice, serve to anchor the Argentineness of Noemí and the sculptor? She bears the wounds of the Argentine government-sponsored terrorism in her flesh and blood, and she cries out to denounce the regime's abuse of power and violation of human rights. She represents not only victimization, but also the vigorous and defiant protest carried out by families of the victims. While the mothers in "El otro cielo" and "Cartas de mamá" represent values the guilty protagonist is struggling to disown—petit bourgeois materialism and Buenos Aires provincialism—Mrs. Bruschtein represents the fight from the trenches that must not be abandoned. By grafting her clipping onto his story, Cortázar expresses his solidarity with the resistance to the arbitrary and barbaric military rule in his homeland. At the same time, it is important to note that France is not represented as a privileged place of civilized escape from barbarism, as it, too, is seen as a place where sadistic violence is perpetrated.

"Diario para un cuento": Anabel/Eurydice Shows Orpheus What a Cad He Was

"Diario para un cuento," the last story in Cortázar's last published collection, represents a significant change in tone from the agonic human rights agenda of "Recortes" as well as from the guilty son of "El otro cielo" and "Cartas de mamá." Now with the voice of a reflective, philosophical old man, the narrator looks back on his last months in Buenos

Aires before his definitive departure for Paris in 1951. He uses Anabel, a prostitute, to accuse himself of cowardly and hypocritical behavior, due, in large part, to his petit bourgeois mentality, which distanced him from her class. In turn, this bourgeois mind-set is directly related to his failure to appreciate the popular movement generated by Peronism. Anabel, a representative of the popular classes to which he turned his back, is given a voice to accuse him.[18]

The basic plot of this multilayered text deals with an Argentine writer who resides in Paris. He is recalling Anabel, a prostitute he knew many years earlier when he was a public translator in Buenos Aires. He translated her correspondence with an American sailor, and eventually became sexually involved with her. When another prostitute is poisoned, he realizes that his knowledge of the scheme via Anabel's letters makes him an accessory to murder, and he takes cover.

The story, which is actually a diary of the writer's desire to write the story, is largely autobiographical. In the interview with Omar Prego, Cortázar explains the story's creation process, conceding "allí hay mucho de autobiográfico. . . . Ése es un episodio de mi vida en Buenos Aires" (51). At the same time, lest we be tempted to take "Diario para un cuento" as pure autobiography, Cortázar also admits that the story was carefully constructed[19] and that the character of Hardy, who originally appeared in "Las puertas del cielo," is fictional (50, 53). With entries dating from February 2 to February 28, 1982, the "diary" becomes a type of confessional for Cortázar, or at least for his authorial construct.

In the first entries of the diary, another Argentine writer, Adolfo Bioy Casares, is evoked. Bioy serves as both foil and imagined interlocutor for the diary writer. The narrator expresses, first of all, his regret that he didn't get to know Bioy better due to "un océano temprana y literalmente tendido entre los dos" (*Cc* 2, 488). The writer's second misgiving concerning Bioy is that he would like to *be* Bioy so he could write about Anabel as Bioy would do, "mostrándola desde cerca y hondo y a la vez guardando esa distancia" (*Cc* 2, 489). However, he knows that he is incapable of maintaining that distance from his character.

I would like to highlight two significant implications of the narrator's references to Bioy. First of all, as noted above, the main story, or perhaps we could call it the story-within-the-story, can be read as a tale of how Cortázar's decision to leave Argentina was a way of turning his back to the struggles of Anabel and her world—the popular classes. However, the story's framing has to do with a loss of quite a different sort occasioned by Cortázar's[20] expatriation: the loss of a literary community. In this sense, Bioy, as an intellectual who stayed in Argentina, is a type of foil for Cortázar—he represents the road not taken. Cortázar's desire to write about Anabel gives him a pretext to dialogue with Bioy—or at least to imagine the dialogue that could have ensued if Cortázar's expatriation had not prevented the development of their incipient friendship. So here Anabel functions to mediate his homosocial desire to hold forth with Bioy on literary topics, as he imagines Bioy comparing her to Annabel Lee. Cortázar then projects what would be his response to Bioy, pointing out the differences between the Anabel he knew and the Annabel of Poe's poem, in particular that the Argentine Anabel was not a "maiden," thus immediately categorizing her according to her sexuality. The woman's body becomes the subject—or, better put, the object—of the imagined "literary" conversation between men. However, this objectification of Anabel will eventually give way as Cortázar allows her to turn the tables on him.

Thus, regardless of his initial motives for evoking Bioy, Cortázar's expressed inability to keep a distance from his character, as Bioy would do, is ultimately an ethical issue, as pointed out by Peter Fröhlicher: "Aparece en el 'centro del espejo' el traductor con los defectos puestos de manifiesto . . . el narrador termina por descubrir su dimensión moral" (*La mirada recíproca* 97).[21] Cortázar's impossibility to portray Anabel without her invading him is related to the fact that he uses the story to criticize his past behavior. It also points to the evolution of his female characters, as discussed in chapter 5: her autonomy is a testimony to Cortázar's greater openness toward women in the latter part of his career. Instead of attempting to control her, Cortázar gives Anabel free rein to expose the narrator's wrongdoing.

Therefore, Anabel's presumptive point of view prevails, something Cortázar acknowledges in the aforementioned interview with Prego: "Es Anabel la que me pone a mí al descubierto, que muestra toda mi cobardía en esa situación con respecto al crimen" (53). In this way, finally, in "Diario para un cuento," the mute Eurydice, the sacrificial woman, is given her voice in the form of Anabel, to show Orpheus, or rather Cortázar, what a cad he was in his cowardly abandonment of her. As the virtual author of the poisoning incident, she exposes the translator's shortcomings—his classist, bourgeois bias, which led him to treat her as an inferior—and she makes him face up to his betrayal of her personally, along with her class. Eurydice's face has changed—she is no longer mamá, nor a Madre of the Disappeared, but a lumpen proletariat. She represents Cortázar's sacrifice of the Argentine popular classes with his departure from Argentina. Now that his personal evolution in matters of politics has led him to embrace socialism and humanistic values, he recognizes he sold Anabel and her type short and regrets: "lo que acaso hubiera tenido que ser de otra manera" (*Cc* 2, 509).

As mentioned above, the narrator's unequal treatment of Anabel is related to the author's failure to understand Peronism insofar as both omissions are a product of the same petit bourgeois mentality. Passages of the story echo statements made by Cortázar in interviews. For instance, in the 1977 interview with González Bermejo, Cortázar mentions his irritation with the loudspeakers broadcasting Peronist propaganda:

> Nos molestaban mucho los altoparlantes en las esquinas gritando: "Perón, Perón, que grande sos", porque se intercalaban con el último concierto de Alban Berg que estábamos escuchando. Eso produjo en nosotros una equivocación suicida y muchos nos mandamos a mudar. (González Bermejo 119)

In the story, the translator complains about those same loudspeakers, as well as the required display of Evita's photo, emphatically stating his aversion to the coercive imposition of Peronism:

> Esos tiempos: el peronismo ensordeciéndome a puro altoparlante en el centro, el gallego portero llegando a mi oficina con una foto de Evita y pidiéndome de manera nada amable que tuviera la amabilidad de fijarla en la pared (traía las cuatro chinches para que no hubiera pretextos.) (*Cc* 2, 494)

Another detail of the story repeats an observation from the González Bermejo interview, creating a parallel between Cortázar's failure to comprehend the political impact of Peronism and his narrator's patronizing attitude toward Anabel:

> Entonces, dentro de la Argentina los choques, las fricciones, la sensación de violación que padecíamos cotidianamente frente a ese desborde popular; *nuestra condición de jóvenes burgueses que leíamos en varios idiomas, nos impidió entender ese fenómeno* [la gran sacudida de masas creada por el Peronismo]. (González Bermejo 119, emphasis added)

> Inocencia de Anabel . . . Fácil tildar a Anabel por esa ignorancia que la
> llevaba como resbalando de una cosa a otra; de golpe . . . la entrevisión
> de algo que se me escapaba, de eso que la misma Anabel llamaba un poco
> dramáticamente "la vida", y que para mí era un territorio vedado. . . . *Sí,*
> *los verdaderos inocentes éramos los de corbata y tres idiomas.* (*Cc* 2, 498,
> emphasis added)

In this way, the story reiterates the paradox that Cortázar put forth in the
interview: that he and his peers who wore neckties and knew other languages, that is, the bourgeois intelligentsia, were the ignorant ones, those
who could not comprehend or appreciate the popular phenomena occur-
ring around them. The juxtaposition of the two passages enables us to
perceive a correspondence between the translator's regret for his failure to
treat Anabel as an equal and Cortázar's misgivings about his earlier scorn
for the Argentine mass movement that took shape under Perón. The regret of Cortázar's narrator, cited above—"lo que acaso hubiera tenido que
ser de otra manera" (*Cc* 2, 509)—could be considered to encompass both
his attitude toward Anabel and toward Peronist populism.

The contrast between the sentiment expressed in "El otro cielo"
and that of "Diario para un cuento" reveals Cortázar's self-reflection as
well as the evolution of his attitude toward Peronism, a development
that he has explained in letters and interviews. We recall that in "El otro
cielo" as well as in the poem "Entronización," the narrator (or lyric voice)
rejects the petit bourgeois values of his family. His disdain toward these
values—the stuffy respectability embodied by mamá and Irma, the bla-
tant materialism evidenced in the refrigerator party—is a contributing
factor in his decision to leave Argentina.

But in "Diario para un cuento," he has to face up to the reality that
he, too, was guilty of petit bourgeois attitudes when Anabel held the
mirror up to him. His bias was brought out by his treatment of Anabel
and his behavior in the aftermath of the poisoning incident. Once he
found out about the homicide, he distanced himself from Anabel and
her life, fearing needlessly that she or her friends would implicate him in
the crime. He admits that he underestimated Anabel's friend Marucha,
not believing that a prostitute would keep her word of honor to remain
silent regarding the source of the poison. His failure to understand
Anabel's world created his removal from her, which prefigured his departure from Argentine due to his disaffection with Peronist populism.
Although his misunderstanding in regard to Anabel and her friends was

not the cause of his ultimate departure, it was symptomatic of the same bourgeois mind-set that repudiated Peronist Argentina. So while "El otro cielo" and "Entronización" point to his repudiation of petit bourgeois values as his reason for leaving, in "Diario para un cuento," his failure to understand the popular classes and, by extension, Peronist populism is implicated in his departure. Now that his experience with the Cuban and Nicaraguan Revolutions has made him appreciate the possibilities of a mass movement, he sees his behavior with Anabel as hypocritical. "Diario para un cuento" represents a gesture of self-reflection and supreme sincerity because he is forced to admit that he possessed the same bourgeois biases he found so reprehensible in others of his social class, and that these came into play in his decision to expatriate. Undoubtedly this is not easy to admit, and it is for this reason he finds writing about Anabel so difficult. It is painful to acknowledge that he, like the refrigerator-party people, was guilty of petit bourgeois classist attitudes.

In the Picón Garfield interview, he explains that while he still distrusts Perón, he has changed his evaluation of the social movement created by Peronism:

> Cuando la primera presidencia de Perón . . . yo fui antiperonista, junto con la enorme mayoría de los intelectuales argentinos que pertenecían también en su gran mayoría a la pequeña o media burguesía. A mí me han hecho falta veinte años y la experiencia de la revolución cubana para comprender hasta qué punto nos equivocamos en aquella época en algunos juicios. . . . [L]o que no comprendí en aquel entonces, es que a Perón . . . las circunstancias y su prestigio personal lo llevaron a crear un movimiento de masas como no se había visto nunca en Argentina. Ese movimiento de masas debió en ese momento haber llegado a una revolución. . . . lo que no comprendimos fue que por primera vez había un cambio de valores y que había todo un pueblo que oscuramente empezaba a tomar consciencia de sí mismo. . . . En realidad nuestro deber hubiera sido no unirnos a Perón pero sí, trabajar paralelamente con ese movimiento. Es decir, habernos mezclado con el pueblo y haber tratado de ayudar en ese camino torpe y confuso y contradictorio en que se movía. (50–51)[22]

Thus, Cortázar believes that he was mistaken in not recognizing and working with the mass movement that arose as a result of Peronism. In "Diario para un cuento," Cortázar's national identity is expressed through his coming-to-terms with his failure to understand and appreciate the masses, symbolized by the body of Anabel. This gesture, at the same time that it is an admission of his past personal investment in the elite versus populist dichotomy that structured Argentina's "guiding fiction," also serves to expose and critique it.

While Cortázar's position regarding Peronist populism is one way of defining his *argentinidad,* the geographical configuration of the story also deals with ways of envisioning Argentine national identity. Like in "El otro cielo," "Cartas de mamá," and "Recortes de prensa," the narrator straddles the Paris-Buenos Aires divide. The distance between the "here and now" of France and the "then and there" of Argentina frames the story. As he begins to recall the incident, the narrator comments that it took place many years ago "en un país que es hoy mi fantasma o yo el suyo" (*Cc* 2, 491) revealing a keen, even painful, awareness of his physical and psychological distance from his country. His connection to his homeland has become increasingly tenuous—in part due to his denunciation of the military regime currently in power.

In contrast to the bidimensional setting—Paris versus Buenos Aires—of the three aforementioned stories, "Diario para un cuento" includes two additional dimensions: an evocation of the pampa and an allusion to the United States. The prior experiences of Anabel and the translator reference the dichotomy between the pampa—Argentina's "barbaric" interior—and Buenos Aires. Their future, on the other hand, holds the promise of leaving Argentina for foreign lands. These spaces, of course, encompass two classical paradigms for imagining Argentine identity. The pampa/Buenos Aires juxtaposition harks back to the civilization versus barbarism polarity, while the abandonment of Argentina for France or the United States reflects Argentina's neocolonized status.

The discourse on the pampa is prompted when the narrator and Anabel, together in her bed, hear the loud music played by one of her neighbors: "*adióóós pááámpa mííía*" (*Cc* 2, 501). "[E]se tipo no acababa nunca de despedirse de su famosa pampa" (*Cc* 2, 500–501), comments the narrator. Anabel complains: "Tanto lío que arma ése por la pampa . . . tanto joder por una mierda llena de vacas" (*Cc* 2, 501). The narrator's snide rejoinder, "Pero Anabel, yo te creía más patriótica, hijita" (*Cc* 2, 501) is a facetious allusion to the pampa's iconic value as a national symbol. Ignoring his crack, Anabel continues: "Una pura mierda aburrida, che, yo creo que si no vengo a Buenos Aires me tiro a un zanjón" (*Cc* 2, 501), and she proceeds to tell the story of her disgrace at the hands of a traveling salesman in her town on the pampa. The nar-

rator has the sensation of having heard this pitiful tale before in a dusty
hotel in Bolívar where he lived for two years. He recalls the violent and
shameful story of a desperate widow who forced her thirteen-year-old
daughter, Chola, to sleep with a lover, a traveling automobile dealer, who
bored of the older woman. "¿Qué le podía decir [a Anabel]?" remarks
the narrator. "¿Qué ya conocía cada detalle . . . ? ¿Qué todo era siempre
más o menos así con las Anabel de este mundo, salvo que a veces se
llamaban Chola?" (*Cc* 2, 502). Thus, Anabel comes to stand for the women
who have lost their virtue to a transient man who passed through their
lives and seemed to represent a better existence elsewhere—a testimony
to the brutality and desperation of the frontier culture.

This incident critiques the pampa as a symbol of Argentine national identity. For Anabel's nostalgic fellow tenant, the pampa represents what was left behind in the phenomenon of rural-to-urban
migration. Moving to the capital city meant greater opportunities for
many migrants, but the neighbor's music sings of something of value
that is lost in the process—a link to the land and his roots, in essence,
his identity. The experience of Anabel and the narrator, on the other
hand, demystifies this romantic or idyllic vision of the pampa. When he
jokes that Anabel's derisive reaction puts her patriotism in question, he
satirizes the sacralization of the pampa as a revered symbol of Argentine
nationalism. Both Anabel's past and the incident recalled by the narrator
expose the pampa as a barbaric culture of male domination where men
can exploit women's bodies without sanctions. This story thus perpetuates the civilization versus barbarism dichotomy described by nineteenth-
century Argentine intellectuals. Both the translator and Anabel clearly prefer
the urban space to the pampa, which they see as boring and more primi-
tive. The pampa meant a dull backwater for the translator, boredom and
a ruined reputation for Anabel. Both had other ambitions for their lives,
and both were relieved to leave the pampa behind for Buenos Aires.

But on the continuum between barbarism and civilization, Buenos
Aires appears to be at midpoint in the road. While Anabel and the translator seem to be more satisfied in the capital city than on the pampa,
both still lead marginal lives. To make a living, the narrator has to translate documents he neither understands nor cares about. Additionally, he
feels annoyed and alienated due to the surging Peronist movement. We
never learn exactly how Anabel envisions her lot in Buenos Aires, but
the narrator does not fail to characterize her marginal status there:
"Anabel se movía en el aire espeso y sucio de un Buenos Aires que la

contenía y la vez la rechazaba como a una sobra marginal, lumpen de puerto y pieza de mala muerte" (*Cc* 2, 495). Life in Buenos Aires for them means corruption of virtue—the translator is an insincere professional, Anabel is a woman who sells her body.

Thus, the third geographic term that comes into play for the translator and Anabel is *el extranjero*—specifically France and the United States. While both the narrator and Anabel must prostitute themselves in Argentina, passage to France or the States holds a promise of sincerity or virtue. We know that Cortázar the translator went to France, and that in Paris, the crossroads of people and ideas, he underwent decisive experiences that enabled him to write his highly acclaimed novel, *Rayuela*, as well as many other works. Cortázar went to France and became a highly successful, "sincere" writer.

In the story, Anabel's sailor friend, William, confides to the translator that he loves Anabel and wants to take her out of "la vida" and to the States with him. Can we surmise that Anabel ended her days as a housewife in a U.S. navy town? After all, the narrator does say that his friend Hardoy never again sees her in the dance halls. Although he refrains from speculating that she could have gone to America with William, this is clearly a possibility.[23] Winning William's love could have meant for Anabel passage to a new life in the United States where, as a married woman in a far-away land, she could distance herself from her past and achieve respectability. In this antinationalistic romance, the love between an American sailor and an Argentine prostitute holds the promise for the latter of escape from the barbarism of the *hampa*, the Buenos Aires underworld, and restoration of virtue through expatriation. Of course, Anabel's escape from the barbarie of Buenos Aires is only projected when the translator hears of William's plan for her—we (and Cortázar) never know whether or not it happened.

In real life, Cortázar left Argentina to escape Peronist "barbarism," and achieved fame and a comfortable life in Paris, realizing success as a writer perhaps beyond his wildest dreams. But his last story focuses on the guilt he felt for his insincere behavior during his last months in Buenos Aires, and for his inability to understand the popular classes. In his life as an expatriate, Cortázar became a sincere writer—guilty, yes, but honest about his guilt.

Does Cortázar's construction of his national identity—as embodied by certain female characters—sustain or break down the traditional schema of Argentine identity: the divisive rhetoric of the dichotomous visions? How can we characterize the evolution in his use of female space as a container for his *argentinidad?* The mother figure in "El otro cielo" and "Cartas de mamá" perpetuates the modernist periphery versus center pattern, by representing the petit bourgeois mentality and provincialism of the satellite culture. "Recortes" is a product of a time of crisis, in which the "Madre" is evoked to express Cortázar's solidarity with the fight against the military dictatorship. The civilization versus barbarism polarity is dismantled by depicting violence as a universal human emotion.

Finally, "Diario" conveys a mixed message in regard to the divisive "guiding fiction" linked to the Argentine national imagination. By evoking a prostitute to "anchor" his *argentinidad* and expressing regret for his treatment of her, Cortázar demonstrates that his "conversion" after he visited Cuba and experienced the revolution has lead him to recant his earlier elitist classism. His identification with Latin American revolutionary movements has caused him to rethink Argentina's potential for transformation through a popular movement. In this regard, we may note that "Diario" was written when Argentina was still in the grips of the rightist military regime that brutally squashed any organization or individual that could have even the remotest sympathy with a popular movement. Could Cortázar possibly have been thinking that Argentine history might have taken a different course—perhaps even have been spared the oppressive rightist regime—if intellectuals like himself had supported and worked with a popular movement? Perhaps this speculation takes us too far afield, but Cortázar's recantation of his petit bourgeois elitism and affirmation of his support for the popular classes constitute the core of his remaining links to Argentina, as embodied by Anabel. At the same time, his evocation of Bioy references the literary community, or high culture, of Argentina, which he also regrets having lost.

However, the story's configuration of geographic spaces—Buenos Aires, the pampa, France, and the United States—perpetuates the dichotomy that fed into the modernist mentality. Both the translator and Anabel abandon the barbarism of the pampa for a better life in Buenos Aires, and the translator continues to pursue his dreams through expatriation to France. It would seem that the only possibility Anabel had of escaping her marginal status as a figure in the Buenos Aires underworld would have been via marriage to a U.S. sailor and passage to the United States. Thus, while the choice of Anabel the prostitute as the sacrificial Eurydice shows that Cortázar would have liked to have done better by her and the popular classes, it seems he never really regrets his departure from Argentina, nor does he show any evidence of rethinking the concept of Argentina as a failed modernity.

Chapter 7

☙

Women and the "Dirty War"

[S]ucede también que escribo cosas que están inmersas en la situación política y que tienen una intención de lucha política.
                    —Cortázar, Interview with Radio France International

[S]abemos los que tuvimos la suerte de ser sus amigos, que Cortázar no era un político y que sus actividades en este terreno eran puramente éticas.
                    —Moyano, "Cortázar y los argentinos"

The female body is the focus of Cortázar's short narratives denouncing the Argentine military dictatorship—young women whose disfigured bodies become maps of the struggle and elderly mothers crazed by sorrow who risk everything to protest the regime's kidnapping of their children. In the stories "Pesadillas," "Graffiti," and "Recortes de prensa," and the essay "Nuevo elogio de la locura," women become the symbolic victim of the abuse of power as well as a voice of defiance against that power. While these works offer testimony to women's opposition during the "Dirty War," it is the female body, not the male, which is invariably depicted as violated and exposed. By featuring women as victims and protesters, Cortázar's narratives rely on gender attributes to articulate a criticism of the regime, using systems of gender identity as a metaphor for the oppressor and the oppressed.[1]

This gender-based denunciation of the abuse of power in Cortázar's writings coincides with the formative role of gender in the ideology of the Argentine military regime. Psychoanalytic theory elucidates the process by which sexual difference is politicized within a patriarchal system. An authoritarian patriarchal regime operates on the pretense that "domination arises naturally from anatomy . . . a biological inscription of patriarchy" (Frosh 87). The masculine then seeks confirmation of its control as it attempts to shore up boundaries, envisioning femininity as a threat to such confirmation. Thus, the feminine, as that which subverts

141

the established order and upsets rationality, becomes the enemy (Frosh 87). Conversely, all entities considered to be the enemy—or in other words, all potential challenges to the military's concept of order—are feminized. These groups come to symbolize excess and irrationality, that which is unacceptable to masculine phallic consciousness. Through this process of feminizing the perceived opponent, the military banishes repudiated parts of self, such as feared weakness, "in the interest of maintaining an identity which feels free of conflict and inferiority" (Minsky 210). The feminized enemy is then hunted down, humiliated, and eliminated.

Ximena Bunster-Burotto and Diana Taylor interpret how the gendered ideology functioned in the case of the Argentine regime; the former explains the military's strongly patriarchal mentality:

> The military state understands itself to be run for the perpetuation and extension of the values of the military, masculinity, power, and public authority to a greater extent than do other patriarchal states. It is founded on the assumption that women and notions of the "feminine" are tools to be used by men; simultaneously, militarism as an ideology purports that women are fearsome threats to public order, to the hierarchy defined and controlled by men. (Bunster-Burotto 300)

Thus, stereotypic gender metaphors were exploited by the military to conceptualize their struggle. The military junta represented itself as the embodiment of masculinity—all insertive, active, and aggressive—and feminized the masses as well as its enemies (Taylor 71, 156). The feminine in abstract was glorified in the image of the *Patria* while real women were split into "good women" and "bad women." The "good women"— mothers and sisters—were those who supported the military's mission and were happiest at home, while the "bad women"—the active women who resisted or transgressed—symbolized evil and the uncontrollable (Taylor 77–79).

Cortázar's narratives mirror, at the same time that they critique, this highly charged scenario in terms of gender identity. In this chapter I will consider how Cortázar uses women, both fictional and real, to embody his denunciation of the regime. In the first half of this chapter, "A War Waged on Women's Bodies," we will look at the differing ways in which the female body reflects the violence of the period in the stories "Pesadillas" and "Graffiti." The second part, "The Politicization of Motherhood" returns to the ubiquitous mother figure as we examine how

Cortázar presents real mothers who struggled against the regime in "Recortes de prensa" and his essay "Nuevo elogio de la locura."

A War Waged on Women's Bodies

"Pesadillas": The Anguished Patria

"Pesadillas" is based on the trope of feminine body as contested national territory. The story focuses on an Argentine family's grave preoccupation over their daughter/sister, Mecha, whose body has been rendered comatose by a viral infection. Although she is unconscious, her body appears to be wracked by repeated nightmares. Through the course of the narration we learn that her brother, Lauro, is involved in some kind of clandestine activity at the university. One day Lauro does not come home, and Mecha finally awakens from her nightmare just as a group of men armed with machine guns are breaking down the door.

Mecha's body becomes a metaphor for the Argentine nation's anguish during the military regime as well as a representation of the site of conflict. This imagery corroborates Taylor's explanation of the military's self-representation as masculine subjectivity while the feminine *Patria* is reduced to the material body (78). Cortázar's portrayal taps into and subverts the military ideology because the regime's penetration of Mecha's body, instead of giving birth to a new civilization, infects it with a terrible disease, leaving it anguished and lifeless. Instead of protecting and defending the *Patria*, they are tormenting it—their targets are not dangerous subversives, as they would claim, but beloved brothers. During the "Dirty War," the military used kidnapping and torture to produce a docile, silent social body. Mecha's comatose body invaded by constant nightmares is Cortázar's hyperbolic symbol for the trauma experienced by the Argentine people during the reign of terror.

Distinctive gender markers structure the story's symbolic discourse. Mecha is imbued with traits associated with essentialist notions of femininity: vulnerability and penetrability, secret interiority, and clairvoyance or intuition. Her name, Mecha (wick), signifies a *conduit* for the spark that will start a fire or activate an explosive device, corresponding to the classic representation of woman as container or empty vessel. Her passive body is at the center of the plot action, but the woman herself, her subjectivity, is absented. She exists only as an inert body that symbolizes the Argentine nation.

The story begins in *medias res*, when Mecha has been in a coma for several weeks, and she has no role in the struggle except as occupied space—her comatose body is depicted as a weight that crushes the family. Her long nightmare is portrayed as an invading force that penetrates and violates the integrity of her body, and neither she, the other family members, nor her doctor can do anything to expel it: "como si Mecha estuviera soñando y que su sueño fuera penoso y desesperante, la pesadilla volviendo y volviendo sin que pudiera rechazarla . . . invadida por esa otra cosa que de alguna manera continuaba la larga pesadilla de todos ellos ahí" (Cc 2, 482). While Mecha's subjectivity is absent, the invading force is personified: "la habitante secreta resbalando bajo la piel," thus representing the female body as harboring a secret interiority. The mother's lament for Mecha could be equally applicable to Argentina: "Dios mío, como puede ser que esto dure y dure . . . está todo el tiempo con una pesadilla y que no se despierta" (*Cc* 2, 484).

Mecha's contortions during the nightmares turn her body into a text to be deciphered. The association of her nightmares with the struggle outside is suggested when the sound of gunshots triggers the onset of a nightmare: "se oyeron los tiros en la esquina . . . vieron pasar el temblor por las manos de Mecha . . . el temblor se repetía en todo el cuerpo de Mecha . . . como una voluntad de hablar" (*Cc* 2, 482). It appears that Mecha is trying in vain to speak or gesture in order to express the horror she senses.

Although the parents and nurse can see no pattern to Mecha's contortions, Lauro perceives them as her futile attempts to give him a message:

> Cada vez que se acercaba a la cama de Mecha era la misma sensación de contacto imposible, Mecha tan cerca y como llamándolo, los vagos signos de los dedos y esa mirada desde adentro, buscando salir, algo que seguía y seguía, un mensaje de prisionero a través de paredes de piel, su llamada insorportablemente inútil. Por momentos lo ganaba la histeria, la seguridad de que Mecha lo reconocía más que a su madre o a la enfermera, que la pesadilla alcanzaba su peor instante cuando él estaba ahí mirándola . . . [é]l no podía hacer nada. (*Cc* 2, 485)

Evidently Lauro had been keeping Mecha informed of his clandestine activities—he exhorts her to wake up because he has so many things to tell her, things he cannot say in the presence of the nurse or his parents. This knowledge is a catalyst for her nightmarish premonition of Lauro's imminent arrest and torture. However her call of warning cannot broach the boundary of her lifeless body, and the impossibility of communicating this urgent message to Lauro torments her. Lauro's reaction, in kind, symbolizes the agony of his generation—his anguish over his inability to do anything to effect Mecha's cure represents the frustration of Argentina's youth who were unable to save their nation from the nightmarish grip of violent military rule.

The parents, Luisa and Eduardo Botto, are representative of the Argentine populace, and their lives reflect the quotidian routine during the dictatorship. Mrs. Botto depicts the women who turned in vain to their religious faith in their search for answers. "[S]anta Virgen ... que se termine este calvario, Dios mío ... sálvala, Dios mío, no la dejes así" (Cc 2, 482), she exclaims, as she prays over Mecha's motionless body. Mr. Botto represents the masses who had a notion that something was going on, but did not want to compromise themselves by coming to grips with the grim reality. His interaction with his son demonstrates how he avoids facing the truth. When Lauro comes home one afternoon, "el señor Botto le hizo [a Lauro] una pregunta casi evasiva sin dejar de mirar el televisor, en pleno comentario de la Copa" (Cc 2, 483), and he accepts Lauro's vague response without insisting on further clarification. Mr. Botto must realize that Lauro is involved in something potentially dangerous because he tells him to be careful, but never asks for an explanation, absorbed as he is in the championship soccer games. Or perhaps the games give him a pretext for not confronting a reality beyond his control. Cortázar's mention of the soccer matches references the World Cup tournament that Argentina hosted in 1978. The regime took advantage of the Argentine passion for *fútbol* to unleash the worst period of government-sponsored kidnapping while the people were diverted with the matches. In this sense, Lauro's father is an accomplice of the regime, taking the bait of the games and choosing to ignore the grave problems of the country. Finally, when Lauro does not return home, Mr. Botto is in a state of denial, making excuses for his failure to notify them: " 'se quedó festejando algo' ...'[e]l pibe andará loco con los exámenes' " (Cc 2, 486). The fact that his two possible explanations for Lauro's remissness are at odds with each other demonstrates that he's grasping at straws to postpone facing the very real possibility that his son has joined the ranks of the "disappeared."

The story concludes with Mecha's awakening from her state of nightmarish unconsciousness to a living nightmare. Lauro had left the house the previous evening without saying good-bye. In the early afternoon the television news reported "otro atentado subversivo frustrado por la rápida intervención de las fuerzas del orden, nada nuevo" (*Cc* 2, 486). Soon, from the within the Botto household can be heard the rising wail of sirens. The reader can conjecture that Lauro has been detained and military operatives have come to search the house for information and/or to detain his family members and torture them in Lauro's presence in order to make him talk about his co-conspirators. As the sirens approach, Mecha opens her eyes and Mrs. Botto, rather than experiencing joy at her daughter's reawakening, clutches her chest and shrieks in horror. Her horrified reaction suggests that she witnesses a type of demonic possession. Instead of recovering the dear daughter she lost to illness, the newly awakened eyes transmit the vision of otherworldly horror, the living nightmare that now surrounds them. Mecha's body shutters in a violent spasm, and she regains her senses in time to hear "la multiplicación de las sirenas, los golpes en la puerta que hacían temblar la casa, los gritos de mando . . . la ráfaga de ametralladora, los alaridos de doña Luisa, el envión de los cuerpos entrando en montón" (*Cc* 2, 487). The military raid on the family home occurs just in time for Mecha's awakening, in time for her nightmare to end so she can finally return "a la realidad, a la hermosa vida" (*Cc* 2, 487). The military have come to claim their occupied territory.

In this ironic reversal, the oneiric vision flows into the horror of the violent regime that shattered the lives of innocent civilians. Cortázar's story portrays an infirm and suffering feminine body to present a version of the national drama that contradicts the military's self-proclamation as saviors of the country.[2] Instead of protecting and defending the *Patria*, their violent abuse of power has rendered it silent and comatose, tormented by a living nightmare.

"Pesadillas" is similar to Cortázar's earlier story "Segunda vez" in that both depict a woman as witness to the abuses of the regime. However, "Segunda vez" is much more indirect and suggestive. María Elena, the story's protagonist, witnesses what may be a "disappearance," but does not really comprehend what she is seeing. Equally indicative of Cortázar's more soft-peddled approach to Argentine politics in this piece, which corresponds to the earlier years of the *proceso*, is the fact that the story depicts no bodily violence. While it is implied that María Elena is a potential victim, her suffering is not portrayed in the story, a major contrast with the violated bodies of Mecha and the female protagonist of "Graffiti."[3]

"Graffiti": The Female Body—Erotic Object versus Cautionary Message

The woman's tortured body depicts the concept of "writing on the body" in "Graffiti." In the triangulation of desire, the body of the female graffiti artist is an erotic object for a male graffiti artist, and for police operatives it is a transgressive enemy to be tortured. The game of flirtation played by the graffiti artists in the story is risky business in a police state that strictly forbids posting of notices and writing on walls. All sketches, even the most innocuous, are quickly removed by crews working at the behest of the police, and those caught inscribing on walls are detained, and face imprisonment and torture. The story's male protagonist begins drawing on the walls for artistic expression, and his curiosity is piqued when he notices other drawings beside his. Certain that they are the work of a woman who is calling to him, he thinks that he loves her and keeps a lookout for her during the night when the graffiti artists venture out under the cover of darkness. One night, at the wall where he had left a graphic message for her, he witnesses the police forcing a woman into a car and finds an unfinished drawing beside his. He agonizes over the fate of the woman, and about a month later, he draws again, reaching out to the woman with a representation of his love and hope. The woman responds with a small drawing of her face, showing it as horribly disfigured by torture. Immediately after the description of this drawing, the narrative voice changes. Up to this point, the story is told in second person from the perspective of the man, thus the reader assumes that it is the voice of the man addressing himself. However, at the end there is a surprising twist: the voice changes to first person, and the woman reveals that she is the story's narrator and that she was imagining the man's life. She concludes the story by saying that her final sketch was her good-bye to him; now she will hide herself in a dark place without mirrors, imagining that he continues sketching clandestine drawings on the walls.

The story conveys the constantly menacing environment during the regime, showing how ordinary actions were interpreted as subversive by the paranoiac military operatives. What would normally be playful courting behavior turns into a dangerous game of cat-and-mouse with the authorities. The budding love relationship cruelly truncated by police intervention points to the diminished prospect for personal fulfillment under the regime, and the woman's fate shows how lives were shattered while others witnessed helplessly. The man, at least before he learns of the woman's torture, has no real political motive. His sole message, which could be interpreted as an allusion to the repressive regime—"*A mí también me duele*" (*Cc* 2, 397)—is the exception that points to the nonpolitical nature of his other drawings. The "*también*" seems to imply that the female graffiti artist had left sketches of a political nature, and he is expressing solidarity with her sentiment.

As in "Pesadillas," the female body is the narrative focus: the woman's body is represented on the wall, imagined by the man (or rather by the woman imagining the man imagining her), disfigured by the torturers, and rewritten by the woman. The triangular relations between the male and female graffiti artists and the woman's torturers are a metaphor of oppression and resistance, the woman's body becoming contested space between the common citizen and the authoritarian power.

Taylor provides insight into the function of torture and its gendered nature during the Argentine military regime:

> Devised, in theory, to wring information from threatening enemies of state, the system of disappearance, torture, and murder of military opponents during the Dirty War served fundamentally to reconstitute the Argentine population and turn it into a docile, controllable, feminine "social" body. . . . The "real" bodies were used as the battleground, the geographic terrain, on which were fought the military's fantasies of Argentina's identity and destiny. (151)

Torture served to write the so-called subversives out of the national narrative and to turn a living body "into a text—a cautionary 'message' for those on the outside" (Taylor 152). Gender hierarchy is reproduced in the act of torture in that the victim's body is penetrated by the military male. Thus, in the all-male system, gender anxiety came into play in the atrocities, which "reaffirmed a masculinist signifying economy" (Taylor 156–157). The phallic signification of the *picana*, the electric prod used in torture by the Argentine state, is stressed by Frank Graziano who singles it out as the instrument empowering the junta (158). He explains that the *picana* as phallus served to stand (in) for the junta's lack of legitimate authority (161). Torture is thus conceived as a masculine, insertive act, a mock of "the act of love by reversing its intent, emptying the sexual structure of affection and filling it with brutality, annulling reciprocity and replacing it with unilateral domination" (Graziano 153).

The body of the female graffiti artist becomes the "object of desire" for both her would-be lover and torturers, and the story's meaning involves the juxtaposition of the multiple uses of her body: the intimate erotic body versus the public political body. She imagines and draws her body as an erotic object for the man, her potential lover. The military see her as a transgressor, and sadistically punish and disfigure her, in an attempt to use her body as a cautionary message. Their act also serves to enforce their (phallic) power over her.

The woman calls attention to her femininity. Initially she flirts with the other artist, provoking his desire for her by conveying her femininity in her drawings: "Cuando el otro apareció al lado tuyo casi tuviste miedo . . . y ese alguien por si fuera poco era una mujer. . . . un trazo, una predilección por las tizas cálidas, un aura" (Cc 2, 397–398). She wants to think that he fantasizes about her body and desires her: "la imaginaste morena y silenciosa, le elegiste labios y senos, la quisiste un poco" (Cc 2, 398). When she is captured by the police, her half-finished drawing remains to convey that she had been representing her body and her desire to consummate their relationship:

un esbozo en azul, los trazos de ese naranja que era como su nombre o su boca, ella ahí en ese dibujo truncado que los policias habían borroneado antes de llevársela . . . había querido responder a tu triángulo con otra figura, un círculo o acaso una espiral, una forma llena y hermosa, algo como un sí o un siempre o un ahora. (Cc 2, 399)

Her drawing is aborted by the police, an anticipation of their disfigurement of her, which will end the flirtation. While she was in the process of saying "yes" to the possibility of love, the police truncated both her representation of this affirmation and her physical body.

The attacks on women's bodies in totalitarian regimes are designed to violate their female human dignity along with their sense of self that comes from their emotional needs (Bunster-Burotto 298, 307). Since the self-representation of the narrator reveals that she conceived of herself as a sexual person, desirable to men, the disfigurement of her face struck at the very core of her being, depriving her of the possibility for emotional fulfillment. The woman's capture and torture mark the transition of her body from an erotic object that she offers to her fellow graffiti artist, to a captive body on which the police will inscribe a political message.

The man represents the Argentine populace who were paralyzed by their fear. In the woman's imagination, he witnesses her detention, hears her shrieks, sees her body being kicked, and sees her dark hair, previously evoked in sensuous terms, being yanked by gloved hands. Thus, when the man finally catches a glimpse of the woman he desires, she is under the power of the police. Since the military are an unassailable rival, he cannot fight for her, or even show himself, but only wait passively in anguish. He has become feminized because he cannot defend his beloved.

The man's knowledge of the fate of political prisoners (again, according to the narrator's imagination) attests to the military's use of tortured bodies as a cautionary tale intended to silence those outside: "Lo sabías muy bien . . . la gente estaba al tanto del destino de los prisioneros, y si a veces volvían a ver a uno que otro, hubieran preferido no verlos y que al igual que la mayoría se perdieran en ese silencio que nadie se atrevía a quebrar" (*Cc* 2, 399).

The woman's final rewriting of her body after she has been returned to society has multiple purposes and meanings. On the one hand, the grotesque image is meant as a farewell to the man, to tell him that the torturers have left her disfigured and she can no longer be his love object because her body is no longer desirable: "viste el óvalo naranja y las manchas violeta de donde parecía saltar una cara tumefacta, un ojo colgando, una boca aplastada a puñetazos" (*Cc* 2, 400). At the same time, she wants to believe that the military's brutal treatment of her will spur him to become politicized, to continue drawing as a way of resisting the regime. She says that she will retire to her hiding place, imagining "que salías por la noche para hacer otros dibujos" (*Cc* 2, 400).

In this sense, the woman subverts the cause of the junta. Instead of becoming docile, she returns to the scene of resistance—the graffiti wall. Instead of displaying her wounded body as a cautionary message, she rewrites it as a battle cry, thus divesting the author-ity of the military leaders, and assuming it for herself. She has lost her function as a sexual woman, but gained as a symbol of resistance.

At the same time, "Graffiti" depicts the struggle for male supremacy waged on the woman's body. Read as an allegory of the national tragedy, the story represents how the military men inscribed their markings on the feminine in order to become the "sole protagonist in the drama of national reorganization" (Taylor 157). While the military embody triumphant masculinity, the male graffiti writer represents the feminized masses who were unable to defend their loved ones and were cowed into behaving as passive witnesses to the horror unfolding in their midst.

An (even) darker side of "Graffiti" speaks of the gender anxiety of the torturers and the link between eroticism and violence. In order to prevent the woman from "cuckolding" them, the torturers "spoil" her, rendering her undesirable to other men, as might a perverse and jealous partner who does not know how to love, only how to mutilate. Initially the woman had imagined her "labios y senos" (*Cc* 2, 398) to be objects of her beloved's fantasy; at the end of the story, her reference to her disfigured face, in particular the "boca aplastada a puñetazos" (*Cc* 2, 400), alludes to a connection between the erotic pleasure invested in the man's fantasizing about her body and the erotic pleasure derived by the torturers in the violent mutilation of her beauty. The female body is the mass on which pleasure and violence are projected or acted out.

Thus, while the woman's body is central to the political metaphor in "Graffiti," also present is the sexist theme of the woman's body as erotic object, mirror of the man's interests (Masiello, "Cuerpo/presencia" 160). During the initial reading of the story, the reader believes that the man is fantasizing about the woman's body, but in the end discovers that all along it was the woman fantasizing about the man fantasizing about her. It seems that she enjoyed imagining that her body could provide erotic pleasure to a man she knew only through his drawings on the walls. Finally, after she was disfigured, she voluntarily withdrew from further contact with the man, thus playing to the *machista* mentality that a woman's looks are fundamental to her desirability. Evidently, the only type of relationship she can contemplate between them is one based on her physical appearance. Clearly, this is a character that serves the author's purpose of denouncing the Argentine military regime, but does not demonstrate the sensitivity to female characters that can be seen in other stories from the latter part of Cortázar's career. In many ways, I find this story painful for the female reader.

To conclude, in this story Cortázar uses the image of the woman's violated body to symbolize the sadistic and arbitrary violence of the military dictatorship and the powerlessness of the ordinary citizen facing the regime of terror. At the same time, her mutilated body will inspire continued resistance. The woman's body becomes a bridge between the junta and civil society, as her detention and torture by military operatives presumably serve to enlist her fellow graffiti artist in the struggle against the regime. In the end, she will remain silent, but the dialogue will continue between men. Ultimately, as in "Pesadillas," the feminine is suppressed and becomes the contested space, the common ground around which the males will position themselves (Taylor 18).

The Politicization of Motherhood

The horrific abuses of human rights during the military dictatorship resulted in the politicization of many mothers whose children were "disappeared." While "Pesadillas" and "Graffiti" illustrate the concept of the war fought on women's bodies, two of Cortázar's most explicit and dramatic denunciations of the regime, the short story "Recortes de prensa" and essay "Nuevo elogio de la locura," focus on the protest mounted by mothers of the disappeared. To some extent, Cortázar's choice of the maternal figure as a vehicle to express his solidarity with the victims is culturally determined because the Madres de la Plaza de Mayo were the most effective voice against the dictatorship. On the other hand, the central role of the maternal figure in these pieces is consistent with Cortázar's emphasis on maternal power and the ubiquitous presence of the maternal attachment throughout his work. My discussion of both pieces focuses on Cortázar's (or his narrator's) *identification* with these mother figures, as well as the significance of this seemingly radical shift compared to earlier stories, which objectified the mother as a source of fear and desire.

"Recortes de prensa": Frustrated Writers, Juxtaposed Mothers, Guilty Revenge

When news of the atrocities of the military dictatorships in the Southern Cone reached his ears, Cortázar undoubtedly felt guilty that he, as a writer of fiction who was distant from his country, was unable to take direct action against the injustices. In one of his speeches, he expressed his pangs of conscience due to his inability to help victims of the oppressive regimes:

> [S]é que puedo seguir escribiendo mis ficciones más literarias sin que aquellos que me leen me acusen de escapista; desde luego, esto no acaba ni acabará con mi mala consciencia, porque lo que podemos hacer los escritores es nimio frente al panorama de horror y de opresión que presenta hoy el Cono Sur. ("El lector y el escritor bajo las dictaduras en América Latina" 90)[4]

As if to confirm his allusion to the superfluousness of writers of fiction in face of these grave situations, in "Recortes de prensa," we see the ominous consequences when the writer acts out that guilt in a moment of passion.

"Recortes de prensa" is an expression of Cortázar's solidarity with the families of the victims of the "Dirty War" as well as a statement about the ethics of writing and the relationship between aesthetic creation and violence.[5] Pervading the story is the narrator's (and thus Cortázar's) sense of guilt and frustration toward the limitations in her ability to help victims of the Argentine military regime due to the fact that she is a writer exiled in Paris. The story's narrator and protagonist, Noemí—a highly successful Argentine writer living in Paris and thus a type of female version of Cortázar—is deeply affected by the heartwrenching testimony of an Argentine mother. Under its influence, Noemí the professional woman is temporarily transformed into a "motheravenger." My analysis of the story will focus on the significance of Noemí's identification with the maternal figure. It is important to note that in his story, Cortázar does not fictionalize the Argentine mother, but incorporates a real-life woman, the implications of which will also be discussed.

Art objects—sculptures representing forms of violence—set the story in motion, but the principal plot action develops around two press clippings, the first of which is real and the second fictional, according to Cortázar's epigraph. Each clipping has to do with a mother seeking justice for acts of violence. In the first clipping an Argentine mother denounces the atrocities the Argentine regime has perpetrated against her family. After reading this clipping, Noemí intervenes to rescue a mother who is a victim of violence, and later reads a second clipping, which chronicles a version of the event. The juxtaposition of Noemí's actions to the Argentine mother's testimony seems to convey Cortázar's attempt to come to terms with his frustration occasioned by his inability to help victims of torture in Argentina.

In the story's opening scene, a sculptor, also Argentine and an acquaintance of Noemí, asks her to write a text to accompany his series of sculptures depicting "man's inhumanity to man." Because she wants to see the figures before she decides whether she will write the accompanying piece, Noemí goes to the sculptor's apartment in a seedy neighborhood of Paris. After she views the sculptures, of which she approves for their abstract depiction of violence, she hands the artist a newspaper clipping which is the testimony of an Argentine woman whose family has been victimized by the Argentine military regime. In face of the woman's horrifying account, the sculptor expresses his frustration at the seeming futility of their esthetic endeavors: "Ya ves, todo esto no sirve de nada. . . . yo me paso meses haciendo estas mierdas, vos escribís libros, esa mujer denuncia atrocidades" (*Cc* 2, 362). Noemí tries to cut him off, saying that she also has those thoughts, but they must both continue to protest through their art—he with his sculptures, and she with her writing. As her subsequent behavior reveals, Noemí's attempt to silence the sculptor's self-recrimination is actually an indication of the profound uneasiness she is struggling to deny. The sculptor, apparently unconvinced with Noemí's attempt at self-justification, laments: "siempre es igual, siempre tenemos que reconocer que todo eso sucedió en otro espacio, sucedió en otro tiempo. Nunca estuvimos ni estaremos allí" (*Cc* 2, 364), thus alluding to their remoteness from the front lines of the struggle.

When Noemí leaves his apartment late at night she notices a little girl sitting alone in a doorway. The child leads her to a shabby room where a man is torturing a woman, slowly burning her manacled and naked body with a cigarette. Noemí, undoubtedly still emotionally shaken by the images of the atrocious torture described in the newspaper clipping, grabs a stool and knocks the man unconscious. She frees the bound woman, and the two women tie up the man, turning the tables as they proceed to torture him. The exact fate of the man is not spelled out by the narrator, but we do learn that Noemí eventually stumbles out of the room and hails a cab. At home, she drinks several vodkas and goes to bed. The next day, she calls the sculptor, tells him what happened, and says that this account will be the text to accompany his sculptures.

A few days later she receives a letter from the sculptor along with a newspaper clipping that recounts the very incident in which she participated. The details are the same as those Noemí experienced, except that it occurred in Marseilles, not Paris, and there is no reference to her participation. What is more, we learn that the man was sadistically killed. Noemí returns to the street, looking for the place where she came across the torture scene, but it is not there. However, she does find the abandoned child, who flees from her. A doorwoman asks Noemí if she is the social worker who is coming to pick up this lost child. As the story concludes, Noemí goes to a café to write the end of the story, and leaves it in the sculptor's mailbox.

The acts of violence, which the sculptor represents in abstract form, are played out in the events related by the two press clippings. Each incident (or series of incidents in the case of the first clipping) features a pair of maternal figures. The story's initial maternal space—in the first clipping—is occupied by the real life Argentine mother, Laura Beatriz Bonaparte Bruschtein, and her daughter Irene who is a mother of two small children. The two subsequent, and fictional, maternal figures are the woman being tortured by her partner, and Noemí herself, who, as I will discuss below, momentarily steps into the maternal space.

The juxtaposition of the two groups of women serves to equate them and their experience with violence and torture. Laura Bruschtein and her family are victims of political violence while the other woman is victimized by her domestic partner. The Argentine mother becomes a foil for Noemí, as Noemí's subsequent actions—after reading the first clipping—are her reaction to the profound impact Mrs. Bruschtein's plight has made on her.

It bears reiteration that the Argentine mother, Laura Bruschtein, is never incorporated into the fictional realm, but left intact in her historical integrity. Mrs. Bruschtein details in her testimony the gruesome particulars of a series of kidnappings and assassinations carried out against her family members. First, in December 1975, her daughter Aída Leonora was kidnapped by the Argentine army in the poor community where she worked as a literacy educator. She was taken to an army barracks where she was tortured; she was then shot to death and buried in a common grave. Her mother describes what took place when she sought information regarding her daughter at a police station, surely the most graphic detail of the list of atrocities she denounces: "De mi hija sólo me ofrecieron ver las manos cortadas de su cuerpo y puestas en un frasco, que lleva el número 24" (*Cc* 2, 362). After this, Mrs. Bruschtein initiated a legal proceeding against the Argentine army for assassination. As a result of her legal appeal, her late daughter's fiancé was assassinated on the street, and the military came to her house, looking for Mrs. Bruschtein and her other children. They kidnapped her husband, who was suffering from a heart condition, and she learned that he died during torture. In September of 1976, the sister of Mrs. Bruschtein's daughter-in-law and her fiancé were arrested and killed. The police notified the dead woman's mother that, regrettably, it had been an error. Then, in March 1977, Mrs. Bruschtein's daughter Irene and son-in-law, Mario Ginzberg, were kidnapped from their apartment by army and police operatives, who left their small children abandoned in the doorway of the building. Mrs. Bruschtein, now exiled in Mexico City, expressing "una firme esperanza de que todavía estén con vida" (*Cc* 2, 364), appeals to all the international human rights organizations that they implement the necessary procedures to free her daughter Irene and Irene's husband, Mario.

Although this woman may not have marched with the Madres de la Plaza de Mayo since by 1978 she had taken refuge in Mexico, she clearly represents the spirit of the Madres. She was unafraid to publicly accuse the Argentine army of assassination while she was still living in Buenos Aires, and continued to launch a vigorous protest against the regime, denouncing the kidnapping of her daughter Irene and son-in-law to international human rights organizations, clinging to the hope that they might still be alive. Her choice of words emphasizes the fact that she is filing this petition in her capacity as a mother. She begins her closing sentence, which demands the restitution of Irene and Mario, with the words "Como madre," and uses the words "mi hija" six times in the declaration. This testimony of the atrocities of the "Dirty War," inserted into the Cortázar story, provides a concrete historical reference for the story and produces a profoundly unsettling effect on the fictional characters as well as the readers.

Undoubtedly, it is Noemí's sense of outrage at the plight of Laura Bruschtein, who has been so horribly victimized and who is unable to take revenge on the torturers, what provokes her to take justice into her own hands when she encounters the torture victim. As an anguished reader of the first clipping who subsequently intervenes in the torture scene in France, Noemí creates the overt link between the two clippings. The reference to abandoned children in both situations serves as a more subtle connection between the incidents and provokes Noemí's initial involvement. In Laura Bruschtein's testimony, we read that the armed forces took Irene and Mario Ginzberg away from their home, "dejando a sus hijitos: Victoria, de dos años y seis meses, y Hugo Roberto, de un año y seis meses, abandonados en la puerta del edificio" (*Cc* 2, 364). Immediately after completing the reading of this clipping Noemí leaves the sculptor's apartment and spots the child. Her description of the little girl recalls the plight of the Ginzberg children: "La nena estaba sentada en el escalón de un portal casi perdido entre los otros portales . . . un camión se alejaba con sus débiles luces amarillas" (*Cc* 2, 365). The mention of the truck, although it apparently has no relation to this child, may recreate in Noemí's mind the image of Victoria and Hugo Roberto's parents being carried off in military vehicles. Noemí could have ignored the little girl like the indifferent passerby: "en la acerca de enfrente un hombre caminaba encorvado, la cabeza hundida en el cuello alzado del sobretodo y las manos en los bolsillos" (*Cc* 2, 365). However, her anguish at the thought of the Argentine toddlers abandoned in the doorway surely plays a role in the interest she takes in the solitary child. "Me detuve, miré de cerca," reports Noemí, and when she realizes the child is crying, she inquires "—¿Qué te pasa? ¿Qué haces ahí?" (*Cc* 2, 365).

Noemí's interaction with the child turns her, at least momentarily, into a maternal figure. The woman and child draw together: "le vi la cara de lleno alzada hasta mí . . . [r]epetí las preguntas . . . agachándome hasta sentirla muy cerca . . . sus brazos se tendieron y la sentí pegarse a mí, llorar desesperadamente contra mi cuello; olía a sucio, a bombacha mojada. Quise tomarla en brazos" (*Cc* 2, 365). Noemí's tender concern for the child—lowering her body to the child's level and receiving her embrace, not caring that she is dirty and smells of urine—liken her to a loving, self-sacrificing mother. This represents an about-face for a women who, a moment before she saw the child, described herself in terms diametrically opposed to the qualities of a "good mother": "tengo fama de muy ocupada, quizá de egoísta, en todo caso de escritora metida a fondo en lo suyo" (*Cc* 2, 365).

Her empathy for the helpless child provokes Noemí to join the ranks of the "mad" mothers who put themselves at risk for the sake of their children. Noemí hesitates before entering the building to which the child has led her: "todas las razones de la razón . . . me mostraban el absurdo y acaso el riesgo de meterme a esa hora en casa ajena," but the sight of the girl—"vi a la nena que me esperaba" (*Cc* 2, 366)—makes her abandon her good sense, her "razón." Thus the writer, whose calculating nature is revealed in her insistence on viewing the sculptures before committing herself to writing the script, behaves in a manner that is out-of-character for her. Overcome by her emotion, she will commit a *"locura"* as she intrudes in a private residence late at night to investigate the cause of the child's anguish, an irrational act foreshadowing her participation in the heinous crime that is to follow.

With this temporary role reversal, Noemí becomes a mirror image of Laura Bruschtein. Mrs. Bruschtein is an anguished mother who momentarily becomes a writer in her attempt to seek justice for her children. This calculated, rational reaction is the only recourse open to her since she cannot physically confront her enemy—the Argentine military establishment. Noemí, on the other hand, is a writer who betrays her typically rational self and assumes the mother's passion. In the sculptor's apartment we sense her frustration with her impotence in face of Mrs. Bruschtein's tragedy, and the torture scene that she encounters presents her with the opportunity to act out her desire for revenge. Mrs. Bruschtein's only recourse is to seek justice through international legal circuits, a quest with a dubious outcome given the circumstances. In contrast, Noemí and the unnamed woman seek, and achieve, revenge by their own hands, outside of the law, but the horrific outcome of her passion shocks Noemí who believed herself to be incapable of the tortuous instincts displayed by the Argentine junta.

Noemí's role as a mother is short-lived because when she returns during the daytime to look for the girl, the child flees from her, and the doorwoman thinks that Noemí is a social worker. The girl's rebuff in their diurnal encounter serves to drive home the realization that she cannot fulfill the maternal function. In the end, Noemí is displaced from her fleeting nocturnal incursion into maternal space and reverts back to a stranger who is taken for a government functionary about to institutionalize the child. In other words, the doorwoman's assumption casts her as a professional woman, a nonmother or even—as the government's pale substitute for a mother—an "antimother." As if to underscore her identity as a professional woman, in the last scene we see her writing again as she pens the end of the story in a café.

Noemí's momentary transformation into a maternal figure and reversion back to a writer seems to portray the divide between professional women and mothers as incompatible roles. In the world of Cortázar's stories, mothers are not career women and vice versa. The traits that form part of Noemí's identity as a successful career woman—selfishness and self-absorption—are the antithesis of traditional maternal qualities. The fact that her behavior was out-of-character when she abandoned her rational self to answer the child's plea serves to reinforce her calculating character. Noemí's short-lived assumption of "maternal thinking" causes us to see her in terms of her maternity—or more precisely, her ultimate lack of it. Maternal values, in contrast to those of a career professional, call for a lack of calculation or secondary interests.[6]

If we interpret the second half of the story as fantastic—that Noemí, in her desire to avenge Mrs. Bruschtein's cruel treatment, transported herself to Marseilles to succor the victim of domestic abuse—the character of Noemí evokes an interesting parallel to the daydreaming protagonist of "Historias que me cuento" (see chapter 4, pages 57–62). Similar to Marcelo Macías—the self-proclaimed Walter Mitty who materialized as Oscar the trucker to rescue a stranded woman at night—Noemí, a self-absorbed writer in quotidian life, metamorphoses into a mother-avenger seeking to right the wrongs. And just like Marcelo Macías, when she views her actions from "este lado," she is shocked by what she sees at the depths of her being. While Marcelo sees a vision of himself as a helpless infant, Noemí sees herself as a sadistic murderer. She realizes that, if she abandons her rational self and acts out the intensity of her anger and frustration, she is capable of extreme violence. After this moment of shocking self-revelation, she reverts back into a writer as she proceeds to transcribe the rest of the story. Perhaps this is Cortázar envisioning what he would be capable of if he were to let his impassioned rage take over. Perhaps this is another example (see chapter 4, page 87) of what he meant when he said "me vi obligado a escribir un cuento para evitar algo mucho peor" (*Último round I*, 69).

The complexity of narrative authority in "Recortes" is unpacked by Aníbal González: "Cortázar's choice of a female first-person narrator also places the question of narrative authority within a *mise en abyme*: Do we read the story as if it were written by Noemí? or by Cortázar writing as Noemí? or by Cortázar writing as Cortázar writing as Noemí?" (240). The ambiguous nature of the narrative authority makes more intriguing this narrator's new relationship to maternal space in comparison to other stories, since, as discussed above, the authorial stance momentarily fuses with the maternal role instead of objectifying her as "Other." The female narrator of "Recortes" so completely identifies with the victimized women/mothers that she steps into the space of the mad mother/frenzied woman to take revenge on a male perpetrator of violence. González points out that in her desire for retribution, Noemí "ends up displaying the same dark impulses as the male power-figures" (244).

Another difference comes into play with Cortázar's decision to use a female narrator: if a male character were to identify with the mother figure, his gender identity would be threatened, but this is not the case with a female character. Thus the narrator's identification with the mother is not a gender issue, rather, her identity as the human being she believed herself to be is turned upside down. In "Recortes," finally, Cortázar's conceptualization of the mother's/woman's role has shifted—instead of a depository for the projection of male fantasies, female space becomes a locus to problematize the divide between the victimizer and the victimized.

"Recortes" can be read as a crisis in Cortázar's personal sense of ethics of writing, as argued compelling by González: "The writer's craft is a sublimated version of the mechanisms of aggression used by those in power and those who wish to have power. To write is to cut, to wound, to hack away at something that is (or seems to be) alive: language, words, texts" (250). In light of González's observations, we can also consider Cortázar's refusal to fictionalize Laura Bruschtein and her family—or any Madre de la Plaza de Mayo for that matter—as an ethical decision on his part. In other words, Cortázar refuses to wield his power as a master writer over a group of individuals who have suffered so much. At the same time, however, he cannot stop writing because it is his way of sublimating his murderous impulses toward the victimizers, impulses that would render him their equal.

Finally, the grafted *recorte* with its horrifying account of the sadistic and brutal violence of the Argentine military regime, along with Cortázar's resistance to the fictionalization of the Argentine victims of violence, throws the story off-balance, tipping it into historical reality, the realm of the testimonial and journalism. This gestures toward Cortázar's personal involvement with the cause of human rights, some examples of which are his essays and speeches and his work on the Bertrand Russell Tribune, which investigated and publicized cases of human rights violations in Latin America. Cortázar's activities on behalf of justice in Latin America recalls a statement from his letter to Roberto Fernández Retamar: "De la Argentina se alejó un escritor para quien la realidad . . . debía culminar en un libro; en París nació un hombre para quien los libros deberán culminar en la realidad" (*Oc* 3, 36). This is another version of his ethics of writing, and his essay "Nuevo elogio de la locura" is an example of his commitment to political reality and human suffering.

"Nuevo elogio de la locura":
Motherhood, Madness, and Cortázar's "zona sagrada"

WHO'S MAD?

"This is a matter of no concern to us. These women are mad," declared an official in the office of the president of the Argentine Republic when questioned about the campaign on behalf of the disappeared (Simpson and Bennett 152). The women in question, when they heard about this derisive remark, quickly assumed the label, calling themselves "*Las locas de la Plaza de Mayo.*"

"*To talk about madness,*" Shoshana Felman tells us, "is always, in fact, *to deny it.* However one represents madness to oneself or others, to represent madness is always, consciously or unconsciously, to play out the scene of the denial of *one's own* madness" (*Writing and Madness* 252).

Who is mad anyway? Is it the government who institutes a campaign to ensure national security by hunting down dangerous subversives? Or is it the weeping mothers of the supposed subversives, who have the audacity to parade around the square in front of the presidential palace, no less, demanding government accountability for their missing children?

In his journalistic essay "Nuevo elogio de la locura," Cortázar plays with the concepts of reason and madness, explaining how the regime's use of the term *locas* to neutralize and ridicule the Madres has boomeranged on the generals, resulting in an outpouring of support for the Madres' cause. Cortázar also points out that the recent change in leadership in the junta—the replacement of the relatively moderate Viola by the hard-liner Galtieri—was provoked by the activity of the Madres, and therefore, Galtieri should be grateful to the Madres for the fact that he ended up in power. After concluding his discussion of this set of paradoxes, which seem to complement one another insofar as they demonstrate the impact of the mothers' campaign, Cortázar exclaims "Sigamos siendo locos, madres y abuelitas de la Plaza de Mayo" (*Oc* 3, 323),[7] thus placing himself squarely in the camp of the Madres by joining them in their so-called madness.

In order to provide context and perspective for Cortázar's focus on the mothers' "madness" to denounce the regime, my analysis will first consider how and why the regime attempted to use the concept of madness to discredit the lamenting women, and how the Madres were able to embrace the epithet to their advantage. We will then look at how Cortázar's essay taps into this dialogue to express his solidarity with the Madres, and discuss the significance of Cortázar's identification with their "maternal madness."

Jean-Pierre Bousquet, reporter for the *France-Press* in Argentina during the military dictatorship, provides an account of the government officials' attempt to convince him of the mothers' madness, and the

Madres' decision to assume the term. In a meeting with government officials in the *Casa Rosada*, Bousquet expresses his concern about the *desaparecidos*, and Captain Corti, director of Public Relations for the Argentine government, and his assistant try to dismiss the issue as nonexistent:

> "¿Qué desaparecidos?" pregunta Corti. "No hay más que en la mayoría de los países." . . . "Usted no pretenderá que nos ocupemos de los divagues de esas locas", me contestó uno de los ayudantes de Corti. "Espero que usted no crea en sus historias. Es suficiente que un joven o una joven se fuguen, para que se los considere como desaparecidos. Sin contar aquellos que formaban parte de una banda de delincuentes subversivos sin que sus padres hayan notado nunca nada. Pasaron a la clandestinidad, donde fueron muertos o secuestrados por sus compañeros cuando decidieron abandonarlos y ahora quieren cargar eso sobre nuestras espaldas . . . [sus padres] habrían hecho mejor ocupándose antes de sus 'chicos'." (Bousquet 56)

Thus, Corti insists that there is no particular problem with disappeared persons in Argentina, and his assistant joins in, exhorting the reporter not to believe the ramblings of those madwomen whose missing children are either runaways or subversives who were kidnapped or killed by their fellow gang members. Casting the blame for the disappearances back on parents who did not notice or correct their children's supposed involvement in delinquent activities, he implicitly accuses the women of "bad mothering."

When Bousquet recounts the words of the government officials to the Madres, one of them seizes on the idea of embracing the label intended as derogatory, and requests of the French reporter that he and other foreign correspondents disseminate it:

> Las locas . . . las locas de Plaza de Mayo, he ahí un bonito nombre de guerra. Está adoptado. Escríbelo así, y que también tus colegas lo hagan. Ustedes, los corresponsales de la prensa extranjera, deben hacer saber al mundo que un grupo de locas no se resigna a sufrir en silencio el yugo de esta dictadura y elevan sus gritos al cielo para reclamar la verdad sobre la suerte de sus hijos desaparecidos. (Bousquet 58)

Bousquet goes on to tell how the image of the "madwomen" caught on in the public imagination: "la opinión internacional que desde hace varios meses ya, se interesa en estas curiosas 'locas', y está más y más inquieta por las informaciones que le llegan de la Argentina y vendrá en su auxilio" (Bousquet 81).

What is the power of the concept of madness that it passed like a hot potato from the government official's lips to the Madres' self-definition and then to the popular imagination? How were the Madres able to take this derisive term and use it to their advantage? What do we make of the fact that Cortázar chose to make madness the focal point of his essay in defense of the Madres? Why is he jumping feet-first into what seems to be the space of female hysteria, which he struggled to disown in early stories, such as "Las Ménades" or "La puerta condenada"?

To proceed in parts, first of all, why did the government officials resort to calling the Madres crazy, a ploy that, as Cortázar and Bousquet explain, turned out to be a major strategical error on their part? The regime's use of the term *locas* to discredit the women's appeal corresponds to a long tradition of claiming mental illness as a way of sublimating unruly women. Frosh's analysis of social organization explains how madness and femininity are aligned: reason is equated with masculinity, and since rationality conventionally demarcates the boundaries of mental health, femininity becomes marginalized as the reverse of mental health. "Where reason breaks down, madness ensues" (Frosh 90). Clearly the Argentine government officials meant to imply that these women were hysterical, the most common understanding of hysteria being a psychical conflict expressed through sudden outbreaks of emotional crises accompanied by theatricality (Laplanche and Pontalis 194). Hysteria has been considered the illness of the Other, typically the feminine Other, and the ancients thought it was caused by a wandering uterus. The recommendation was marriage and pregnancy—thus a cure by submission to the yoke of patriarchy (Bernheimer and Kahane 1–3). The regime, presuming to speak from a righteous position of patriarchal power, attempted to cast the seemingly hysterical women as sick, unbalanced deviants, individuals in a position of powerlessness. Due to the high respect afforded mothers in Argentine culture, coupled with the fact that the regime called for a return to Occidental and Christian values,[8] considering the mothers as enemies of the state would be much too risky. On the other hand, calling them *locas* would serve to marginalize them while still retaining them within the community. Thus the government officials played the gender card in their attempt to deny the truth behind the mothers' appeal, upping the ante of the prevailing sexual politics.

Another justification for calling them crazy is that from a stand-point of political strategy, the Madres' campaign was indeed irrational insofar as they rejected a conventional political model of participation based on the rational calculation of costs and benefits, substituting it with one based on sacrifice (Taylor 196). As unarmed elderly women who openly confronted a vicious military regime, they were putting themselves at grave bodily risk for the sake of their children.

What fascinated the public with the madwomen? The suspicion that they were not really mad? The realization of the sheer desperation that must have driven them to this point? The fact that any parent can empathize with the mothers' anguish? As we have seen, the Madres' subversive tactic of appropriating this derogatory label turned out to be a shrewd move on their part. In so doing, they agreed that they were indeed crazed by the government's refusal to provide information regarding the whereabouts of their missing children. Embracing the term *locas* deflated its negative connotations at the same time that it communicated the intensity of their grief. And, to reiterate Felman's observation, to talk about madness, no matter how one represents it, is always to *deny one's own madness* (*Writing and Madness* 252). Therefore, by assuming the discourse of madness, the Madres admitted that their rash and desperate behavior may have merited their inclusion in the category of seemingly hysterical women, but with the underlying implication that their actions were an appropriate and justifiable response in view of the extreme and cruel situation in which they found themselves. The mothers' move was subversive because they appropriated the regime's own language to further their antigovernment campaign. Their new battle cry served to call attention to their weakness and underdog status as well as to publicize the plight of their children and the government silence about the kidnappings (Navarro 250).

The Logic of Maternal Madness, or Celebrating the "zona sagrada"

In "Nuevo elogio de la locura," Cortázar conceptualizes the internal conflict in Argentine society—manifested through the clash between the mothers' demand for an explanation for their missing children and the junta's claim that these women are crazy—as a confrontation between two antagonistic orders. The contours of these opposing realms— the Mothers and the generals—are sketched when he speaks of what happened when the "hired assassins of the Argentine military junta" called the Madres *locas* to neutralize and ridicule them:

Estúpidos como corresponde a su fauna y a sus tendencias, [los generales] no se dieron cuenta de que echaban a volar una inmensa bandada de palomas que habría de cubrir los cielos del mundo con su mensaje de angustiada verdad. (*Oc* 3, 321)

Lo irracional, lo inesperado, la bandada de palomas, las Madres de la Plaza de Mayo irrumpen en cualquier momento para desbaratar y trastocar los cálculos más científicos de nuestras escuelas de guerra y de seguridad nacional. (*Oc* 3, 322)

The generals represent a rigid and limited order that bases its claim to "esa rázon que tanto enorgullece al Occidente" (*Oc* 3, 321) on science and technology, the "knowledge and logic" of the military schools. They use their "slogans de orden, disciplina y patriotismo" (*Oc* 3, 323) to justify their kidnappings, torture, and assassinations. Their flaw, their stupidity, according to Cortázar, is their failure to take into account the powerful order from which the mothers emanate, characterized as "[l]o irracional, lo inesperado, la bandada de palomas, las Madres de la Plaza de Mayo" (*Oc* 3, 322) disseminating "su mensaje de angustiada verdad" (*Oc* 3, 321). This submerged realm, the mothers' truth, which has burst forth to undermine the calculations of the generals, speaks of the human emotion vested in the mothers' tragedy of their missing children, and of the maternal love that has driven them to their bold and desperate protest.

At first glance, Cortázar's depiction of this struggle seems to be consistent with the order versus irrationality paradigm that runs throughout his work, beginning with the stories of *Bestiario*. At the same time, the conflict between the generals and the Madres reflects the binary configuration characterizing a basic mode of perceiving reality whereby the masculine self represents reason and order, and the feminine other is equated with the irrational and chaotic (see page 6 of chapter 1). The patriarchy attempts to assert its pretense to domination based on anatomy, while the subversive feminine element threatens to upset their control (Frosh 87). But Cortázar's description of the current situation in Argentina focuses on the *crisis* in the patriarchal narrative based on the generals' loss of control over the female space. He further undermines the insidious gender polarity by identifying himself—gendered male— with the mothers' so-called madness, and by pointing to the truth underlying their "madness."

Cortázar sets forth his approach to reality in his now-classic treatise on the fantastic short story, "Algunos aspectos del cuento." He explains that he suspects there exists another more secret and less accessible order that has guided his search for a literature transcending the false realism that believes that all phenomena can be described and explained by the philosophical optimism of the eighteenth century (*Oc* 2, 368). As discussed in chapter 1, Noé Jitrik employs the term "*zona sagrada*" to describe the presence in Cortázar's work of this secret, truer order, which is at odds with a more limited and circumscribed mentality. Citing the basic paradigm structuring the stories of *Bestiario*, Jitrik describes a conflict between opposing spaces, which he calls "la zona sagrada" and "el mundo de los otros" or "la anti zona sagrada." The zona sagrada, as Jitrik characterizes it, is inner irrationality, which must hide itself from "la racionalidad de los otros" (49).[9] For example, in "Carta a una señorita en París," Sara the maid insists on imposing her sense of order on the untidiness caused by the mischievous little rabbits that the protagonist vomits from time to time. Sara, Jitrik points out, illustrates "la estúpida dureza y arbitrariedad frente al alumbramiento que supone la aparición de una zona sagrada" (56).

The expulsion of this invading force, or uncontainable emotion, explains Jitrik, breaks a state of equilibrium. The characters must operate within the confines of the zona sagrada and "los otros." The tug-of-war between the two opposing forces results in an unequal struggle with dramatic consequences. The triumphs of the "zona sagrada sobre el mundo de los otros son efímeros, pero son los que valen" (56), and when it is exteriorized, "la zona sagrada . . . termina por resplandecer y . . . se generaliza al transmitirse cubriendo todo el vivir del que la contenía" (52). For instance, in the conclusion of "Omnibus," the emergence of the two passengers hand in hand means that "juntos pueden resistir, una reivindicación respeto de un orden opresivo y limitado, más arbitrario todavía en el odio del conductor" (59). And at the end of the story "Bestiario," when the tiger roaming the estate kills sadistic El Nene, the zona sagrada emerges, Jitrik comments, in an almost glorious and indisputable recognition of justice (58).

In "Nuevo elogio de locura," the manner in which Cortázar portrays the so-called madness or irrationality of the Madres makes their protest resemble a manifestation of the zona sagrada that clashes with the logic of the generals who become "los otros" or the "anti zona sagrada." Not unlike the miniature rabbits in "Carta a una señorita en París" or the tiger in "Bestiario," the Madres' truth is envisioned by Cortázar as a flock of doves that burst forth from a hidden, but truer sphere, shattering the false quotidian reality that attempted, unsuccessfully, to conceal or repress or them. Thus the logic of the military corresponds to Cortázar's concept of a naive, false realism that was ignorant of the power of the submerged, but truer realm of the Mothers' logic, "la lógica de la locura" (*Oc* 3, 322). The Argentine people, then, are analogous to Cortázar's fictional characters that are caught in the tug-of-war between the two polarized forces. Both the Madres and the generals presume to represent the nation: the generals proclaim their "slogans de orden, disciplina y patriotismo" (*Oc* 3, 323), while the Madres are "las palomas de la verdadera patria" (*Oc* 3, 323). Thus the Argentine people must take a stand with one of these two opposed and irreconcilable versions of true nationhood. Of course, Cortázar ends the essay by taking his stand with the Madres and urging all Argentines to do the same.

While the above comparison draws a parallel between the portrayal of the zona sagrada in *Bestiario* and in "Nuevo elogio," a closer examination brings out their differences, which reveal the dramatic evolution in Cortázar's thinking. In the stories of *Bestiario*, the protagonists' relationship to the zona sagrada was highly conflictive. This zone of inner irrationality was zealously safeguarded and seemingly shameful to those who experienced it; and to the "others"—the rest of society—it was antisocial and unacceptable. Its exteriorization invariably resulted in ominous consequences. My analysis in chapter 1 identified it as a phobic symptom of the censored desire for the maternal womb. Thus, as repudiated sexuality, it carried the opprobrium of regressive narcissism (Frosh 112).

However, in "Nuevo elogio de la locura" it is no longer *repressed*, but rather *expressed* as the representation of a luminous truth. No longer a phobic *symptom* of the shameful incestuous desire, now it is a celebrated *symbol* of the maternal bond of love. Here, where Cortázar employs the zona sagrada paradigm in a nonfictional piece to describe historical reality, his concept of this "secret realm" takes on a new, political, meaning, and no longer represents a threat to gender identity. Within this context of collective political action, the mother-infant bond becomes a force for human rights. A symbol of the mothers' bold and seemingly irrational protest against the crimes of the military regime, it is exteriorized and exhibited publicly for all to see. It has a positive, life-affirming value, testifying to Cortázar's personal commitment to the cause of human rights in Argentina. As Jitrik observes, the zona sagrada concept could have lead to "una vía muerta de enroscamiento y narcisismo de no haberse producido una ampliación" (62), and in "Nuevo elogio" it opens up to the concerns of mankind, an identification with the victims of torture, as Cortázar reaches out to embrace humanity. Of course, this transformation of the zona sagrada parallels Cortázar's personal metamorphosis from an elitist, apolitical stance in the 1940s and early 1950s to the deep political commitment that he came to embrace after he moved to Paris and which he describes in terms of a religious conversion.[10] It was Cortázar's belief in socialism and advocacy of human rights that gave him hope, and faith in a better way for humanity.

Following the tracks of Cortázar's imagery in "Nuevo elogio," we uncover evidence that points to the essence of this sacred, irrational zone as the primordial bond between the mothers and their children as infants. Cortázar's symbol for the Madres is doves; first he refers to them as "palomas de angustiada verdad," and later as "palomas de la verdadera patria." The "anguished truth" is the mothers' right to an explanation for their missing children. The "palomas," in addition to their traditional iconic value as bearers of peace, are an allusion to the *pañuelos* or white headscarves worn by the Madres, which became one of their highly visible symbols. Originally, these head scarves were *pañales*—the diapers of their missing children, which Argentine mothers keep as mementos, according to the testimony of the Madres.[11] This information allows us to expand the list of metaphors and metonymies Cortázar sets up in the appositive he uses to characterize the Madres: *lo irracional, lo inesperado = la bandada de palomas = Madres = pañuelos = pañales.* This is a highly charged string of associations, with the symbolic (or real) diapers calling to mind the bond formed between the mothers and their children as infants. Thus ultimately, this primordial tie is the fiercely unrelenting and implacable emotional element that the generals, with their short-sighted and naive military logic, based on blind faith in science and technology, did not take into account, and which finally would bring them down.

Therefore, that which was a strongly censored taboo in *Bestiario*, the essence of the zona sagrada, is extolled here as the mother-infant bond, the connection to the pre-Oedipal mother. The Madres, Las Locas de la Plaza de Mayo, defiantly display it in public by wearing the diaper on their heads. The diaper is surely a "loaded" symbol. Once it hugged the babies' bottoms and collected their excrement; now the mothers demonstrate their self-effacing devotion to their children as they wrap it around their heads. It is noteworthy that Freud considered the baby's feces, its precious internal contents, as a gift. These diapers—which the mothers have kept as a remembrance of that gift and now parade in the street—symbolically testify to the lasting quality of the mother-infant bond. While the regime considers their children—now young adults— nameless subversives who agitate against the interests of the country, the mothers' demonstration resists and confronts that characterization by showing that they are loved children of grief-stricken mothers. The irrational element that drives "la demencial obstinación de un puñado de mujeres" (Oc 3, 322) is that implacable bond. And the logic of the mother-child bond—"la lógica de la locura"—transcends the cruel and cold logic of the generals. Thus the diapers/head scarves in Cortázar's essay symbolically metamorphosize into "palomas de la verdadera patria," doves that will spread the message of the anguished truth to other Argentines and the rest of the world. Indeed, the revelation of these crimes did deal a severe blow to the junta's credibility and legitimacy.

The conclusion of the essay represents a climactic moment in the development of Cortázar's thinking,[12] as he steps unhesitatingly into the zona sagrada, identifying with the Madres in their "madness":[13]

> Sigamos siendo locos, madres y abuelitas de la Plaza de Mayo . . . Sigamos siendo locos, argentinos: no hay otra manera de acabar con esa razón que vocifera sus slogans de orden, disciplina y patriotismo. Sigamos lanzando las palomas de la verdadera patria a los cielos de nuestra tierra y de todo el mundo. (Oc 3, 323)

Assuming for himself the madness of the mothers and exhorting all Argentines to do the same, Cortázar breaks down the gender-based strategy of the generals who attempted to belittle the Madres by reducing them to a clutch of hysterical women. Cortázar's use of parallel structure: "Sigamos siendo locos/Sigamos lanzando las palomas de la verdadera patria" functions to equate "being mad" with "telling the truth to the world about what is happening in Argentina." The identification of all Argentines with the "locura" will expose the hidden truth of the kidnapped, tortured, and murdered Argentines. In the dangerous atmosphere of the military regime, this sinister and repressed truth—which the generals attempted to deny or to justify with their appeals to national security and Western and Christian values—could only be expressed as the locura of aggrieved mothers made bold by their desperation.

Cortázar's closing declaration juxtaposes two concepts of national allegiance: the generals' patriarchal order based on "slogans de orden, disciplina y patriotismo" must be engulfed and obliterated by "las palomas de la verdadera patria," the maternal order that speaks of the power and truth of the maternal bond. In the context of the military dictatorship in Argentina, where patriarchal thinking was carried to a sinister extreme, the traditional "male" sphere represents the cruel excess of authoritarian control. Feminine space, on the other hand, becomes a camp from which to contest this abuse of power and call for justice.

Cortázar's self-inclusion in the Madres' "madness" in "Nuevo elogio" is the culmination of his evolving depiction of female space. Mother is no longer the threatening Other; instead he embraces and identifies with the maternal bond. In fact, we all become aggrieved mothers as we identify with their cause to fight against the cruelty of the military regime, expose their lies, and discover the truth behind the missing persons. In the situation of the dictatorship in Argentina, when the military regime becomes a loathsome embodiment of paternal authority, Cortázar fuses with the female sphere to find truth and justice, "la verdadera patria." Cortázar's maternal imagery has come full circle. No longer the dreaded pre-Oedipal mother who is a product of narcissistic fantasizing, the mother figure is embraced as a life-affirming force, an activist for human rights. Ultimately, with the mediation of the collective political agenda—his commitment to human rights—Cortázar overcomes his guilty obsession with the maternal body and envisions the maternal bond as a life-affirming value.

Conclusion

❧

As the present study has attempted to demonstrate, Cortázar's conception of the feminine, or female space, plays a pervasive and crucial role in his literary universe. Initially, female space means that "first bond"—the maternal womb. Cortázar's yearning to return to this utopian space, combined with the fear of his forbidden desire, resulted in a futile attempt to delimit the feminine within rigid boundaries. Futile because Cortázar's keen intuition sensed the fissures in these boundaries, that he was invaded by "the feminine." His ambivalence in regard to female space, the struggle to expel "the feminine within" and separate from the powerful, engulfing mother, generated many memorable fantastic stories. This ambivalence carried over to his depiction of love relations, as would-be lovers became another version of the desirable yet dangerous mother.

Gradually, he became more at ease with female subjectivity and less controlling with his female characters—he gave them greater latitude in his stories, at times allowing women to expose the chauvinism of their male counterparts. Of course, this literary development was an outgrowth of his personal evolution: he retracted his earlier male chauvinistic pronouncements, apologizing repeatedly to women for having coined the term *lector hembra* to refer to the passive reader. At the same time, his rapprochement with the feminine was uneven, with setbacks along the way.

Cortázar's female space is key to his conceptualization of his national identity. The changing portrayal of certain female characters dramatizes the evolution in how he, as an Argentine residing in France, conceived his relationship to his country. The Argentine female characters who embody his abandoned homeland first represent the abandonment of his mother(land), next the guilt and frustration of the exiled

171

Argentine during the military dictatorship, and finally, his regret for his previous failure to understand and connect with the popular classes in Argentina.

The culmination of Cortázar's use of female space occurs with his new access to the feminine via the political sphere. As he praises the mothers' bold protest against the repressive regime in Argentine, the feminine takes on an expansive significance in his essay. Joining in the so-called madness of the justice-seeking Madres, he fuses with maternal space to denounce the abuses of patriarchal rule, finding truth and power in the maternal bond. With this new valorization of female space—a camp from which to contest state-sponsored terrorism and rally for justice—his depiction of femininity evolves from "woman as problem" to "woman as solution."

Cortázar's life and works encompass a dramatic evolution in his personal relationships and political attitudes. In the early 1950s he was a self-admitted elitist. His "discovery" of the Cuban Revolution in 1963 marked the beginning of his deep commitment to popular political causes: social change and human rights in Latin America. His highly autobiographical literary work reflects the development in his thinking, and through it we can detect the "crisis" in the master narrative: the male narrator who no longer is certain that he is in sole possession of reason and truth, who has "lost control" over "the feminine," is no longer able to expel the irrational from himself and banish it to the margins. Ultimately, we witness a breakdown in the insidious gender polarity—male versus female is no longer a charged category as Cortázar reaches out to embrace humanity. This changeover in sensibility, of course, was not isolated or unique to Cortázar, but rather a product of his keen sensitivity and attunement to the changing times in which he lived.

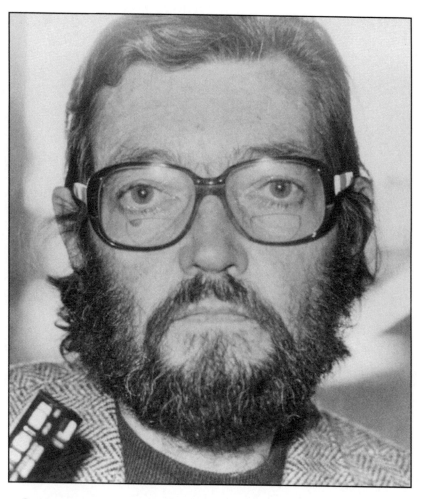

Cortázar c. 1982. "Anabel sería incapaz de imaginar este cuento—si vive, si todavía anda por ahí, vieja como yo" ("Diario para un cuento"). Courtesy of Carmen Balcells Literary Agency.

Anabel would never imagine this story—if she's alive, if she's still out there, old like me. (Diary for a story, translation mine).

Notes

∾

Chapter 1. Introduction: Cortázar's Female Space and the Configuration of Masculinity

1. For a full account of the controversy surrounding Cortázar and his "political literature," see the chapter entitled "The Brawl Outside: Literature and Politics" (121–150) in *Understanding Julio Cortázar* by Standish. For his polemic with Liliana Heker regarding his exile and his remark about "genocidio cultural," see Heker's "Polémica con Julio Cortázar." Cortázar's polemics are also discussed in newspaper articles by Mudrovcic, "El baúl de los insultos," and Mazzone, "Maneras del exilio."

2. Carlos J. Alonso, ed. Also in line with new revisionist readings of Cortázar is Sorensen's article "From Diaspora to Agora: Cortázar's Reconfiguration of Exile."

3. Cortázar, *Cartas* (3 vols.).

4. Two critics who have discussed the change in Cortázar's depiction of women are Sommer, "A Nowhere for Us," and Cedola, "El oficiante y el acólito."

5. "Notas sobre la 'zona sagrada' y el mundo de los 'otros' en *Bestiario* de Julio Cortázar," in Jitrik, *El fuego de la especie. Ensayos sobre seis escritores argentinos.* Pagination is from this edition. First published in *La vuelta a Cortázar en nueve ensayos,* Ed. Carlos Pérez.

6. Since Jitrik's article was initially published in 1969, prior to the publication of Cortázar's last four story collections, he was referring to the entirety of Cortázar's work published up to that moment. However, Jitrik's statement proved to be visionary because—as will be borne out by the present study—Cortázar's work did continue to evolve along the lines Jitrik indicates.

7. Presented initially in 1975, this study predates Cortázar's last three collections of stories.

8. "A Nowhere for Us: The Promising Pronouns in Cortázar's 'Utopian' Stories."

9. Articles by Standish ("Another Glance at Marini's Island") and Morell ("Para una lectura psicoanálitica de 'La puerta cerrada' y 'No se culpe a nadie' ") previously analized the presence of the birth trauma in "La isla al mediodía" and "No se culpe a nadie," respectively, but Prieto was the first to identify and systematize its pervasiveness in Cortázar's work. Prieto's analysis of the generative mechanism of Cortázar's recurrent obsessions is first presented in his article "Cortázar's closet" (1998), and further developed in the chapter dedicated to Cortázar in his book *Body of Writing* (2000).

10. One of Cortázar's remarks reported by Peri Rossi seems to confirm that he subscribed to the reason versus emotion concept of gender difference: "A mí me gusta hablar con las mujeres –decía a menudo Julio, con más frecuencia en sus últimos años—. Los hombres son demasiado serios, demasiado racionales. Las mujeres hablan con el lenguaje de la emoción, eso que nos cuesta tanto reconocer a los hombres de mi generación, por lo menos" (Peri Rossi 19–20).

11. For one of Cortázar's statements about his mistrust of reason, see "Algunos aspectos del cuento," *Obra crítica/ 2*, pages 365–385; for statements regarding dreams as the origin of his stories, see, for instance, the interview with Picón Garfield, page 89, or the interview with Prego, pages 48, 79, and 99. Sosnowski's extensive studies of Cortázar's *oeuvre* present illuminating readings of how Cortázar's texts play out his profound distrust of Occidental reason. See, for instance, *Julio Cortázar: una búsqueda mítica*, "Conocimiento poético y aprehensión racional de la realidad. Un estudio de 'El perseguidor,' " and " 'Una flor amarilla', vindicación de vidas fracasadas."

12. Regarding *Las armas secretas*, Sommer considers its last two stories, "El perseguidor" and "Las babas del diablo," as belonging to "a distinct period, a moment of unprogrammed self-consciousness," page 239. For my purposes, I will locate it in the second phase, based on the characteristics of the mother figure in "Cartas de mamá."

13. For Cortázar's statements about his story writing as therapy, see, for instance, the interview with Prego, pages 255–257 or the González Bermejo interview, page 31.

14. For the purpose of my study, I include *Las armas secretas* in stage two, and collapse the stories categorized by Sommer as belonging to stages three and four into a single third and final stage.

15. The terms of these categories come from Frosh, page 42.

16. My analysis of the narrator's complicity with the feminine excess in "Las Ménades" is indebted to Borinsky's article, "Figuras furiosas." See this article for an analysis of "female fury" and the narrator's contamination by it in Cortázar's works.

17. Charles Bernheimer and Claire Kahane, editors.

18. This passage is quoted by Frosh on page 23.

19. These descriptions of defensive male behavior, which is characteristic of Cortázar's protagonists, come from Frosh, pages 81 and 112.

20. Sommer discusses this phemonenon in "A Nowhere for Us," page 244, and it is also the focus of her earlier article "Playing to Lose: Cortázar's Comforting Pessimism."

21. Pratt, "Women, Literature, and National Brotherhood," and Masiello, "Women, State, and Family in Latin American Literature of the 1920s."

Chapter 2. The Personal and Cultural Context

1. Biographies of Cortázar have been published by Mario Goloboff (1998) and Miguel Herráez (2001); also in 2001 Cristina Peri Rossi published a personal account of her friendship with Cortázar. Karine Berriot's1988 book, *Julio Cortázar, l'enchanteur*, is a cross between a biography and an essay.

2. "La señorita Cora" and "Ud. se tendió a tu lado" will be further discussed in chapter 4.

3. It has been reported that Cortázar practiced bisexuality at one point in his life. For instance, Stavans says, "After his divorce from Aurora Bernárdez . . . he had been involved with a number of men and women, engaging in bisexual affairs" (61).

4. Letter to Graciela Sola in response to her request for biographic information.

5. Letter to Manja Offerhaus.

6. Letter to Eric Wolf.

7. Letter of Pierre Mertens cited by Berriot, page 258.

8. Goloboff reports that both Dunlop and Cortázar died of leukemia, acknowledging but discounting the rumor that they died of AIDS (285). Peri Rossi presents circumstancial evidence to support her belief that they died of AIDS, which Cortázar acquired when he underwent a massive blood transfusion in southern France. Despite the fact that Carol was much younger than Cortázar, she succumbed more quickly, according to Peri Rossi, because earlier she had had a kidney removed (12–15). Herráez calls the claims that Cortázar died of AIDS "speculative and sensationalist," and cites as cause of death the diagnosis of one of his doctors: chronic myloid leukemia. Herráez adds that this diagnosis is supported by Aurora Bernárdez and other close friends (262–263).

9. Herráez remarks the personal change in Cortázar, from a closed, private man into an outgoing, expansive person, a metamorphosis that Herráez links to Cortázar's infatuation with Cuba (164, 174, 200).

10. In an interview he gave during his visit to Argentina, about two months before his death, he reiterated the unambiguous apology and also criticized Latin American machismo: "En lo que me equivoqué—y ya he pedido disculpas a muchas mujeres—fue en ese concepto de lector-hembra, un lector pasivo. Me lo criticaron con mucha razón pues aceptaba la noción de pasividad, tan típica de nuestro machismo latinoamericano. . . . [E]l machismo es una de las lacras

en América Latina. Nadie se da cuenta de que es machista hasta que alguien lo pone contra la pared y descubre eso" (Bedoián 25).

11. See, for instance, the critiques made by Taylor, pages 183–222, and Rossi, page 146.

Chapter 3. The Omnipotent Mother

1. An earlier version of this analysis was read at the State University of West Georgia International Conference on Despair and Desire in Literature and the Visual Arts in 1996.

2. Benjamin explains and reelaborates the omnipotent mother theory in several of her works, specifically *The Bonds of Love* (1988), "The Omnipotent Mother" in *Representations of Motherhood* (1994), *Like Subjects, Love Objects* (1995), and *Shadow of the Other* (1998).

3. This detail evokes a characteristic of Cortázar's family: biographer Herráez notes the "hipocondría crónica" of his family, along with "un clima de alarma," probably caused the father's sudden and unexpected departure (29).

4. The idea of the marginalizing "unruly women" by claiming they are insane is further developed in chapter 7 in reference to the "mad" Mothers of the Plaza de Mayo, pages 160–170.

Chapter 4. Mothers and Lovers

1. The first version of my analysis of "Historias que me cuento" and "Deshoras" was read at the 1995 meeting of the Latin American Studies Association.

2. A point underlined by Prieto is that Cortázar constantly and artfully masks the forbidden yearning for the mother by using substitutes for the desired mother (*Body of Writing* 59, 61, 63, 65).

3. Sommer tells us that in Cortázar's fourth and last period (according to her categories), which consists of the 1981 and 1983 short story collections, he arrived at "an acknowledgment of the ways in which language can and cannot coincide with the desire for utopia. . . . In Cortázar's last period . . . [h]armony belongs to the Imaginary realm, where the child perceives its mother as an extension of itself, so there is no contradiction between self-love and love for the other. Language, or the Symbolic order, breaks that dyadic relationship and dooms the child to frustrating attempts to recover the paradise of being at one with the other. Cortázar may always have had his doubts about the human capacity to attain harmony, but he understood that desiring and striving after it was constitutive of the human condition. . . . We can think of his utopia therefore, as the site of construction, the very space in language that divides desire from realization and that provides the possibilities for happy slippage" ("A Nowhere" 232). Using Sommer's terminology, we can say that these two stories, which articulate the

longing to return to a state of oneness with the mother, deal with the utopian theme in its purest, literal, sense. The narrators experiment with creating, through the "slippery" discourse of their fantasies, the "utopia [that] will never materialize in a fixed space, nor should it" ("A Nowhere" 234).

4. Of course, the character of Walter Mitty comes from James Thurber's short story, "The Secret Life of Walter Mitty" (1939), about a timid man who dreams of being a hero. There is also a 1947 movie based on the story and with the same title, directed by Norman Z. McLeod and starring Danny Kaye in the role of Walter Mitty.

5. Sommer speaks to the ominous consequences linked to the resolution of desire in reference to Cortázar's stories: "With *Glenda*, and also *Deshoras* (1983), he [Cortázar] apparently learns that no true homecoming is possible, unless it is death" ("A Nowhere" 238), and "While some of the stories [in the 1981 book] in fact reach a resolution of desire, the harmony that they produce is grotesquely homicidal or simply untenable over time" ("A Nowhere" 251).

6. Marcelo's adventures can also be seen as protection against over-stimulation from the mother, as explained in the following passage: "Freud implicitly explains that masculine activity originates in the defensive reversal of passivity, the helpless subjection to overwhelming stimulation. It is this very helplessness in the face of overstimulation from which the mother's activity—nurturing and containing—originally protected the child" (Benjamin paraphrasing A. Christiansen, *Like Subjects* 101).

7. For a detailed analysis of the temporal structure of "Deshoras," see Abdala's article, "Secuencia y temporalidad en 'Deshoras' de Julio Cortázar."

8. My discussion of Sara in the role of nurse is indebted to Sprengnether's analysis of the relationship between Freud and his nurse, page 21.

9. Benjamin revises the traditional theory that the third term that breaks up the mother-child dyad must always be the father. Instead, she views this third term as an effect generated by a symbolic space between the mother and child (*Like Subjects* 96).

10. I am indebted to Benjamin for the terms of the analysis of this phase of Aníbal's relationship with Sara (*Bonds* 151, 164).

11. Sprengnether makes this statement in the context of her discussion of Otto Rank's reinterpretation of the father's role in the castration complex.

12. It is noteworthy that Cortázar says *his mother sent him* to be seen by this dentist, thus, perhaps unwittingly, making his mother an accomplice of sorts of the young female dentist who seduced and tortured him.

13. For a detailed analysis of Cortázar's experimental technique of shifting the personal pronoun in "La señorita Cora" and "Ud. se tendió a tu lado," see Standish, "Adolescence in the Stories of Julio Cortázar."

14. For an insightful analysis of how "Las babas del diablo" enacts Cortázar's theory of the short story, see Schiminovich's article, "Cortázar y el

cuento en uno de sus cuentos." For an incisive comparison of the role of the witness in "Las babas del diablo" and "Apocalipsis de Solentiname," see Sosnowski's article "Imágenes del deseo: el testigo ante su mutación."

15. Apparently Boby's obedience is another autobiographical allusion. Martha Gavensky, an Argentine artist and writer who knew Cortázar as a child, recalls: "Era un chico ingenuo y obediente." (In a cultural section of *Tiempo Argentino*, February 19, 1984, page 8.)

16. For a discussion of "Circe" and Cortázar's use of the Circe myth in his fiction, see Ana Hernández del Castillo, pages 17–41.

17. For a detailed and fascinating analysis of "Los venenos," see Prieto's *Body of Writing*, pages 44–49.

18. The story does not spell out exactly what Pierre did to Michèle, but some type of violence is clearly implied. But at least it was Cortázar's intent to have her killed by Pierre, as he explains in an interview: "el muchacho consigue finalmente acorralar a la chica, la viola y la mata antes de que lleguen los amigos. El cuento termina antes de que se descubra todo, pero todos los datos están dados" (Prego 115).

19. Sommer's statement also applies to the stories "Historia con migalas" and "Las caras de la medalla."

20. My understanding of "Orientación de los gatos" is indebted to Lohafer's superb study: "Preclosure in an 'Open' Story: Julio Cortázar's 'Orientation of Cats.'"

Chapter 5. *Defiant Women, or Coming to Terms with Difference*

1. Larsen, "Cortázar and Postmodernity: New Interpretive Liabilities."

2. Studies presenting these depictions of women include Cedola, "El oficiante y el acólito: roles femeninos en la obra de Cortázar"; Ibsen, "Hacia la puerta del infinito: El papel de la mujer en *Rayuela*"; de Mora, "'Orientación de los gatos' (apuntes para una poética)"; Gyurko, "Art and the Demonic in Three Stories by Cortázar"; Hernández del Castillo, *Keats, Poe, and the Shaping of Cortázar's Mythopoesis*; Borinsky, "Fear/Silent Toys"; Branco and Brandão, "Circe: o Feitiço e o Enigma"; Francescato, "The New Man (But Not the New Woman)"; and Pita, "Manipulaciones del discurso femenino: 'Yo y La Otra' en 'Usurpación' de Beatriz Guido y 'Lejana' de Julio Cortázar."

3. See Muñoz, "El derecho al goce erótico de la mujer en 'Anillo de moebius.'"

4. See note 20, chapter 4.

5. Ferré, in her analysis of "Cambio de luces" explains the social dimension afforded by the *radionovelas*: "Las radionovelas les dan la oportunidad de escapar al mundo pacato y represivo de la clase media a la que pertenecen y refugiarse en un pasado romántico y aristocrático" (*Cortázar, el romántico en su observatorio* 107).

6. As noted in chapter 4, in earlier works, such as "Circe" and "Manuscrito hallado en un bolsillo," the spider imagery was used to evoke the dreaded yet desired female who threatened engulfment and annihilation, but in "Cambio de luces," it is used to describe the crafty, possessive male. Perhaps this gender switch of spiderlike attributes could be considered another indicator of Cortázar's evolution.

7. For an insightful analysis of the representation of art in Cortázar's work see Lanin A. Gyurko's article, "Art and the Demonic in Three Stories by Cortázar."

8. The concept of a woman distanced by art is inspired by Castillo's article "Reading Over Her Shoulder: Galdós/Cortázar."

9. For an analysis of Tito's double, see Chanady's article, "The Structure of the Fantastic in Cortázar's 'Cambio de luces.' "

Chapter 6. "Éurídice, Argentina": Women and the Guilty Éxpatriate

1. This letter is also published in *Cartas 1964–1968*, vol. 2.

2. Sorensen's subtle reading of the 1967 letter to Retamar spells out how Cortázar's construction of his notion of exile was part of his constant negotiation and adjustment of the problematic relationship between culture and society, the intellectual and his audience: "It is in this sense [making Paris the site of a (re-)discovery of Latin America via the ideological commitment to the Cuban Revolution] that he resemanticizes diaspora as agora: it is a peripatetic construction of subjectivity which does more than meets the eye. For the agora which exile turns into has freed itself of the communities needing exclusion in his homeland—the 'negros achinados,' the petits bourgeois . . . The continental leap is operated by this paradoxical transformation of exile into the bridge mediating between hitherto irreconcilable positions. By undergoing a process of de-nationalization, he can erase a class position which blocked solidarity" ("From Diaspora to Agora," 386).

3. For a discussion of women as territory or as national iconic signifier, see for instance, Taylor, *Disappearing Acts*, pages 16 and 95; and Kristeva's essay, "Women's Time." For this portrayal within Latin American literature, see Masiello, *Between Civilization and Barbarism*, and Pratt, "Women, Literature, and National Brotherhood."

4. My sources for the details of the Orpheus myth are Strauss, pages 5–6 and Hasty, page xiv.

5. While Cortázar does not evoke Orpheus' eventual demise to the Maenads in his poem, their mention in regard to the Orpheus myth recalls Cortázar's most gripping depiction of feminine hysteria in the story "Las Ménades" (see chapter 1, pages 14–15).

6. The concept of "passionate patriotism" comes from Sommer's *Foundational Fictions*, which will be discussed in greater detail in regard to the analysis of "El otro cielo."

7. While Cortázar's major novel, *Rayuela*, lies outside the scope of this study, it is important to note its role in this process. Perhaps the most pertinent assessment of the male and females roles in *Rayuela* comes from Colás, who sees female character la Maga as the representation of nature, and Horacio Oliveira (boyfriend of la Maga and *Rayuela's* protagonist) as culture. Colás states that their relationship "might follow a centuries-old trope in writing about Latin America in which it is associated with the body and materiality or immanence and Europe with the mind and spirituality or transcendence. . . . In this tradition, la Maga might represent an American solution, and culture a European solution to the same problem of alienation. In la Maga's case, this would reinforce the gendering of that nature/body as female. . . . This seems especially appropriate considering the respective 'sides' of the novel that each dominates. La Maga occupies the central role in the side entitled 'Del lado de allá.' That is, in Paris, immersed in culture, Horacio seeks as his remedy la Maga, distinguished by her 'lack' of culture and, precisely, by her body. On the other hand, the desire for *cultura* springs from existence on 'this side,' that is, from Buenos Aires. There, European 'civilization' has always seemed to hold the cure for what ails Argentina" (30).

8. See McGuirk for his fascinating reading of the story's psychological, poetico-erotic, and sociopolitical dimensions.

9. This defensive aversion to domesticity which drives the narrator of "El otro cielo" out of Buenos Aires is equally a motive of Horacio Oliveira's flight from Buenos Aires in *Rayuela*, as pointed out by Ortega: "Cortázar turns time and again to the subject of 'the Great Habit,' repeatedly satirizing the everyday routine, the established orders, and conformity . . . Could it be that Oliveira is afraid that he himself may derive from one of the established orders, be it called the family, work or history? . . . His satirical attitude toward a brother who chastens him and toward old people, bosses, or simple women, etc., also indicates the irritated presence of a defense mechanism in Oliveira, who is also the product of a traditional Buenos Aires full of aunts from whom he has fled" (47–48).

10. This refers to the military regime that governed Argentina from 1943 to 1946. A 1943 coup put General Pedro P. Ramírez in power. In 1944, a group inspired by Perón replaced him with General Edelmiro J. Farrell (Di Tella 261–263).

11. For a discussion of literary figures in "El otro cielo," see the articles of Rodríguez Monegal and Young ("La poética"), as well as Schwartz's book, *Writing Paris*, pages 47–48.

12. For an analysis of Cortázar's Parisian stories as a critique of Latin American colonized mentality, see Schwartz, chapter 2, "The Interstices of Desire." Viñas's seminal works present the classical analysis of the meaning of Paris, and the "viaje a París" within Argentine culture.

13. Another parallel between Cortázar and Lautréamont is the ambivalence of the maternal images. In passages from Lautréamont's *Maldoror* we find

the presence of the "Terrible Mother," the enveloping, tender mother, and the fear of incest and castration (Zweig 58–60).

14. Carmosino points out the identification of the narrator with Laurent, explaining it in these terms: "Se mueve en los mundos paralelos del deseo reprimido y el deseo desatado y brutal. El doble funciona como un recurso para violar las barreras impuestas por la sociedad al sexo y al crimen. . . . Por lo tanto se puede decir que el doble aquí abre las puertas a lo prohibido" (90). Reichardt characterizes the connection in the following manner: "la [identificación] del narrador con el joven Cortázar quien—por escritor y sudamericano—se proyecta sobre aquel Lautréamont/Laurent . . . parece compensar sus irrealizables deseos sexuales con la literatura" (206).

15. It is interesting to note that Cortázar uses the Jekyll-Hyde image to describe himself in the interview with Soler Serrano, page 70, and also in the interview with Kerr: "I do not doubt that Jekyll sometimes takes the place of Hyde, or vice versa, and that like every human creature, I am a hodgepodge of contradictions" (Kerr 40).

16. For a discussion of the evolution of Cortázar's political commitment, see Standish's article, "Los compromisos de Julio Cortázar," as well as chapter 6 of his book, Understanding Julio Cortázar, "The Brawl Outside: Literature and Politics."

17. This generalized attitude is explained by Alonso in The Burden of Modernity, page 172.

18. I am indebted to Fröhlicher's observation that Anabel is the virtual author of the story (La mirada recíproca 100). See Sorensen's article "From Diaspora to Agora" for an illuminating reading of Cortázar's fictional texts that mark his separation from the popular classes. Sorensen presents an incisive analysis of how Cortázar's multiple subject positions ultimately serve to revise his initial stance regarding the intellectual's impossibility of social cohesion.

19. Specifically, Cortázar says of "Diario para un cuento": "es un cuento muy pensado" (Prego 50).

20. Trying to keep separate the story's narrator from its author seems like a useless circumlocution, as least in the section that evokes Bioy. For this reason, I will momentarily dispose with the authorial construct, if there is one at this point in the story, and simply call the narrator "Cortázar."

21. I disagree with Fröhlicher's study in one point: specifically, Fröhlicher's assertion that Cortázar is criticizing Bioy. While it may be true that Cortázar ultimately comes off as more ethical than Bioy due to his sincere self-reflection, which allows him to face up to his shortcomings, I do not believe that Cortázar's intention is to pass judgment on Bioy.

22. Cortázar reiterates this sentiment in respect to Peronism in the González Bermejo interview, page 119.

23. Cortázar's anti-imperialist stance surely is not conducive to a speculation that engages the myth of the United States as the land of golden opportunity for immigrants.

Chapter 7. *Women and the "Dirty War"*

1. My understanding of the use of gender metaphors in literature dealing with the military regime is indebted to Masiello's article "Cuerpo/ presencia: mujer y estado social en la narrativa argentina durante el proceso militar."

2. For an analysis of the rhetoric of the Argentine military regime, see Feitlowitz, *A Lexicon of Terror*, especially pages 19–62. Feitlowitz explains that "[t]he generals arrived with a plan, called the Process for National Reorganization. . . . This was a fight not just for Argentina, but, the generals stressed, for 'Western, Christian civilization.' By meeting its 'sacred responsibility' to forever rid the earth of 'subversives,' Argentina would join the concert of nations." (7)

3. For an analysis of "Segunda vez," see the article by Hemingway and McQuade, "The Writer and Politics in Four Stories by Julio Cortázar."

4. This essay is contained in *Argentina: años de alambradas culturales*, pages 82–91.

5. My understanding of "Recortes" as a statement of Cortázar's ethics of writing is indebted to Aníbal González's compelling article, " 'Press Clippings' and Cortázar's Ethics of Writing." Lois Parkinson Zamora's article, "Deciphering the Wounds: The Politics of Torture and Julio Cortázar's Literature of Embodiment," presents an insightful study of the ethical issues of the writer and embodiment of pain, as well as the significance of the female identity of the narrator in "Recortes."

6. The concepts of maternal thinking and maternal values come from Ruddick (see chapter 2, pages 32–33).

7. Nuevo elogio de la locura" is published in *Obra crítica/3*, as well as in *Argentina años de alambradas culturales*. The pagination of my quotations refers to *Obra crítica/3*.

8. Feitlowitz analyzes the rhetoric used by the military to justify their actions; see note 2 of this section.

9. See note 5 of chapter 1.

10. "París fue un poco mi camino de Damasco, la gran sacudida existencial," he tells González Bermejo (12).

11. In *Ni un paso atrás*, the Madres tell how they first chose to use diapers to identify one another: "Entonces empezamos a ver cómo nos identificamos. . . . 'Y, che, y si nos ponemos un pañal de nuestros hijos' (que todas teníamos esa cosa de recuerdo, que una guarda). Y, bueno, el primer día, en esa marcha a Luján, usamos el pañuelo blanco que no era otra cosa, nada más ni nada menos, que un pañal de nuestros hijos" (Madres de Plaza de Mayo 19).

12. In her article, "From Diaspora to Agora," Sorensen explains that Cortázar's role during the seventies and eighties as "a continental spokesperson for the Cuban and Nicaraguan Revolutions and against the brutality of the dictatorships plaguing Latin America—his identity as a public intellectual" allowed him to bridge the gap between himself and his audience (384–385). "For Cortázar has come a long way in shedding the obsession with distinction which we noted in his earlier works," Sorensen points out, "replacing it with a keen sense of the pain and collective anguish which spread not only over his own country, but over the rest of Latin America as well" (386). Thus, Sorensen's reading of Cortázar's nonfictional political texts serves to elucidate the social dimension of Cortázar's essay.

13. It is interesting to note that Cortázar actually did walk with the Madres when he visited Argentina shortly after the collapse of the military dictatorship. Argentine writer Daniel Moyano describes Cortázar's encounter with the Madres: "Acaso por haber acudido tantas veces a él en Europa para que ayudara a denunciar a través de *Amnesty* los asesinatos de la dictadura, las Madres de Plaza de Mayo lo reconocieron, cuando Cortázar se acercó a dicha plaza para ver manifestarse a las madres, lo abrazaron, besaron e incorporaron a la manifestación" (163).

Bibliography

⚛

Works by Cortázar

Cortázar, Julio. *Argentina, años de alambradas culturales*. Ed. Saúl Yurkievich. Barcelona: Muchnik, 1984.

———. *Cartas*, 3 vols. Buenos Aires: Alfaguara, 2000.

———. *Cartas a una pelirroja*. Ed. Evelyn Picón Garfield. Madrid: Orígenes, 1990.

———. *Cuentos completos*/1 and 2. Madrid: Alfaguara, 1994.

———. *Libro de Manuel*. Buenos Aires: Sudamericana, 1973.

———. *Obra crítica*/1, 2, and 3. Madrid: Alfaguara, 1994.

———. "The Present State of Fiction in Latin America." *The Final Island. The Fiction of Julio Cortázar*. Eds. Jaime Alazraki and Ivar Ivask. Norman: University of Oklahoma Press, 1976. 26–36.

———. *Rayuela*. Madrid: Cátedra, 1996.

———. *Salvo el crepúsculo*. Madrid: Alfaguara, 1994.

———. *Último round*. Mexico, D.F.: Siglo XXI, 1974.

Dunlop, Carol and Julio Cortázar. *Los autonautas de la cosmopista o Un viaje atemporal París-Marsella*. Barcelona: Muchnik, 1983.

Interviews of Cortázar

Aguilera, María Dolores. "La escritura, ese exorcismo." *Quimera: Revista de Literatura* 8 (1981): 12–16.

Bedoián, Juan. "Cortázar, el optimismo y la cautela." *Clarín*. 3 December, 1983: 24–25.

Berg, Walter Bruno. "Entrevista con Julio Cortázar." *Iberoamericana: Lateinamerika* 14.2–3, 40–41 (1990): 126–141.

Blázquez, Adelaida and Ramón Chao. "Cortázar: 'Rayuela' fue un libro machista e inocente." *El País. Libro*. Año IV, no. 268. (9 December 1984): 1 and 4.

(Contains portions of interview conducted by Radio France International. Other portions of same interview are published as "Cortázar: La transgresión permanente." *Las Palabras y las Cosas* 2 (3 October, 1991): 11–14.

González Bermejo, Ernesto. *Conversaciones con Cortázar*. México, D.F.: Hermes, 1978.

Harss, Luis. "Julio Cortázar, o la cachetada metafísica." In *Los nuestros*. Buenos Aires: Sudamericana, 1971. 252–300.

Huasi, Julio. "Los bellos mundos de Julio Cortázar." *Nueva Estafeta* 28 (1981): 50–62.

Kerr, Lucille. "Interview/ Julio Cortázar." *Diacritics* 4.4 (1974): 35–40.

Kohut, Karl. "Julio Cortázar." In *Escribir en París*. Frankfurt/Main: Verlag Klaus Dieter Vervuert, 1983. 193–232.

Picón Garfield, Evelyn. *Cortázar por Cortázar*. Jalapa, Mexico: Universidad Veracruzana, 1977.

Prego, Omar. *Julio Cortázar (la fascinación de las palabras)*. Montevideo: Trilce, 1990.

Soler Serrano, Javier. " 'Mis personajes favoritos' Resumen de las más famosas entrevistas en el programa 'A fondo': Julio Cortázar." Tomo I. *Revista Tele/Radio*, Altamira S.A. (n.d.). 67–74.

Sosnowski, Saúl. "Julio Cortázar: Modelos para desarmar." *Espejo de escritores*. Ed. Reina Roffé. Hanover, NH: Eds. del Norte, 1985. 39–62.

Studies of Cortázar's Works and Life

Abdala, Marisa. "Secuencia y temporalidad en 'Deshoras' de Julio Cortázar." *Hispanic Journal* 7.2 (1986): 115–120.

Ainsa, Fernando. "América y Europa: Las dos orillas de identidad en la obra de Julio Cortázar. Significados del viaje iniciático." *Inti: Revista de Literatura Hispánica* 22–23 (1985–86): 41–54.

Alazraki, Jaime. "Doubles, Bridges and Quest for Identity: 'Lejana' Revisited." *The Final Island*. Eds. Jaime Alazraki and Ivar Ivask. Norman: University of Oklahoma Press, 1978.

———. *En busca del unicornio: Los cuentos de Julio Cortázar. Elementos para una poética de lo neofantástico*. Madrid: Gredos, 1983.

———. "From *Bestiary* to *Glenda*: Pushing the Short Story to Its Utmost Limits." *The Review of Contemporary Fiction* 3.3 (1983): 94–99.

———. *Hacia Cortázar: aproximaciones a su obra*. Barcelona: Anthropos, 1994.

———. "Los últimos cuentos de Julio Cortázar." *Revista Iberoamericana* 51.130–131 (1985): 21–46.

Alazraki, Jaime and Ivar Ivask, eds. *The Final Island*. Norman: University of Oklahoma Press, 1978.

Alonso, Carlos J., ed. *Julio Cortázar: New Readings*. New York: Cambridge University Press, 1998.

Aponte, Barbara Bockus. "El niño como testigo: La visión infantil en el cuento hispanoamericano contemporáneo." *Explicación de Textos Literarios* 11.1 (1982–1983): 11–22.

Arrigucci, Jr., Davi. *O Escorpião Encalacrado (a Poética de Destruição em Julio Cortázar)*. São Paulo: Perspectiva, 1973.

Béjar, Eduardo C. "Cartas de/para mamá: Urtexto de dos cuentos de Cortázar." *Discurso literario* 5.2 (1988): 375–388.

Berg, Mary G. "Obsesionado con Glenda: Cortázar, Quiroga, Poe." *Los ochenta mundos de Cortázar: Ensayos*. Ed. Fernando Burgos. Madrid: Edi-6, 1987. 211–219.

Berg, Walter Bruno. "De convergencias, confesiones y confesores ('Diario para un cuento')." *Inti: Revista de Literatura Hispánica* 22–23 (1985–1986): 327–336.

Berriot, Karine. *Julio Cortázar L'Enchanteur*. Paris: Presses de la Renaissance, 1988.

Borinsky, Alicia. "Fear/Silent Toys." *The Review of Contemporary Fiction* 3:3 (Fall 1983): 89–94.

———. "Figuras furiosas." *Río de la Plata Culturas* 1. Centro de Estudios de Literaturas y Civilizaciones del Río de la Plata. 1985: 113–124.

———. "Juegos: una realidad sin centro." *Estudios sobre los cuentos de Julio Cortázar*. Ed. David Lagmanovich. Barcelona: Hispam, 1975. 59–72.

Branco, Lúcia Castello and Ruth Silviano Brandão. "Circe: o Feitiço e o Enigma." *A Mulher Escrita*. Rio de Janeiro: Casa Maria Editorial, 1989. 37–41.

Buchanan, Rhonda Dahl. "El juego subterráneo en 'Manuscrito hallado en un bolsillo.' " *Los ochenta mundos de Cortázar: Ensayos*. Ed. Fernando Burgos. Madrid: Edi-6, 1987. 167–176.

Burgos, Fernando, ed. *Los ochenta mundos de Cortázar: Ensayos*. Madrid: Edi-6, 1987.

Carmosino, Roger. "Forma y funciones del doble en tres cuentos de Cortázar: 'La noche boca arriba,' 'Las armas secretas' y 'El otro cielo.' " *Texto crítico* 2:2 (1996): 83–92.

Castelo, Carla and Leila Guerriero. "El largo camino hacia Europa." *El País Cultural*, no. 258 (14 October, 1994): 2–5.

Castillo, Debra A. "Reading over Her Shoulder: Galdós/Cortázar." *Anales Galdosianos* 21 (1986): 147–160.

Castro-Klarén, Sara. "De la transgresión a lo fantástico en Cortázar." *Lo lúdico y lo fantástico en la obra de Cortázar*. Vol. 2. Coloquio Internacional. Centre de recherches Latino-Americaines, Université de Poitiers. Madrid: Fundamentos, 1986. 181–190.

———. "Desire, the Author and the Reader in Cortázar's Narrative." *The Review of Contemporary Fiction* 3.3 (1983): 65–71.

———. *Escritura, transgresión y sujeto en la literatura latinoamericana.* México, D.F.: Premia, 1989.

———. "Ontological Fabulation: Toward Cortázar's Theory of Literature." *The Final Island.* Eds. Jaime Alazraki and Ivar Ivask. Norman: University of Oklahoma Press, 1978: 140–150.

Cedola, Estela. "El oficiante y el acólito: roles femeninos en la obra de Julio Cortázar." *Nuevo Texto Crítico* 2.4 (1989): 115–128.

Chanady, Amaryll B. "The Structure of the Fantastic in Cortázar's 'Cambio de luces.'" *The Scope of the Fantastic: Theory, Technique, Major Authors.* Eds. Robert A. Collins and Howard D. Pierce. Westport, CT: Greenwood, 1985. 159–164.

Cohen, Keith. "Cortázar and the Apparatus of Writing." *Contemporary Literature* 25.1 (1984): 15–27.

Colás, Santiago. *Postmodernity in Latin America. The Argentine Paradigm.* Durham: Duke University Press, 1994.

Coloquio Internacional. Lo lúdico y lo fantástico en la obra de Cortázar. Centre de recherches Latino-Americaines Université de Poitiers. Madrid: Fundamentos, 1985. Vols. 1 & 2.

Concha, Jaime. "'Bestiario,' de Julio Cortázar o el tigre en la biblioteca," *Hispamérica: Revista de Literatura* 11.32 (1982): 3–21.

Cunha-Giabbai, Gloria da. "Cortázar y su diario de amor, de locura y de muerte." *Estudios en homenaje a Enrique Ruiz-Fornells.* Erie, PA: ALDEEU, 1990. 123–130.

Dixon, Paul B. "Ficción sobre ficción: 'La salud de los enfermos' de Julio Cortázar." *Crítica Hispánica* 8.2 (1986): 137–143.

Domínguez, Mignon. *Cartas desconocidas de Julio Cortázar, 1939–1945.* Buenos Aires: Sudamericana, 1992.

Fazzolari, Margarita. "Una muñeca rota con una sorpresa 'adentro.'" *Lo lúdico y lo fantástico en la obra de Cortázar.* Vol. 1. Coloquio Internacional. Centre de recherches Latino-Americaines, Université de Poitiers. Madrid: Fundamentos, 1986. 195–202.

Ferré, Rosario. *Cortázar: El romántico en su observatorio.* Hato Rey, Puerto Rico: Literal, 1990.

———. "Cortázar y el sentimiento romántico." *Nuevo Texto Crítico* 3 (1989): 117–133.

Filer, Malva E. "El texto, espacio de la vida y de la muerte en los últimos cuentos de Julio Cortázar." *Lo lúdico y lo fantástico en la obra de Cortázar.* Vol. 1. Coloquio Internacional. Centre de recherches Latino-Americaines, Université de Poitiers. Madrid: Fundamentos, 1986. 225–232.

———. *Los mundos de Julio Cortázar.* New York: Las Américas/Anaya, 1970.

———. "Spatial and Temporal Representation in the Late Fiction of Julio Cortázar." *The Centennial Review* 30.2 (1986): 260–268.

Francescato, Martha Paley. "The New Man (But Not the New Woman)." *The Final Island*. Eds. Jaime Alazraki and Ivar Ivask. Norman: University of Oklahoma Press, 1978. 134–139.

Fröhlicher, Peter. "El sujeto y su relato: 'Argentinidad' y reflexión estética en 'Diario para un cuento.'" *Inti: Revista de Literatura Hispánica* 22–23 (1985–1986): 337–344.

———. *La mirada recíproca. Estudios sobre los últimos cuentos de Julio Cortázar.* Bern: Peter Lang, 1995.

———. "Leer un libro de cuentos: *Deshoras* de Julio Cortázar." *Actas del X Congreso de la Asociación Internacional de Hispanistas.* Ed. Antonio Vilanova. Barcelona: Promociones y Publicaciones Universitarias, 1992. 611–616.

Fuentes, Carlos. "Julio Cortázar, 1914–1884." *La Nación* (Buenos Aires) 15 April 1984, Sección 4a: 1.

Gertel, Zunilda. "Funcionalidad del lenguaje en 'La salud de los enfermos.'" *Estudios sobre los cuentos de Julio Cortázar.* Ed. David Lagmanovich. Barcelona: Hispam, 1975. 99–114.

Giacoman, Helmy F., ed. *Homenaje a Julio Cortázar. Variaciones interpretativas en torno a su obra.* New York: Las Américas/Anaya, 1972.

Goloboff, Mario. *Julio Cortázar. La biografía.* Buenos Aires: Seix Barral, 1998.

González, Aníbal. " 'Press Clippings' and Cortázar's Ethics of Writing." *Julio Cortázar: New Readings.* Ed. Carlos J. Alonso. New York: Cambridge University Press, 1998. 237–257.

———. "Revolución y alegoría en 'Reunión' de Julio Cortázar." *Los ochenta mundos de Cortázar: Ensayos.* Ed. Fernando Burgos. Madrid: Edi-6, 1987. 93–109.

González, Eduardo. *The Monstered Self. Narratives of Death and Performance in Latin American Fiction.* Durham: Duke University Press, 1992.

González Echeverría, Roberto. " 'La autopista del sur' and the Secret Weapons of Julio Cortázar's Short Narrative." *Studies in Short Fiction* 8:1 (1971): 130–140.

Gutiérrez Mouat, Ricardo. " 'Las babas del diablo': Exorcismo, traducción, voyeurismo." *Los ochenta mundos de Cortázar: Ensayos.* Ed. Fernando Burgos. Madrid: Edi-6, 1987. 37–46.

Gyurko, Lanin. "Art and the Demonic in Three Stories by Cortázar." *Symposium* 37.1 (1983): 17–47.

———. "Artist and Critic as Self and Double in Cortázar's 'Los pasos en las huellas.'" *Hispania* 65 (1982): 352–364.

———. "Cortázar's Fictional Children: Freedom and Its Constraints." *Neophilologus* 57.1 (1973): 24–41.

———. "Destructive and Ironically Redemptive Fantasy in Cortázar." *Hispania* 56 (1973): 988–999.

————. "Fury in Three Stories by Julio Cortázar." *Revista de Letras* 12 (1971): 511–531.

————. "Man as Victim in Two Stories by Cortázar." *Kentucky Romance Quarterly* 19.3 (1972): 317–335.

Harvey, Sally. "Dominator-Dominatrix: Sexual Role-Play in Julio Cortázar's 'La señorita Cora.' " *Love, Sex & Eroticism in Contemporary Latin American Literature.* Ed. Alun Kenwood. Melbourne/Madrid: Voz Hispánica, 1992. 99–106.

Heker, Liliana. "Polémica con Julio Cortázar." *Cuadernos Hispanoamericanos* 517–519 (1993): 590–604.

Hemingway, Maurice and Frank McQuade. "The Writer and Politics in Four Stories by Julio Cortázar." *Revista Canadiense de Estudios Hispánicos* 13.1 (1988): 49–63.

Hernández del Castillo, Ana. *Keats, Poe, and the Shaping of Cortázar's Mythopoesis.* Amsterdam: John Benjamins, 1981.

Herráez, Miguel. *Julio Cortázar. El otro lado de las cosas.* Valencia: Institució Alfons el Magnànim, Diputació de València, 2001.

Ibsen, Kristine. "Hacia la puerta del infinito: El papel de la mujer en *Rayuela.*" *Mester* 18.1 (1989): 33–40.

Jaffe, Janice A. "Apocalypse Then and Now: Las Casas' *Brevísima relación* and Cortázar's 'Apocalipsis de Solentiname.' " *Chasqui* 23.1 (1994):18–28.

Jitrik, Noé. "Notas sobre la 'zona sagrada' y el mundo de los 'otros' en *Bestiario* de Julio Cortázar." In *El fuego de la especie. Ensayos sobre seis escritores argentinos.* Buenos Aires: Siglo Veintiuno Argentina, 1971. 47–62. Also published in *La vuelta a Cortázar en nueve ensayos.* Ed. Carlos Pérez. Buenos Aires: Viamonte, 1969. 13–30.

Jones, Julie. *A Common Place. The Representation of Paris in Spanish American Fiction.* Lewisburg: Bucknell University Press, 1998.

Kason, Nancy M. "Las 'Pesadillas' metafóricas de Cortázar." *Los ochenta mundos de Cortázar: Ensayos.* Ed. Fernando Burgos. Madrid: Edi-6, 1987. 149–156.

King, Sarah E. *The Magical and the Monstrous. Two Faces of the Child-Figure in the Fiction of Julio Cortázar and José Donoso.* New York: Garland, 1992.

Lagmanovich, David. *Estudios sobre los cuentos de Julio Cortázar.* Barcelona: Hispam, 1975.

Larsen, Neil. "Cortázar and Postmodernity: New Interpretive Liabilities." *Julio Cortázar: New Readings.* Ed. Carlos J. Alonso. New York: Cambridge University Press, 1998: 57–75.

Levinson, Brett. "The Other Origin: Cortázar and Identity Politics." *Latin American Literary Review* 22.44 (1994): 5–19.

Lohafer, Susan. "Preclosure in an 'Open' Story: Julio Cortázar's 'Orientation of Cats.' " *Creative and Critical Approaches to the Short Story.* Ed. Noel Harold Kaylor, Jr. Lewiston, NY: Edwin Mellen Press, 1997.

Mac Adam, Alfred. *El individuo y el otro. Crítica a los cuentos de Julio Cortázar*. Buenos Aires: La Librería, 1971.

"Martha Gavensky lo evoca como ingenuo y obediente." *Tiempo Argentino*, Cultura (19 February, 1984): 8.

Masiello, Francine. "Grotesques in Cortázar's Fiction: Toward a Mode of Signification." *Kentucky Romance Quarterly* 29.1 (1982): 61–73.

Mazzone, Daniel. "Maneras del exilio." *El País Cultural*, no. 258 (14 October, 1994): 14.

McGuirk, Bernard J. "La semi(er)ótica de la otredad: 'El otro cielo.' " *Inti: Revista de Literatura Hispánica* 22–23 (1985–1986): 345–354.

———. "On the semi(er)otics of alterity. Beyond Lacanian limits: Julio Cortázar's 'The Other Heaven.' " In *Latin American Literature. Symptoms, risks and strategies of post-structuralist criticism*. London: Routlege, 1997. 139–155.

Mora, Carmen de. " 'Orientación de los gatos' (apuntes para una poética)." *Coloquio Internacional. Lo lúdico y lo fantástico en la obra de Cortázar*. Vol. 2. Madrid: Fundamentos, 1985. 167–180.

Mora Valcárcel, Carmen de. *Teoría y práctica del cuento en los relatos de Cortázar*. Sevilla: Escuela de Estudios Hispanoamericanos de Sevilla, 1982.

Morell, Hortensia R. "Para una lectura psicoanalítica de 'Después del almuerzo.' " *Discurso Literario: Revista de Temas Hispanas* 2.2 (1985): 481–485.

———. "Para una lectura psicoanálitica de 'La puerta cerrada' y 'No se culpe a nadie.' " *La Torre* 33:123 (1984): 188–199.

Morello-Frosch, Marta. "El discurso de armas y letras en las narraciones de Julio Cortázar." *Lo lúdico y lo fantástico en la obra de Cortázar*. Vol. 1. Coloquio Internacional. Centre de recherches Latino-Americaines, Université de Poitiers. Madrid: Fundamentos, 1986. 151–162.

———. "Espacios públicos y discurso clandestino en los cuentos de Julio Cortázar." *Los ochenta mundos de Cortázar: Ensayos*. Ed. Fernando Burgos. Madrid: Edi-6, 1987. 75–83.

———. "*Octaedro*: O los puentes circulares." *Revista Hispánica Moderna* 39.4 (1976–77): 198–209.

Moyano, Daniel. "Cortázar y los argentinos." *Araucaria de Chile* 26 (1984): 162–164.

Mudrovcic, María Eugenia. "El baúl de los insultos." *El País Cultural*, no. 258 (14 October, 1994): 20–21.

Muñoz, Willy. "El derecho al goce erótico de la mujer en 'Anillo de moebius.' " *Love, Sex & Eroticism in Contemporary Latin American Literature*. Ed. Alun Kenwood. Melbourne/Madrid: Voz Hispánica, 1992. 107–116.

———. "La alegoría de la modernidad en "Carta a una señorita en París." *Inti: Revista de Literatura Hispánica* 15 (1982): 33–40.

Ortega, Julio. *A Poetics of Change. The New Spanish-American Narrative*. Austin: University of Texas Press, 1984.

Paulino, Maria das Graças Rodrigues. "A Perfeição Mortal." *Cadernos de Linguística e Teoria da Literatura* 7.14 (1985): 125–132.

Pérez, Carlos, ed. *La vuelta a Cortázar en nueve ensayos.* Buenos Aires: Viamonte, 1969.

Peri Rossi, Cristina. *Julio Cortázar.* Barcelona: Omega, 2001.

Picón Garfield, Evelyn. *Julio Cortázar.* New York: Frederick Ungar, 1975.

Pita, Beatrice. "Manipulaciones del discurso femenino: 'Yo y La Otra' en *Usurpación* de Beatriz Guido y *Lejana* de Julio Cortázar." *Crítica: A Journal of Critical Essays* (San Diego) 2.2 (1990): 77–83.

Planells, Antonio. *Cortázar: Metafísica y erotismo.* Madrid: Porrúa, 1979.

———. " 'La autopista del sur' o la dinámica de la incomunicación humana." *Explicación de Textos Literarios* 12.1 (1983–1984): 3–9.

———. "Represión sexual, frigidez y maternidad frustrada: 'Verano,' de Julio Cortázar." *Bulletin of Hispanic Studies* 56 (1979): 233–237.

Prieto, René. *Body of Writing. Figuring Desire in Spanish American Literature.* Durham, NC: Duke University Press, 2000.

———. "Cortázar's Closet." *Julio Cortázar New Readings.* Ed. Carlos J. Alonso. New York: Cambridge University Press, 1998. 76–88.

Pucciarelli, Ana María. "Análisis de 'Cartas de mamá.' " *El realismo mágico en el cuento hispanoamericano.* Ed. Angel Flores. México, D.F.: Premia, 1985. 257–274.

Pucciarelli de Colantonio, Graciela. "Los símbolos de la culpa de 'Cartas de mamá.' " *Letras (Univ. Católica Argentina)* 19–20 (1988–89): 79–90.

Puleo, Alicia Helda. "La sexualidad fantástica." *Lo lúdico y lo fantástico en la obra de Cortázar.* Vol. 1. Coloquio Internacional. Centre de recherches Latino-Americaines, Université de Poitiers. Madrid: Fundamentos, 1986. 203–212.

Rama, Angel. "Julio Cortázar, constructor del futuro." *Texto Crítico* 7:20 (1981): 14–23.

———. "Julio Cortázar en su cielo narrativo." *Revista Nacional de Cultura* (Caracas, Venezuela) 34: 2218 (1975): 27–39.

Reichardt, Dieter. "La lectura nacional de 'El otro cielo' y 'Libro de Manuel.' *Inti: Revista de Literatura Hispánica* 22–23 (1985–86): 205–215

Rix, Rob. "Visions of Blighted Youth: Buenos Aires Remembered in the Tales of Julio Cortázar." *A Face Not Turned to the Wall.* Ed. C.A. Longhurst. Leeds: University of Leeds, 1987. 257–276.

Rodríguez Monegal, Emir. "Le 'Fantome' de Lautréamont." *Revista Iberoamericana* 84–85 (1973): 625–639.

Schiminovich, Flora. "Cortázar y el cuento en uno de sus cuentos." *Homenaje a Julio Cortázar.* Ed. Helmy F. Giacoman. New York: Las Américas/Anaya, 1972. 307–317.

Schmidt-Cruz, Cynthia. "De Buenos Aires a París: Los cuentos de Julio Cortázar y la reformulación de su identidad cultural." *Actas del XIII Congreso de la Asociación Internacional de Hispanistas de Madrid 1998.* Vol. 3. Madrid: Castalia, 2000: 411–419.

Schulz, Bernhardt Roland. " 'La señorita Cora' a la sombra del mito." *Tropos* 14.1 (1988): 1–8.

Schwartz, Marcy E. *Writing Paris. Urban Topographies of Desire in Contemporary Latin American Fiction.* Albany: SUNY Press, 1999.

Shafer, José P. *Los puentes de Cortázar.* Buenos Aires: Nuevohacer, 1996.

Sommer, Doris. "A Nowhere for Us: The Promising Pronouns in Cortázar's 'Utopian' Stories." *Discurso Literario* 4.1 (1986): 231–263.

———. "Pattern and Predictability in the Stories of Julio Cortázar." *The Contemporary Latin American Short Story.* Ed. Rose S. Minc. New York: Senda Nueva, 1979. 71–81.

———. "Playing to Lose: Cortázar's Comforting Pessimism." *Chasqui* 8.3 (1979): 54–62.

Sorensen, Diana. "From Diaspora to Agora: Cortázar's Reconfiguration of Exile." *MLN* 114.2 (1999): 357–388.

———. "Presencia de la otredad en *Octaedro*." *The Contemporary Latin American Short Story.* Ed. Rose S. Minc. New York: Senda Nueva, 1979. 44–53.

Sosnowski, Saúl. "Conocimiento poético y aprehensión racional de la realidad. Un estudio de 'El perseguidor', de Julio Cortázar." *Homenaje a Julio Cortázar.* Ed. Helmy F. Giacoman. New York: Las Américas/Anaya, 1972. 427–444.

———. "Cortázar's Other Texts." *The Review of Contemporary Fiction* 3.3 (1983): 100–106.

———. "Imágenes del deseo: el testigo ante su mutación ('Las babas del diablo' y 'Apocalipsis de Solentiname', de Julio Cortázar)." *Inti: Revista de Literatura Hispánica* 10–11 (1979–1980): 93–98.

———. *Julio Cortázar: Una búsqueda mítica.* Buenos Aires: Noé. 1973.

———. "Los ensayos de Julio Cortázar: Pasos hacia su poética." *Revista Iberoamericana* 39 (1973): 657–666.

———. "Pursuers." *The Final Island.* Eds. Jaime Alazraki and Ivar Ivask. Norman: University of Oklahoma Press, 1978. 159–167.

———. " 'Una flor amarilla', vindicación de vidas fracasadas." *Estudios sobre los cuentos de Julio Cortázar.* Ed. David Lagmanovich. Barcelona: Hispam, 1975. 179–190.

Standish, Peter. "Adolescence in the Stories of Julio Cortázar." *The Modern Language Review* 82.3 (1987): 638–647.

———. "Another Glance at Marini's Island." *Neophilologus* 60:4 (1976): 389–396.

———. "Cortázar's Latest Stories." *Revista de Estudios Hispánicos* 16.1 (1982): 45–65.

————. "Los compromisos de Julio Cortázar." *Hispania*: 80.3 (September 1997): 465–471.

————. *Understanding Julio Cortázar*. Columbia, SC: University of South Carolina Press, 2001.

Stavans, Ilan. *Julio Cortázar: A Study in the Short Fiction*. New York: Twayne, 1996.

Teitelboim, Volodia. "Julio Cortázar, violentamente dulce." *Plural* 14-1.157 (October 1984):12–25.

Tittler, Jonathan. "Los dos solentinames de Julio Cortázar." *Los ochenta mundos de Cortázar: Ensayos*. Ed. Fernando Burgos. Madrid: Edi-6, 1987. 85–91.

Trastoy, Beatriz. " 'La salud de los enfermos' de Cortázar: Notas sobre la ficción teatral." *Latin American Theatre Review* 26.1 (1992): 103–110.

Turner, John H. "Sexual Violence in Two Stories of Julio Cortázar: Reading as Psychotherapy?" *Latin American Literary Review* 15.30 (1987): 43–56.

Tyler, Joseph. "El elemento infantil en la ficción de Julio Cortázar." *Los ochenta mundos de Cortázar: Ensayos*. Ed. Fernando Burgos. Madrid: Edi-6, 1987. 157–165.

————. "Repression and Violence in Selected Contemporary Argentine Stories." *Discurso: Revista de Estudios Iberoamericanos* 9.2 (1992): 87–97.

Vargas Llosa, Mario. "La trompeta de Deyá." Prologue to *Cuentos completos*/1. Madrid: Alfaguara, 1994. 13–23.

Villardi, Raquel. " 'Grafitti' Leitura refletida." *Revista Brasileira de Língua e Literatura* 5.11 (1983): 49–52.

Viñas, David. *De Sarmiento a Cortázar: Literatura y realidad política*. Buenos Aires: Siglo Veinte, 1974.

Volek, Emil. " 'Las babas del diablo', la narración policial y el relato conjetural borgeano: esquizofrenia crítica y creación literaria." *Los ochenta mundos de Cortázar: Ensayos*. Ed. Fernando Burgos. Madrid: Edi-6, 1987. 27–35.

Weitzdörfer. Ewald. "¿La patria o las patrias? Observaciones acerca de la concepción del exilio en el cuento 'Cartas de mamá' de Julio Cortázar." *Letras de Deusto* 16:34 (1986): 163–183.

Young, Richard A. "Cuentos de Cortázar entre la historia y la ficción." *Revista Canadiense de Estudios Hispánicos* 15.3 (1991): 531–544.

————. "El contexto americano de un cuento de Cortázar ('El otro cielo')." *Explicación de Textos Literarios* 16.1 (1987–88): 8–17.

————. "La poética de la flor en 'El otro cielo,' de Julio Cortázar." *Kentucky Romance Quarterly* 39.3 (1992): 347–354.

————. *Octaedro en cuatro tiempos (texto y tiempo en un libro de Cortázar)*. Ottawa: Ottawa Hispanic Studies, 1993.

————. "Prefabrication in Julio Cortázar's 'Lugar llamado Kindberg.' " *Studies in Short Fiction* 28.4 (1991): 521–534.

———. " 'Verano,' de Julio Cortázar, 'The Nightmare,' de John Henry Fuseli, y 'the judicious adoption of figures in art.' " *Revista Canadiense de Estudios Hispánicos* 17.2 (1993): 373–382.

Yovanovich, Gordana. "Character Development and the Short Story: Julio Cortázar's 'Return Trip Tango.' " *Studies in Short Fiction* 27.4 (1990): 545–552.

———. "The Role of Women in Julio Cortázar's *Rayuela*." *Revista Canadiense de Estudios Hispánicos* 14.3 (1990): 541–552.

Yurkievich, Saúl. *A través de la trama. Sobre vanguardias literarias y otras concomitancias.* Barcelona: Muchnik, 1984.

———. "Julio Cortázar: Al calor de su sombra." *Lo lúdico y lo fantástico en la obra de Cortázar.* Vol. 1. Coloquio Internacional. Centre de recherches Latino-Americaines, Université de Poitiers. Madrid: Fundamentos, 1986. 9–24.

———. *Julio Cortázar: Mundos y modos.* Madrid: Anaya/Muchnik, 1994.

———. "Màte, tango y metafísica." *Inti: Revista de Literatura Hispánica* 22–23 (1985–86): 17–27.

Zamora, Lois Parkinson. "Deciphering the Wounds: The Politics of Torture and Julio Cortázar's Literature of Embodiment." *Literature and the Bible.* Ed. David Bevan. Amsterdam: Rodopi, 1993. 179–206.

———. "Movement and Stasis, Film and Photo: Temporal Structures in the Recent Fiction of Julio Cortázar." *The Review of Contemporary Fiction* 3.3 (1983): 51–65.

———. Review of *Deshoras*, by Julio Cortázar. *Hispanic Journal* 5.2 (1984): 172–173.

General Bibliography

Alonso, Carlos J. *The Burden of Modernity. The Rhetoric of Cultural Discourse in Spanish America.* New York: Oxford University Press, 1998.

Archetti, Eduardo. "Multiple Masculinities. The Worlds of Tango and Football in Argentina." *Sex and Sexuality in Latin America.* Eds. Daniel Balderston and Donna J. Guy. New York: New York University Press, 1997. 200–216.

Bassin, Donna; Margaret Honey; and Meryle Mahrer Kaplan. Introduction to *Representations of Motherhood.* Eds. Donna Bassin, Margaret Honey, and Meryle Mahrer Kaplan. New Haven: Yale University Press, 1994. 1–25.

Benjamin, Jessica. *The Bonds of Love. Psychoanalysis, Feminism, and the Problem of Domination.* New York: Pantheon, 1988.

———. *Like Subjects, Love Objects. Essays on Recognition and Sexual Difference.* New Haven: Yale University Press, 1995.

———. "The Omnipotent Mother: A Psychoanalytic Study of Fantasy and Reality." *Representations of Motherhood.* Eds. Donna Bassin, Margaret Honey, and Meryle Mahrer Kaplan. New Haven: Yale University Press, 1994. 129–146.

———. Shadow of the Other. Intersubjectivity and Gender in Psychoanalysis. New York: Routledge, 1998.

Bernheimer, Charles and Claire Kahane, eds. *In Dora's Case: Freud-Hysteria-Feminism.* New York: Columbia University Press, 1985.

Bousquet, Jean-Pierre. *Las locas de la Plaza de Mayo.* Buenos Aires: El Cid Editor, 1983.

Bouvard, Marguerite. *Revolutionizing Motherhood: The Mothers of the Plaza de Mayo.* Wilmington, DE: Scholarly Resource Books, 1994.

Bronfen, Elisabeth and Sarah Webster Goodwin. Introduction to *Death and Representation.* Eds. Sarah Webster Goodwin and Elisabeth Bronfen. Baltimore: Johns Hopkins University Press, 1993. 3–25.

Bunster-Burotto, Ximena. "Surviving Beyond Fear: Women and Torture in Latin America." *Women and Change in Latin America.* Eds. June Nash and Helen Safa. South Hadley, MA: Bergin and Garvey, 1986. 297–325.

Cassem, Ned H. "Bereavement as Indispensible for Growth." *Bereavement: Its Psychosocial Aspects.* Eds. Bernard Schoenberg, Irwin Gerber, Alfred Wiener, Austin H. Kutscher, David Peretz, and Arthur C. Carr. New York and London: Columbia University Press, 1975. 9–17.

Coulson, John, ed. *The Saints. A Concise Biographical Dictionary.* New York: Hawthorne, 1958.

Daly, Brenda O. and Maureen T. Reddy. Introduction to *Narrating Mothers: Theorizing Maternal Subjectivity.* Eds. Brenda O. Daly and Maureen T. Reddy. Knoxville: University of Tennessee Press, 1991. 1–18.

Di Tella, Torcuato S. *Historia social de la Argentina contemporánea.* Buenos Aires: Troquel, 1998.

Dinnerstein, Dorothy. *The Mermaid and the Minotaur. Sexual Arrangements and Human Malaise.* New York: Harper & Row, 1976.

Feitlowitz, Marguerite. *A Lexicon of Terror. Argentina and the Legacies of Torture.* New York: Oxford University Press, 1998.

Felman, Shoshana. *What Does a Woman Want? Reading and Sexual Difference.* Baltimore: Johns Hopkins University Press, 1993.

———. *Writing and Madness (Literature/Philosophy/Psychoanalysis).* Ithaca: Cornell University Press, 1985.

Freud, Sigmund. *Beyond the Pleasure Principle.* Trans. and ed. James Strachey. New York: Norton, 1961.

Frosh, Stephen. *Sexual Difference. Masculinity and Psycholanalysis.* London and New York: Routledge, 1994.

Giannangelo, Stephen J. *The Psychopathology of Serial Murder. A Theory of Violence.* Westport, CT: Praeger, 1996.

Graziano, Frank. *Divine Violence: Spectacle, Psychosexuality, and Radical Christianity in the Argentine "Dirty War."* Boulder: Westview Press, 1992.

Guy, Donna J. "Mothers Dead and Alive. Multiple Concepts of Mothering in Buenos Aires." *Sex and Sexuality in Latin America.* Eds. Daniel Balderston and Donna J. Guy. New York: New York University Press, 1997. 155–173.

Hasty, Olga Peters. *Tsvetaeva's Orphic Journeys in the World of Words.* Evanston: Northwestern University Press, 1996.

Holweck, F. G. *A Biographical Dictionary of the Saints.* St. Louis: B. Herder, 1924.

Irigaray, Luce. *The Irigaray Reader.* Oxford, U.K. and Cambridge, MA: Basil Blackwell, 1991.

Jardine, Alice. *Gynesis. Configurations of Woman and Modernity.* Ithaca: Cornell University Press, 1985.

Kahn, Coppélia. "The Hand That Rocks the Cradle: Recent Gender Theories and Their Implication." *The (M)other Tongue. Esssays in Feminist Psychoanalytic Interpretation.* Eds. Shirley Nelson Garner, Claire Kahane, and Madelon Sprengnether. Ithaca: Cornell University Press, 1985. 72–88.

Kristeva, Julia. "Women's Time." *Feminisms. An Anthology of Literary Theory and Criticism.* Eds. Robyn R. Warhol and Diane Price Herndl. New Brunwick: Rutgers University Press, 1993. 443–462.

Laplanche, J. and J.-B. Pontalis. *The Language of Psycho-Analysis.* Trans. Donald Nicholson-Smith. New York: Norton, 1973.

Madres de Plaza de Mayo. *Ni un paso atrás.* Nafarroa, Spain: Txalaparta, 1997.

Masiello, Francine. *Between Civilization and Barbarism: Women, Nation and Literary Culture in Modern Argentina.* Lincoln: University of Nebraska Press, 1992.

———. "Cuerpo/presencia: mujer y estado social en la narrativa argentina durante el proceso militar." *Nuevo Texto Crítico.* 4 (Special Issue). Eds. Mary Louise Pratt and Marta Morello Frosch. Stanford: Stanford University Press, 1989. 155–171.

———. "Women, State, and Family in Latin American Literature of the 1920s." *Women, Culture, and Politics in Latin America.* Seminar on Feminism and Culture in Latin America. Berkeley: University of California Press, 1990. 27–47.

Minsky, Rosalind. *Psychoanalysis and Gender.* London and New York: Routledge, 1996.

Moi, Toril. "Patriarchal Thought and the Drive for Knowledge." *Between Feminism and Psychoanalysis.* Ed. Teresa Brennan. London: Routledge, 1989. 198–205.

Navarro, Marysa. "The Personal Is Political: Madres de la Plaza de Mayo." *Power and Popular Protest*. Ed. Susan Eckstein. Berkeley: University of California Press, 1986. 241–258.

Polatnick, M. Rivka. "Why Men Don't Rear Children: A Power Analysis." *Mothering. Essays in Feminist Theory*. Ed. Joyce Trebilcot. Totowa, NJ: Rowman and Allanheld, 1983.

Pratt, Mary Louise. "Women, Literature, and National Brotherhood." *Women, Culture, and Politics in Latin America*. Seminar on Feminism and Culture in Latin America. Berkeley: University of California Press, 1990. 48–73.

Rank, Otto. *The Incest Theme in Literature and Legend. Fundamentals of a Psychology of Literary Creation*. Tr. Gregory C. Richter. Baltimore: Johns Hopkins University Press, 1992.

Rich, Adrienne. *Of Woman Born*. 10th ed. New York: Norton, 1986.

Rossi, Laura. "¿Cómo pensar a las madres de Plaza de Mayo?" *Nuevo Texto Crítico*. 4 (Special Issue). Eds. Mary Louise Pratt and Marta Morello Frosch. Stanford: Standord University Press, 1989. 145–153.

Ruddick, Sara. "Maternal Thinking." *Mothering. Essays in Feminist Theory*. Ed. Joyce Trebilcot. Totowa, NJ: Rowman and Allanheld, 1983. 213–230

———. *Maternal Thinking: Toward a Politics of Peace*. Boston: Beacon Press, 1989.

Schwartz, Murray M. "Leontes' Jealousy in *The Winter's Tale*." *American Imago* 30 (1973): 250–273.

Shumway, Nicolas. *The Invention of Argentina*. Berkeley: University of California Press, 1991.

Simpson, John and Jana Bennett. *The Disappeared and the Mothers of the Plaza de Mayo. The Story of the 11,000 Argentinians Who Vanished*. New York: St. Martin's Press, 1985.

Sommer, Doris. *Foundational Fictions. The National Romances of Latin America*. Berkeley: University of California Press, 1991.

Sprengnether, Madelon. *The Spectral Mother. Freud, Feminism and Psychoanalysis*. Ithaca: Cornell University Press, 1990.

Stevens, Evelyn P. " 'Marianismo' The Other Face of Machismo in Latin America." *Female and Male in Latin America*. Ed. Ann Pescatello. Pittsburg: University of Pittsburg Press, 1973. 89–101.

Strauss, Walter A. *Descent and Return. The Orphic Theme in Modern Literature*. Cambridge: Harvard University Press, 1971.

Taylor, Diana. *Disappearing Acts. Spectacles of Gender and Nationalism in Argentina's "Dirty War."* Durham: Duke University Press, 1997.

Vázquez-Rial, Horacio. *El enigma argentino (descifrado para españoles)*. Barcelona: Ediciones B, 2002.

Zweig, Paul. *Lautréamont: The Violent Narcissus*. Port Washington, NY: Kennikat Press, 1972.

Index

ᕽ